Ma

Enjoy ⸻

It Just Gets Better With Time

[signature]

An original publication of Tongue Untied Publishing, PO BOX 822 Jackson, Georgia 30233

First Printing 2004 by Tongue Untied Publishing

ISBN 0-9745783-0-4

For more information regarding special discounts for bulk purchases, please contact Tongue Untied Publishing at (678)576-2768 or www.tongueuntiedpublishing.com www.maseyree.com

Cover Design by McKinley Mitchell Jr.

Photographer- Justin Lee

Printed in USA

Acknowledgements

First of all, I'd like to thank my mother. I love you mom with all my heart. All that I do is for you. Thank you for all the love and support that you've shown me over all the years. Thank you for always pushing me to be my best. You're the best mother I could ever want.

RIP my father Willie Richardson Jr. My memories of you will live on forever.

God Bless my grandparents, Willie and Vera Richardson, my brothers Willie Richardson II, Marcus Lofton, and Milton Lewis Kennebrew, Jr., my sisters, Yatanya Thompson, and Angel Boston. Thanks to all my aunts, uncles, cousins, nieces and nephews. I love you all.

Very special thanks to my Uncle Danny for always being there for me. You have been a wonderful role model, and I admire the fact that I can talk to you about anything. Thank you for wanting to be a part of my life. Also, thank you for coming to my college graduation. I knew I could count on you if no one else. I love you.

God Bless Mr. Large, my high school Algebra teacher whose words of wisdom I've carried with me since the day he held me after class to tell me that I wasn't a follower even though I had start hanging out with some knuckleheads. Obviously, you saw potential that I never knew existed. You told me, "There is no limit to the amount of information my brain could consume and for me to take advantage of the opportunity whenever I could." Since that day, I've never stopped being hungry for knowledge and information.

Special thanks to Mrs. Bernice Brown who told me to stop allowing fear to consume my dreams of being a writer. If you had never told me to "just do it" I would still be doing hair, hoping for the day to become that world famous Celebrity Stylist. If it wasn't for you, I would have missed my true calling.

To my good friend, Danne Johnson who I always call on for prayers, and to have my spirit lifted when I'm feeling discouraged. Thank you for talking me into staying in Atlanta after my second day. I remember when I called you crying because I was so overwhelmed by the changes of moving to a new city. You told me to stay, because God had sent me here for a reason that I couldn't see at the time. You were right because my dream to write this novel has finally came true. God Bless You.

Thank you, Sandra Mitchell, for being my support when I needed it most.

I'd also like to thank all those whose input help make this book a success. Thank you, Debbie Ellison, Krystal Sessoms, and Rhae-Ann Booker. Big ups to my Tongue Untied Publishing Staff. My cover designer, McKinley Mitchell Jr., my photographer, Justin Lee, and my Graphic Designer, Emaunel Johnson, and also Latrece Morris.

Contents

A New Beginning

The eager and impatient woman sat in the uncomfortably padded chair in the housing office. She had been called to see a town home they had for rent. Dorothy had been on the subsidized housing waiting list for over a year and had almost forgotten about applying until Margaret called her to see if she was still interested. The leasing agent apologized saying that they were undergoing renovations so everything around the office was really backed up. Dorothy was delighted that the woman called her because she couldn't wait to get away from the apartment she lived in now.

Finally, she would have the chance to live someplace halfway decent and affordable. Dorothy knew her children would object to moving into the projects so she hadn't mentioned it to them yet. She wanted to make sure everything was official before she spread the news. If she got the place, Dorothy wasn't sure how she would break the news to her children.

As she waited in the crowded office filled with whining babies and slang-talking baby mamas, Dorothy wondered, why did the girl sitting to her left have to come to an appointment with bedroom shoes on. She was profiling a hand full of flea market jewelry, and had a colorful scarf wrapped around her big ghetto fabulous hairdo. She was the loudest one in the place too. She was talking with another girl about how somebody else's man was trying to talk to her at the American Legion two nights before. They were talking about how no good he was and about the banging new, candy apple red, Cadillac SUV he drove. She stated that him being a "Baller" was the only reason she'd holla' at him because he wasn't too cute, although she heard he had it going on in the bedroom. The girl was loud and ignorant, a true ghetto queen. She was so caught up in the conversation about someone else's man that she wasn't even paying attention to her three bay-bay's running around the place, conveying that they had no home training. After she got an ear full, Dorothy turned and tried to tune out the sack chaser and her accomplice. If she liked the place and decided to move in, she would get a big discount on rent. With the money she would save, she could buy her children some of the name brand clothing they always talked about. Usually, she shopped at the ten-dollar store for her daughters and could find some pretty good deals on some nice things. Now that they were older, her girls were asking her to buy them Baby Phat, Apple Bottoms, J-Lo, and all those popular, name brand clothing.

Her son Dwayne never complained, but she couldn't buy cheap clothing for him; you just didn't dress little boys in cheap clothes. You could dress girls cute for little or nothing, but not boys; you had to keep them dressed fresh. To buy Dwayne name brand clothing without going broke, Dorothy shopped at TJ Maxx. His feet grew so fast it seemed like Dorothy was buying him shoes every other month. If she moved into the projects, the money she saved on rent could buy more Nikes.

Dorothy waited at least thirty-five minutes before a slender, flat-assed white woman finally approached her.

"Hi, my name is Margaret Kavinaw," said the woman, smiling. She extended her hand. It was the middle of May, and in Michigan, the snow had barely melted, yet her skin was so tan it looked like she'd just been out on Venice Beach. She had wide friendly blue eyes and mid-back length, wavy auburn hair. Her frame was frail, and she weighed about one hundred-twenty pounds. She walked as if it almost killed her to carry around those bony legs and carrot stick arms. Dorothy stared pleasantly at Margaret and rose from the chair. After their handshake, the woman said, "If you are interested in the place after seeing it, I'll be the person you will contact with any problems or concerns." Dorothy relaxed her lips, turning them into a comfortable smile. She politely exaggerated what a pleasure it was to finally meet Margaret as they walked toward the bright EXIT sign."Now, the place I'll be showing you," Margaret said, "is just a little ways up the street- about a five minute walk to be exact." Dorothy was excited but ashamed to reveal how happy she was, so she held back her joy and continued walking.

As they stepped out of the air-conditioned building, the warm breeze slapped them in the face. After waiting for a vehicle to pull out, the women walked through the parking lot and up the hill toward the townhouse. Dorothy wiped away the sweat running down her forehead, and Margaret noticed how nervous she was. She wasn't sure if her perspiration was from the heat, the extra fifteen pounds she was carrying, or her anxiety.

The ladies continued up the hill past a playground in the middle of the complex. Margaret mentioned that the playground was new and would be a nice play area for Dorothy's children. A large swimming pool next to the play area had a separate fence around it. Margaret said the complex only had one pool, so guests were not allowed. "It's only for the residents," Margaret stressed.

As Dorothy surveyed her surroundings she nodded and continued walking, barely hearing what Margaret was saying. Dorothy was pleased with the appetizers, but the main course was yet to be approved. Lost in a daydream, Dorothy continued up the hill. She was sick of renting from her slum lord, whom she despised, and eager to get her children out of the drug infested neighborhood. She didn't want them growing up in that environment, and they could certainly use the extra space. Upgrading from the overstuffed two bedroom, to a four bedroom she could afford would be a dream come true.

"Here we are," Margaret announced, startling Dorothy, as she jolted into reality. The chaperone stepped up the two stairs cautiously. Dorothy patiently waited for the woman to open the door. Margaret fiddled with her keys. She had at least three-dozen on the circular chain and each one had a different number welded into it. "I'm in charge of twenty-four separate units, so I stay pretty busy around here," Margaret said as she turned the silver key in the stainless steel lock and pushed open the front door. "After you," she smiled and moved to the side so Dorothy could be the first to enter the newly remodeled place. Dorothy gasped in disbelief as she walked into the huge living room. She marveled at the freshly painted white walls, the newly carpeted and tiled floors, and the large picture window that looked out into the parking lot. The window was in a perfect spot to be nosy. She would be able to see everything going on outside.

Margaret told Dorothy that the place was approximately 1600 square feet as they walked down the narrow hallway leading to the kitchen. There was plenty of counter space, two standard sized windows, lots of cabinets, and an adjoining dinning area. Dorothy's bright brown eyes glowed with approval. When she saw the matching refrigerator and stove, she almost jumped out of her skin. She felt like doing the "funky chicken" in the middle of the kitchen floor. She'd never had a matching refrigerator and stove. "I must say," Margaret volunteered. "I love this kitchen. It has plenty of space and the windows allow the morning sunlight to shine right in." Dorothy smiled as she continued the tour. "Over here to your right is your bathroom, which is full sized, but is a bit smaller than the upstairs one," Margaret continued.

The bathroom was pastel yellow with miniature yellow ducks scattered throughout the wallpaper that stood out like "the golden arch" on the McDonalds sign. It was the perfect size for her and Dwayne. There was a white tub with an attached stainless steel shower head and matching manila toilet. "Nice," Dorothy mumbled as she glanced in the humongous mirror. Exiting the bathroom, the women entered a spacious eleven by six downstairs bedroom. The room across the hall was the same size. Both bedrooms had walk-in closets twice as big as her closet at home. Dorothy decided which bedroom would be hers and which would be her sons.

Dorothy followed Margaret to the basement, which was

right off the kitchen. It was divided into two sections and the cement floors and walls caused the room to be a bit chilly. One side of the basement was a laundry area, perhaps Dorothy could fix up the other side as a den or recreation area for her kids. Dorothy had no idea the projects were so well kept and spacious. She would see the third floor of the townhouse before giving Margaret her final approval.

From the basement, they headed upstairs to the third level. By the time they reached the top floor they were huffing and puffing from the long climb up two flights of stairs. The bathroom was at the top of the staircase. To the right of the bathroom was a linen closet and down the hall were the bedrooms. They were larger than the two downstairs. Dorothy looked heavenward, closed her eyes, and silently mumbled, "Thank you." She couldn't wait! She and her children would finally have their own bedrooms. They were so cramped now they were always in each other's way. More space would alleviate a bit of the sibling rivalry.

"The bedrooms up here are approximately thirteen by four, which is quite a bit larger than the ones downstairs," Margaret commented. Dorothy followed her down the hall to the two bedrooms.

"I love the place," Dorothy blurted, "Where are the papers you need me to fill out? As far as I'm concerned, you can consider this one rented."

Margaret pulled a small black handbook from her folder and handed it to Dorothy. The book read in big gold letters, "Rules and Regulations." Margaret suggested that Dorothy take it home and read it carefully. She also held a form with red ink marking the paragraphs that Dorothy needed to read and sign.

"This one you can get back to me later, just as long as it is filled out before you get ready to move in. It's just a list of rules that we have to make sure you understand, so that's why those in particular require a signature," Margaret said before asking

Dorothy if she had any questions.

"No ma'am," Dorothy happily replied.

Margaret explained that the security deposit was two hundred dollars in addition to the first month's rent. Dorothy could move in as soon as she signed the papers and paid. "I'll have all the money in your office before you close on Friday evening."

"Well," Margaret replied, "since everything is set, we can head back up to the office."

The leasing agent noticed Dorothy's gigantic smile as they went outside. Back at the office, the two women waved at each other as Margaret headed toward the building and Dorothy hopped into her vehicle. Dorothy was so excited and nervous her hands were shaking. She tensed as she wondered how she would break the news to her children.

The more she thought about it, the more determined she became. She liked the place, and as long as neither child was paying the bills she wouldn't worry about pleasing them. As long as they had shelter, they should consider themselves lucky; some children didn't have that. Dorothy knew she could afford the rent since it was based on income. Her take home salary wasn't much, so this place would definitely land her in the low-income bracket. As her car approached a yellow light, Dorothy stopped to reflect. Her mind raced, deciding where everything would go in the new place. She decided that Keisha and Tonya would share the bedroom upstairs across the hall from Monet, who was the oldest of the three. She recently turned sixteen and was always complaining that she needed her privacy. Now she was going to get her wish and Dorothy was dying to see her expression when she told her the good news. She knew the younger girls would resent sharing a bedroom, but it was better than being crammed in one with Monet.

Keisha, who was almost fourteen, and the youngest daughter Tonya, who was twelve, were constantly bickering about who acted the oldest. By being upstairs, they could both close their bedroom door and Dorothy would no longer have to hear the drama. Dorothy knew they both would hit the roof when they found out Dwayne would also have his own bedroom.

Dorothy turned the corner onto the street where she lived. She looked at the dilapidated tenements as if this were her first drive down this road. Suddenly, the neighborhood appeared filthy and run down. She could not wait until the end of the week to pay her money, pack, and move. Dorothy pulled up in front of her apartment, cut the engine off, and sat in the car reminiscing. She thought about the day she moved into her apartment six years ago. Ever since that day, she prayed that God would bless her and her children with some place better to live. Now, her prayers were answered, and it was a great feeling.

Dorothy climbed out of her vehicle and walked up the pathway to her front door. The closer she got to the door the louder the aggravating sound of Monet's stereo rung in her ear. Monet had the stereo up sky high again and Dorothy could not wait to get inside and push the power button off. Her daughter's bedroom was at the back of the apartment, but you could hear the music as loud and clear as if the speakers were on the front lawn. For Monet's birthday, her dad, Tony, who hadn't seen her since her fifteenth birthday, gave her two hundred dollars. Instead of buying the school clothes or shoes she always complained about needing, Monet bought a loud ass stereo that was real close to being thrown out on the front yard. Disturbed, Dorothy proceeded into the apartment. The windows vibrated and her crystal figurines had fallen from the bookcase to the floor. Dorothy was so angry she couldn't get down the hall fast enough to see her hardheaded daughter. Dorothy was going to disconnect the entire component and silence the room instantly. Monet had been warned often about having the music up so loud. She must have figured she could do whatever she wanted, with her mother gone, typical teenage thinking.

Enraged, Dorothy headed to Monet's room. She burst through the door to see Derrick, the punk who hung out at the corner store hustling, and the same one Monet knew she couldn't stand, posted beside the bed pulling his pants up. Dorothy's eyes raced back and forth from the boy to her daughter. Monet was lying in her bed under the covers. She jumped up wearing only an oversized T-shirt. Dorothy's words were like fire burning, "Boy, you better get the hell out of my house!" When she reached out to grab the gangster boy, he ducked and dashed out of the bedroom. He was lucky that she didn't get her hands on him. Dorothy wrapped her hands around her daughter's neck as she screamed for mercy. Realizing what she was doing, the raged mother released her frightened child and left the room. Dorothy was upset and didn't want to argue with Monet because she might end up seriously hurting the girl. She was so disappointed, tears streamed down her face. She had lost total trust in her daughter. She didn't know what she had walked in on, or what she had missed. Monet was supposed to be looking out for her younger siblings, but now she would have to be watched. She was too old to whip, so Dorothy would put Monet on a strict punishment. She wouldn't allow her to leave the house for a month, except for school. She would only be allowed to utilize her bedroom, the kitchen, and the bathroom. Monet sat in the back for about ten minutes before Dorothy called her into the living room. Before she could say a word, Monet walked up, "I'm sorry, Mom."

Dorothy took a deep breath, trying desperately to stay calm. She counted to ten, then changed the subject. "Where are your brother and sisters?" "They said they were going down the street to watch a fight."

"Did they finish their homework?"

"I don't know. I didn't get the chance to ask them because they all ran out of here. They said them bad kids down the street gang banged somebody at school yesterday, and today that girl who they jumped came around here with her cousins. They are supposed to be down the street trying to beat down whoever jumped their cousin yesterday so Tonya, Keisha, and Dwayne went down there to watch the big brawl."

Dorothy thought, she probably told them to leave so she and Derrick could be alone in the apartment. "Them damn kids gone get enough of always trying to run and see something," Dorothy said. "Did you take them chicken wings out of the freezer like I asked you to?"

"Yes ma'am," Monet answered without hesitation. "They should be thawed by now."

"Good," Dorothy said stomping out toward the kitchen. "Go down there and tell them that I said to get their nosy behinds home right now before I come down there with my belt and give everybody down there something to see. I have something to tell you all, so hurry up back," she demanded.

Less than an hour later, the girls were sitting in the living room watching television. In the kitchen, Dorothy waited for her cornbread to finish baking and for her son to come back from the store. She'd sent Dwayne to the store for some Kool-Aid more than twenty minutes ago and he hadn't returned. Dorothy knew his little hard head butt was somewhere out there monkeying around.

Dwayne walked through the front door as Dorothy was about to tell the girls to go look for him. "It's about time you came back," Tonya yelled. "You got us waiting on your slow butt before we can eat."

"Shut up, nappy head," Dwayne teased as he swerved his leg to avoid Tonya's punch as he walked past her toward the kitchen. "Mama," he yelled, "Tonya hit me when I walked past her nappy head butt."

"Y'all two cut it out," Dorothy snapped as she evil-eyed

Dwayne when he walked into the kitchen. "What took your behind so long?"

"I went up there and came right back Mama," Dwayne explained. Since her temper was short, Dorothy calmly turned the knob on the cold water tap. She stood there waiting as the warm water turned cold. She smiled as she reflected on what Dwayne said before. He had called Tonya "nappy head" and he was not lying. Of all four of Dorothy's children, Tonya was the only one who inherited bad hair from her daddy's side of the family, straight-up kinky. Her smile vanished and Dorothy poured the Kool-Aid into the pitcher before filling it with cold water.

"You all go and wash your hands, then come in here and eat. The food is ready." They all competed to be the first one to the bathroom sink, creating a commotion. Later, all four children gathered around the kitchen table. Monet silently poured every-one drinks while Keisha passed her brother and sisters their plates as Dorothy stood at the stove fixing them. Tonya and Dwayne were still aggravating each other by staring one another down with a devilish demeanor.

"I am going to kick your cry baby butt as soon as Mama leaves again," Tonya whispered to her tattle tale brother.

"I'm telling," Dwayne moped, making sure his mom could hear him.

Dorothy interrupted! "Now this is the last time I'm gone say this, so listen up. The next time I'm not going to talk. I'm just going to start swinging and y'all can try me if you want to. Now I said, cut out the mess okay?" Dorothy grabbed her plate from the counter, told the children to say grace, and walked toward the living room. She stared at Monet for a long time with a hateful expression. She was so disappointed in her, she didn't know what to do. The children dug into their fried chicken, mashed potatoes, corn, and homemade cornbread. The only sound was clanging forks and smacking jaws. When they finished eating, the children scraped their plates into the trash and placed their soiled stoneware in the kitchen sink. Dwayne headed toward the television in the front room, and Keisha was right behind him. As Tonya entered the living room, she noticed her mother's annoyed expression and paused. Dorothy's look meant "don't even try to come in here and think that you are about to watch T.V. when you know that it's your dish night."

Tonya did a one hundred and eighty degree turn in the middle of the floor and headed back toward the kitchen. The water running in the kitchen sink reminded Dorothy how well trained her children were. Even though Tonya tried to be slick, she realized her foolishness wouldn't get her far. After she washed the dishes and swept the kitchen floor, Tonya joined her family watching television.

Dorothy twiddled her fingers, trying to figure out a way to break the news to her children. She couldn't wait to get her income tax refund so she could upgrade her living room furniture. She hadn't noticed how run down, dirty and dingy, everything looked. She knew she could do better. She felt good knowing that when she spent her hard earned money from now on, she could relax in a comfortable place. Dorothy was tired of paying her slum lord four hundred and seventy-five dollars a month for a raggedy, squeaking floor, leaking ceiling, and dumpy apartment. God was blessing her with the extra earnings that she'd soon bring home so she could refurnish her new place.

Monet was only sitting with the family because Dorothy wanted to talk to them. She hoped her mom wasn't about to tell her business. Even though Monet was wrong, she didn't want her siblings to know about her and Derrick. She felt embarrassed and guilty. "What are you thinking about, Mama?" she asked. Blinking back to reality, Dorothy faked a smile and began to speak.

"I bet you guys are ready to move out of this apartment and move into something three times as good."

"Yeah," they responded simultaneously.

"Well, the place that I went to go and look at today is three times better than this one."

"Where is it, Mama?" Keisha blurted out impatiently.

"Well," Dorothy mumbled, letting the words slide slowly off of her tongue.

"Where, Mama?" Dwayne shouted.

She hesitated. "It's downtown near the West Side." Her oldest daughter was beginning to object.

"Please, Mama, don't say the Campau Projects," she exploded. Judging from her mother's expression Monet had guessed correctly. Monet's head dropped in disappointment.

"But, you will be able to have your very own room, Monet," Dorothy said, thinking that this would make her smile. Dorothy informed Keisha and Tonya that they would have to share a bedroom, and told Dwayne that he'd have his own bedroom. The younger girls were totally for the idea. They figured anything was better than their current living arrangements.

Dwayne jumped up as if attempting a slam-dunk. He was overjoyed at the prospect of having his own room. Monet was shaking her head. Confused, Dorothy stared at her ungrateful child. How could the girl not be excited about getting her own room when sharing a room had always been her biggest complaint?

"Does the new place have a basement, Mom?" Dwayne asked. Dorothy nodded, and her son ran around the room like a wild child. She said they could all drive over Friday and look at it together. Again, the ungrateful one interrupted. "Y'all acting all happy and stuff to be moving into the projects, knowing good and well that they have roaches."

"Girl, shut up," Dorothy demanded. "Have you ever been to the projects and seen any roaches?"

"No, but everybody at school says that the Campau

Projects are full of roaches."

"Well, that just goes to show you that you don't need to believe everything that you hear, and whether they have roaches or not we're moving there regardless, so you might as well start getting used to the idea." Monet turned away, rolling her eyes and mumbling, "I'd rather stay here than move into the funky projects." Dorothy told the children to take their baths and get ready for bed. As they marched off, Dorothy sat contently in the living room thinking about her new place.

Before going to sleep, Dorothy called her friend Punkin and told her about the place. Punkin told Dorothy that she would help her get situated. Dorothy rushed off the telephone saying she was tired and needed to get to bed. She grabbed some blankets from the hall closet and walked into the living room and made a small pallet. Dorothy was happy, exhausted, and anxiously anticipating the days to come. She changed into her pajamas and fell asleep.

———————

The grudge that Caroline had for her sister manifested after their mother died, when they were nine and thirteen years old. After the funeral, they had to leave the neighborhood they'd grown up in to live with Aunt Linda, their mother's sister. She was their next of kin, since the girl's father had never been in the picture. Aunt Linda spoiled and pampered Dorothy because she was the baby. Her baby sister was always excused for her wrongdoings and Caroline got blamed. When Aunt Linda questioned Dorothy about being insubordinate she would burst into fake crocodile tears and Auntie Linda would apologize. She would grab Dorothy and hug her while chanting the same pitiful explanation for not whooping her. "I know you're only doing this because you miss your mama, baby. It's gone be all right." Caroline would roll her eyes at the both of them and walk off.

Auntie Linda never said that when Caroline did something wrong.

No matter how hard she tried, the pain wouldn't go away. She tried to love her sister unconditionally, but the grudge manifested as the years passed. Dorothy had always been The Golden Child, even in their mother's eyes. Because Caroline always felt second to her baby sister, she made it her business to outdo everything Dorothy did. Dorothy had all the glory when they were coming up, now it was Caroline's time to reign. She wished Auntie Linda could see her pride and joy get pregnant, drop out of high school, and marry a bum without a pot to piss in or a window to throw it out of. If only Auntie Linda could see how successful she'd become. The one she had failed to pay attention to had grown up and landed a blue collar job as a line-production worker at a GM plant, right out of high school, the same job that was now paying her a decent seventy-thousand a year. Also, Caroline would have liked for her auntie to meet her wonderful husband. They met at the job two years after she started working there. Thomas had a business/management and marketing degree, and served as the Senior Marketing Supervisor of Assembly and Production at the plant. He didn't work in the hot factory like she did. He was in an air conditioned office all day. She and her line partner Adell met him one day as he walked through the plant showing their product to a potential customer. From that day on, Caroline made it her business to get his attention whenever he came into the production department. He finally asked her out, leaving her competition Adell to revel in her success. She and Thomas were married two and a half years later and moved to an upscale neighborhood, one of three black families in the area. They'd purchased an extravagant custom made 4500 square foot Mediterranean home. A turret, two story with plenty bay windows. Rich amenities furnished the inside. Her living room with fireplace had breathtaking views. The formal dinning room was highlighted by a tray ceiling, and curved-glass windows. The expansive kitchen had a tiled island, ten foot ceilings, and an adjoined sky-lit breakfast nook. There was a spacious bath in the hall leading to the living room with equipped wet bar for entertaining. The bay windowed den was next to the guest room that opened up to a rear garden situated around her royal blue fiberglass, above ground pool. Upstairs, there were three bedroom suites. The master suite had a lush bath, two walk in closets, a walk out terrace and a two person whirlpool tub. Two split bedrooms with study and bath equipped with two sink vanities took up the other half of the upstairs. Their home was beautiful. Between her husband's $125,000 a year salary, and her lavish salary, the couple was soon ready to start a family. Caroline wouldn't have time to play daddy to her sister's children while Delvin was in and out of jail. Caroline thought her family was perfect. Unlike her sister, her husband was very good looking, smart, and a dedicated father. His wife and two precious daughters ran his house and emptied his wallet. Caroline's days now were nowhere near as depressing as they were when she was a child because she was in control of everything. She had the man that every woman at GM wanted and she reveled in her glory five days a week on her job. Since they were such a closely knit family, she always brought up what they did on the weekend to her line partner Adell, who like the others, wanted Thomas from day one.

Drama

Thomas was sitting in his office waiting for his secretary to return when he heard a knock on the door. Judith was not around to let him know he had a visitor. Thomas sat up straight in his Lazy Boy office chair, straightened his collar and called to the visitor to enter. Judith must have still been gathering the information he needed. The door opened slowly revealing the uninvited intruder.

He gasped as if seeing a ghost. Earlier, he'd asked his secretary to check on an employee. Adell Brown had not shown up for work for three days, nor had she called. This was unusual for her and Thomas was worried, so he asked Judith to call her to see if everything was okay. Adell had worked for the company almost fifteen years and had never done anything like this. If Judith didn't get an answer, she was to ask around the plant to see if anyone heard from her. Now, here was Adell, her face bruised and her eyes filled with tears. The woman had confided in Thomas weeks before about some personal problems at home. Adell felt close to him since they'd worked together so long. Caroline despised their friendship, even though it was strictly platonic.

As Adell tiptoed to Thomas' desk, he rose, his hand covering his mouth. "Adell, what happened?" he asked sympathetically. Adell burst out saying that her boyfriend had gone on one of his drunken binges, then came home and jumped on her. Thomas walked around his desk and gave her a comforting hug. This was not the first time he'd heard about Adell's boyfriend beating her, but he'd never seen her bruised like she was now. With tears running down her swollen face Adell looked like a victim of a Mike Tyson fight.

"Adell, how long are you going to keep putting up with his mess?" Thomas asked.

"Thomas, I want to leave him," she interrupted. "I've wanted to leave him for quite some time, but I just don't know how. Please help me. I don't know what else to do. When Fred got off work Monday, he started trippin' again. He asked me to give him twenty dollars and I told him I didn't have it. After that, he snatched my purse and took my wallet. I didn't say anything, I just stared at him. He then got pissed off and started punching me after he discovered there was no money in it. After he jumped on me, I ran to my car and tried to pull away but he snatched my keys out of the ignition, threw them off into the dirt, and drug me by my neck all the way back into the house." Adell was hysterical. "I got away again and went outside to find my car keys. I started up the car and was driving a few blocks on my way to work but I lost courage and pulled over to the side because I couldn't come to work in that state." Tears dripped into her mouth and she took short breaths as she continued. "I wouldn't have been productive at all, so I just sat there and cried trying to figure out what to do next. I'm scared of going back home because as soon as I ask him about my wallet, he's going to start again," she paused. "All week I've been trying to let my face heal from the weekend fight." She paused, exhaled and collapsed into the chair beside her, "Thomas I don't have anywhere to go."

He stood by the desk contemplating what to do. He glanced at his wristwatch, then back at Adell, wondering if there was something he could do to help her. Thomas snapped his finger and told Adell he had an idea. "There is a hotel about ten minutes from here that I can take you to. I can charge your room on my credit card for a week, but that is about all I can do," he exhaled. "Why didn't you call me?"

"I was too ashamed. I've been spending the last couple of days trying to figure out how to leave this man, but I still have not come up with a suitable idea. I don't know what to do," Adell continued. Thomas looked at his wrist watch again to determine if he had time to drive Adell to the hotel, check her in, and make it back to work in time to meet his wife for their routine lunch. Thomas grabbed her arm and escorted her out. He told her to take the rest of the week off and return Monday after she recuperated.

Judith was not back at her desk so Thomas left her a note that he ran to the cleaners, but would be back in less than thirty minutes. Thomas escorted Adell to his Lexus. They jumped in and pulled out of the parking lot. He was nervous because he didn't want anyone at work to see him and Adell riding off together. He knew Caroline would flip the script, especially if she heard it from one of her colleagues.

The two co-workers rode off silently. Thomas avoided looking at Adell because it hurt to see her bruised face. He wished he could see the punk that did this to her. There was one thing he could not tolerate, and that was a woman beater.

At ten minutes after eleven, Thomas and Adell pulled up to the Ramada Inn across the street from the Steak and Shake restaurant where he and his wife sometimes had lunch. Thomas pulled up to the lobby door and told Adell to sit in the car while he checked her in. He didn't want her to go through the embarrassment of people staring at her face. Adell sat in the car with her head down, looking up often to see if Thomas was coming or if her boyfriend was in sight. Adell was glad to have a friend like Thomas to help her get away from her controlling boyfriend. It was a good thing she'd left her car at the job; that way if Fred was stalking her he would be sitting at the job all night. Thomas came out of the lounge almost running. He jumped into the car and handed Adell the hotel keycard. He was paranoid and ready to get Adell situated so he could get back to the job without being seen. "It's room two, two, one and they said it was right around this corner." Thomas pointed in the direction. Thomas told her to call him as soon as she decided what to do. She gave Thomas a big hug and thanked him for all he'd done to help her. As she approached the door of her room Adell paused, looked back, and said to Thomas, "I owe you one." She slid the card through the magnetic slot, waited for the green light on the key pad to shine, and opened the door. Adell turned and watched Thomas speed away. She closed the door. Through a small opening in the curtain, she could see Thomas racing over the speed bumps and into the street. His car hit the highway cruising at seventy-five miles an hour.

Thomas slipped through the plant, trying to get back to his office before Caroline clocked out for lunch. His secretary was sitting at her desk staring at the computer monitor. Judith looked up with a wiry expression on her face. "Did you get my memo?" Thomas asked.

"Yes, I did. Did you get what you needed from the cleaners?"

"As a matter of fact, I did," he answered in a guilty tone, wondering if Judith knew anything or if she was just being courteous.

"Good, your wife is in your office waiting on you."

Thomas's eyes grew wide as he froze next to Judith's desk.

"How long has she been in there?" Thomas asked his secretary.

"Maybe ten or fifteen minutes," Judith answered. Thomas checked his Rolex. It was forty-five minutes after eleven and Caroline punched out for lunch at eleven thirty.

"Damn," he mumbled, and thanked Judith for the information.

He stepped in with a gigantic smile. "I'm sorry to have kept you waiting, Baby, but I'm ready now." Caroline's face didn't look as cheerful as her husband's. She didn't even answer. Instead, she handed him the memo that he'd jotted down on a post-it note. She must have gotten it from Judith.

"You went to the cleaners?" Caroline inquired.

"Yeah," he mumbled softly.

"I guess you had to take items others than the ones I drop off every Saturday, huh?"

He stared at her intently, his thoughts on a rampage. Thomas had no clue what his wife was fishing for. He wondered why Judith hadn't told him that Caroline found his note.

"So, you've been to the cleaners, huh?" she asked again in an angry, speculating tone.

He hunched his shoulders, with a fake-it-till-you-make-it smile.

"Baby, I didn't have to go to the cleaners for myself. I gave Vernon from sales, on the fourth floor, a ride to the cleaners. He had to pick up some work suits that he took there a couple days ago," Thomas tried to convince his wife, but he knew from his wife's expression that Caroline was not buying his story.

"Thomas, don't lie to me."

"I'm not lying," he said, digging himself deeper into his fabricated hole. Thomas nervously continued, "You want to call upstairs and ask Vernon?" he asked as he walked toward his desk and reached for the telephone. He hoped Caroline wouldn't call his bluff. Her eyes turned red. She tried to remain calm, but Thomas was pushing it. "This lying bastard is trying to play on my intelligence," she thought. She decided to go along with his story and grabbed the telephone.

"No, that's okay," she warned. "I won't call Vernon, but let me call Brenda to see if she was sure that it was you she saw no more than thirty minutes ago, pulling up into the Ramada Inn Hotel with Adell in your motherfucking car. How about I do that, Thomas?" Caroline snatched the phone from his hand and dialed. Thomas pressed the disconnect button with his index finger and stared at Caroline with her hurt eyes.

"Okay, I'll explain the whole story to you."

"No, you won't," she yelled, cutting him off. "You've said quite enough, so now it's my turn to talk. I'm taking the rest of the day off, boss, and I suggest you do the same. Instead of going home, how about you start looking for a new one? Maybe now

Adell will let you come fuck her at her house instead of the two of ya'll creeping off to a hotel in the middle of lunch, when you were supposed to be having lunch with me."

Thomas tried to interrupt but she threw her hand in the air. Caroline stormed to the door sobbing and shaking her head in disgust. "Unh, unh, unh," she pouted. "Fifteen fucking years!"

"Caroline!" he yelled. His wife left, slamming the door behind her.

"Damn! Damn! Damn!" Thomas screamed, pounding his hand on the desk. He desperately wanted to run after her and tell her the truth, but Thomas didn't want to make a scene at work. Instead, he plopped down in his chair. He needed a way out of this one quickly. Why did she think he was having an affair with Adell? Ever since he and Adell started working together, there'd been animosity between Caroline and Adell for no apparent reason. "Damn," he said to himself. "How was he going to clear this up? "Shit," he remarked and dashed out of the office. He had to find Caroline before she found another ride home. He rushed past Judith and told her he would be out for the rest of the day. She replied, "Yes, boss," with a frustrated expression. She thought whatever was going on between the couple wasn't good because they both came out of the office upset and slamming the door. "Unh," the woman thought, "that's the reason companies don't hire spouses or family members."

When Thomas got home, Caroline was already there. She'd gotten a ride before he could make it outside the plant. He raced into the house to try and work everything out before their daughters got home from school. Caroline was in the bedroom on the edge of the bed. When he walked in the bedroom she cried, "Thomas, I want you to gather up your things and leave this house right now."

"Caroline, honey, I know that I lied at first, but please allow me the chance to tell you the truth."

"How dare you, Thomas! How dare you sneak around with her right up under my nose. All this time my speculations have finally manifested into truths and you've been denying the affair from day one."

"Caroline, I promise that Adell and I are not having an affair. I was helping her find a place to stay because her boyfriend beat her up again and she desperately needed someplace to go. I swear to you that our relationship is strictly platonic and it has always been that way."

"If that was the case, then why did you leave a note saying that you were going to the cleaners, Thomas, huh?" His face reflected his grief. "Why did you have to lie about it if you are not hiding anything?"

"Because!" He answered without justifying his answer.

"Because you are fucking her, Thomas, that's why." Caroline was yelling at the top of her lungs. "I don't want to hear anymore. Thomas, just please get out!" Caroline rose from the bed angrily and headed toward the bathroom. Thomas sat on the bed and placed his head between his legs. He heard his wife in the bathroom unrolling tissue. He heard her blow her nose and flush the toilet. Caroline unrolled more tissue and returned to the bedroom. "I want a divorce!" she demanded.

"A divorce! What do you mean you want a divorce?" Thomas stood directly in front of his wife.

"I'm sitting here telling you that nothing happened between me and Adell and you don't believe me. Caroline, I was only gone away from the plant for maybe twenty good minutes. Is that enough time to be having an affair?" Caroline cast an evil eye at her husband.

"Hell, yeah! That's long a fucking-nuff!" Caroline shouted casting an evil eye at her husband.

"Come on now, Caroline," he begged, "let's be realistic."

"Be realistic," she interrupted. "I am being realistic. First of all, you sneak away from work leaving notes with your secretary saying that you were going to the cleaners. Not only did you lie on paper, but when I asked you about it you told me some bullshit story about riding with somebody to the cleaners, when in fact you were at a hotel lying up with that ugly ass tramp. You chose to do that rather than being on time to have lunch with your wife. What the fuck do you mean be realistic?" Caroline paused and caught her breath. "I just want your lying ass the hell out of my house and out of mine and my girls' lives."

"What? Now wait just a damn minute. You are talking crazy! The girls don't have anything to do with this Caroline, keep them out of it."

"Don't tell me what to do about my fucking kids," she fussed. "My kids are staying with me."

"Damn right," Thomas interjected, "right along with their father, who in case you forgot, took a part in bringing them into this world as well."

"Like I said, Thomas, I want you out! Everything will be settled in time, but you best believe it's going to be based on a judge's decision," Caroline interrupted by jumping into Thomas's face, and pointing her finger between his eyes. Right now I want you to get your two timing ass out of my house."

"I'm not going anywhere, Caroline," he repeated, stepping away from her. Her fist slammed into the side of his face! Thomas grabbed his jaw and tried to shake off the numbing effect that Caroline's punch had on the side of his mug. He looked up in time to duck the second punch. On reflex, he snatched her up in a bear hug and firmly pushed her away. Thomas grabbed his aching jaw again, checked for blood in his mouth, and massaged it in a circular motion to make sure it wasn't fractured. Now, Caroline had pissed him off. Shaking his head in disgust, Thomas turned and started to walked out. She rushed him from behind. When he felt her jump onto his back, he swung around to block her, but instead his arm knocked her to the floor. She collapsed into the corner of the bed, screaming mercilessly.

"I'm gone kill you," Caroline yelled as she got up and charged at her husband. Thomas surrounded her body with his. He held her firmly. She continued swinging and yelling about what she would do to him when he let her go. She called him every name in the book and said that as soon as he released her she would call the police. Thomas pushed his wife out of the way and headed toward the dresser, angry enough to kill! Caroline maneuvered onto her feet. She watched Thomas while he fumbled through the drawer like he was looking for something.

He pointed in her direction. "Unh huh, you just stay right there. You want me to leave? Then I'm getting ready to leave. You just stay right there and let me get my stuff together. I promise you, Caroline, that you are making a mistake though, a big mistake."

"Yeah, I know. My mistake was marrying your cheating ass, but that's all going to be over very soon."

Thomas grabbed his gym bag from the closet and stuffed it with his clothes. Before he left the bedroom he turned to her.

"Caroline, I still love you," said Thomas trying to save his marriage. Caroline fell silent. "Well, answer this," Thomas pleaded. "Don't you think I should stay so we can work this out?"
"I'm filing for a divorce on Monday," Caroline interrupted.

"What?" he asked.

"You heard right, MONDAY," Caroline fussed. Thomas just bowed his head and walked out of the bedroom. Caroline stood silent, doubting that he would leave. Minutes later, she heard his car engine and saw him back out of the driveway at what seemed to her a hundred miles per hour.

Drama Part 2

Thomas was angry enough to kill someone. He was hurt that his wife didn't trust him. Thomas' Lexus glided so smoothly, he didn't notice the eighty-seven miles per hour speed he'd picked up. Glancing at the speedometer, Thomas eased his right foot off the gas petal and onto the brake. He eased his way to the far right lane, veering to the shoulder of the highway and stopping on the side of the road. He was about twenty minutes away from home. He resisted going to a local strip club and got back onto the road. He would go to the first bar he saw and drink until he had the nerve to go back home and apologize to his wife. A few drinks would help clear his mind and ease his aching heart.

Thomas drove to a small sports bar called Shackers, on the other side of town. The fluorescent billboard in front almost blinded him as he turned onto College Street. He'd never seen this place nor driven through this neighborhood before. There were very few cars in the lot, but that was cool, Thomas needed seclusion. He pulled into a parking space on the side of the building, got out, and locked the doors. Jogging toward the door, he hoped his stress would dissolve in the wind. He stepped inside and grabbed a seat at the end of the bar, away from everyone else. The place was half empty with maybe only twelve other guests. He sat comfortably on the stool trying not to look uptight. The bartender, muscular, dark-skinned, and bald, asked Thomas what he wanted to drink. Thomas stared at Herbert's close-cut, shining mane and said to hook him up with whatever was most popular. "Dark or light?" Herbert asked. Thomas sat silently covering his face with his hands.

Minutes later, the mangy-looking bartender returned with a cranberry colored drink. Thomas slapped his credit card on the counter and told the man to run a tab.

Herbert took his Platinum Visa and returned shortly mumbling in a baritone voice. "Wave if you need me. I'll be right down at the other end," he pointed.

"As a matter of fact," Thomas began. "Why don't you bring me another one so I won't have to bother you right away! This one will be gone before you know it." He sighed, and gulped down half of whatever his drink was. Thomas watched the bartender fix his second drink, some sort of Vodka mixed with cranberry juice, and deliver it.

He hadn't noticed the woman standing next to him. She was attractive but reeked of grocery store perfume. Thomas stared at her before inviting her to sit down. Lowering herself onto the barstool, she introduced herself. "I'm Shelia." She watched him gulp down the liquor. He didn't offer his name, but asked if she wanted a drink. Shelia waved for the bartender. Herbert arrived with a drink and sat it in front of Sheila. She was a regular. She smiled and thanked him. Herbert nodded and went to the other end of the bar where he and another regular were watching a football game on television.

Sheila flirted coyly, telling Thomas how attractive he was. He nodded, the liquor making him angrier. He tried listening to his newfound friend but his mind was preoccupied.

Sheila whispered in his ear, which tickled and made him smile, but he said nothing. They sat at the bar for a couple of hours and Thomas bought Sheila three or four drinks. He'd lost count after his sixth drink and now either his head was spinning or everything around him was. Drunk, he rocked to the music. The numbers on his watch were blurry. It was seven, something, or maybe the big hand was on the eight; Thomas wasn't sure. All he knew was that he was drunk and Shelia was whispering some interesting propositions in his ear. Before he knew it, they were leaving the bar holding each other up.

Thomas woke up the next morning still intoxicated with the smell of cheap perfume. The aroma blended with the tainted smell of liquor and sex. His head was pounding. After trying to sit up and realizing his head was too heavy, Thomas plopped back down on the pillow. Discovering he was butt-naked made him happy. He realized he'd made it home safely and figured his wife had undressed him and helped him into bed. Although his head was spinning, he was relieved. He knew he and his wife had reconciled since he was exhausted and his shaft felt as if it had put in some serious work. He and Caroline had gone a couple of extra rounds, and Thomas was definitely feeling it.

He sat up and looked at the snoring woman lying next to him. But it wasn't the bed he was used to waking up in, and as he looked closer, the woman wasn't his wife. "Shit," he thought. He remembered meeting Sheila the night before but how he ended up in bed with her was a total blank. Thomas didn't even know where he was. He jumped up searching for his clothes. He dressed quickly and headed for the door. He saw that Sheila was waking up and he told her he was sorry and had to go. He had to muster up the courage to face his wife. He would stay at Vernon's until he and his wife came to an understanding. After two days at Vernon's, Thomas and his wife grew tired of being apart and reconciled as if nothing ever happened.

Two and a half months later, the shame and guilt he felt from being unfaithful was getting to him. He'd been holding this secret for a long time and he needed to tell his wife about that night before she found out through another source. He loved Caroline too much to keep the secret from her any longer. He tried to tell her one morning on their way to work, but couldn't find the words. Thomas had to tell his wife that Sheila had gotten in touch with him to tell him about the baby she was going to have in seven months. He rehearsed for days how to break the news to his wife. "Baby," he would say, "I know this is going to hurt you and I'm sorry, but please don't interrupt me until I'm finished." He would continue, "If you feel like you don't want to be with me after this, then I will understand." But he couldn't say that and allow her to act negatively. He knew Caroline would want a divorce and he wasn't about to let that happen. He loved her and their children too much. Thomas decided to tell Caroline that he was going to be a father and deal with whatever came up. She cried all night when she found out her fairytale family no longer existed. Since then, Thomas and his wife could not have a decent conversation without her bringing up Sheila's name. Caroline spent most nights in bed crying. She couldn't tell her sister Dorothy what was going on because she was too ashamed.

Caroline contemplated foolish thoughts of doing what Francine Hughes did to her husband in the movie "The Burning Bed." Caroline couldn't believe her husband would have unprotected sex with that sleazy, whore-ass Sheila and risk bringing a disease home to her. She couldn't believe that in seven months another woman would have her husband's baby. Caroline was unable to have more children, so she accused her husband of getting Sheila pregnant on purpose to have the son she couldn't give him. Thomas said that was foolish. The first time they had sex after the ordeal, Caroline told Thomas to use a condom. "I don't know what you have been doing," she fussed. Thomas caught an attitude, turned away from her and went to sleep. What put the icing on the cake was when Caroline made an appointment with her gynecologist to check for STD's. She told Thomas that while he was making babies there was no telling what else he could have gotten. Their marriage was becoming a disaster.

As her marriage began changing, so did her oldest daughter Andrea. Since becoming a teenager, the girl had gone slap out of her mind. Caroline hoped she wouldn't have to go through the same thing with her younger daughter. Andrea did whatever she felt like doing, whenever she felt like doing it. She became distant from Caroline when she got her first boyfriend. She was determined to have a so-called boyfriend even though Thomas forbid it. She swore she was in love with the young punk. When Andrea had her first menstrual cycle, her parents rushed her to the doctor for birth control pills. They weren't taking any chances. Thomas told Caroline that kids these days got into too many things that their parents didn't know about. Thomas was determined that neither of his girls would get pregnant until they graduated from college and married.

They caught Andrea skipping school and sneaking out of the house late at night. The most embarrassing thing was picking her up from the juvenile center for shoplifting. Caroline was crushed. Andrea had no reason to steal. She and Taylor received a fifty-dollar allowance every week and neither of them had chores. All that was expected of them was good grades. The two girls got everything they wanted, Sega, Nintendo, nineteen-inch television sets, bicycles, scooters, skates, not to mention computers. What more could they want? Apparently, Andrea didn't appreciate what she had.

Caroline's nieces and nephew weren't as fortunate as Andrea and Taylor. Dorothy was raising four children alone, since her husband was in prison. Her children only got what they needed. Dorothy busted her butt every day as a manager at Kentucky Fried Chicken to take care of her family. If it wasn't for the monthly Social Security check she received for her son's learning disability, Caroline didn't know how her sister would make it.

Of the fourteen years Dorothy and her husband had been married, he'd been locked up at least eight. Caroline could not understand why Dorothy didn't find someone else since Delvin was serving a ten-year sentence. He knew Dorothy would wait for him. Dorothy had been with the man forever and he hadn't changed at all. Caroline knew her sister could get a decent man if she made herself available. Her sister wasn't bad looking nor was her one-hundred and seventy pound body out of shape. She just needed to get out of those cheap clothes that made her look ten years older. She was such a plain Jane. If Dorothy wasn't wearing some mammy made dress, she would wear old jeans and a t-shirt with dusty black flip-flops Caroline wished she could bury. Dorothy didn't know what a regular pair of shoes looked like. She just needed to get out more. Caroline prayed for the day that her sister would get over Delvin and go on with her life.

The next morning, Caroline woke up to the annoying sound of her gold trimmed alarm clock ringing loudly. She called out to make sure her daughters were up and getting ready for school. Caroline scuffled into the bathroom to wash her face and brush her teeth. Thomas was already in the bathroom placing Remembrant tooth polish on his toothbrush. After freshening up, Caroline left the bathroom and went down the hall to Taylor's bedroom to help her get dressed. When they dressed and had eaten cereal and toast, the whole family headed out. After dropping the girls off at the bus stop, Thomas and Caroline rode to the General Motors plant.

Thomas suggested that they make an appointment with a marriage counselor. For the next couple of blocks, they remained silent. Thomas broke the monotony.

"I really do hate the way things have been between us lately, Caroline. All we seem to do is argue all the time and we never talk the way we used to. What's happening to us?"

As her husband spoke, Caroline's mind wandered. She was able to focus on only one thing. "It's real hard for me, Thomas," her eyes filled with tears. "I'm having a hard time trying to adapt to all this. Try putting yourself in my shoes. If I'd gone out and came home pregnant with another man's baby, how do you think that would make you feel? After all we've been through Thomas, this has to be the only thing that constantly nags me to reconsider our marriage."

"But, I've told you time and time again that none of this was intended or planned, Caroline, you know that. As a matter of fact, this is one of the biggest mistakes I've ever made in my life.

You just don't know how much I wish that I could turn back the hands of time, but I can't. Do you know how much of me wishes that I could have been more responsible? You're my wife and I love you. There's no one who can take your place and that's why I suggest we see a counselor. I can't even see myself being with anyone besides you."

Thomas' words were sincere, but Caroline would not let her guard down. She didn't say anything because her heart ached. She could not stomach the fact of someone else being intimate with her husband. Caroline knew that in time she would probably forgive Thomas, but not now. She'd never forget his life changing mistake.

The car eased into the General Motors parking lot. Thomas moaned. "Yes, Caroline, I do know exactly how you feel. I know what I did was wrong, but lack of communication and holding that grudge that you have is not going to help either." Thomas pulled the car into an empty parking space. He could tell Caroline still had some things on her mind that hadn't been said. He closed his eyes and relaxed in his seat.

"What's going to happen with Sheila?" Caroline asked. "Why do we keep talking about the situation, but not about the other person who is involved? Not only, Thomas, do I have to accept your child into our life, but also I have to accept its trifling ass mother interfering. How can we go on pretending that everything is okay when so much has changed?"

"Caroline, if we are going to remain a couple then we simply have to learn to deal with what has happened. If that's not the case then we need to be meeting with a lawyer instead of a counselor!" he shouted, sliding out of the vehicle and slamming the door.

"There is no leaving the past behind!" she shouted out the window after Thomas was long gone. How dare he jump out without letting her have the last word.

Sorting Things Out

Dorothy parked the U-Haul in front of her new place. Today nothing could upset her, she thought, as she stepped out of the truck. "Finally, after all the years, hard work is paying off."

Two men climbed out of the passenger side eyeing their friend's new place.

"Nice crib," James said to Dorothy as his eyes scanned the townhome.

"This ain't nothing. Wait until you see the inside," she bragged.

James and Tyrone were friends of her husband who as a favor to him, volunteered to help her move. As she unlocked her front door, Dorothy stepped out of the way so the guys could carry in her furniture. She took a deep breath, exhaled, and wondered what her sister would think of this. Dorothy was sure Caroline would say something negative even though she should be happy that her nieces and nephew would be living in a decent place. Dorothy's new duplex didn't compare to the beautiful home her sister and brother-in-law owned. She didn't have cathedral ceilings or fancy, custom made window treatments. She didn't have his and her sinks in her private bathroom adjourning her bedroom, nor did she have a custom-made jacuzzi, or a big swimming pool in her backyard, but she did have a nice place. She used to be so self-conscious when her sister came over to the old place because it was so run down compared to Caroline's. Even though Dorothy kept the place spotless, it wasn't appeasing to her older sister. Every time Caroline came over she would say something like, "I'll be so glad when you move away from here," or, "When are you going to start saving money to buy your own home?" Once she even said, "Do all those boys hang around outside all times of the day and night? Doesn't that bother you?" She acted as if she was above living in the hood, you know, like the ghetto wasn't where she came from. A little money sure can change a person.

The two movers maneuvered through Dorothy's front door, straining under the weight of her couch. "Where do you want this to go?" Tyrone asked. "Just sit it over there for now. As soon as everything is inside I'll situate it where I want it to go. My friend Punkin is supposed to be coming over here to help me."

"You talkin' bout' yo' thick ass friend Punkin?" Tyrone said as he placed the end of the couch on the floor and stared at Dorothy.

"Whatever," Dorothy giggled, "if that's what you call her."

"Yeah," Tyrone continued. "I remember her from that birthday party you had a couple years ago. Won't you hook me up?"

"Now I don't know nothing about hooking nobody up. If y'all two get hooked up, it's not going to have anything to do with me." Dorothy laughed and left the room.

It was evening when the guys finished moving Dorothy's things and she still had to take the truck back and get her children. Dorothy thanked her husband's friends for helping her move. She fumbled through her purse and whipped out two twenty-dollar bills and handed one to each mover. It was all the spare money she had. "Here y'all, you guys can at least go and get yourselves something to eat. Y'all done worked hard today, I have to give you that. I know you weren't charging me anything but it wouldn't be right if I didn't offer y'all something." James reached for the money.

"Well, I guess I can get me some grub and a couple of cold ones. Thanks, Dorothy." Dorothy turned on a few lights, and they all headed outside toward the truck. She dropped the guys off at Tyrone's house, then drove the U-Haul back to the lot and got her eighty-dollar deposit and her car.

The girl at the U-Haul place took forever, talking on a cordless telephone while inspecting the truck. Dorothy waited patiently while the weave-headed Maybeline Queen took twenty minutes to type her information into the computer. After signing the final document, Dorothy rushed to her vehicle and zoomed out of the lot. Tonight was going to be her first night at her new place.

Monet and Derrick were standing outside the apartment when Dorothy pulled up. Derrick was the same punk she'd come home and caught with her daughter. Monet was still claiming they didn't do anything wrong, but Dorothy didn't trust him or her daughter. Derrick hung out all day in front of the convenience store down the street. That was one reason Dorothy couldn't stand him. He and his friends stood out there on that corner all day acting tough. It was intimidating to see a group of thugs hanging in front of a store you were trying to enter. They would stand in your way with their pants hanging half off their butts. They made Dorothy's skin crawl. None of them attended school regularly and seemed to think standing on the corner was going to get them somewhere. It was obvious that the guys were selling drugs. Heck, they did it in broad daylight. Dorothy tried to make sure that her son wouldn't be one of those guys. Monet had been calling Derrick her boyfriend for the last couple months and he'd been hanging around their apartment, when Dorothy wasn't home. At first Dorothy forbid Monet from seeing him but it was hard to monitor the situation when she wasn't home. Since she started seeing the boy, Monet grew courage and had an episode where she wanted to buff up and act grown. She mouthed off to Dorothy on one occasion and her mother reminded her who was boss with a back hand slap to her mouth. It snapped the girl back into reality. Dorothy was an old fashioned mother who didn't allow her children to talk back and be disrespectful. If her children had something to say, they asked for permission. As a single mother she knew she had to keep them under control. Dorothy was delighted that her family was moving to the other side of town and was sure Derrick would never visit or even think about Monet anymore. Dorothy knew he was the main reason Monet objected to moving. He was also the reason Monet wasn't allowed to have company inside the apartment when her mother wasn't home. "Y'all might as well say y'all good-bye's because today is the last time you will be seeing each other." Dorothy looked at Monet. "I think you need to get inside and start getting the last of your things together because we'll be leaving in a little while."

"Man, she be trippin'," Monet complained as her mother walked away.

"Yeah, I know," Derrick agreed. "You know she only acts like that because of me." Derrick hugged Monet and told her he would see her later.

"I'm gone miss you, Boo," she whined. Derrick kissed her and walked up the street toward the store. As she opened the front door of her apartment, she heard her mother tell the others to get their things together. Depressed, Monet walked through the living room with a dismantled smile on her face. Dorothy was sweeping the hallway. "While you were out there talking to that knuckle head boy, you could have been in here getting your things together." Monet put her head down, mumbling, and headed to the bedroom.

"What did you say?" Dorothy asked. She'd stopped sweeping and placed her hand on her hip.

"Nothing," Monet answered quickly.

"Okay. You can act like you grown if you want to Monet. Don't make me come in there and slap the taste out of your mouth." The girl knew better than to say anything else.

They all squeezed into the car with the last of their belongings and Dorothy started the engine. She told her children to wave to the old apartment. Everyone except Monet waved and shouted, "Bye, old house!"

That Saturday, Dorothy and her best friend Punkin went to Ionia prison to see their men. The ride seemed longer than ever. Dorothy and Punkin drove up twice a month to visit and Dorothy couldn't wait to get there. She was tired of listening to Punkin go on and on about some new guy she met, her new "cut" buddy. Dorothy listened without expressing her opinion.

In the waiting room Punkin was still talking about this man as if she wasn't about to visit Bruce. "Girl, Colby is about the sweetest man I done met in a long time. He came over last night and we sat up talking for about four hours. After that we watched a good movie on HBO until I fell asleep. Girl, instead of him trying anything, he woke me up and let me know that I had fallen asleep on him, and to let me know that he was about to leave. He didn't even try to get none," she bragged. "Ooh, Dorothy. I think this one might be around for awhile."

As long as Dorothy had known Punkin she had been the same way. She could sniff a "dirty dick" twenty miles away and would get it before she recognized the stench of him being a tri-fling, no good parasite. She would play with it for a couple months, then suddenly find an excuse to ramble on to the next. Punkin was her girl, but Dorothy always teased her about being whorish. Dorothy could not figure out why Punkin wasted her time visiting Bruce, even though he was the best man she'd ever seen Punkin with. He gave her everything she wanted. He was a shy, pushover type who was madly in love with Punkin and thought she could do no wrong even though she wasn't faithful.

Dorothy was worried how her husband would handle the news that he can't stay with her when he is released from prison. She knew Delvin would be upset, but she had to do what was best for her and her kids. Margaret made it clear that the new place was only for her and her children. Dorothy could not have any-one staying with her who wasn't on the lease or she would lose her place and her benefits. They'd been in the waiting room over twenty minutes before the guard called the visitors' names. Punkin was called in before Dorothy. As she stepped through the heavy glass door, Punkin turned to Dorothy. "Now, don't you go in there upsetting that man, girl." Dorothy waved her hand in the air oblivious to Punkin's chattering. But who was Punkin to be giving someone advice?

Going With The Flow

It was 3:47 a.m. and Monet was the only one in the house still awake. She was bent over the toilet, throwing up her guts. She had been up all night running to the bathroom. Her stomach ached before the puking started. Monet calculated that the last time she had a period was two weeks before they moved, about two months ago. Monet worried that she might be pregnant. She sat alone on the bathroom floor, beside the tub, crying. Later that morning as she was getting dressed, Monet decided she would skip school to go to the clinic for a pregnancy test. She would ask her friend Brandy to go with her. Once she signed in and was called to the back, Monet took the cup the nurse gave her and walked into the ladies room to fill it with urine. She and her friend sat in the waiting room afterwards, quiet and frightened. Monet prayed the results would be negative.

A medium built, tall black woman came from the back and walked toward Monet. Monet could tell she had bad news. The lady escorted Monet to her office and told her the test results were positive and that she was about nine and a half weeks pregnant. The nurse handed the girl a brochure of reputable OB/GYN's to start prenatal care, if she planned to continue the pregnancy.

Monet and Brandy dragged out of the clinic and walked down the narrow pavement with their heads down. Brandy tried comforting her friend by saying that everything would be okay, but Monet wasn't listening. She kept saying her life was over. All her hopes and dreams were fantasies now because she would soon have a snotty-nose baby riding her hip. The number four bus pulled up to the stop and both girls got on, paid their fare, and walked to the back. "Girl, how am I supposed to go to my mom and tell her that I'm about to have a baby?"

"If it'll make you feel better, I'll ride over to your house with you; either way you're gonna' have to tell her sooner or later." Monet assured Brandy that it was a good idea to come with her.

"Before we go to my house, though, I'd like to stop over

by the way and talk to Derrick."

"Cool," Brandy answered, then sat back in her seat staring out the window. The girls transferred to the number six bus. It would take them to where Derrick hung out.

When they got off the bus, Derrick noticed the girls right away. "What's up?" he asked. "How come y'all ain't in school, y'all skipping or something?" Brandy walked over to the store to give them some privacy. Monet and Derrick sat on a tree stump. He could tell something was on her mind.

"What's wrong?" he asked, staring into her watery eyes. Monet burst into tears. Derrick grabbed her up against his chest hugging her. "What's wrong with you, Monet?"

"I'm pregnant. I don't know what we're going to do. Derrick, I'm so scared," Monet boo-hooed and looked at her boyfriend.

"What do you mean you're pregnant?" Before Monet could answer he pushed her away and yelled, "Stop playing!"

"I'm not playing. Me and Brandy just came from Planned Parenthood. The nurse said I was about nine and a half weeks pregnant. That's why I came to find you. I wanted you to be the first to know." The girl dug into her bag and pulled out the paper with the results.

"Why are you telling me this, Monet?"

"Why do you think?" Derrick looked furious. He sat on the tree stump seemingly in denial of everything that she'd told him. He seriously thought Monet was playing.

"Yo' moms know about this?"

"Not yet. I told you, Brandy and I just came from the clinic." She shoved the paper toward him. "Read it for yourself." Derrick glanced at the paper as he licked his bottom lip like LL. He glanced at it quickly and handed the paper back to Monet.

"How are you gone be sitting up here telling me you're

pregnant by me and I ain't been with you in a couple of months? How do I know if that baby is mine?"

Monet lost her temper.

"You know why you haven't seen me, so don't even try it. You know my mama wasn't trying to let me come over this way after we moved." The girl's neck jerked out of control as she swung her finger in his face. "Yes, I am for sure that this is your baby, so don't sit there and get ignorant with me. When you and me done something, that was my first time, and you know I ain't been with no one else besides you, so don't play wit me." Monet rested one hand on her hip and pointed the other in Derrick's face.

Derrick stood quietly. Monet's tears had dried and she felt totally opposite from the way she felt earlier. It was probably because she was about to bust Derrick in his face if he said one more time that the baby wasn't his.

"Damn," he finally mumbled. "I'm gone be a daddy."

"Me and you need to work this thing out before I go home and tell my mother," Monet pleaded. There was silence. Derrick glanced at the store and saw his boy Jamil talking to Brandy. He was probably trying to get his game on with her.

"So what are we gonna' do?" Monet asked, distracting her boyfriend. "You remember just like I do the day this all happened. It was the same day my mom caught us in my room together, so don't front. I know you remember that."

"Well, Monet, since you say the baby is mine, I on' have no other choice but to take care of my responsibility." Derrick was acting macho again. Monet could tell he was as nervous and scared as she was. "Do you want me to come with you so we can tell yo' mama together?"

"I don't know."

"What you mean you on' know? Either you do or you don't."

"My mother is at work right now, but me and Brandy are

on our way over there to wait for her to get off."

"What time she get off?"

"Three o'clock," Monet answered. "She normally would have been off today, but she got called in and doesn't get off until three. I'm glad she got called in. That way, I know she didn't talk to anyone from the school. I know she is not going to be home before the school calls to let her know that I have not been there today."

"Well, I'ma get my homie to shoot me over that way bout three-thirty. Maybe now your mother will stop trippin' and give me some respect. You know, I'm glad you ain't come over here talking about no abortion cause you ain't gone be killing none of my seeds."

"Well, actually," she blushed. "I had not given that option much thought at all. The only thing I'm trippin' about is the fact that I ain't but sixteen, I have two more years of high school to finish before I graduate, and I don't know for sure if I can handle being a mother."

"I ain't but seventeen my damn self. Do you think I know something bout being a daddy? Hell, naw, I guess it's something we both gon' learn to do."

"How are you going to help me so much Derrick when you don't even have a job?"

"That don't stop my pockets from being fat, besides I still got plenty of time to look for a job." He looked out the corner of his eye and nodded. "You know, I'm gone always get my hustle on." Monet hissed while sucking her teeth.

"Well, that ain't the only thing I have a problem with," she snapped. "At least I can transfer to a school for pregnant teens and still go while I'm pregnant, but you don't even go. Now, what do you think you'll possibly be able to teach our child?"

"Damn, Monet. You talkin' like I'm dumb or something. Just in case you didn't remember, I only have one more year to go until I graduate, so don't be frontin'."

"So, when do you plan on finishing that year?" she asked.

"Aw, Monet," he sighed. "All that don't got nothing to do with me being no dad...."

"Well Derrick, she interrupted I'm just making you aware of the things you need to start taking more seriously, that's all. You need to leave this corner alone and start concentrating on getting yourself together so that you can help me take care of this baby." Monet looked over Derrick's shoulder and saw Brandy walking in their direction.

"Do you think your mother will start lettin' me come see you now?" Derrick asked.

"That depends on you," Monet told him. "That depends on how long it's going to take for you to get yourself together. You're gonna have to prove to her that you can handle what you have gotten yourself into." Derrick pecked Monet on the lips and told her he would see her at three-thirty. He ran toward Brandy and tried to hit her on her head, but she ducked and yelled, "You punk!" Monet felt like one burden had been lifted off her shoulders. The only thing she feared now was facing her mother.

Brandy and Monet got on the number five bus. It would drop them off on the corner of Division and Franklin, across the street from The Campau Projects. It was almost two o'clock when they arrived. As they stepped off the bus, Monet burst into tears. Her friend tried to calm her as they walked into the house and headed upstairs to Monet's bedroom. Monet and Brandy heard Dorothy come in. Dorothy was unaware that Monet and her friend were upstairs. She dropped her purse in a kitchen chair and headed to the bathroom to prepare a hot bath. Brandy told her friend, "Dry your eyes! If you don't, she'll know right off that something's wrong." Monet tiptoed into the bathroom to wash her face.

Dorothy came out of the bathroom and saw Monet and her

friend sitting at the kitchen table. Dorothy jumped, gripping her chest, her heart racing. "You scared me," she said. "And what are you girls doing home from school so early?"

"I have something to tell you, Mom," Monet whispered. "Mom, I was sick this morning, so instead of going to school, Brandy, and I, we, we, went down to the clinic." Dorothy's eyes bounced from Monet to Brandy. "Well, what's wrong?" she asked. The girls looked at each other, then at Dorothy. "Will somebody tell me what's going on? I'm growing impatient, so just come on out with it."

"Mom, I'm pregnant," Monet blurted. Tears rolled down her face as she waited for her mother's response. Dorothy's eyes enlarged.

Did she believe what she was hearing? Was her sixteen-year-old daughter telling her she was about to have a baby, the same daughter she knew to be on the pill?

"Mom, I'm sorry to disappoint you!" Monet shouted. Brandy looked at her friend and back to her mother; this was her cue to leave. Brandy headed up the stairs. Soon she came down with her backpack on her back. She waved goodbye to Monet and said she would call later. She let herself out. Dorothy left the kitchen, walked into her bedroom, and closed the door. Monet sat alone in the kitchen unsure of what to do.

Dorothy fell into bed asking herself if she heard what she thought she'd heard. Why was she hearing this nonsense when she was just about to get on her feet? It was hard enough raising her four children. Now there would be another mouth to feed. And who was the father? Dorothy didn't recall her daughter hanging around any boys. Since they'd moved, Monet kept to herself. Even though Monet swore she wasn't doing anything, the clinic had given her a three months supply of pills. So, why was Monet pregnant? Was the girl trying to get attention or what? Monet tapped on the bedroom door, barging in before her moth-

er answered. "Can we talk about this, Mom?" she asked.
Dorothy sat up and wiped the tears from her face. "How could you allow this to happen, Monet?" she asked, disappointed. "You know how hard it is on me already, and I'll be damned if you ain't went and added fire to the flame." Monet didn't answer. Dorothy continued, "Well, who is the father?"

"Derrick," Monet answered boldly. Dorothy was shocked.

"Oh, my Lord, him of all people." Her mind raced back to the day she'd found the two of them together. "Oh, Lord," she murmured again, covering her face in shame.

"And just how long do you think he's going to stick around when he finds out?"

"He already knows," Monet answered quickly. Dorothy threw her head back in disbelief.

"You know what, Monet? All I'll say is you'll find out for yourself just how boys are. As soon as you get pregnant, they don't want to have nothing else to do with you. You are going to end up stuck, just like me." Monet let her mom do all the talking.

"What happened to you taking the birth control pills we went and got?"

"They were making me sick, so I stopped taking them."

"That's no excuse because if you had told me, we could have gotten them changed and you wouldn't be in the situation that you're in right now," Dorothy said. She wouldn't yell or fuss because it was too late for that and besides, Monet was pregnant and that was enough stress for her to deal with. Instead, Dorothy said to her. "Listen, Monet. I know I raised you to be responsible and I know that you know right from wrong, but everybody makes mistakes, some just seem bigger than others. I have faith that you will make the best decision for you because this is about you. It's your body, and your life. I cannot sit up here and say that I want you to do this, or I think you should do that, because it's not about me. I am your mother, and I love you. I will support whatever decision you make because I know that you are capable of handling yourself. I can't say that this is the smartest thing you've ever done but I have faith that in the end you'll overcome this situation because you're a product of me which means you're a trooper." She smiled and shook her head. "This situation can only make you, or break you, if you let it. Don't let nobody tell you what you can and can't do because you can do whatever it is you want to do as long as you believe you can, and if you work hard enough at it. I got your back one hundred percent. But I'll tell you now, a baby comes with great responsibility," she paused. "So when did Derrick find out about this?"

"I seen him today and he told me he was coming over at about three thirty." Dorothy shook her head and rolled her eyes. She tried to hold back the tears.

"How far along are you?" Dorothy asked.

"The nurse said about nine and a half weeks."

"Girl, you done missed two periods and I didn't know anything about it." She stared at Monet in astonishment. "Unh, unh, unh," Dorothy moaned to herself, "and you think you know your kids." Dorothy closed her eyes, no longer able to hold back the tears. "Well, I'll tell you what," Dorothy cried. "I'll help you out as much as I can, but this is your baby, not mine. The only thing I can say now is we have to take this one day at a time." Dorothy hugged her daughter and reassured her that even though she was disappointed, she still loved her.

The doorbell rang and Monet jumped to answer the door.

"That's probably Derrick." When she opened the door Derrick was facing the street. He didn't want to risk being face to face with Dorothy if she answered. He stepped inside relieved that Monet had answered and not her mom. She told him that her mom already knew. They walked over to the couch and sat next to each other. Derrick's hands were shaking. He couldn't wait to get the whole thing over with.

Dorothy walked into the room and managed to ease out a fake, "Hi, Derrick." She sat on the sofa across from them and began lecturing the two teens. "I'm going to go ahead and make a long story short. You two have a lot of growing up to do and not a whole lot of time to do it. Once this baby gets here it'll be up to you all to be responsible for its well being." She looked at Derrick. "I guess you plan on being a good father for this child, Derrick?"

"Well, Mrs. Johnson," he answered nervously and unprepared. "I already told Monet that I was gone start looking for a job right away. I also told her I was going back to school. I realize that I might as well do what I got to do since I'm gone be havin' a lil' shorty coming." He sounded as dumb as he looked. He stuttered as he talked. "I don't want my son having no dummy for a daddy," Derrick said. He acted as if he was sure Monet was going to have a boy. "I promise you, Mrs. Johnson, I promise I'm gone be there for mine, that is, if you'll allow me to have some visitation rights with the baby and your daughter. I know that we've had our problems before, but hopefully now, due to the circumstances, things will change."

Dorothy's eyes met Derrick's. She knew the boy was full of it. Her instincts told her that his story sounded fictitious, but she didn't want to be judgmental. Dorothy let him talk. Then she spoke slowly and carefully.

"I don't know if you're telling me the truth or not, Derrick, but I promise you one thing. If you leave my baby alone to raise this child on her own, I'm going to make sure you pay." Her words were harsh. Out of respect, Derrick gave her his undivided attention. Monet's eyes met her mother's. She didn't defend her boyfriend.

Mrs. Johnson informed the boy how to conduct himself from now on, for the sake of the child. Derrick promised Monet and her mom that he would stick to his commitment.

Dorothy went into her bedroom and closed the door. Within moments, she was in tears again. Her daughter's pregnancy was too overwhelming. Monet gave Derrick a big hug and a peck on the lips before he left. She jotted down their telephone number and gave it to him. "Promise me you'll call."

"I promise," Derrick said as he walked to the parking lot toward his friend's car.

Changes

It seemed like only yesterday that Sheila gave birth to her precious little son, but he was getting bigger and more independent each day. Thomas Jr. was almost four months old and she was still enjoying him. Sheila smiled as she watched her son wiggle in his playpen. She wished things with his father had turned out differently, but there was nothing she could do now, although she knew one day she would have to explain to her son why his dad wasn't around. She loved her baby, but she wished her life could be like it used to be. If she could go back, things would have turned out a lot different. She never intended to have her child with someone else's husband. Sheila sat back in the recliner and reflected on the day it all went down.

She remembered Thomas sitting at the bar, looking handsome, and tossing down drinks like they were water. Sheila sat across the room observing him for about twenty minutes before she finally approached him and introduced herself. He didn't tell her he was married, but she observed the gold band glistening on his finger. Her only thought was getting down with him, no shame, no strings attached, and no hard feelings.

After that night, Sheila heard nothing more from Thomas and didn't expect to. After discovering she was pregnant, Sheila tracked Thomas down. It was a good thing she had gone through his wallet and memorized the information on his driver's license. He was so drunk, she could have taken him for everything he had, but he was too fine and the sex turned out to be the bomb, so she couldn't do him like that. The morning after they'd slept together Thomas told her he'd made a big mistake and for her to not to plan on seeing him again. He confessed to being in love with his wife and Sheila was cool with it because she was in it for the same thing he was, a one night roll in the hay.

It took a long time to locate her soon-to-be-baby's daddy, which pissed Sheila off. Every time she called his office, that damn Judith would say, "He's not in, may I please take a message?" Sheila knew the woman had given Thomas the messages, and he was simply avoiding her. That's the main reason she decided to keep the baby, along with the fact she didn't have the four-fifty to get rid of it. Since he was playing games, Sheila hoped to ruin Thomas's marriage and make him as miserable as she was. During her pregnancy, she worried about having to do everything in vain. There was no one to rub her swollen feet or comfort her aching stomach and back. It was horrible working all the way through her pregnancy. She worked as an accounting manager at a small law firm. Due to their busy schedule, Sheila had to put in overtime. Her job required her sitting down all day, and by lunchtime, her bottom was numb. If she had a man, she could have taken the last three months of her pregnancy off, but she couldn't afford to do that.

Thomas didn't easily agree to support her decision, but because it was too late for her to get an abortion, there was nothing to do but have the baby. She wouldn't give it up for adoption after carrying it for nine months. Sheila enrolled in a Lamaze class and asked Thomas, out of spite, if he could give her a ride home after the classes every Wednesday night. He declined, saying she was out of her mind, she didn't even want to go to the class. She just wanted to see what he would say.

Even though Sheila felt she had made the biggest mistake of her life by having her son, at the wrong time, and by the wrong person, she couldn't imagine her life without his handsome behind now. She loved having someone who needed her. She loved kissing his tiny little feet and hands. She loved his unique smell and those big brown eyes she saw looking up at her every night before she went to sleep. Sheila loved being a mother. She figured it must have just been her time. Hell, she was thirty-one years old. Her son slowed her down and made her look at life from a new perspective. She'd learned her lesson and decided not to travel that same road again.

Sheila never forgot the day she had to call Thomas to tell him she was in labor. Caroline answered the telephone and was really pissed that she was calling. Thomas had to leave home to be with her, and there was nothing Caroline's arrogant ass could do about it. Knowing that Sheila was having a boy only irritated her more. Sheila remembered yelling into the mouthpiece, to Caroline, "Tell your husband his son is on the way and he needs to get to Spectrum Hospital as soon as possible."

Sheila didn't know they would both show up at the hospital a half hour later. They sat outside the room listening to Sheila screaming during her six hours of labor. Caroline wouldn't allow him to stay in the delivery room after Sheila requested she leave. The doctor finally came out and announced the arrival of a seven-pound, twelve- ounce boy. Thomas walked into the room to see the baby with his wife beside him. Caroline looked at the newborn, hoping it had no resemblance to Thomas. While Thomas admired his child, Caroline was almost in tears. The baby looked like her husband had spit him out. Even though Caroline knew the baby was her husband's just by looking at him, he was still going to take the scheduled DNA test.

Sheila's mom and her friend Elaine were in the delivery room. The grandmother asked her friend loudly, "What is the purpose of her being here?"

"This is my husband," said Caroline. "Your trifling ass daughter got involved with a packaged deal. That's why I'm here. I may not have been there when the shit went down, but I'm gone be here from now on and that's a promise.

"Caroline, calm down, honey," Thomas mumbled. Caroline became enraged and walked closer toward the girl's mother. Elaine walked up in Caroline's face and said. "I bet we ain't worried about you doing a damn thang to nobody up in here." Thomas stepped between his wife and Elaine because both of them were loud and out of control. The nurse advised the women to leave.

Embarrassed by his wife's behavior, Thomas grabbed Caroline and led her out of the room. They left before the police were called. Sheila was in no position to argue, but she vowed not to forget. She owed Caroline one for disrespecting her mother.

Thomas was denied getting acquainted with his newborn son because of the feuding. He was so upset he didn't say anything to his wife during the ride home or after they arrived. He walked into the bedroom after Caroline. "Why are you so damn quiet?" Caroline asked. His silence made her furious. "It's your damn fault this shit happened anyway. If you wouldn't have been out there fucking with that bitch, then I wouldn't be at the hospital showing my ass." He stared at her with enough venom in his eyes to kill. Not only had she acted foolish, she had disrupted his time with his son. "Don't try and blame me for your immaturity. You were at the hospital acting totally ignorant. You have yourself to blame for that," Thomas said. Caroline was up in his face invading his comfort zone. He clutched her arm.
"Caroline, I'm warning you," he yelled. "Get out of my face before you make me do something I'll regret later."

"Let go of my damn arm," she warned. "If you want, you can move in with that bitch and that damn baby." After the harsh words fell from her mouth Thomas pushed his wife aside and walked away. "I told you a long time ago to get the hell out and what did you do afterwards, Thomas? You came back," she bragged. Thomas ignored her, grabbing pajamas from the drawer and walking into the bathroom, locking the door behind him. "You were the one calling here and begging me to let your ass back in. I didn't call you, Thomas! Caroline yelled." The bathroom door swung open and Thomas' slender frame passed his agitated wife as he left the bedroom. "Did I call you and ask you to come back, Thomas?" Caroline asked. Thomas slammed the door in her face. Caroline's body jerked to avoid it hitting her. "Did I call you?" Andrea and Taylor were standing outside their bedrooms and Thomas instructed them to go to bed. Taylor wanted to know what was going on. "Nothing," Thomas told her, "Now, go back to bed." Thomas slept in the guest bedroom that night so he wouldn't lose control. He sat up all night thinking. Although his wife often acted crazy, he loved her to death. He hadn't decided what to do, but he knew a lot of things had to change. He was determined to be a part of his son's life. The little time he'd spent with his son they established a bond. He felt the same as he did with his two girls. A genetic force connected him with the little boy. Thomas was positive Sheila would name the little one after him. He wouldn't see it any other way. Thomas wanted to hold his son and tell him what they were going to do when he was older. He was so excited, he couldn't sleep. He was going to have a relationship with his son, no matter what. Caroline would have to accept that. It was her who got him into the situation in the first place. She put him out of the house, accusing him of something he didn't do, which drove him to the other woman. If she hadn't put him out, he would have been at home that night in bed with her.

Three days later, Thomas showed up at Sheila's apartment with clothes, toys, and pampers. He was so proud of his only son, he went overboard. He kissed and cuddled his son, admiring his tiny fingers and cottony soft skin. Caroline was so insecure that she came with Thomas and impatiently waited in the car. Sheila looked out the window and saw Caroline sitting in the car. Sheila thought Thomas' visit would be short, but Thomas didn't appear to be leaving any time soon. Sheila sat across from Thomas and the baby. She looked toward the window thinking Caroline was lucky she didn't run outside and snatch her prissy ass out of the car for disrespecting her and her mother, and creating a scene at the hospital. She needed to get over the jealousy. It wasn't her fault Caroline couldn't provide her husband with his first son. "Doesn't she trust you anymore?" Sheila asked, taking

Thomas' attention away from the baby. Thomas ignored her and continued directing his attention to his little boy, who was wiggling in his arms, yet sound asleep.

Jealousy played tricks with Caroline's mind as she wondered what her husband was doing inside that whore's apartment so long. She wondered if this baby would tear Thomas further apart from her. It was eight-forty when she and her husband arrived, and Caroline looked at the digital clock in the wood grained interior of the car. It was five minutes to ten. Caroline rose up and looked toward the apartment. She didn't see any movement inside. This pissed her off. Caroline broke into a sweat and pushed her body back into the seat. Ten seconds later, she lost her cool and said, "Fuck this, Thomas is trippin'." Caroline blew the horn like she should have done ten minutes ago.

The telephone rang, waking Caroline from her catnap. Although she needed to start dinner, she hated being awakened. Since no one else was in the house she had to answer. Andrea was at the mall with her friends, and Taylor went with her father to see Thomas Jr. Caroline didn't feel like going today, but she always sent one of her girls. If anything went on between her husband and the slut, the girls were old enough to come home and tell her.

As she picked up the receiver, Caroline accidentally knocked over a small plant on the nightstand beside the bed. She cursed it for falling on the floor. The caller asked if he could speak with Mr. or Mrs. Smith. "This is Mrs. Smith," Caroline answered, not recognizing the voice. The man explained that he worked for the Wyoming County Police Department and her daughter Andrea Smith was in custody. The man said Andrea had been picked up at the mall in Dayton's Department Store for shoplifting. Caroline's heart dropped. She could not believe what she was hearing. She had given her daughter fifty dollars to go shopping. "You must be mistaken," she told the officer.

"Ma'am, this is no mistake," he argued. "Mrs. Smith,

Andrea is sitting right here in my office and all of her paperwork has been processed. What we need to know is if you're able to come down here to pick her up. If not, we'll have to take her to...."

"You don't have to take her nowhere," Caroline said cutting off the smart- mouthed cop. "I'll be right down there!" Caroline slammed down the phone angrily and jumped to her feet. He pissed her off! Andrea being wrong, didn't mean no one cared about her. Caroline fumbled around gathering her things. She slipped into a pair of Gucci jeans and Faragamo heals, grabbed her Louis Vutton purse, and was down the stairs in minutes. This was Andrea's second offense in less than six months and Caroline was fed up with Ms. Sticky Fingers.

Caroline entered the garage, jumped into the Escalade and backed out of the driveway. She called her husband's car phone, but he didn't answer. As soon as she got her hands on her daughter, Caroline was going to knock some sense into her. She didn't know where Andrea had picked up such a bad habit, but if the girl knew what was good for her she'd drop it. Caroline had given her money before she left and if Andrea didn't have enough for what she wanted, she should have waited. Caroline was so angry, she could feel a headache coming on. She warned Andrea the first time, but obviously that didn't matter. She halted at a yellow light and banged on the steering wheel, shouting, "No, no, no!" She wasn't going through this shit with Andrea. The girl had pushed her to the limit and Caroline was going to punish her. The first time Andrea misbehaved she got off easily. Thomas did nothing but yell at her and send her to her room. This time, things would be different. Caroline had her own way of handling things.

She pulled into the parking lot at the police station. There was a sign outside the gate, "No Available Parking," so Caroline pulled out of the entrance and found a metered parking space. She dug into her purse for change as she waited for someone to pull out of a parking space. A man was driving in slow motion, so Caroline blew her horn to make him aware that she was waiting for the parking space. She could see him mumbling into his rearview mirror, but she didn't care. Impatiently, she pulled into the empty space and pulled down her vanity mirror to check her appearance. "Oh my God!" she screamed, realizing she was still wearing her head scarf. She ripped the scarf from her head, dug into her purse and whipped out her feathering comb. She combed out her wrap and dabbed on some Fashion Fair's Berrylicious lipstick. She gathered a dollar and twenty cents worth of change and jumped out of the SUV. Caroline dropped the coins into the meter, then dashed across the street toward the police department.

She approached the information desk to find out where to go. The clerk listened carefully to Caroline's story and gave her directions to Officer Willinsky's office. Nervously, she walked faster than usual. Picking her child from the police station was embarrassing. When Caroline arrived at Officer Willinsky's department, the receptionist told Caroline to have a seat and the officer would be out in a few minutes.

After announcing her name, the officer approached Caroline in the waiting room. He shook her sweaty palm and asked her to follow him. She felt like a criminal. Everyone was either in a police uniform and carrying a gun or plainly dressed in everyday attire and carrying guns. They walked down the hallway and turned left, stopping at the second door on the right. The man turned the knob, pushed the door open, and stepped to the side so Caroline could enter. Caroline's eyes watered when she saw Andrea in handcuffs.

"You can have a seat right over there next to your daughter, Mrs. Smith," said the officer, pointing to the chair next to Andrea. Even though she felt sorry for the girl, Caroline was still angry. She felt like knocking the girl out for embarrassing her. Caroline closed her eyes and counted slowly from ten to one. She would deal with Andrea at home.

"Well, Mrs. Smith," the officer began firmly. "It looks like your daughter will have to appear before a judge this time." When Caroline had talked to Officer Willinsky on the phone, he seemed like an arrogant you-know-what, but he was an ordinary man who took pride in his job. He wasn't as bad as Caroline had imagined. Maybe she'd just been upset because he was punishing her child. Until she knew the whole story, he was still the enemy. "Let's see here," the officer said. "Your daughter was caught with"— he paused, glanced at the paperwork, then resumed, "she was caught with $570.00 in stolen merchandise." Caroline's pupils dilated like a uterus giving birth when she heard the amount.

"Under the circumstances, with this being her second offense and all, Andrea will have to see a judge on June fifteenth, at two o'clock in the afternoon," he continued.

"Well, do you know what type of punishment she should be expecting?" Caroline asked. "Considering that she's only fourteen years old, she may be sentenced to serve time in boot camp, community service, or maybe she'll just be responsible for a bunch of court costs and prosecution fees. I'm not to say for sure, but the store presses charges to the fullest extent of the law. They want to make sure whomever is caught has to pay severely for their mistakes; besides, this has become an increasing problem with teenagers these days. It's common now for them to cut school and go to the mall to shoplift. I don't understand these children."

"I don't understand either, Officer," Caroline acknowledged, looking at her daughter. "My husband and I are well off and our children have no reason to steal. I don't know what has gotten into her. She has everything. I don't understand why Andrea would do something like this."

"It's probably just a phase," the officer said sympathetically. "Sometimes it's who your children hang with that gets them into trouble."

"Lord, have mercy," Caroline gasped, as the officer placed X's on the forms for Caroline's signature. He handed her a black pen. He grabbed a Polaroid and snapped Andrea's picture, then uncuffed her. Andrea rubbed her wrists. After signing the forms, Caroline shook the officer's hand and thanked him for all his help, then took her daughter down the hall. Caroline yelled at Andrea, asking her why she was dragging behind. Andrea didn't answer. Caroline lowered her voice and walked toward her. She glanced around the hallway to see if anyone was watching as she scolded her. "You are in a lot of trouble," she said. Andrea rolled her eyes and quickened her step. Caroline continued talking about how she should have left Andrea down there. The girl tuned her mom out because she knew she would have to hear her fuss the rest of the day.

At home, Andrea walked into the kitchen before Caroline got out of the car. Caroline told Andrea to go to her bedroom.

"What's going on with you guys?" Thomas asked, looking at his wife's mean expression. "Taylor and I were sitting here wondering where you all were."

"Your daughter has been caught stealing again," Caroline said as she kicked off her shoes. "I just came back from picking her up at the police station."

"Didn't you give her money this morning?" Thomas asked.

"Yes, I did," Caroline answered, "but apparently fifty dollars wasn't enough. Andrea wanted five hundred- seventy dollars worth of clothes."

Thomas shook his head as she was about to go to battle with her thieving daughter. Once Caroline got to the top of the stairs, Thomas walked into the family room where he and Taylor were watching a movie. He'd have to wait until Caroline came back down to ask any questions.

Caroline stomped into her daughter's bedroom. Andrea

was sitting on the edge of her bed. The girl noticed that her mom had one of her father's thick leather belts. She stood up as the belt came toward her.

"Now you know you had no business out there stealing when I gave you fifty dollars this morning," Caroline fussed, while the leather strap wrapped around Andrea's arm. She screamed as the strap stroked her repeatedly.

"Okay, mama!" she yelled.

"Oh, Mama, nothing," Caroline fussed, striking the child with the belt.

"I promise, Mama, I'm not going to steal anymore."

The girl fell back on the bed, protecting her legs. Caroline did not stop swinging. Once, she swung so hard, the belt boomeranged and she hit herself. This made her angrier. She threw down the belt and grabbed her daughter's shirt. The girl squirmed out of her mother's reach just as she got ready to swing. Her hand met the side of Andrea's face, and it stung. The girl cried out like her mother was trying to kill her.

"The next time you get caught stealing, you are going to be on your own, because I'm not going to pick you up," Caroline said angrily. Caroline left the room. She was tired and out of breath.

Caroline burst out crying in the hallway. She hated to whoop her children, but Andrea was overdue for that one. She didn't want Andrea to think she could get away with stealing. Upset, she charged into her bedroom and sat on the edge of the bed. Tears poured down her face as she thought about her sister. They had not talked in a long time, but she needed to talk now. They had a lot of catching up to do because Caroline had never even told Dorothy about Thomas Jr.

Thomas walked into the bedroom and asked if she was okay.

"Yeah, I'm all right," she answered. "I just hope this phase will be one that passes because if there is a next time I'll probably kill the girl."

"Are you ready to tell me what happened?" he asked.

"Thomas, can you believe Andrea was caught with almost six hundred dollars in stolen merchandise? What's worse than that, we have to take her to court in two weeks. The officer said the judge might place Andrea on probation, or even worse, she could be sent to a juvenile boot camp. I can't believe she would try this a second time."

"Whatever has gotten into her, I hope it's out," her husband commented.

"Well, you can decide a punishment for the little thief because I don't want to see her face anymore today," Caroline said lying across the bed on her stomach. Her husband sat down and rubbed her legs. "It's going to be all right, baby," Thomas assured his wife. He told her dinner was downstairs, if she was hungry. Although Thomas was one hell of a cook, Caroline had no appetite. She sat straight up in bed, wanting to be held. Thomas hugged his wife, then their tongues joined. The kiss was like an electrical wire touching a charged battery. Her body jolted as she leaned back and they embraced in a long, wet, passionate kiss.

Without letting go of her tongue, Thomas laid his wife's body on the bed and began taking off her blouse. "Where is Taylor?" she asked.

"She's downstairs watching cartoons on television. We don't have to worry about her."

Thomas continued kissing his wife. With his available hand, he slipped her pants down her thick legs. Her underwear shortly followed. Caroline relaxed while her husband undressed. She was so turned on that she unzipped his pants. They fell to the floor. Her husband licked her belly button, fascinated with her pleasure zone. She squirmed and let out a soft pleasing moan as his pallet licked her pudding. Thomas' tongue raced up and down between her legs, setting her on fire. Refusing to wait any longer, she begged him to enter her anticipating womb. Slowly, he climbed on top of his wife. He rocked his way inside, while slowly maneuvering himself comfortably within the mounds of her walls. Caroline moaned with satisfaction and wrapped her legs around her husband's strong body. While Thomas worked his body in and out of hers, she rocked back and forth, as their bodies swayed in a smooth, rhythmic motion. He paused just when the feeling was getting great. He asked her to turn around as he penetrated her heaven from behind. He eased inside like a snake into its hole. She cried out his name as the great pleasure of his lovemaking prepared her for climax, something she hadn't experienced in over three months.

Caroline felt energized and climbed on top. On his cane, her body swayed in a sensual dancing motion. He moaned, "Work it, Baby, work it!" She smiled and looked into her husband's face, but his eyes were closed. She knew that expression. It meant he was almost ready to blast off in ecstasy. It meant he was filling all of her. She knew exactly what to do next. She straddled up and rode her husband like a cowgirl. In no time, he cried out, stiffened up, and released his bodily juices inside her. Caroline stayed on top motionless. When she finally rolled over, she felt the liquids escape from her body and roll between her buttock cheeks, landing on the sheets.

Thomas headed to the bathroom to take a shower. His wife stayed behind enjoying her euphoria. It was like she and Thomas had made love for the first time. Their romance had been rekindled by their daughter getting into trouble. How ironic was that. After about five minutes she jumped up and pranced into the bathroom to join her husband.

Thomas smiled as his wife peeked through the white curtain. She slowly stepped into the shower, grabbing her husband's arm so she wouldn't fall. Caroline took the soap from his hand and placed it into the soap dish. Thomas pulled his wife close to him as the water danced off their bodies and down the drain. Fondling led to foreplay and more lovemaking inside the shower stall.

After the second time, Thomas climbed out of the shower before his wife and headed for the bedroom. He was dripping water all over the floor. Caroline stepped out to put her wringing wet hair into a ponytail. Tomorrow she would go to the beauty salon and have her hair re-wrapped because she and her husband had worked a hurting on her hairdo. Happily, she pulled a scrunchie from a drawer and pulled her hair into a ponytail, then headed for the bedroom. She dried herself, slipped into a night-gown, and headed downstairs to enjoy the food her husband had prepared. Thomas walked to Andrea's room to talk to her.

Caroline had worked up quite an appetite. She popped her plate into the microwave and went into the family room to check on Taylor. The cartoon was watching her! Caroline woke Taylor and instructed her to go to bed, then went back to the kitchen and got her plate from the microwave. She grabbed the telephone. For some reason she felt like talking to her sister.

Dwayne answered the telephone on the second ring. "Hi, Dwayne, how have you been doing?" Caroline asked.

"I'm fine. How are you doing, Auntie Caroline?"

"I'm fine, Boo," she replied. "Where is your mother?"

"Hold on a minute and I'll go and get her for you." Caroline heard her nephew yell in the background, "Mama, tele-phone. It's Auntie Caroline." Dorothy picked up the receiver from her bedroom and Dwayne hung up.

"Hey, girl," Dorothy answered in a sad tone.

"What's wrong with you?"

"Girl, too damn much. I received some hurtful news and I've been a little upset every since."

"What's wrong?" her sister asked. "Don't tell me that you lost your job?"

"Girl, I think my situation is much more serious than that. Right now, I'd probably rather deal with that then to be dealing with what I have to."

"Girl, what is it?"

"Caroline, your niece, Monet, is about to have a baby. She's nine weeks pregnant, girl."

"You better take her to get an abortion. I know a really nice clinic where she can get the procedure done this week for only three hundred dollars."

"This is between her and Derrick. I am not going to make her do anything. She has to learn from her mistakes and I don't believe that having an abortion would teach anything. She knew before she laid down that screwing with no protection could result in pregnancy and what did she do about it. She laid up there and fucked. If she knew the difference between right and wrong she should have made that punk get up, or use protection. She can't say she didn't know any better because I've talked to my kids about sex and they all know what I went through. If I spend my hard earned money to get her an abortion, then how do I know this won't happen again? I don't want her to think an abortion is a form of birth control. Mama always used to say, "don't make your bed hard, because you are the one who has to lie in it." My daughter is the one pregnant. It's her body, her baby, and her life and she has to be the one to make the decision about what she wants to do. She has decided to have this baby and the only thing I can do is support her one hundred percent. I'm not worried about how hard it's going to be, but I believe in God all things are possible. We are going to take it one day at a time."

"She ain't grown. Your daughter is sixteen years old, unmarried and is not finished with high school. There is no need for her to ruin her life by having a baby," Caroline said, pleading with her sister."I don't believe her life will be ruined, only hindered. A baby don't stop no show," Dorothy replied."Well, if either one of my daughters get pregnant, I bet you they're going straight to the clinic. I will not have a child of mine having children out of wedlock. I refuse to be a grandmother of any bastard children, how is that going to make you look? It would be a different thing if the one she is pregnant by was possibly marriage material but he ain't nothing but a lil' knuckle head punk. Do you want Monet to follow in your footsteps?" Caroline asked.

"Ain't that a bitch?" Dorothy snapped. "What do you mean? You act like I have this fucked up life or something. Yes, I dropped out of school when I got pregnant, but I did go back and get my GED. I have a job that's taking care of me and my children, although you might not consider it to be the best. You think you have the perfect little life over there in your big castle, but let me tell you something. You may enjoy living in that cosmetically superficial world you live in but some people enjoy just keeping shit real. My shit may not look so pretty but it's the way it is and I'm going to deal with. Around my neck of the woods we deal with our problems head on. We don't put as much effort as you do in trying to cover them up. Everybody ain't as lucky as you to have all the finer things in life, and our money doesn't get us or our kids out of trouble. We're normal people just like you used to be and we don't live in a daydream world cause we all know everything ain't always as perfect as it may seem."

"I ain't saying that my life is without flaw. Shit, I had to get with Andrea today so how can I say that my family is perfect."

"I bet you don't run and tell your high and mighty friends when your children fuck up, do you?" She interrupted, "What I was saying is that Monet could be ruining the rest of her life."

"Whatever, Caroline," Dorothy argued. "Your ass needs to watch how you say shit to people." Caroline always carried on like her children were angels. In her eyes, those two girls could do no wrong.

"I know one thing, though," Caroline tried to change the

subject since she knew she had struck a nerve with Dorothy. As bad as I got in that ass today, Andrea will think twice before she tries me again. Thomas says that she's going through a phase of rebellion. I don't know what it is." Changing the subject, her sister asked, "Does Tony know that he's going to be a grandfather yet?"

"No, girl, and it ain't no telling when was the last time we've seen or talked to him. Derrick is the only one besides Monet's friend Brandy who knows about the pregnancy."

"Do you think that the boy is going to stick around?"

"Girl, please. He came over here talking about he's going to enroll back in school and start looking for a job. You know they always talk that I'm gone do shit in the beginning."

"Do you think he's really serious, though?"

"I don't know. Only time will tell; but just like I said, they all talk a good game at first."

"I hope Monet knows that having a baby ain't gone be easy at all. Didn't you tell her how hard you and I had it trying to raise her?" That was another thing about Caroline that pissed her off; she always wanted to take credit for everything. She had helped Dorothy out with Monet when she was a baby, and how could Dorothy forget when her sister brought it up every chance she got. "Well, hopefully she'll graduate soon, then her and her crumb snatcher would be on their way." Caroline giggled as her sister joked about her daughter and soon-to-be grandbaby.

"Well, Sis, at least one good thing happened today after all the drama."

"What?" Dorothy asked.

"I got my groove on so good today that I felt like a naive school girl getting her groove on for the first time. Thomas really put it on me."

"Aw, you stanking tramp."

"Don't player hate on me cause yo' shit is all dried up and

decrepit," Caroline laughed.

"That's all right because when my man comes home we gone be putting in some overtime."

"Girl, you crazy," Caroline laughed. It made her feel good to talk to her sister and be able to laugh after all the bad news. "I hate to say this, but my food is getting cold, so I got to go. I'll talk to you later."

"You know," Caroline said, "I have to build back up all my energy that I lost today from my strenuous workout."

"Fuck you," Dorothy said and hung up the telephone. Caroline was cracking up. She would be happy when her husband came home so she could get her some sex. Right now, Dorothy could use the comfort of a man.

Break the Rules Pay the Price

Monet's pregnancy became more obvious as the months went by. Now that she was almost six months, Monet noticed dramatic changes in her body. Her face was swollen, her nose was a big deal larger, and her butt stuck out voluptuously. Checking herself out in the full-length mirror on her closet door, Monet noticed her entire body had changed.

She stared at her naked body. Her two sisters sat on the edge of her bed in amazement. Monet had just bathed and was about to get dressed to go the movies with Derrick. Neither of her sisters could believe how Monet had expanded over the last couple months. Tonya had a clue about the pregnancy process, but Keisha wasn't sure how it had gotten there. When Monet became pregnant neither of her sisters could tell, but now she looked totally different.

"Derrick wants a boy," Monet stated. She stared at Keisha through the mirror, rubbing her bare swollen belly. "I'm not for sure if I want a girl or a boy, but whatever it is I just hope it hurry up and comes. I am tired of looking like this. Being pregnant is the most uncomfortable feeling you could imagine. Not only do you look different, but you feel different. You walk funny, and all throughout the day you're tired but can't get any sleep because you're uncomfortable because this big ole sack is in your way." Monet rubbed her stomach to demonstrate. "Y'all better not ever let no boy talk y'all into going through this until after your wedding ceremony," Monet scolded her sisters.

"I ain't getting pregnant," Tonya replied. Then both girls shook their heads, assuring Monet this was not going to happen to them. Monet said a prayer every night for God to look over them. She did not want them ending up like her.

"Monet. Telephone!" Dwayne yelled from downstairs. She already knew it was Derrick, so Monet slipped on her robe and tied the belt on her way out of the room. When she left the bedroom, Tonya told Keisha.

"I can't see how Monet got pregnant," Tonya told Keisha, "and she ain't nothing but sixteen years old. If she was ready to be messing with boys then she should have went to the Planned Parenthood to get her some birth control pills. She could have got some without mama even finding out."

"What is the Planned Parenthood?" Keisha asked naively.

"It's a place where teenage girls and women can go and get birth control pills, female exams, and education on diseases like HIV."

"How do you know, Tonya?"

"We had an assembly at school one time where some people from the clinic came to talk to a group of us who wanted to listen. No students could come unless their parents filled out the permission slip, because they were going to be talking about sex. Mama filled out mine and said that I could go because she thought it was good for me to learn about my body as early as possible." Tonya explained.

"I'm gone go there too, so I can't get pregnant." Her little sister stared at her, listening intently. Keisha didn't want to end up like Monet either.

"Hello," Monet huffed into the receiver when she reached the telephone.

"What's up, Boo?" he asked.

"Nothing much, I was just upstairs about to slip on my clothes. I just got out of the shower, so I'll be ready by the time you get here."

"Well, see," Derrick hesitated. "I was calling you to let you know that there has been a slight change in plans tonight."

"What?" Monet was disappointed.

"Well, see, I was calling you to tell you that I think it would be better for us to go to the movies tomorrow instead of today." He continued, "See, my boys changed their minds about going to the movies and want to go bowling instead. I told them that you can't be bowling with that big ole belly sticking out so I figure you can just chill tonight, and I'm gone chill wit them. Tomorrow me and you can go to the movies together cause that's when they gone be chillin' wit' they girls."

" After he'd spoiled their plans and hurt Monet's feelings, Derrick had the nerve to say, "You know you got to be careful. You can risk hurting my son by bowling and you know I ain't having that." Monet eased out an artificial okay as the tears filled her eyes.

"Well, call me tomorrow then." Monet didn't give him the chance to say anything else before hanging up the telephone. She was pissed because going to the movies was all that she'd been talking about all day. Derrick had a lot of nerve calling her thirty minutes before it was time to go. She mumbled to herself, "The least he could have done was called and asked me if I wanted to go or not, instead of making decisions for me."

The baby must have known she was mad, because it started kicking and wiggling. Monet stuck her hand through the robe and rubbed her belly where she'd felt movement. After the first four months of her pregnancy, Derrick had been acting different. He acted as if being around her was contagious. The more she thought about it, the more her stomach hurt. She tried to stop thinking about it and walked into the living room. She relaxed her big butt on the couch and switched on the T.V. She flicked the remote, looking for a good movie. When she felt the baby move again, she rubbed her belly and said, "Your daddy makes me sick.

"Derrick stepped out of the phone booth and hurried to the car where his friends were waiting. Jamil and his girl were up front and Jamil's girl brought along her friend, who was sitting in the backseat waiting to meet him. Derrick jumped into the backseat and joined his date. "Let's roll," he sang with a huge smile on his face. "My mom said I'd better be home by one or else I'm not getting in," he joked, hitting the back of Jamil's seat.

"Yeah, man, yo' moms be trippin'," Jamil responded, as rehearsed. Everything was cool. The girl beside Derrick sat quietly as they car drove down the street.

The car of teens arrived at the bowling alley. They all climbed out and headed inside in couples. Jamil and Derrick told the girls to grab a seat while they rent bowling shoes and a lane. The girls said they were going to the bathroom to freshen up.

"Were going to put our jackets at that table over there, and I wear a size seven," Nicky said. She pointed to a table. While in line, Jamil told his friend. "Man, I don't know what you gone do but when we leave here, me and Keyla are going to the hotel. She's about to give me some.

" Derrick chuckled. "Man, slow yo' roll. You was just with that honey Anetra last night. She should have tied you over for a while."

"Don't trip like you ain't gone try to push up on Nicky's fine ass while yo' woman is at home mad cause you ain't taking her to the movies. I wonder if Monet knows that Nicky is here filling in for her."

"Man, you know that a player's got to do what a player's got to do. You can't please 'em all at the same time."

"Can I help you?" the girl at the register asked when it was their turn. Derrick and Jamil paid for one lane and walked away.

The guys bowled two games, beating their dates both times, and enjoying it. The girls didn't care; they were still full of smiles. They were all hyped up like they hadn't been out of the house in months. Keyla had a nine-month old son at home and kept reminding everybody how happy she was about convincing her mom to baby-sit for her. Keyla was only sixteen but she acted older. Nicky said she was a year younger than her friend. They both were acting shy. Nicky didn't have any kids but was glad to get out of the house as well. Otherwise she would be stuck at home watching her two little brothers.

An hour later the guys got bored and said they were ready to leave. The group headed out to the car. Derrick and Jamil walked slowly behind the girls. "Man we should drive up by the way to see if someone up there can rent us a couple of rooms for the night. Them fiends are always game to earn an extra bump." Derrick whispered a plan to his friend. The boys were determined to get their dates into a room before the night was over.

The boys jumped into the car and Jamil drove out of the parking lot doing about sixty-miles an hour. After circling a few blocks, he spotted a crack-head they called Pepper. She spent money with him and Derrick all the time and Jamil knew she wouldn't mind doing them the favor. As much as she hollered,

"Let me get the twenty for sixteen." Jamil knew she better not have had complaints with providing a favor. The boy threw his ride into park and jumped out of the front seat, leaving the car running. Derrick climbed out of the back seat and told Nicky they had to handle something and would be right back. Jamil called out to Pepper as he and his friend walked toward her.

She headed in their direction strutting like she was the shit. Pepper used to have it going on, but she fell off after her big time boyfriend got locked up. Rumor had it that she used to be the finest, and sharpest dressed female around, and everybody wanted her. Now, she was always trying to turn tricks by begging to do various jobs so she could get high. She had on a wrinkled, dingy black skirt with a red cotton T-shirt and a beat up mustard colored, leather jacket. She was always sporting them off white, leather like, K-Mart pumps, even in the winter. You couldn't tell her that she didn't still have it going on.

The boys explained what they wanted her to do, and she happily agreed. Jamil was like, "cool". They all walked back to his ride and Pepper jumped in the backseat.

She climbed into the back seat and her funk came right with her. Her body reeked, filling the whole car. Nicky plugged her nose and stared an evil stare at Derrick, thinking, now why did they have to let her stanking ass ride with them?

They cruised down the rode as the fumes became more unbearable. Eventually, Jamil and Keyla caught a whiff of the funk, because they suddenly began rolling down their windows. The wind coming inside the car was ice cold but the smell had to go.

Jamil finally remarked, "Pepper, you back there living fouler than a mother-fucker, and that's real."

"Man, y'all chill out," she said. "I'm going to change my clothes. I been hustlin' all night and ain't had the chance to freshen up yet."

"Man, it's almost another day now. If you been funky this long you must have intended on being that way. I just hope yo' scent don't stay inside my ride after you get out," Jamil laughed. The others in the car were cracking up laughing too. Jamil was so bold.

"I know y'all ain't trying to be funny and I'm doing y'all punk asses a favor," Pepper said, getting louder. "Yeah, I might smell like dope but what do you expect when I been smoking the shit all day, and gone smoke some more too when I get these rooms for y'all, and get my shit."

"Man, you have been doing more than just smoking dope all day. You smell like you have been fucking all day without washing yo ass," Jamil replied.

"Nigga,' whatever. I'm from the old school and this shit y'all doing, showing out in front of these girls, this ain't shit. It don't bother me cause y'all too young to know anythang any ways." Derrick was cracking up laughing because they'd made Pepper mad, and Pepper would cuss you out in a minute. She was one of the most respected fiends around. She was talking mad shit knowing good and well they could put her out on the side of the road and keep on rolling. Knowing Pepper, she wouldn't have cared. She would have just walked back to the hood and cussed Derrick and Jamil when she was ready to spend her money with them.

After being told there were no vacancies at the first two stops, Pepper had to get two rooms at a hotel on the corner of 28th and Division. The woman came back to the car with the keys to the room. Before Jamil gave her the dope he promised, he told Pepper to run across the street to the liquor store to get them some drinks.

As she walked across the busy strip, Derrick yelled, "Call you a cab while you're over there too!" Pepper turned in the middle of the street and shot Derrick the bird, then ran into the liquor store. Minutes later the junky came out of the store carrying a brown paper bag. Jamil checked the bag when she handed it to him. It had everything they ordered, Tangeuray, Rose's Lime Juice, and a six pack of Colt forty fives in the can. Jamil gave the woman a satisfying look, then handed her a small piece of rock, a ten dollar bill, and four ones. Pepper placed the dope in her mouth, the money inside her cheap, dirty bra, and was on her way down the strip.

The crew climbed out of the car with their belongings and headed toward their designated hotel rooms. At the top of the stairs, Jamil looked back and saw that Pepper had stopped walking and was standing down the street in one spot. He could see her lighter flickering. She was down there trying to smoke. "Damn," he grunted. "She could have at least waited until she got to a side street or something."

He stared at her, then realized she had not given him his change. It probably wasn't but a couple of dollars, but he knew it wasn't an accident that Pepper forgot to give him his change. Since he didn't say anything about it, neither did she.

Nicky stood behind Derrick, waiting for him to unlock the door to their room. She turned her head and looked down where her friend Keyla and Jamil were before, but they had already gone inside.

"I ain't trying to get all sloppy drunk, so I don't know why you bought all these drinks," Keyla told Jamil as they entered the room.

He ignored her and took the drinks out of the paper bag. He placed them on the table and walked over to the counter and grabbed the complimentary guest cups. He handed one to Keyla. She had taken her jacket off and laid it across the bed. Jamil noticed they needed ice, so he got up and grabbed the ice bucket, then left the room.

Keyla was happy to be spending time with Jamil. They had been kicking it for over two months and she wanted to ask him if he felt strongly about her, like she felt about him. She sat on the sofa and tried to warm up and relax while she waited for Jamil to come back. Even though she was glad to be away, Keyla wondered what her baby was doing at home. She knew he would be in bed by now.

Jamil came back into the room with the small bucket filled with ice cubes. He sat it on the coffee table and took off his shirt. The boy stretched his arms, yawning then poured their drinks, making sure Keyla's was eighty percent liquor. That Tang always made the honey's real anxious. He smiled and handed the girl her drink. Jamil sipped and joined his girlfriend on the sofa.

They sat there for a minute, just chilling. Keyla quickly gulped down her first drink and asked Jamil to fix her another one. She took a few sips from her second drink and confessed to Jamil that she was bored. "What else can we do besides sitting here drinking and staring at the walls?" she asked.

Jamil smiled and sat his drink on the table. He rose and reached for her. She got up and followed his lead to the bed. He took her drink, sat it on the table, and said, "Let me show you."

"She sat on the neatly made bed and their lips joined.

When he stuck his tongue into her warm mouth she could taste the gin. Jamil stood by the bed with her head in his hands. His tongue danced inside her mouth. Keyla unfastened his Sean Jean jeans. She could feel his manhood growing strong against the zipper; desperately trying to get out so she let it. Once he had her jeans down, Jamil stuck his fingers inside her. She wiggled onto his index and softly spoke his name. The boy was excited, he couldn't wait to explore his discovery. He gently pulled away and climbed into the bed on top of her.

When Keyla felt Jamil enter her secret chamber, she closed her eyes and focused on what she was doing. She began to move her body as if sex was nothing new to her. Jamil began pumping faster and faster, letting out loud annoying noises. Keyla felt his manhood when he entered, but could no longer feel him. She stopped moving. He had turned into a tiger. He was acting like he was about to lose his damn mind inside her, and she wasn't feeling it. Keyla rolled her eyes. This was her first time having sex since she'd had her baby, and if this was what sex was like after giving birth than she'd never get pregnant again.

Nicky and Derrick sat on the sofa in their room sipping drinks, smoking on a blunt, and talking. Nicky told Derrick about all the talk going around about him. She told him about the many times she'd heard that he was a player.

He said, "Man, don't listen to everything you hear. A lot of people be hating on me, but I'm a good guy." He smiled seductively, hoping to ease her mind. "If you want to know anything about me, I'm right here. Ask me whatever you want to know."

"I've got to go to the bathroom," she confessed, changing the subject. Derrick watched her as she staggered to get up. She felt him watching her and she was embarrassed. Nicky didn't want Derrick to think she was immature so she hurried into the bathroom.

She pulled her jeans off, squatted on the toilet, peed, and

wiped herself. Nicky flushed the toilet and stood up to wash her hands. She glimpsed in the mirror to see if her eyes were red. She laughed when she noticed they were halfway closed. She grabbed one of the new looking, white linen towels, and proceeded to freshen up. She finished quickly, then reached into her purse and pulled out two condoms. Even though she planned on giving Derrick some, he wouldn't be giving her anything she didn't want, and she damn sure wasn't trying to get pregnant. She'd just met him. The liquor had her feeling kinky, so she hyped herself up for what she was about to do.

Derrick could not believe his eyes when he saw the girl come out of the bathroom in her birthday suit. Her dark skin was smooth, and her body perfectly sculptured. The five foot two inch girl pranced her beautiful body to the table and grabbed her drink. She took a big sip and began dancing to her own music. He watched as she wiggled and dipped her body with a smooth rhythm that made his manhood erect. She danced like she was auditioning for a strip club. Derrick licked his lips and pushed down his protruding penis. He did not want its enlargement to appear too obvious. Nicky threw the condoms to him and asked what he was waiting on to get undressed. She sashayed around in front of him as if she could hear music playing. Her body was so tight. Her ass was plump and chocolate and Derrick was watching it bounce, move, and shake up and down as she danced. He couldn't wait to get all up in her.

His game plan had been to sweet talk Nicky into giving him some, but it wasn't necessary. She was more bold and blunt than he was. Taking her lead, Derrick stood up and began to undress. Nicky picked up a condom and ripped the pack open. She accompanied him as he slipped himself into the latex. She jumped into the bed and pulled back the bedspread and sheets. Derrick slid the cover over their bodies. Nicky closed her eyes as he climbed on top of her and stuck his stiffened pole into her moist hide-away. Erect and strong, he pushed his way through the tight walls until he discovered the end of the tunnel. Nicky moaned pushing his weight off her. Derrick eased up, allowed her to relax, and gently slid back in. They rocked together gently as their bodies perspired. She pulled the covers off and they switched positions. She rode him strenuously into a climax, then they collapsed side by side next to each other. Derrick was better than Nicky heard he was.

That Saturday morning Monet woke up looking forward to spending the day with Derrick. About 11:30, he called her and said he would be by to get her at about four o'clock. The rest of her family was gone shopping so Monet was alone in the house when Derrick called. She was still mad at Derrick from the night before. She couldn't wait to ask him why he didn't ask her if she wanted to go before he voluntarily counted her out. Derrick thought she didn't know, but she knew he wasn't as attracted to her as he was before she got pregnant. Before, Monet had a shapely figure that he adored. She weighed a hundred and seven pounds and everything was in the right places. Now, her face and feet were swollen. She could no longer wear her old shoes, she'd gained thirty-seven pounds and had a little more than two months to go before she would be full term. If any of her friends from school could see her now, Monet swore they wouldn't recognize her.

When Derrick pulled up in front of the house and blew, Monet rushed right out the front door. She locked the door behind her and wobbled to the car. Derrick planted a big kiss on her lips and asked the soon-to-be mother how she was doing.

"Fine," she grinned. "Mother and baby are doing fine."

"Are you guys hungry?" he asked rubbing Monet's belly.

"No, I just finished eating a hamburger," Monet answered,

removing his hand from her belly. He was going to start the baby kicking and she didn't feel like being bothered.

"Dang," he remarked. Derrick was shocked by her actions. "I can't let my shorty know his daddy is here?" Monet stared him down with an evil glare. She didn't say anything. "All right, that's cool. We can go to the mall first, and afterwards we can catch a movie. Now is that going to change the look on your face?"

Monet finally eased out a smile. Spending time with Derrick did make her happy. Monet wiggled comfortably into her seat, gripped her purse, and relaxed while the car glided down the street. Derrick noticed her satisfied look and sighed in relief. After the night he'd had, he wasn't in the mood to argue with no pregnant and moody ass female.

They seemed to be walking through the mall forever. Monet's feet hurt but Derrick was running in and out of stores. He was convinced that she was having a boy, so he was purchasing blue everything. Derrick even bought her two outfits at Mother's World. They walked to Gymboree and bought a blue jean jumper with a blue shirt to go under it, and another sleeper outfit for his son. Their final stop was at the Foot Locker. Derrick had to buy the new Jordans that came out the day before. He bought a pair for himself, a pair for their soon to be coming son, and bought Monet a comfortable pair of all white Reebok Classics.

They left the mall and went to the movies. When the movie was over, Monet was tired and hungry, so they went to IHOP. When they were seated, Derrick told Monet to order them some drinks while he used the phone. He needed to call back whomever was paging him. The waitress finally came to take their drink orders. When she returned with the drinks, she asked Monet if they were ready to order. Monet was mad at Derrick for taking so long so she snapped on the waitress by saying. "How are we going to be ready and he ain't even here?" The lady left the table saying she would give them a few more minutes. Monet sipped up some of her Sprite and sat patiently. She looked up to see if Derrick was coming, but he wasn't. She said to herself. Even though Derrick gets on my nerves, he is still good to me. She was overwhelmed with the amount of money he'd spent on her and the baby. She knew he would be a good father because he was already making sure his baby was freshly dressed. Monet thought tonight would be a good time to discuss her and Derrick moving in together. She'd mentioned it to her mother a couple of months ago, but Dorothy objected to Monet moving out before graduation. She said if Monet moved in with that boy before she graduated she'd probably never finish school. Monet tried to convince her mother that she was making too much of a simple situation. Monet said Derrick could handle everything without her help. Dorothy told Monet that she was talking crazy.

"How are you going to be moving out, with a baby, on a drug dealer's salary?" her mom fussed, even though Monet told her mother that Derrick was getting a job. Her mom said, "He's been singing that same song ever since you've been pregnant and doesn't have a job yet. How much longer is it going to take before he gets one?" Monet dropped the subject and never brought it up again. She was just saying those things because she didn't like Derrick. Sooner or later Monet would be old enough to make her own decisions.

Dorothy tried explaining to her hard-headed child that Derrick was no good for her. Everything he'd promised at the beginning of her pregnancy was a lie. The only thing Derrick was good at was standing Monet up. After hurting her feelings he would take her shopping or out to eat. He would splurge her with all kinds of gifts and stuff for her and the baby. Dorothy knew it was to cover up for hidden dirt and soon Monet would wake up and see for herself. She would learn through her own experiences, not based on what her mother said. Mothers didn't know everything.

Derrick came back from the telephone and eased in the booth across from his girlfriend. He'd taken so long coming back that Monet ordered him a steak, egg and pancake platter. The food came a few minutes before he sat down. Derrick quickly scuffed down his meal without looking up once at Monet. He finished eating and went to use the phone again. When he came back he said he had to take Jamil his car back. He paid and Monet followed him out of the restaurant with her doggy bag in her hand. She wasn't quite ready for their day to end, but apparently it was over.

They pulled up in front of Monet's house and Derrick gave her a big kiss and said he'd call her tomorrow. Monet got her bags from the backseat and struggled up the walkway. Derrick pulled off.

Monet was tired and couldn't wait to get inside and rest her aching feet. It was a quarter to nine and Dorothy said she and the kids had been home since around seven. When Monet came in her mother was on the couch watching a program on television. She said, "Girl, what do you have in all of those bags?"

"Oh, just some more stuff Derrick bought for me and the baby," she answered. Her mom shook her head and called for Dwayne to help Monet carry the bags upstairs to her room.

When Dwayne brought the bags into her bedroom he said, "Dang, Derrick bought you all kind of stuff." Monet didn't say anything. She was too happy to see her bed. When her brother left the room she slipped into her favorite gown and climbed into bed. She was too tired to put any of her new things away; that would have to wait until tomorrow.

Surviving the Circumstances

She was in a state of shock when her friend Punkin told her she was about to have a baby. Sitting in a chair beside her, Dorothy said,

"I just can't believe, after all these years, you managed to get yourself caught up- and by the way, who is the father?"

"I'm not telling you," Punkin blushed.

"That is probably because you don't know," her friend laughed.

Punkin's eyes caught the attention of a Hispanic woman playing with her little boy. The toddler was full of energy.

"At least this will only make your second one. I got four with one on the way," Dorothy said.

"Girl, I'm still trying to figure out what to tell Bruce. I haven't figured out how to tell him I'm pregnant, but I have to."

"You'll figure out something, I'm sure."

"Oh yeah, what am I supposed to tell him? Baby, I'm about to have a baby even though you, my man, and ain't had the coochie."

Dorothy held her hands over her mouth to keep from laughing. Punkin looked very serious as she talked. "I can't believe you. You're sitting up here laughing in my face, Dorothy."

The security guard called out her name and others. Dorothy got up to visit her husband. Punkin yelled as she walked through the sliding glass door, "It ain't funny girl."

The guard searched her when she walked through the door. She was happy she had been called in before Punkin. Dorothy couldn't wait to see her husband. After being patted down thoroughly, she waited patiently until the next door opened. The visitors stepped through the sliding glass door, one by one, into the visiting area. Delvin walked cordially into the waiting area. His hair was low cut. He was well groomed. He'd been anticipating seeing his wife's gorgeous smile. "The days are growing shorter, baby," he said after kissing her." In thirteen more months our family will be back together again. It ain't no way I'm messing up this time. I owe my kids and you more than that. I've realized I don't need those drugs and it has taken me this long to figure that out. All I need is to get my family back," Delvin pleaded.

Dorothy smiled as she listened to her husband's promises while smiling. She'd heard it all before, but this time she felt he was sincere.

He continued, "I know you've heard all this before and I'm sorry that things didn't turn out the way they should have last time, but I've changed. I know we can work out our problems, and in no time we'll be out of the projects, and in a house of our own."

She cut him off, "I hope you plan on finding yourself a new set of hanging buddies. All of your old friends are all still doing the same thing, and while you're trying to get yourself back together, I think you need to stay away from them."

"If that's what you want, baby, then that's what you're going to get."

The rest of the visit Delvin went on and on about doing things differently when he got out.

An announcement said the visitors had one minute to wrap up their visits. Dorothy gave her spouse a long passionate kiss and told him she loved him. On the way to his cell, Delvin told himself, "This is the last sentence I'm gone serve for these motherfuckers, that's fo' sho'." He was determined to put his family back together and stay clean. He had to be strong and stay away from his old buddies.

Delvin had always been good to Dorothy and the kids. The problems started when he started getting high. Before being locked up, Delvin had reached the point of not caring about anything except getting high. He knew in his heart that if he hadn't been on the crack, he'd have never robbed that liquor store. This time he was determined to keep himself afloat. All he needed was his family's help and support.

Dorothy rode home in silence. She wanted to believe her husband, but she still had her doubts. Her mind was made up. If her husband didn't do what he was supposed to do this time, he wasn't getting another chance. She'd overcome too much to let him drag her down. If he did, they were through. She was still paying off debts he'd accumulated when he was out getting high. It hadn't been easy, but most of the bills were paid.

Monet stood in the front door holding the phone. Dorothy rushed to get the telephone; it was Punkin. Dorothy had just dropped her off at home. "What, girl?" Dorothy asked.

"Girl, I finally told Colby I was pregnant."

"For real," Dorothy gasped as she pulled a chair away from the kitchen table and sat down. She was anxious to hear the juicy gossip. Dorothy wiggled into the chair to hear the whole story.

"Girl, he came running some bullshit to me about he ain't ready to settle down and start no family. I told him he should have been thinking about that before he let his contaminated juices flow into my body. His no good ass hung up on me. Girl, what am I going to do?"

"Girl, please," Dorothy remarked. "You better do like the rest of us and take care of your baby yourself. I'm the mother and father of mine. Just make sure you got his address and social security number for child support purposes," she joked. Call waiting interrupted their conversation. "Hold on for a minute, Punkin." Dorothy clicked the line.

"Hello." After a minute of silence the operator came on asking if Dorothy wanted to accept a collect call from an inmate at a correctional facility. She said, "Yes." Dorothy asked Delvin to hold on while she freed the line. She clicked over and told Punkin she would call her back.

"Dang, we just left from up there," Punkin said and hung up. Dorothy clicked over to her husband.

"Who was that on the other line?" he asked.

"Punkin!"

"Oh," he paused. "Well, baby, I was calling you to let you know that they changed my release date."

"What do you mean?" She questioned.

"Well, it's getting so crowded in here they have to get rid of two hundred-forty people in order to make room for new inmates and since I was getting out in a little over a year they gave me nine months advancement." Dorothy couldn't believe what she was hearing. She thought of having long, passionate sex.

"Hot damn," she shouted. Her dick would be home sooner than she thought.

"My, my, my, this has to be the best news I've heard all day," Dorothy blurted.

"I ain't gone keep you long Boo, but I had to call and tell you the good news. Right now it's time to go to dinner, so I have to go."

He hung up and rushed to his bunk for count. Delvin's stomach was growling and he couldn't wait to get to the cafeteria to eat. The food was horrible, but enough nourishment to keep you going.

A tingle in Dorothy's vagina moistened her satin, flowered underwear. She imagined her body locked with Delvin's. She ran to the bathroom to take a shower to cool off.

———

Two months later Monet was closer to her delivery date. She awakened feeling queasy. She sat up on the side of the bed with her knees up and her head buried between her legs. She hoped this position would bring her comfort. The sleepless nights she'd been having lately were getting on her nerves. She got up from the floor and paced.

Dorothy woke up hearing footsteps upstairs. It had to be Monet. Weary, she glanced over her shoulder and looked at the clock. It was four twenty-eight in the morning. Dorothy got up, grabbed her robe, and headed upstairs to see her pregnant daughter. She was worried about Monet going into labor. "Are you okay?" Dorothy asked.

"Yeah, I guess. My stomach is really hurting so I got up to walk around hoping to alleviate the pain. It feels like something heavy is pressing on my stomach making me feel like I have to go to the bathroom. It's just sitting right there and won't move."

"That's probably the baby turning into its position to come out."

"Mom, I can't wait until I have this baby. I am so tired of being pregnant," Monet complained. "I didn't start feeling this uncomfortable until these last few months."

"Well, baby, this is the way it's going to be from here on out. You might as well get used to it. Rather you realize it or not, this is still the easy part. Wait until that baby starts crying in the middle of the night, waking you up out of your sleep. That is going to get on your nerves much worse than this." She persisted. "No, wait until you get your paycheck and plan what you're going to do with it, but end up having to spend the majority of it on pampers, milk, Oragel, or Penicillin. That's what's going to get on your nerves."

Dorothy sat on the side of the bed near her daughter. She observed all the horrible faces Monet made while rubbing on her lopsided belly. The baby was turned in some strange position and had Monet's belly looking deformed. Monet listened to her mother but silently disagreed.

"I bet you'll think the next time before you lie down and spread them legs," Dorothy said. "You were talking about those birth control pills made you sick, I wonder what you're gonna do after this. Are you going to try and take a different kind?"

Monet just rubbed her aching back. Dorothy rose, laughing a tired laugh. "I'm going back downstairs so that I can at least sleep till about eight or nine. The only thing I can tell you is this part will be over soon." Dorothy left the room and closed the door. She paused and said, "My poor baby," then continued down the stairs to her bedroom.

Seven-thirty the next morning Monet awakened in a hot sweat. A sharp pain raced from her abdomen. She tried to pull herself up from the bed, but another pain hit her, the second one about two minutes after the first one. The pain raced from her abdomen down her legs. Her muscles tightened like the arm strap used to test blood pressure. Monet let out a loud frightening scream because the pain was so overbearing. As she climbed out of bed, Monet opened the bedroom door and crept down the hallway to the stairs. Another contraction shot through her body. The girl took a seat on the top of the stairs and tried to catch her breath. Her heart was pounding and sweat was dripping from her body. She couldn't think or move. The throbbing pain shifted from her legs to her stomach and down her back. Monet knew she was too delirious to make it down the stairs.

"Mom!" she cried. "Mom, please help me!" the girl yelled down the stairwell.

Dorothy jumped up from bed as if it was on fire and raced toward the stairs where she found the girl with her head between her legs. Monet looked up and tried to call out to her mom, but the words would not come out.

"Oh my God!" Monet screamed. The pain was so excruciating she could no longer move. She had never been in so much pain. She cried, hoping to relieve some of the misery.
In a panic, Dorothy ran up the stairs and helped her daughter down to the kitchen table. She sat Monet down and rushed into

the bathroom and grabbed some wet towels. She ran back and placed them on Monet's forehead because she was burning up. Dorothy ran to the kitchen sink and poured a glass of cold water for her daughter, but ended up drinking it herself. She filled the glass again and rushed to the girl. Dorothy noticed a puddle of liquid slowly forming on the floor under her daughter's chair.

"Oh Lord," Dorothy griped. "Your water done broke. Oh Lord," tears fell from her eyes. "Baby, I've got to get you to the hospital."

Monet screamed as each contraction raced through her body. Dorothy grabbed the first pair of jeans she came across. The soon-to-be grandmother slipped into the jeans and tucked her nightgown inside. She threw on a t-shirt over the gown since she wasn't wearing a bra. Dorothy zoomed up the staircase to get Monet's overnight bag from her bedroom. "Calm down, Dorothy, calm down," she told herself. "You have to be able to drive." Monet knew her baby was coming soon and she was petrified.

"Keisha," Dorothy called, hoping one of her girls in the next room would wake up. No one answered so Dorothy raced back down the stairs. She would call the kids from the hospital. She helped her daughter out of the chair, and escorted her to the door.

"Mom," Monet stopped walking. "I have to call Derrick." Dorothy looked bothered but didn't say anything. She led Monet back to the chair and reached for the telephone. Dorothy called the doctor to let her know that Monet was on her way to the hospital.

Dr. Harris asked how far apart the contractions were. "Her water broke," Dorothy explained. The doctor said she would meet them at the hospital. Dorothy keyed in the numbers of Derrick's pager as Monet called them off. She waited impatiently for the recording so she could leave the phone number.

She punched in her home phone number and 911 after it. Dorothy told her daughter they didn't have time to wait for her boyfriend to call back. Then they left the house immediately.

Derrick was asleep when his pager buzzed. He reached for it and glanced at the display to see who was paging him so fucking early in the morning. If it was one of his customers, they was gone get cussed out as soon as he got on the block. It was Monet's phone number and 911 after the digits. Derrick knew he needed to call back right away. She might be in labor.

Dorothy's telephone rang about twelve times before Keisha answered it. Derrick could tell she had just gotten up because she sounded distant and groggy. "Hello," Keisha eased out.

"This is Derrick. Can I speak to Monet?"

Keisha hesitated and called out for her sister. "Monet," she called again with an attitude. Keisha was upset that Derrick was calling so early in the morning and because she had to go all the way upstairs to get Monet. She was surprised her mom hadn't answered and cussed him out.

"Monet, telephone," Keisha called. She would have to deliver a message because Monet wasn't answering. "Why are you calling here this early anyway?"

"Girl, don't start trippin'. Monet is the one who paged me. I was just calling back to see what she wanted."

"Dang, let me go upstairs and wake her up." She told Derrick to hold on.

Keisha took a deep breath and dashed up the stairs to her sister's bedroom. She knocked on the door and went in but found Monet's room empty. She called her sister's name. Monet didn't answer. Keisha glanced in the bathroom and Monet wasn't there either. The bewildered little sister ran back downstairs to her mother's bedroom, which was also empty. She walked into Dwayne's room and found him asleep. Keisha closed his door and walked to the front to look out and see if her mom's car was outside; it wasn't. Frustrated and uneasy, Keisha told Derrick that Monet was no where to be found.

"Dang, girl, how come you had me on hold for so long?"

"Derrick, I don't know where Monet is but wherever she is my mom must be with her because neither of them are here. If Monet paged you she must have done it before she left. They must have gone to the hospit..." He hung up before she could get the rest out!

Derrick jumped up from bed and into his oversized blue jeans. He grabbed his t-shirt, hanging on the bed post. He rushed out of the house and into his friend Jamil's ride. Derrick jumped in, started the car and pulled off in a hurry.

Keisha hung up the telephone and walked into the kitchen to see if her mother had left a note. As Keisha turned the corner she slipped in a pile of water on the floor she hadn't seen. "Aw," she yelled as her one-hundred pound frame slammed into the floor. "Ouch!" she shouted as she lifted herself from the pool on the floor. Keisha fussed all the way to the utility closet. She grabbed the mop and angrily walked over to mop up the hidden water puddle that had her pajamas soaked. "I wish whoever spilled this water would have gotten it up. If it had been me, mama would have been on me like white on rice."

After cleaning up the mess, the girl placed the mop back in the closet and went into her mother's room to see if Dorothy had left a note there. When Keisha turned to walk out of the room, Dwayne startled her. He was standing in the doorway rubbing his eyes. "You scared me, boy," she gasped.

"What you doing?" Dwayne asked.

"Mopping up this water. Did you spill it?"

"No."

"I think Monet is probably at the hospital having her baby."

"For real," the boy said as he walked back to his room. He

jumped into bed and buried himself under his covers, then yelled, "Keisha, can you fix some breakfast?" His sister didn't answer. She headed up the stairs to wake up Tonya.
"Forget you then!" Dwayne shouted.

———————————

   Yvette walked into the bedroom and looked around for Derrick. She didn't see him. She called his name and he didn't answer. Something told her to look out the window and that's when she noticed Jamil's car was gone. Yvette couldn't believe it. She heard tires screech when she was in the other room with Asia but she hadn't paid any attention. Now she knew it was Derrick. "No, he didn't" she yelled. "That lil' no-good bastard. He could have at least had the nerve to tell me that he was about to go." He'd spent the night and they'd gotten busy until the break of day and he didn't have the decency to tell her that he was leaving.
   After talking to Keisha, Derrick forgot to tell Yvette he had to go. Yvette would definitely be bitching the next time he talked to her. He would just have to make it up to her later. He had to stay on good terms with Yvette, his older female, because she had her own crib. It was convenient not to have to spend any money on a hotel when he wanted to get some from her. At her apartment, he and Yvette could lay as long as they wanted to, for free. It was better than the twelve o'clock check-out he was accustomed to, although being with Yvette had its downfalls too. Her daughter Asia got on his last nerve. She was two years old and spoiled rotten. She whined more than she pissed. The only time that baby didn't cry was when she was asleep, and that was when Derrick tried to come over. He would call and ask Yvette if she was asleep before going over so he and Yvette could have their privacy.
   At the hospital, nurses and doctors gathered around Monet to prep her for delivery. Dorothy tried to calm her child's scream-

ing but to no avail. Dorothy wished she could ease Monet's pain.

"Aw!" the girl shouted when a contraction raced through her back. The pain was so intense she cried, begging the doctors to help her. "Please make the pain go away!" she cried.

"Monet, listen to me, honey, the nurse coached. "We need you to calm down before you hurt yourself or your baby. The crying and moving is only causing more stress to your cervix, which will make labor much more difficult. I don't want you pushing until I say so. You have to calm down now sweetheart,"

Monet didn't want to hear what the nurse was saying because she was experiencing horrendous trauma. As a contraction caused her uterus to contract, she cried out again. "Please can you give me something?" the girl begged. The only relief she knew was to soak in a warm tub of water, but that wasn't possible. The spasms shot through her body like shocks of lightening. The throbbing aches were more intense than menstrual cramps. It felt like the baby was trying to exit her front and rear at once. The girl tried to wiggle away the hurt, but that didn't work. She tried sitting up but her head was too heavy.

"How much longer until it comes out?" Monet asked.

"Well, baby, we don't know," the nurse answered.

"Please nurse lady, please give me something," she begged. "I can't take much more of this torture. I'm going to die if I don't get rid of this pain. Ooh, please give me something. It hurts so bad. Don't you all have something that will numb my whole body, you know the epider...?

" Her words ceased. Monet had begged and pleaded with the last of her strength. Her hair was wringing wet and sticking like a magnet to her face. Her eyes were buck and her lips were dry and chapped. The young girl was starting to look like Shug Avery on the movie The Color Purple on the stormy night when Albert brought the drunken woman home to stay with him.

"Can y'all please give her something for the pain?"

Dorothy begged. "It's hard for me to see my baby like this."

"Ma'am, we're not going to give Monet anything because she's already dilated to seven."

Dorothy stuck her nose in the air and rolled her eyes at the smart mouthed woman, and then tried to get Monet to relax. Dorothy thought about her other children at home. She had to call and let them know where she was.

Dorothy also needed to call her sister Caroline. Until then, she hoped the baby would pop out soon because Monet's outbursts were working on her nerves.

Derrick made it to the maternity floor. He headed straight for the nurses' station and asked which room Monet was in. The lady at the desk instructed him how to get there. As Derrick rushed down the hallway, he could hear delivering mothers screaming all the way down the corridor. His pace slowed and he became very nervous. The reality of this baby coming hit him! He wasn't sure if he was prepared for the responsibility of being a father.

The boy soon regained his composure and crept down the hall way. He eased open the door to the delivery room. Dorothy and a nurse spotted him. Dorothy turned away and the nurse asked his identity. When she realized he was the father, she took him to put on a sanitary robe.

Monet tried to calm down so she wouldn't embarrass herself in front of Derrick. She was able to fake for a minute, but as soon as another contraction hit she began yelling louder than before. Derrick finished in the bathroom and stood by her side. He grabbed her hand and held it tight.

The screeches and howls kept coming. There was staff coming in and out of the room. A man in a white overcoat came in and picked up the clipboard hanging on the side of the bed, looked at it, jotted down something and left the room without saying anything. The nurse was busy with her head between Monet's legs, as she probed around inside the womb. The girl cried out for her mama while unconsciously squeezing Derrick's hand. She clenched his hand as if her life depended on it. The boyfriend whispered for Monet to loosen up the grip. He gently pried his hand away from hers. "You are making my hand go numb, Monet."

Dorothy instructed Monet to take a deep breath and to push until the nurse told her to stop. The mother-to-be looked down between her legs and yelled, "Is it almost out?"

"Just a couple more pushes, Monet. You're doing real good," the nurse assured her.

Dorothy peered at Derrick holding her daughter's hand and felt sick. She thought, how could Monet be interested in someone like him? He was sorry and had no class. Dorothy didn't know why he came to the hospital with his pants sagging the way they were. He wasn't groomed at all. The boy was about five foot seven and had very dark skin like her husband. His hair was short, kinky-curly and untamed. He looked like he'd just jumped out of bed and came straight to the hospital.

Monet looked at her mom and then at her boyfriend. She wondered why either of them were there, if they could do nothing to help her.

Another contraction hit her! Monet screamed and Derrick held her. She was embarrassed but the pain was too strong to hide. She wanted to rub her stomach, but she didn't have a free hand. It felt like her insides were coming out. She wiggled and moaned, hoping the pain would go away, but it didn't. She tried thinking of something else but nothing could relieve it. She prayed. "Oh God, please let it go away. I will never, ever do this again if you just let the pain go away now."

Even prayer didn't work. Monet stretched her legs hoping her muscles would loosen, but they were getting tighter. She was getting a Charlie horse from her waist to her feet. If she could rock, she knew the pain would go away at least for a couple minutes. Her legs throbbed becoming an overbearing nuisance. The soon-to-be mother yelled, "Rub my legs, Derrick. Rub them."

"Rub what?" he asked

"My legs, rub my legs! They're going stiff and it hurts! Please, Derrick, rub them!" Derrick rubbed her legs, which sent pain up to her back and stomach.

"STOP!" She yelled. "That's enough, you're making it worse, that's enough!"

Derrick pulled his hand away quickly and his mind went blank; he didn't know what to do. Monet wiggled and moaned. She hadn't eaten anything so her stomach was hurting and growling. Her mouth was dry and she vomited. The girl leaned to the side of the bed and a clear slimy fluid ran from her mouth to the sheet. The nurse pointed to the bucket of ice, telling the father,

"Give her those to suck on."

After the fourth hour of labor Monet's legs were weaker and stiffer. She wished she could walk off some of the stiffness, but she was strapped to the bed. The only thing she could do was cry. The young lady tried convincing herself it would all be over soon, and no matter what, this was never happening again. From now on she was going to leave the babies wherever they came. She had no idea that labor was such trauma. She wondered why men didn't have to go through anything like this. They always had an easy way out of everything.

Derrick glanced at his girlfriend's player-hating mother. He wasn't trying anymore to impress her because he knew she didn't like him. As long as she respected him he would respect her and that would be the extent of their relationship. Derrick reached down and gently kissed Monet's hand and cheek. He did it mostly to aggravate her mother and let Monet know that he was there to support her no matter what. Like he'd told the girl in the beginning, he was gone be down for his.

Derrick never would have believed that a woman's vagina could stretch as wide as Monet's. After Monet pushed, the doctor began stretching her wound preparing it so the baby's shoulders could come out. This was the most difficult part of the labor. The practitioner exercised her hands around the baby's frame. She took a metal instrument and maneuvered it around the lining of the patient's womb. Her body went limp. She was sweating like a frozen coke in a hundred and ten-degree weather, and her mouth was as dry as Las Vegas desert. Derrick continued to feed Monet the ice as her mother patted her forehead with a small white towel. The young girl in labor cried out with all the air left in her lungs. All her strength was gone and her de-energized frame collapsed onto the elevated mattress. All she could finally mumble was,

"Ooh, it hurts! Ooh, mama, it hurts." The hardest part was over.

"It's almost over, baby. In a few more minutes it's all gone be over." Dorothy had been saying that for the last four and a half hours and it still wasn't over yet. Monet's eyes played peek-a-boo. Every now and then she would appear less delirious and open them while glaring around the room. Monet laid silently on the bed until the nurse instructed her to do something different.

Derrick glanced into the mirror above the bed. He was observing his baby sticking half way into the world, and halfway in the dark lonely tunnel. He could not believe what was happening! His eyes dilated more every time the nurse twirled the metal instrument inside his girlfriend. Tears crowded his eyes. His mind wasn't registering what was going on. As a result of him and Monet having sex and combining internal fluids they produced a living, human being.

One... more... big... push, "Ooh," Monet screamed, and the baby popped into the hands of the doctor at one thirty-eight p.m. Monet's little boy welcomed the world with soft whimpers as the cool air hit his fragile body.

"It's a boy," Derrick said while almost jumping to the ceiling with excitement.

"I knew it was," he shouted. As he secretly wiped away the tears he wanted no one to see.

"I knew it was going to be a boy." Dorothy shed a few tears when she got her first close up view of her brand new grandson. Monet got a good look at him and closed her eyes, sighing in relief. She was happy that he was healthy.
Throughout the delivery, her baby had worn her out and now she was about to get some sleep. Monet had been going through the emotions all morning and she was happy that her labor was finally over.

Two nurses worked on prepping the newborn while Dr. Harris stitched Monet's slightly torn womb. The baby weighed six pounds and seven ounces and was born on June 5th, 2003. Dorothy was able to slip away and call her sister Caroline and tell her about her new grandbaby. Caroline said she was on her way up there. Dorothy called her children to deliver the news. She told Keisha she would be home in about an hour.

Derrick and Monet announced the name they'd chosen for their son, Deshawn Marquise Anderson. The nurse made the bracelet for the baby while Dorothy checked him thoroughly. She wanted to know him from head to toe, in case things around the hospital got screwed up. She'd seen Switched at Birth on Lifetime and Dorothy wasn't going to risk the possibility of her precious grandson going home with anyone else.

A Whole New World

Monet's friends greeted her when she walked into the house with her newborn. She never had a baby shower but Dorothy's living room was packed with gifts. She was delighted to see her friends. Everybody except Derrick was there, but Monet was used to him being late. She was so tired, no one stayed long, but they all held the baby before they left to let him and his mother get some rest. An hour later, the house was clear and Monet hurried to her bedroom to go to sleep. Having Deshawn drained her energy and she needed rest.

The first night back home in her own bed, Monet was sleeping like a baby until the first time her son woke her at two seventeen in the morning. Monet was half asleep and half awake, as she lay there feeding the baby his bottle. She burped him and Deshawn fell back to sleep, but Monet was out before he was. At four thirty-one Deshawn whimpered again. It took her a minute before she heard him, but Monet finally awakened to tend to her newborn's needs. He wanted another bottle, which she had to go downstairs to fix. Monet was so tired she could barely see to make her way down the stairs. Half asleep, Deshawn was still crying, wanting to be fed. In the kitchen Monet poured some milk into a small pot and placed it on the stove. She prepared her son's bottle and went back upstairs. She fed and burped him again, but Deshawn wasn't ready to go to sleep. Instead, he lay in her arms and looked out the window toward the mid morning light.

Monet was not ready to sit up. She wanted to sleep. She rocked her son, hoping he would go to sleep. She looked down at him and whispered, "Please, baby, go to sleep so Mommy can get some rest." If that worked, then it wouldn't have been five forty-one in the morning when she looked at her digital clock.

She was so restless she started to cry. Monet stared into those dreary eyes Deshawn had like his father, then rubbed her hand across his oval shaped head. Her baby was a few shades lighter than her. The baby wiggled in his mother's arms and sometimes cried softly. Monet glanced at the thick eyebrows her son inherited from her. He was so precious. She still couldn't believe he was hers. As she drifted off to sleep, Deshawn squirmed around trying to familiarize himself with his mother's comforting arms. He finally fell asleep at about six-thirty and didn't wake again until about ten.

For the first couple of weeks Derrick visited the baby and Monet often. When he held Deshawn, Derrick called him "Daddy's Little Man". Monet adored the two of them together. Derrick was always talking about all the things he and Deshawn were going to do together when he started walking. She'd just had a new baby, and the father was still around. That was more than she could say about most of the girls her age with babies. Half the girls from her school hadn't heard from their babies' fathers since they donated the sperm. Derrick always found time to spend with his son.

After her six-week check-up, Monet walked out of the clinic with a gigantic smile after Dr. Harris told her she was doing fine. The doctor said all of Monet's stitches had healed and her body was back to normal. Monet couldn't wait to get home to call Derrick. He'd promised to take her out and she was more than ready to go. When she got home and called him, Monet discovered that Derrick already had plans for the night. Monet demanded to know with whom, and where. He claimed he and his friends were going to the skating rink.

"I know how to skate," she fussed. Derrick didn't respond but then he said,

"Let me call Jamil. I'll call you back." Derrick hung up the phone and dialed Jamil's number. He asked. "Man who all riding with you tonight?"

"Just us fellows. Why?"

"Monet wanted to come with us, but I told her it was only

gone be us guys going."

"Tell her to meet us there."

"Naw' man. I ain't trying to have no female up under me all night. I might see something new at the skating rink," Derrick laughed. "I'll just have to call Monet back and let her know the car is gone be full wit dudes and she can't go. She'll just have to wait until next time. Let me hit you back after I get everything straightened out with her." He laughed as he dialed his girl-friend's phone number. Derrick knew Monet would not to be able to go because she had no transportation, so he was delighted to return the call.

Monet answered the telephone on the second ring. Derrick told her that if she could meet them at the skating rink, she could still go. He said Jamil didn't have enough room for anybody else in his car. "All right Derrick, whatever. I'll talk to you later." Her boyfriend could sense her disappointment.

"Don't be acting all mad, girl," he said in a sympathetic voice.

"You know if I had a ride you could go, but I'm riding with somebody else. Call one of your friends and see if y'all can come to the skating rink together then call me ba..." Monet hung up before he finished talking.

Derrick sat there for a minute thinking. He felt badly for the way he treated Monet. He knew she deserved a break and he had promised to take her out. He decided to call Jamil and tell him that he'd changed his mind about going skating. Jamil called him a sell-out but told Derrick to handle his business.
"I'll get up wit you later then man," Jamil told Derrick.

"All right," Derrick said and hung up. He called Monet and told her to catch a cab to his house and he would pay for it when she got there. He felt real bad.

Dorothy agreed to baby sit, so everything was set.

"I'll be back by one, Mom," she slammed the front door

and rushed out to the cab.

When she pulled up in front of Derrick's house, Monet told the driver to blow the horn. Within a couple minutes Derrick's frail, dark skinned frame ran toward the car. He jumped inside and told the driver to go to 539 Sigsbee. They were headed to Derrick's older brother Mike's house. Mike had his own place, but was out of town. He'd left his house key with Derrick so he could check up on the place.

"Right here," Derrick yelled, as the driver was about to pass the apartment. The tires screeched as the man hit the brakes. The driver threw the car in park, turned the meter off, turned around in his seat, and said, "That'll be $14.70." Derrick paid the man and he and Monet jumped out of the cab.

Derrick walked behind Monet to get a good look at her backside. She was wearing jeans that snugly fit her small, shapely figure. She looked good in the outfit he'd bought her. Monet was wearing onyx black Baby Phat jeans with the matching jacket. Underneath, she wore a white t-shirt that advertised Baby Phat. Monet wanted to hurry inside but Derrick dragged slowly behind. She swayed up the stairs seductively which really caught Derrick's attention. His mannish eyes were seriously checking her out. She was looking good. Monet wasn't but five foot one and weighed a hundred and ten pounds. She had small bulging hips and a round behind. She was 36-27-28. Her boyfriend was becoming aroused. When he got to the porch, Derrick gave Monet a kiss before opening the front door. Her beautiful brown eyes sparked as the porch light glistened, casting a silhouette on their cuddling bodies. Derrick unlocked the door and walked inside. He fanned his hand across the wall in search of the light switch. Derrick turned on the light and Monet accompanied him inside the empty apartment. She was on cloud nine.

The apartment was small and cozy. The two piece sofa and loveseat was nothing to brag about, but it was typical for a bachelor's pad. The couch was an off- white linen material accentuated with dingy pink and blue flowers. The apartment had no pictures and no extra home decorating items, just the essentials; the couch, a coffee table, and a television on a plain old dusty TV cart. You could tell this was a man's apartment and it definitely longed for a woman's touch.

"Are you hungry?" Derrick asked.

"A little bit," Monet mumbled, as she plopped on the couch.

"Well, I'm gone go ahead and order a pizza anyway, just in case we get hungry later."

"That's fine."

Derrick pointed toward the VCR tapes on the television cart under the TV. "My brother has a lot of movies we can watch. Look through them and pick out a good one for us to watch."

He went into the kitchen and Monet eased back and got more acquainted with the sofa. She couldn't remember the last time she and Derrick spent private time together. She was glad to be on birth control because she knew Derrick would want some when he got situated. This time she was going to be prepared. There was no way she was getting knocked up again. "It doesn't matter," she huffed, in an unconcerned tone. In two weeks she would be seventeen years old and she definitely wasn't trying to have more children.

Her young lover boy came from the kitchen with two glasses of bubbling beer. It appeared as if he'd poured the beer straight into the glasses, creating a whipped cream look on top. She smiled shyly and said, "I don't want any." The last thing Monet wanted to do was go home with the smell of alcohol on her breath. That would give her mother a legitimate reason not to baby-sit for her again.

"I guess I'll have to drink both of them then," Derrick chuckled as he put the extra glass of beer down on the table and took a big gulp from his glass. After sipping from it he placed his glass on the wood table and headed toward the television. Since Monet hadn't picked out a movie, he decided to choose one for them. He fumbled through the movies and came upon a couple that he thought were good. "Do you want to watch Life, Kingdom Come, or a porno?" he laughed. "This one is hella funny," he sighed then popped a cassette into the VCR and pressed the PLAY button. "Bro needs to upgrade to a DVD player. The next time somebody come through with one I'm gone get it for him."

During the previews, Derrick wrapped his arms around Monet and asked how she liked being a new mother.

"I'm just now starting to get used to Deshawn waking up in the middle of the night," she said. "At first it was hard but now that I know his schedule I'm more prepared for it. I have the bottles lying under the pillow beside me so when he wakes up I don't have to go all the way downstairs to fix him a bottle. I just grab one from under the pillow and pop it into his mouth. I prepare them before I go to bed, that way by the time he wakes up they are still pretty warm. I pop one in his mouth, turn him over on his back and burp him, then I keep on patting him until he goes to sleep. Everything is so different. Now I have to worry about him first and then myself. Now it is Deshawn, and then Monet. Putting someone else's needs before your own really takes some getting used too. You should try keeping him for a whole twenty-four hours so you can see what it's like." Monet gazed at Derrick. She could tell the reality of being a father had not hit him yet. Having a son was no big deal to him. Derrick took another sip from his cup.

"I think I'm gone wait till my lil' man gets a little bigger before I keep him overnight," he said. "Right now he's too small. It seems like if I touch him the wrong way I might hurt him." His remark pissed Monet off, but she didn't say anything. She wasn't about to make a big deal about it when she knew how

Derrick was. If she did let Derrick keep Deshawn, he'd probably just drop him off with his mother and keep on going. He and Jamil would be in the streets somewhere.

"Derrick, where do you see us in about five years from now?" Monet asked.

"What do you mean?"

"I mean, do you soon see me and Deshawn as your family or do you just consider me as being your baby's mother, and him your son?"

"Aw, come on now, Monet. You know that you are my woman, so I don't even know why you'd ask me something like that. I love you."

"Yeah, right," she replied.

"Look Boo, I'm gone be straight up with you. When you first got pregnant I was thinking about ending our relationship, but the situation turned out to be more serious than that. I couldn't just walk out on mine like my daddy did with me. I felt like I had an obligation to you. In the beginning I thought you were on a scam to tie me down."

"Don't even try that, Derrick. You know good and well that getting pregnant was not a part of my plan, even though it was a mistake that you and I both made. You just don't know how having Deshawn has changed my whole life. Having my son has caused me to grow up quickly. You know there was a time when all I had to have was my mom's permission to go somewhere. Now if I want to go somewhere, I have to get my mother's approval, and find a babysitter. Instead of having money to spend on me, I have to see if Deshawn needs anything, which he always seems to need something. Before, I used to depend on my mom to take care of me, now I have to be responsible for myself plus one more even though I solely depend on my mother." Monet paused, took a deep breath, and continued.

"I knew my mother was already struggling and I didn't

make the situation any better by bringing in an extra mouth to feed. You just don't know how bad that makes me feel."

Monet sat on the edge of the couch staring at Derrick. "So, while you're sitting around enjoying being a part time father, I'm suffering and struggling to be a full time mother. Besides all that, I have to work extremely hard to get caught up in school before graduation. Don't get me wrong, I love my baby with all my heart, but caring for him is a big job, as well as a lifetime commitment."

Derrick stared apologetically at his girlfriend. Her voice was scratchy like she was about to cry. He had not realized how much Deshawn had affected Monet's life. It didn't seem like his life had changed much. The only thing that changed was that he had to pick up something for his lil' shorty every time he went to the mall, instead of just buying something for himself. Since Monet had their son, Derrick hadn't lied to her about coming over like he sometimes used to do. To him being a father was making sure his son stayed dressed in the freshest gear and making sure he had everything he needed. Derrick figured Monet could handle the rest. Their son would soon be two months old and Derrick had not spent over three hours at a time with him. If his intentions were to be a decent role model, Derrick wasn't that yet.

He eased up on the couch and pulled Monet closer. The movie was just beginning. "Come here, baby," Derrick mumbled.

As Monet slid closer, his tongue slid into her mouth tasting like beer. After their first kiss the girl started feeling butterflies in her stomach. She yearned for Derrick's attention, but Monet didn't know if she was really ready to go all the way, until they kissed again. Derrick's kisses were so warm and welcoming, Monet didn't want to stop. Not paying attention to what Jada, Sedric, or Whoopi were doing, Monet climbed onto Derrick's lap. As she positioned her body comfortably on his, Monet felt the increasing of his manhood. "Are you on the pill?" Derrick asked.

"Yeah," she answered. "Plus, I have some condoms."

"We ain't using no condoms if you on the pill," he answered.

"Of course we are. I ain't trying to get caught up with nothing I didn't come with."

Derrick took off her shirt and pulled one of her breasts from her bra, teasing the nipple with his tongue. After arousing one of them, Derrick switched to the other. He gently sat her lightly tanned, brown skin body on the couch as he got up to take off his clothing.

When he finished undressing, Derrick took Monet's hand and led her into the bedroom. He pulled back the Michigan Wolverine's comforter to unveil the matching sheet set. Monet got a good look at the sheets before she laid down in the bed. She asked her boyfriend, "Are these sheets clean?"

"Yeah, girl," he proceeded to climb in the bed on top of her. He tried to enter her but Monet stopped him and handed him the condoms she'd taken from her Coach bag he'd also bought for her. Derrick looked amazed because Monet never came to him like this.

"Girl, you really trippin' with these condoms ain't you?"

"If we're going to be doing anything we're gonna' be using these," Monet replied. "My doctor didn't give them to me for nothing." His palm was unaccepting but Monet shoved the condom into it anyway. No matter how hot and horny she got Monet was not about to be no fool. She and Derrick hadn't had sex in a long time and she didn't know who he'd slept with since then.

"So, is it that you don't trust me, or have you been fucking wit somebody else?"

"I ain't been sleeping with nobody," she answered. "All I'm saying, Derrick, is if we're going to be having sex, you gone be putting on that condom. If not, we might as well go back in there and watch the movie."

He was a little ticked off, but obeyed her. He sat up to put on the condom, climbed back on top of Monet, and rubbed her naked body. Her words had depreciated his manhood and he had to get back up so they could continue. Everything was fine until Monet started trippin' about him putting on a condom. Derrick climbed on top of his girlfriend. His penis probed around her center in search of the hole. To Derrick it shouldn't have been so hard to find considering how much it had stretched when Deshawn came out.

Finally, Derrick hit the right spot and Monet jerked. Derrick eased partially back out and jolted back inside her. He entered and Monet jerked and moaned because it hurt like hell. Her moan caused Derrick to pause and ask if everything was okay. She sounded as if she'd flashed back to the delivery room. When she told him she was okay, he continued.

Their love session ended about twenty minutes later. Derrick laid beside her for a minute before he got up and walked into the bathroom. He walked into the bathroom and looked in the mirror as sweat raced down his face and body. He snatched off the liquid filled condom and dashed it into the toilet. He reached into the closet and pulled out two washcloths. Monet walked into the bathroom and grabbed one of the towels from Derrick, then turned the water on in the sink. Derrick washed up and exited the bathroom where Monet was trying to fix her hair, "I'm about to go and call the cab," he said.

The cab pulled up and blew, and Derrick gave Monet a big kiss and some money. He told her he was spending the night at his brother's and would talk to her tomorrow. The girl ran toward the cab and her boyfriend stood in the doorway until the car was out of view. After Monet left, the pizza came, but Derrick was so tired he placed it on the kitchen counter and fell asleep on the living room sofa.

One More Chance

Delvin woke up nervous and excited. He had been waiting for this day for a long time. Today was the day he was going to be released from prison. He climbed out of his top bunk and stripped the bed. He folded his borrowed wool blanket and sheets and placed them at the end of the bed. After showering, Delvin took his time shaving. He washed the whipped residue from his face, then dabbed on after shave. Back in his small cell he stood in front of the small square mirror. Dorothy had sent him black slacks and a printed cotton shirt to wear home, so he put on the outfit and gathered his belongings. He took one last look at the place he'd called home for nearly seven years. When the officer came to escort him out, Delvin said a final prayer, held his head high, and proudly exited with the guard close behind.

As he walked past their rooms, his buddies said their final farewells. Delvin promised to keep in touch. The female officer who gave him the rest of his belongings asked Delvin for his ID. Delvin gave it gladly as a cold chill rushed through his body. He had been behind bars so long, he didn't know how to act. He knew he was headed through the gate to freedom.

As he entered the area where his wife was waiting, Delvin was so nervous his hands trembled. Through the glass he could see his wife sitting in a pretty black dress. Her face was glowing and her hair was beautifully styled. Delvin couldn't wait to touch her soft firm body. As he proceeded through the last door, Dorothy rose. She wanted to be the first thing her husband saw when he entered.

Delvin ran to his wife lifting her off her feet. He planted a kiss on her red painted lips. Dorothy smiled and took a sexy stance. Her sleek hips bulged, defining her plus size, hourglass figure.

He undressed her with his eyes. "I can't wait to get you out of that dress, baby." He moaned and used his hand to conceal his swollen manhood. Dorothy smiled as they joined hands and walked out of the prison.

"I am so glad that you're finally coming home," Dorothy replied. Her husband stopped and grabbed her in his arms. From lack of a man's touch, Dorothy's body quivered in his arms. He released her and Dorothy stood in front of him staring directly into his eyes. She hadn't seen this much of him in a long time. His muscular frame was more in tact than she remembered. It was obvious he'd been working out. His sexy dark skin, those beautiful brown eyes, and bow legs were her weakness. Those features turned her on the most about her husband and they had her weak at the knees.

They arrived at the car and Delvin helped Dorothy in the driver's side. Walking to the other side of the car, Delvin took a deep breath, inhaling the fresh morning air. His ears enjoyed the soft chirping of nearby birds. He had not seen trees, or heard birds sing in years, and the melody sounded so nice.

"Come on, baby, we got time to make up for," she smiled. Dorothy anticipated spending a lot of time together in the bedroom. She wanted him so badly her underwear was damp. Before she pulled off, Dorothy slipped out of them. "We gone have to make a quick stop."

"Where?" he asked as he grabbed the underwear and pulled them toward his nose.

"At the first hotel we can find." She pulled away from the prison parking lot. "I'm glad I don't have to worry about seeing this place anymore."

Delvin leaned over and kissed his wife on the cheek. She smiled. His naughty hand rubbed her legs. "What are you doing?" she asked naively.

"Wanting you too damned bad," he answered.
She tried to pay attention to the highway while Delvin's warm anticipating tongue licked the back of her earlobes. His tickling

palate felt so good Dorothy almost ran her dusty Celebrity off the road. She moaned sweetly, "Stop before you make us crash into something."

In a sweet devilish way, Delvin ignored her no's that were meant to be yes's and continued. He lifted her skirt. Since she wasn't wearing underwear, it was easy access to her private tunnel. While Dorothy drove, Delvin's strong fingers played inside her baby maker. She wiggled in the seat. The pleasure was so overbearing she could hardly drive.

About thirty miles down the highway, Dorothy pulled over at a small motel. She turned off the engine and they embraced in a long intoxicating kiss. They climbed out of the car and headed up the pathway toward the office. The motel was small and secluded with about fifteen rooms. The place didn't appear dirty or run down, just like it wasn't occupied very much. A bell rang alarming the clerk when Delvin opened the office door. The old white man placed his fat, stinky cigar into the ashtray and rose as they approached the counter.

"Can I help you?" he asked in a dull, but friendly tone.

"Yes, sir. We would like a room," Dorothy said

"A room is thirty-nine, ninety five a night, plus tax." The man handed Dorothy a form to fill out. "I will also need to see at least one form of identification."

Delvin waited patiently while Dorothy filled out the form. The clerk took another pull from his cigar. Delvin's eyes scanned the dark room. There was nothing fancy about the place. There was not what you called a waiting area nor were there flowers or brochures anywhere. The place was plain and simple; no vending machines, or pretty pictures. Delvin enjoyed not seeing any steel bars or police officers standing around.

Dorothy paid the money and took the key. The clerk said the room number was 107 and it was seven doors down from the office. The lovebirds exited the darkened office and walked outside. They rushed to their room. Dorothy threw her purse on the small round table and kicked off her shoes. Her husband undressed. She locked the door, and ran into her husband's anticipating arms.

Delvin pulled off her black dress and unfastened her lace bra. He laid her down on the bed gently, and kissed her nipples. She closed her eyes and enjoyed his caresses. Her husband kissed her body from cheeks to feet and Dorothy moaned softly as her body squirmed around on the bed. Delvin's palette touched her center sending a shock wave through her body. She was very sensitive but anticipating. She curled her red polished toes into a tight ball. The bed became wet with the juice Delvin's mouth didn't catch, the white cotton sheets were soaked. Her body craved his. He grabbed his bulging rod and wiggled it between her legs. He was only a quarter of the way in when she whined. He eased out and carefully danced his way back through her tight walls. Her gates opened up and let him enter. The path was warm, wet, and snugly barricaded around his piece. She whimpered kindly as he explored deeper into her mound. They rocked in a slow motion together.

Delvin cried out like a car stricken animal when Dorothy rocked up and down on top of him. "Oh, Dorothy, I missed you so much."

She'd brought the tiger out of him and he was ready to explore the forest. He enjoyed the real thing instead of his hand, a small substitute for pleasure. Her whimpers and outbursts turned into tears of delight. Delvin licked the tears from her face and lifted her body. She turned on to her hands and knees and he re-entered his magic stick. He maneuvered in and out, and back forth. They moaned and groaned together.

"You saved it all for me, didn't you, mama?" he asked. "It's real good too. Work it for daddy," Delvin gripped her hips and pulled her body into his. "Whose is it?" he whispered.

"It's yours," she cried out. "It's yours, baby." Sweat dropped from his body and on to her back. Juices released from her satisfied body as she rocked faster and became louder. Suddenly, she developed cotton mouth and was sweating like a chilled 40 ounce on a hot summer day. Delvin burst his pleasures into his wife and his manhood went limp. Dorothy collapsed at his side wringing the water from her hair. Delvin laid next to her for twenty minutes then they were at it again.

They stayed at the hotel all night. Dorothy called home to check on her kids and let Monet know she would be home in the morning. Later that evening, she went out to get something to eat, and drinks. When she came back the couple took a shower together, sipped slowly from a bottle of wine while they laid in the bed and talked. They made love again and by the end of the night they were worn out. The following morning they checked out the hotel and headed to greet the rest of the family.

They arrived at Delvin's sister house and Shirley cursed them as soon as they pulled up in her driveway. "Y'all lil' horny asses are a day late. I was about to put a missing report on my brother," she said as they got out of the car.

The couple apologized as the three of them headed into the house. Shirley, Delvin, and Dorothy sat down at the table chit chatting for an hour. "Delvin, we've got to get going," Dorothy said. "I have to go home and check on the children." Delvin told his sister he would be back later, and they left. Dorothy promised Shirley she would have her brother back before dark.

Everything looked as if he were seeing it for the first time. A lot had changed since he went to prison. He'd been gone for so long, he felt like a foreigner in his own neighborhood. As his wife drove toward the house, Delvin looked at the tall, beautiful, green trees, the newly remodeled homes, and the happy faces of children playing. Delvin felt like a blind man given sight. Everything looked so pretty and alive, so colorful and happy. He admired the smell of the air because it was like him, fresh and free.

Before he went to prison, the projects where Dorothy lives now were infested with crack heads and drug boys. He'd heard that the old tenants had been evicted and the city renovated. He heard they were accepting a new genre of tenants and that the community had improved. When they pulled into the complex, Delvin noticed how much better everything looked. The Campau Projects looked no different than any regular old townhouse subdivision. Before, there were paper, junk, and broken windows everywhere, not to mention all the loose bay-bay kids and two dollar prostitutes running around. Delvin was worried when his wife said she was moving into the projects, but now he could see how the place had improved. He was convinced that his children were living in a better neighborhood. This neighborhood used to be his hanging spot when he got high.

Dorothy pulled into her parking space and turned the car off. They got out and she walked up the stairs after her husband. Keisha was the first of the children to discover they had arrived. She screamed, "Daddy's home" and ran toward Delvin and jumped into his arms. The other children jumped in his arms and kissed all over him. Dorothy stood to the side and let the children welcome their father. She smiled because she had already had her chance. Monet was on the telephone when they came in, but even she jumped up and gave her stepfather a welcome hug. Tonya rushed to get Deshawn out of his car seat so he could meet her daddy. She brought the baby into the front room and held him up in Delvin's face. "Here is Monet's baby, Deshawn, Daddy," Tonya said as Delvin smiled.

"Unh, unh, unh. Look at you, lil' man," Delvin took his first look at the baby. Deshawn sucked his Gerber cookie, and had it all over his face and hands. As Delvin started talking, the baby stopped gnawing the cookie and cried. Delvin handed him to his mother.

"I don't even know why Tonya gave him to you," she said.

He has this cookie everywhere," Monet said rolling her eyes at her sister as she walked into the kitchen to put Deshawn in his high chair. Tonya didn't say anything, just looked away.

"It's all right," Delvin said. "He just needs some time to get used to me."

He sat on the couch, as his children crowded around him. Delvin was excited to be home with his family and, judging their smiles, they were happy as well. There was no way he could stay away from all this love ever again.

Monet observed her mother's happiness. The girl hadn't seen a smile so large on her mother's face in a long time. Monet really didn't have a problem with Delvin. It wasn't until he started using drugs that she started disliking him. After that, he and Dorothy argued all the time. He used to leave and stay out all night, then he'd come home the next day begging for money and wanting to argue. If they weren't fussing about him staying out all night, he and Dorothy were shouting about how he misused their money. Monet hoped he'd changed his ways. She felt it was necessary to give him another chance as long as he was trying.

Her long lost partner had dinner with the family. Then, Dorothy drove him back to Shirley's where he was staying. Before she left her husband, she got her a little bit. She didn't know if she could stand living away from him knowing he wasn't locked up anymore. If his probation officer wasn't coming over the next day Dorothy would have let Delvin spend the night. Since he was paroled to his sister's house Delvin had to be there when the man came.

The next day was a normal one. Only Dorothy and Deshawn were at the house. She got up and cleaned the house real good before "Young and the Restless" came on at 12:30 p.m. While watching the conversation between Victor and Nicky, Dorothy laid Deshawn across her lap and changed his diaper. He was wiggling and squirming so much she couldn't focus. At the commercial, she got up, threw the baby over her shoulder, and threw the dirty diaper away. Dorothy was glad she didn't have to go through this all the time. She was happy her baby days were over. Even though Dorothy wasn't fond of babysitting, she did it because she wanted Monet to finish high school. She didn't want anything standing in the way of her daughter getting her diploma. When she was her daughter's age, she didn't have anyone to baby-sit, so Dorothy had to drop out when she was sixteen. As soon as she was able, she got her GED. Although she never made it to college, she wanted to make her children aware of it. If not college, Dorothy prayed they would all at least graduate from high school and find a decent job. Monet wanted to go to college and Dorothy strongly supported that. She didn't want Monet to feel like having a baby would stop her from being successful. Dorothy encouraged her children to believe in themselves and told them they could be anything they dreamed of if they believed in it.

The telephone rang as Dorothy was on her way back to the couch. She picked up the receiver and greeted the caller. It was Delvin. He called to tell her he'd been hired at the job where his sister worked. He said the job paid only nine-fifty an hour, but it was full time. She couldn't believe he'd gotten a job so soon, one that was going to be paying him just a dollar less than she was making as a manager. He told his wife he would be starting the next day, and he would be working second shift, from three til eleven. "That way we will have some time to spend together," Delvin told his wife.

Dorothy congratulated him and rushed him off the telephone so she could get back to her soaps. After hanging up, Dorothy realized that everything was starting to work itself out. If her husband stayed clean, everything would get better with time.

Bad Girl

Monet walked into the house about two-forty. She yelled to her mother as she walked through the front door. Deshawn was asleep in his car seat on the kitchen floor, so Monet lowered her voice. She followed the aroma into the kitchen where Monet discovered her mother cooking. The girl asked, "Was my baby good today, Mama?"

"He was the same old Deshawn, honey," her mother said, looking at her daughter and then to her simmering pot. Monet unfastened Deshawn from his car seat and laid him down. She kissed him several times on his cheek and walked upstairs toward her bedroom. When it was time for Dorothy to go to work, Monet came downstairs to see what her daily chores were. By this time her siblings were home.

"Make sure that your sisters and brother do their homework," her mom instructed.

"Mom, can I go to the library with Andrea? We both have research papers to finish." Tonya asked.

"Is your Aunt Caroline going to drop you guys off?"

"No. We planned on catching the bus." Dorothy stood silent about twenty seconds before answering. She was trying to make up her mind.

"Be home by six o'clock!" Dorothy left for work.

Everyone gathered at the kitchen table for smothered pork chops, mashed potatoes, broccoli spears, and corn on the cob. Dorothy always tried to have dinner ready before she left for work everyday. Although two of her girls could cook very well, Dorothy wanted them to focus on homework after school. They could cook on the weekends when she didn't feel like it. Monet had her hands full with Deshawn and keeping an eye on her sisters and brother. Most of the time, Dwayne was just as much a baby as his nephew.

Tonya quickly demolished her food so she wouldn't be

late meeting her cousin Andrea at the library. After eating, she washed her hands, grabbed her book bag and jacket, and was soon on her way.

It was quite chilly outside and she felt every bit of the thirty something degree temperature that whipped through her thin nylon jacket. According to the bus schedule she would only have to wait two or three minutes before the city bus would arrive. Once it finally did show up Tonya paid her fare and headed to the back of the bus.

Andrea got off the bus right in front of the library. She looked at her watch and turned to check out her surroundings. It was almost four-thirty and apparently her little cousin had not arrived yet. Andrea ran toward the building to get out of the cool weather. When she got inside she stood in front of the window facing the bus stop. Within minutes another bus pulled up. When it pulled away Andrea saw Tonya walking toward the library and ran outside to meet her.

"What's up, cuz?" Andrea said.

"Nothing much," Tonya answered. She closed her jacket to block the wind. "I guess we better get on in here and get started on these papers," Tonya suggested. Andrea's smile dropped.

"Girl, now I know you don't think we're going to the library for real." Her head bobbed as she spoke.

"Yeah," Tonya answered with a wiry expression.

"I was just using the library as an excuse for us to go to the mall." Tonya's eyes widened with amazement.

"What reason do I have to go to the mall? First of all, I don't have any money, and second of all, I really do have a paper to turn in." Andrea smacked her lips and rolled her neck. She let out an annoying sound as her eyes scanned her cousin up and down. She didn't know Tonya was so lame. She had to fill Tonya in on how everything was about to go down. She threw her arm around her cousin's neck.

"Look girl," she said, "as long as I have a bag we don't need no money to go to the mall." She pointed toward her empty duffle bag. "A lot of older guys occupy the mall around this time. It's kind of like a hang out spot."

"Andrea, I know you don't steal do you?"

"Girl, you're late," she bragged," I'm damn near a professional."

"As much stuff as you and Taylor have I don't see you having a reason to be stealing."

"Child, please, I do whatever I want to do. My parents don't run me. I know my mom has told Aunt Dorothy about... Oh yeah, I forgot, my mom only tells what she wants to tell. If it ain't nothing to brag on, it ain't nothing to talk about."

Tonya stood in silence. She could not believe what she was hearing. Why would Andrea be stealing?

"Andrea, I think I'm gone have to pass on the mall thing. I don't want to get into trouble because if my report isn't turned in on time my mom will kill me."

"Forget it then," Andrea said as she prepared to stand solo. Not only are you missing the chance to meet some cute guys but you're also turning down the chance to get a new outfit."

"I guess I will have to catch you later then." Tonya walked toward the library waving a goodbye to Andrea and stepping through the oscillating glass door.

Once inside Tonya realized she only had forty-five minutes of research time. She tried to locate reference materials so she could copy the information she needed to complete her report. When she finished copying information from the library books Tonya gathered her belongings and threw them into her Busta Rhymes notebook folder and stuck the folder into her backpack. She didn't want to miss her bus. She still had Andrea on her mind throughout the ride home.

She unlocked the front door and walked into the house.

The fresh smell of baby lotion filled the air. Monet was giving Deshawn a bath and Derrick was sitting beside her. Tonya walked toward the kitchen and Monet followed her holding a soiled pan of water while Derrick held Deshawn. Tonya followed Monet into the bathroom. "Guess what Andrea went to do today," she said.

"What?" Monet answered with little concern.

"She asked me to meet her at the library so that we could go study, but when we got there she said she was using the library as an excuse to go to the mall."

"Okay, Tonya, she told a lie. What's the big deal?"

"The big deal is that she wanted me to go to the mall with her so she could steal."

"Who went to the mall to steal?" eavesdropping, Keisha blurted from the other room.

"Quit dippin'," Monet told her. Keisha mumbled.

"Y'all make me sick."

"So, did you go with her?" Monet asked.

"Naw. Do you think I'm stupid or something? I really did have a research paper to do. Besides, I ain't about to be at no mall stealing."

"Well, don't worry about it then," Monet told her younger sibling." If Andrea gets caught, then that's on her. Did you get your paper finished?"

"I have all of the information I need."

"Good! Andrea will learn her lesson as soon as her butt gets caught. If Aunt Caroline or Uncle Thomas finds out she's going to be in big trouble."

Keisha listened secretly to the conversation. When Monet came out of the bathroom she faked doing something. She hadn't heard every juicy detail, but she'd caught quite a bit of information. "Ooh wee."

Derrick sat on the couch rocking the baby to sleep and rubbing his back. Monet sat beside him. "He is getting so big, ain't he?"

"Yep," Monet answered, her eyes still in her books, and don't wake him up either." Derrick admired the fact that Monet was serious about graduating and going to college. He was pleased to know his baby's mother wasn't a dummy.

Monet finished her homework and sat with Derrick until his ride came. As car lights flooded the living room, they looked out the front window to see if it was Jamil. As he got up to leave, Derrick handed Monet a fifty dollar bill so she could get Deshawn's pampers and other things he needed, kissed her and told her he would see her later.

As soon as he could get in the car, Jamil asked Derrick if he wanted to go to the movies with some honey. "Naw, man," Derrick answered. "I think I'm just gone chill tonight. I ain't really in no macking mood."

"Man, you a sell out," Jamil teased. "You done been over here with Monet now you want to be jumping back into that, I'm a good boy mood. Fuck that punk ass shit, Derrick."

"Man, fuck you," Derrick said punching his friend's shoulder. Monet is my boo, you know that. Don't none of these other females I fuck wit compare to her."

Jamil dropped Derrick off at home and asked what was up for tomorrow. Derrick said he didn't know, but he would hit Jamil up on the pager when he got up. Jamil told his friend he wanted to go look at pre-paid cell phones. "I heard you can get one without ID or credit check."

Before his friend pulled off, he said, "We can't be fucking around and miss all that loot that's gone be out there. You know tomorrow is the first so we got to check on the phones early."

"Fo' sho'," Derrick said. He gave Jamil some play and headed up the cement path toward his mother's house.

Party Time

Before getting off work, Dorothy called home to check on her kids. Monet answered on the third ring.

"Hey baby, how is everything going?" Dorothy asked.

"Dwayne is in the bed sleeping and the last time I checked Keisha was sitting upstairs on her bed. Tonya is in the bathtub."

"Where is my grandson?"

"Oh, he's been sleep. He went to sleep about an hour ago, right after I gave him a bath."

"I was calling to tell you that I am going over to Punkin's house when I get off of work. I'm going to stop by and get Delvin on my way."

"Well, I guess I won't see you until in the morning because I'm sure I'll be sleep by the time you get home."

"Yeah, I'll probably be in pretty late."

"Have fun then," Monet told her mom.

Punkin was having a small get together at her house. Since she'd had the miscarriage she wasn't herself. All week the girl had been acting strange. God knew what was best for that baby! Punkin was so wild, she wasn't cut out to be a mother. One was more than enough for her. Dorothy didn't know that losing the baby would affect Punkin the way it had. During the short time she was pregnant Punkin had been drinking. When she called Dorothy Tuesday to tell her about the party, she was drinking. It seemed that since the daddy didn't want the baby, she didn't either, or at least that's how she was acting. Maybe she was going through the guilt phase and trying to hide her feelings by throwing a party to forget about it.

Dorothy brought a change of clothes to work. She made sure her employees completed all their closing duties, then went into the office to call her husband. Shirley answered and told her sister-in-law she would tell Delvin she was on her way. Delvin was already dressed and on his way up. He had been out of prison almost three weeks and hadn't been able to get his party on yet. Though it was a cool night, Delvin was wearing short sleeves and black jeans. He knew it would feel like a hot summer day inside Punkin's.

Dorothy freshened up and changed out of her work uniform, put her clothes into a plastic grocery bag, and she and the closing employees left the restaurant together.

When she arrived, Delvin was at the front door waiting for her. He jumped in the car. Before heading to Punkin's house, they stopped at a nearby liquor store to grab some drinks. They didn't want to go to the party empty-handed.

Her favorite song began to play on the radio. Dorothy pumped up the volume and snapped her finger to the song. She sang, "Give me that tasty love." Her Celebrity came to a sudden halt as the traffic light turned red. She hadn't been paying attention and was about to ride through it. Delvin grabbed the dashboard for security. Most of the time Dorothy listened to gospel music, but every now and then she listened to her favorite old slow jams. She reminisced what she and Delvin were doing when the song playing was popular. When that song first debuted, they were madly in love. "Do you remember the first time you heard this song?" she asked. He smiled without saying anything. Dorothy said, "I remember it like it was yesterday."

"We were at our old friend Camille's birthday party. Everybody and their mamas were getting high. Remember Delvin?" she asked tapping his leg. It was the first time I ever smoked weed. I sat there with Camille while she rolled up a fat joint in her kitchen. She had gotten me so high I laughed all night long." Delvin didn't seem interested, so Dorothy dropped the subject and continued driving.

They pulled up in front of Punkin's house and saw a big crowd. Dorothy parked her car and cut the engine off. She and her husband got out and walked toward the house. Inside, Dorothy had to push through the crowd until she saw Punkin who was on the dance floor pumping it up. The living room furniture was stacked in the dining room and the dining room table was in the kitchen, so there was a nice sized dancing area. Punkin was out there in her skin tight jeans bumping her big butt in some man's face. Dorothy let Punkin know she was there and headed to the kitchen to put the E&J and the rest of the drinks on the counter. She placed the twelve pack of Colt 45's in the cooler with the rest of the beer. She'd lost Delvin as soon as they walked in the door. He was somewhere amongst the crowd. Punkin walked off the dance floor and into the kitchen where Dorothy was. On her way to the bathroom, she said to her friend, "Girl, that damn beer gone have me pissin' all night."

"You don't need to be drinking," Dorothy told her. Punkin waved her hand at her friend as she went into the bathroom.

"Don't start!"

When Punkin finished, she came out of the bathroom trying to force the zipper on her jeans to go back up. She took a deep breath, sucked in her stomach and zipped her pants.

"Where is Delvin?" she asked.

"Oh, he's probably in there speaking to everybody. You know it's been a long time since he's seen anybody in there. How are you feeling?"

"I'm feeling fine, and don't start because I don't want to hear about what I don't need to be doing." Punkin snapped her fingers dancing in place.

"I'm trying to get my party on, girl. I ain't got time to be sad." Before she left the kitchen, Punkin said, "I guess I will get my hug when I see him." She wiggled toward the dance floor with Dorothy right behind her.

Punkin and her friend headed back into the kitchen to get a drink, after the song went off. A chic named Niecy walked into the kitchen. She was a friend of Punkin's. The two of them were

tight hanging buddies, and had a lot in common. Niecy and
Punkin had become tight when Dorothy turned jive, if you let
Punkin tell it. Niecy was a tall, slender, fairly brown skinned
woman about five feet nine. She had bulging eyes with sad
droopy brown sacks underneath. She looked to be in her forties
but she had to be around twenty-nine or thirty. Hard life was writ-
ten all over her face. She was wearing an all black Lycra sport
outfit. The shirt didn't cover up the wrinkled obstacle course on
her belly. She wasn't wearing a bra and the way her behind was
sagging she couldn't have been wearing any underwear either.
Her hair was relaxed, but the natural kinkiness came through. It
was pulled back into a kitchen ponytail with lots of styling gel
keeping her natural African roots from being fully exposed. With
sweat and make-up running down her face she looked like a hot
mess. She needed to dip off into the bathroom to freshen up
because she did not have it going on like she thought she did. She
was cool, so when she approached and spoke, Dorothy smiled
and said a fake,

"Hey, girl."

"What's up," Niecy said to Dorothy. "This party is jam-
ming," she then said to Punkin.

"Thanks," Punkin replied. Niecy stood beside her guest of
honor and fumbled through her purse. She whipped out a fat joint
and lit it up. Niecy pulled off of it once and passed it to Punkin.
Punkin took a long pull and held it in for about ten seconds, then
exhaled. When she felt lightheaded Punkin smiled. "This is the
chronic." Punkin passed it to Niecy and she hit it. They both
coughed at the same time. Niecy tried handing it to Dorothy and
Dorothy snapped.

"Don't pass that mess this way. I don't mess around."

"Oh, yeah, I forgot you was square," Niecy said before she
hit it again. Dorothy protested.

"As a matter of fact, I'm about to get up out of here before y'all pollute my lungs with that mess." Dorothy left the kitchen and her two friends continued smoking. When they finished, Niecy put the joint out in the ashtray and whipped out a pack of Newports. She took the roach and placed it inside the cellophane covering her cigarette pack, then pulled out a cigarette. She lit it, blew out the contaminated smoke, and snapped her fingers to the beat of the music.

"Now I'm ready to go back out there and get my dance on," she said to Punkin. They both rocked toward the dancing area.

The heat in the house was almost overbearing. Punkin had three fans going but it felt like they were all blowing out hot air. She mingled with a couple of the people she hadn't seen in awhile. Dorothy eased back to the cooler area of the house, walked into the kitchen, and grabbed a paper towel. Dorothy took the cloth and blotted the sweat on her face, then grabbed a can of beer from the cooler and headed back toward the dance floor.

About an hour later, the party really started jumping. The dance floor was packed and the hostess was in the middle of the crowd getting her party on. Punkin had been dancing for a long time. Every song the D.J played she swore it was her jam. She was dancing like she was on stage performing. This woman was a disco fiend. Drunk or sober, just let her hear music and she would get to dancing, no matter where she was.

"Rock, rock, to the Planet Rock, don't stop," went the lyrics of the song. The bass pumping from the loud house speakers had the whole party hype. Punkin was screaming, "Party over here, party over here," at the top of her voice. She was the center of attention. Tyrone, Delvin's friend, was dancing with her, and they'd practically taken over the dance floor. Tyrone was doing his best to keep up with her, but she was hard to keep up with. The dances Punkin were doing were dances no one in the room could do anymore. It was hard to break it down like Punkin was doing.

She had the energy of a teenager.

Dorothy glanced around the room to find her husband. She saw him and waved her hand to get his attention. He stepped away from the man he was talking to and eased toward his wife. He met her on the dance floor and they grooved together to the rhythm of the music. Delvin was on Dorothy like white on rice. She wiggled her behind around his frontal area as he grabbed hold of her hips and they continued swaying to the music.

The D.J stopped the music and announced it was time to slow things down. The crowd cleared the dance floor for those who were about to get their bump and grind on. The D.J put on a slow cut and wobbled his three hundred and something pound body toward the restroom. A hand towel hung across his shoulder. He used it to wipe away his constant sweating.

When Delvin and Dorothy finished dancing he told her he was going to the store with a couple of his partners to get more drinks. She rolled her eyes with an artificial grin. She knew that Delvin and his boys were probably up to no good. He kissed her on her cheek and left with his buddies.

Dorothy glanced around at all the people sitting or standing around fanning themselves. They all looked miserably hot, but heat apparently wasn't stopping anybody from partying. Most of them were so drunk they didn't know if they were coming or going anyway. Dorothy shook her head and headed outside to go get some fresh air. On the porch, she took a seat in one of the plastic patio chairs. The cool breeze whipped through her sweaty hair. Dorothy enjoyed the fresh brisk breeze as she sat bumping to the music.

The screen door swung open and blinked her from her daze. Two women staggered out and wobbled down the steps. "You all leaving or just trying to get a little air?" she asked.

"Naw, girlfriend, we're leaving," one of the women answered.

"Why so soon?"

The woman who answered had a familiar face. Dorothy didn't know her but had seen her before. She was wearing an old, red sweater dress that looked like it was "the shit" about fifteen years ago. She turned to Dorothy and said, "We done had enough. I'm fucked up and she's fucked up, so we best be going. We had fun though." The lady threw her hand in the air waving goodbye to Dorothy and stepped down the stairs to her red Cadillac parked at the end of the driveway.

"Y'all sure you don't need someone to drive you home?"

"No. She lives down the street and I live on the next block over. We're straight! Thanks anyways."

Dorothy burst out laughing about nothing in particular. She rose and headed back inside. She was happy no one was out there to see her or they would have sworn she was crazy.

Tyrone and Delvin came back from the store with plenty of drinks. It was close to four a.m. and nobody should still be drinking at that hour. All the party animals needed to sober up so they could drive home safely.

Punkin was still on the dance floor grooving with this guy named Percy Collins. Punkin met him when she and Dorothy were at the gas station a week ago. Punkin was all hyped when she met him too, she was going on and on about how fine he was. Percy was very slim and had sexy dark brown eyes. Other than that, he was nothing to brag on.

The lady of the house was drunk as a skunk. After five, the partiers cleared her house and Dorothy was ready to go. She helped Punkin clean up by picking up the trash and empty cups. After separating the junk bottles and cans from the ones with the ten cents refund, Dorothy exited the kitchen. She asked one of the guys to help her husband put the furniture back in place. After saying bye to Punkin, Dorothy and her husband closed the door and headed home.

"That was an all right party." Delvin said. His wife said she enjoyed herself too. She didn't feel like dropping him off so Dorothy took Delvin to her house and would take him home in the morning. She was tipsy and definitely not going to bed without getting her some first.

Deshawn was screaming so loud he woke his grandmother from her sleep. He was her automatic alarm because every morning around nine-thirty he was crying. When Dorothy drug herself from the bed Delvin woke up. Monet had not left a bottle in the room so Dorothy had to fix one. Thank goodness the milk was already prepared in the refrigerator.

Delvin went into the bathroom when Dorothy left the room. She wondered why he had left Deshawn on the bed by himself. She said, "Baby, could you please stay in the room with Deshawn until I come in there? He might fall off of the bed."

Delvin exited the bathroom and walked back into the bedroom. When she went back to her room, Dorothy decided she should take Delvin home before she got back into bed. She and her grandbaby were going to be in bed all day because she was hanging over big time.

When they pulled in front of Shirley's house, Delvin gave his wife a big kiss and told her he would talk to her later. When he got out of the car, she pulled off. Shirley was sitting on the couch watching television when Delvin came in. He waved to her as he rushed to his room in the basement. She looked oddly at him, then zeroed back in on the television.

Delvin waited all night and the next morning to test the stuff Tyrone had given him the night before. He impatiently unfolded the one-dollar bill. Tyrone had given him only enough for a one on one so Delvin took the dollar bill and laid it flat on the dresser. He whipped out his ID pressing it down on the creased dollar bill. Before taking his first hit, he paused. He was tremendously paranoid. He wasn't giving much thought to his promise to his wife and family. He hadn't been out a month and he was already falling prey to the powerful. He looked at the temptation and then in the mirror. He said, "I promise this will be the only time. This is to celebrate my homecoming and after this I won't need anymore."

Afterwards he opened the homemade envelope and scooped some powder onto it. He sniffed up a small amount of the finely ground drug and up his nostril it went. Delvin paused for a second and waited for the powder to work its magic in his system. The rush came quickly. He closed his eyes and waited for it to stimulate his central nervous system. He shook his head, trying to calm the atomic rush. It was a wonderful feeling. A few minutes after the first hit, Delvin scooped up the last of the powder and forced it down his nose. His buzz came on so strong after the second toot that Delvin had to sit down on his bed. His tongue curled around his lips as his body relaxed into a featherish euphoria. Even though he'd promised Dorothy otherwise, Delvin couldn't resist getting a little hit since it had been so long; He didn't pay for it, which was his only reason for accepting it. This was not something he was going to start back doing on a regular basis. When his high mellowed Delvin decided to take a shower. He felt guilty and needed to rid his mind of the awful devil that had gotten into him.

Disobedient Child

Caroline and her husband sat in the reception area of the doctor's office. This was their very first visit; a friend had referred them. Caroline hoped this doctor could help her and Thomas rekindle their love, before it was too late. Dr. Marshall walked into the office and her secretary introduced the couple to her. She extended her hand and apologized for being late as she led the couple into her private office.

The large room was decorated in cherry oak wood with antiquated burgundy leather chairs. Certificates and plaques covered the back wall accentuating the large wooden desk in front of them. The off-white wallpaper was speckled with burgundy tulips that added depth to the room, making it appear larger than it was. To the right was a large bookcase covering the entire wall filled with thick, colorful books. The woman flipped through a folder on her desk. Caroline stared at her trying to get a feel of her personality. The doctor looked nothing like Caroline envisioned. She was a fair skinned black woman, very petite, only five feet tall. She had almost microscopic freckles on her face that were about three shades darker than her skin, with far set, dark brown eyes and a short auburn afro. The couple waited in silence as the doctor asked questions to get more acquainted. She asked that they answer the questions to the best of their knowledge. She paused and smiled at the couple. She told Caroline, "What I need you to do is fill in the blanks to this sentence. Thomas, you know that I love you with all my heart and I cherish our marriage but what makes me unhappy is the situation involving_____. In order to overcome this obstacle and move forward I think we should work on_____."

After reciting the sentence with the blanks filled in Caroline stared at her husband and then the doctor, who asked Thomas the same thing. It felt weird, but the counselor said the uneasy feeling would go away after a couple visits. "I know it sounds stupid right now, but trust me, before long, filling in the blanks will become easy."

The doctor explained her agenda and the strategy she used to help her clients with their issues. She estimated an amount of the time it would take before they would notice any progress.

The doctor told the couple that their succession depended on how badly they wanted to regenerate their marriage. The lost souls felt so relieved by the end of the session, they decided to schedule another appointment with Dr. Marshall for four weeks later.

Andrea ran up the path leading to her house. She let herself in through the side door and headed straight for her bedroom. She knew her parents and sister would be home soon and she had to hurry. She rushed to her walk-in closet, frantically digging through her shoe boxes searching for one particular box she'd hid in the closet under her favorite blanket. When Andrea opened the box, her joint was sitting inside where she left it. She'd copped the weed from one of her friends at school. The girl took some matches from her backpack, walked to the window, and opened it. She lit the joint and exhaled the smoke out the window. She made sure the smoke went out of the window so the smell wouldn't linger. She lit up a cigarette and took a few puffs from it. She grabbed a bottle of air freshener and sprayed it in the bedroom and bathroom. She turned on the ceiling fan so the fumes would circulate. She pulled a small bottle of Visine from her desk drawer and squirted a few sprinkles into each of her eyes. She wiped away the residue running down her face, then grabbed some tissue and wrapped the other half of the joint up. She placed it back into its secret hiding place.

She heard footsteps downstairs and wondered if it was her sister. Mrs. Rodriquez always dropped Taylor off at home on Mondays after ballet. Andrea became paranoid. She sprung open the bedroom door and ran downstairs to greet Taylor. "Hi Taylor," she smiled.

"What are you grinning about?" Taylor asked dumbfounded. Andrea didn't answer, but stood there grinning. Taylor walked to the kitchen sink and filled her small hands with the liquid soap on the counter. She turned on the faucet and massaged them. She dried her hands and ripped off another paper towel and laid it on the table. She was about to fix a peanut butter and jelly sandwich.

"Do you have any homework?" Andrea asked.

"Yeah, and I am going to start on it as soon as I'm finished with my sandwich." Andrea didn't say anything, but headed to her private domain to see if it had completely aired out.

Caroline pranced into the house after her husband. She peeked into the den and saw Taylor working on her homework.

"Did you find something to eat?" she asked.

"I ate a peanut butter and jelly sandwich." Caroline smiled at her daughter and left the room. She walked into the kitchen to start dinner. Thomas kissed her and said he was going upstairs to take a shower. When he reached the top of the stairs he peeked into Andrea's room. He knocked on the door and asked.

"How was school today?"

"It was okay," she answered without turning her head away from a book she was pretending to be reading. "How was the meeting?"

"It was okay," he informed. "We have to go again next month."

"That's cool, dad," she answered. "I ain't trying to rush you out or anything, but I am trying to study for a history test."

"Oh, I'm sorry," he said as he exited, and closed the door. As he marched down the hallway, Thomas smiled and thought. Andrea was a bright young lady as long as she could stay focused. This semester her GPA had gone from a three point nine to a two point six, and he knew it was because she spent too much time with her friends. He was happy to see her studying.

Her dinner was on the stove simmering, so Caroline went upstairs to see her daughter whom she hadn't seen since morning. She was curious to know how her day had gone. The prying mother walked into the bedroom and observed Andrea sitting at her desk. The girl's eyes were fanning through a book and her neck was cocked to the side as she talked hands free on her private line. When Caroline walked in, Andrea swiveled around in the chair and faced her mother with an aggravated expression. She looked at Caroline and held her homework papers in the air so her mother could see them and wouldn't interrupt her phone conversation. Caroline nodded her head as if to say excuse me, then she left the bedroom with a satisfying grin on her face. The strong powdery smell coming from the bedroom was so strong it made Caroline sneeze. She didn't know why Andrea always had to spray so much of that darn air freshener.

Caroline opened the door and crept across the plush Swiss Coffee colored carpet. Her husband was sitting on the edge of the bed with a towel wrapped around his waste. She smiled at him as she headed for the dresser to change into something more comfortable. She stood in front of the dresser and undressed. As she bent over to take one leg from her pants Thomas shimmied over to her and started massaging her butt.

"Stop," she yelled bashfully as she turned to face her husband. "Don't start none, and it won't be none," she playfully fussed.

"You are the one trying to start something. You know that I'm easily enticed." He wrapped her body in his arms.

"I am not enticing you, all I'm trying to do is change my clothes so I can go back downstairs to finish cooking."

"You know that beautiful body of yours always turns me on." He smiled mischievously, took a step backwards, and said, "Go ahead and finish taking it off while I watch. You can even sway your hips back and fourth a little bit, you know the way you do when you walk."

Caroline undressed as his eyes seduced her. She was sympathetic to his needs, but she killed his thrill.

"Sorry, baby, but I must get back downstairs and tend to our dinner before we have to eat cold cuts when it burns up. Can you take a rain check?" Thomas stared at her with a pitiful expression as Caroline left the room. She left him stiff and lonely. Disappointed, he walked toward his closet. Realizing he wasn't about to get none, Thomas grabbed a pair of sweats from the closet and slipped them on, then went to his dresser and grabbed a fresh t-Shirt. He had to wait for his protruding manhood to go back down before he could leave the room to go downstairs. Caroline knew she was wrong.

When they finished dinner the family headed into the den to watch television. After the movie started Caroline snuck into the kitchen to call her sister to see what was up with her. She'd already seen Dr. Doolittle twice.

"What's up, girl?" Caroline asked when her sister answered the telephone.

"Nothing much, sis. I'm just sitting up here going over my children's homework before they get ready to take their asses to bed. Don't start, little boy," she warned Deshawn as he squirmed in her lap looking like he was about to start crying. Monet was upstairs taking a bath and had left her son's worrisome behind downstairs to get on his grandmother's nerves.

"Girl, do you want him?" Dorothy asked. Caroline laughed. Deshawn fussed because he couldn't grab the telephone cord. "If somebody don't come and get him, Grandma is going to hurt him," Dorothy said while playfully squeezing his jaws. She rubbed her nose behind his ears and the baby laughed. Caroline laughed too. She was as excited as Deshawn was.

"I can't wait to see him and Delvin. Hopefully, if you guys come over to dinner next Sunday, after church I'll get the chance to see them both," she said.

"Oh, you're cooking for us Sunday?"

"I'm cooking Sunday and if you come over here after church you're welcome to eat some of everything I cook. I invited my good friend Denise and her husband over here and I want you and your family to come also. You remember Denise don't you?"

"Yeah, I think so," Dorothy answered. "Isn't she the doctor that lives near you?"

"She and her husband are psychiatrists," her sister corrected. But anyways, guess who else will be there?"

"Who?" Dorothy asked.

"Thomas's little boy." Dorothy was silent then asked,

"What little boy? You don't have a son." Caroline became silent. "Girl, I know yo ass ain't pregnant."

"No, girl, Thomas has a son." She'd finally let go of her secret. This was the first time Dorothy heard anything about a baby. She thought, that's what she gets from thinking her husband is perfect. Dorothy automatically knew what her sister was about to say, how her husband had an almost grown child pop up from his past who recently came into the picture wanting quality time and back child support payments to catch up for all the years he wasn't around.

As she waited for her sister to tell her what she already knew, Dorothy said, "What's up, big sis? Caroline sat silently on the other end of the telephone.

"Girl, when did Thomas have a baby, and who is it by? Better yet, have you started divorce procedures? I mean, I know you ain't happy about the shit." She was happy to recite those words, anxious to give Caroline a taste of her own medicine.

"Well, I wasn't happy at first, but the baby is almost one and I'm slowly learning to accept him."

"One, girl, I cannot believe that you are just now telling

me this. How long have you known?"

"I've known since the girl was a couple months pregnant but I was too ashamed to tell you when I first found out. I had to have time to deal with it myself, and yes I was considering divorcing Thomas but now I've changed my mind because we have too much together."

Dorothy felt as if she'd been hit with a ton of bricks. She couldn't believe Caroline kept the child a secret for so long. How dare her.

"Thomas and I have been seeing a marriage counselor and she suggested we get better acquainted with the baby since he is definitely going to remain a part of our lives. It makes no sense for me to go on acting as if the little boy doesn't exist." Dorothy didn't comment. She sat on the other end of the phone in shock. She knew her sister had to be joking.

"Dorothy, Dorothy, girl are you still there?" Caroline said. She was in awe. Dorothy was prepared to hear about a child from Thomas' past, but not one from the present.

"Honey!" Thomas yelled from the den.

"Girl, I've got to go," Caroline said. "I'll talk to you later," Caroline didn't tell Dorothy the details about the dinner on Sunday. She was happy that Thomas called her. He'd rescued her just in time.

Dorothy couldn't wait until Sunday. She was anxious to get to her sister's and hear about this baby. That's probably all she would tell because the dirt on her family was usually hush, hush.

It was a warm Saturday afternoon and the frantic woman peeked nervously at the wooden clock on the kitchen wall one more time. She mumbled, "Three-seventeen." Any minute Thomas would walk through the door with his son. This would be his first time bringing the baby to their house. She was so nervous her cocoa buttered hands were trembling. When she heard the garage door open, she ran to the end of the staircase and yelled for Taylor. When her youngest daughter came to the top of the stairs, Caroline yelled, "Come on down here to greet your little brother!"

Andrea was supposed to be home at three and she had not shown up yet. That girl just couldn't do the right thing to save her life. Sometimes Caroline felt like snatching the girl up by her neck and shaking her until she possessed good sense, but these days that could get you locked up. She let the girl hang out with her friends for a change, and still Andrea hadn't done what she was told. She hoped the girl wasn't getting into trouble.

Thomas walked into the house with the baby in his arms. His wife and daughter greeted them with smiles. "Nice to meet you again little brother," Taylor said with a friendly grin as she shook his small hand. Thomas Jr. was looking at his stepmother and sister like he wished they would get out of his face. The little boy looked around the room. The place was unfamiliar to him and so were the faces. His eyes watered. When Caroline reached for him, he turned toward his dad. She pulled her arms back to her side. If the baby didn't want to come to her she wasn't going to force him. She stood to the side, feeling resentment. Thomas sat down and Taylor stood close to him aggravating the little boy. Caroline stood there quietly. She could not believe how much the baby resembled his father. Even his complexion was the same. Taylor familiarized herself with the baby and Caroline went into the den. She decided to call around and see if anyone had seen her disobedient child.

The first call she made was to Dorothy's house even though Caroline figured that was the last place Andrea would be. When no one answered she dialed one of Andrea's friends.

Mrs. Gilbert answered on the second ring and said she had not seen Andrea and that her daughter Rochelle wasn't even home. Caroline asked her to please send Andrea home immediately if she stopped by there. Mrs. Gilbert laughed and told her she would deliver the message if she saw the girl.

"Thanks," Caroline said and hung up.

Now she was really worried. Where was that daughter of hers? All sorts of bad ideas ran through her head. Caroline always told herself when her children were smaller that she couldn't wait until they grew up, but now Caroline wished they were still babies. At least she would know where they were all the time. If Andrea didn't come home soon Caroline was going to start looking for her.

After hanging up the phone she headed back into the den with the rest of the family. The baby was laughing uncontrollably. Obviously, he was getting more acquainted with his new surroundings and his playful big sister, who was making crazy faces and gestures.

Andrea, Tonya, Lisa, and their friend Tim from school were sitting in his vehicle, in an abandoned building's parking lot getting messed up. Tim was a fine, bronze skinned, hip white boy who listened to nothing but rap and hip-hop, and sold nothing but the fire-ass bud.

Tonya was snuggled in the back seat beside her cousin's friend Lisa. Between them was a stack of stolen merchandise they'd lifted from the mall. They were trespassing and getting high. Tonya had never smoked anything in her life and hadn't planned on it now but peer pressure was a terrible thing! To stop everyone in the car from signifying on her and calling her square, Tonya sided with the majority. She took a few light pulls from the blunt. She hacked and exhaled the smoke, then passed it to the next person. "Take this stuff," Tonya fussed. The other kids were laughing at Andrea's cousin who was trying to catch her breath. Her eyes turned red and she patted her chest, breathing hard.

"She can't hang. She can't hang," Andrea teased when

Tonya stopped coughing. Her cousin asked, "Are you okay, girl?"

The younger cousin rolled her eyes and turned away, staring out the window. They could tease her all day and she wasn't changing her mind. She didn't see what the hype was all about.

"Whatever," Tonya answered offensively. "Y'all can smoke all of it, 'cause I don't want any more. Y'all are the ones who's going to have long term bronchial chest problems."

It was Lisa's turn. Lisa went to school with Andrea and the two of them were in the same grade, but her face was painted with so much make-up she looked every bit of twenty-one. She was another cool Caucasian. She had a nice personality and was fun to hang around. One would never guess that she got into as much dirt as she did because she appeared so innocent. Lisa giggled before hitting the blunt and said, "Next time around I'll take your turn. We can't let good shit go to waste." She took a professional pull and exhaled the smoke in circle rings.

Tim didn't say anything, just listened to the girls and chilled. The blunt went around one more time until it was gone. Tim threw the remainder out the window and he and Andrea exchanged curious smiles. His piercing blue eyes gleamed in her direction as he pulled out of the lot. He had a huge crush on Andrea but didn't know if she knew it or not.

When The Marvelous Music Master Greg from radio station 104.7 came on the air and announced the time, Andrea was reminded of her curfew. Her pupils dilated as she loudly announced, "Man, you guys, I was supposed to be home over an hour and a half ago. My parents are going to be trippin because I'm supposed to be there to meet my brother. He is supposed to be coming over to spend the weekend with us."

"What brother, Andrea?" Tonya asked. She wondered why her cousin was lying about having a brother.

"Oh yeah, cuz," Andrea began. "You didn't know my daddy cheated on my mom a little while back and now some hoe is saying she's got a baby by him." Tonya's eyes bulged. She never heard this before. Andrea continued, "I'm surprised you didn't know as much as my mama and Aunt Dorothy gossip. She makes me mad always trying to act like she's more than what she is. You know that fake shit. I don't know why she acts like that. Her and Aunt Dorothy are like night and day."

"I don't believe you."

"I promise, and my parents are acting like I am supposed to be pressed to run and go to see the little bastard. If I ain't seen him in all this time I don't know what makes them think I'm supposed to be all overjoyed about meeting him today."

Tonya couldn't believe what she was hearing. Tim interrupted. "Sorry we have to ride out y'all but I got to make a run."

"That's cool, I need to be on my way home too," Lisa moaned.

"Girl, can you take the stuff I racked home with you?" Andrea asked her friend. "You know my moms' be trippin' every since I caught that case."

Her friend said she would and her kin folk sat in the back seat in total disbelief. She was finding out lots of secrets that Aunt Caroline hadn't told her mother. She knew her cousin stole but she had no idea she'd been arrested for it. It was a good thing Tonya told them she would meet them back at the car in two hours. She knew her cousin was going to steal and she didn't want to have anything to do with it. When she finished shopping she waited at the car until they came out of the mall. Tonya would never hang with her cousin and her crew again.

Tonya sat silently in the back seat of the car feeling paranoid. She didn't enjoy getting high. She wished they would drop her off first, but they were in Lisa's neighborhood. Lisa reached into her purse, pulled out Visine and dropped it into her eyes. It ran from her eyes like tears. She held the bottle in the air and asked if anyone else wanted some. The other two girls used the

Visine, but Tim passed. He said he wasn't going straight home so it didn't matter if his eyes were red or not.

"If they see my eyes red they'll know that what I have is proper and that equals moe money, moe money, moe money."

Tim dropped Lisa and Tonya off first. Since, Andrea didn't live far from where he was going, he could drop her off last. As they neared her house Tim became nervous. He planned on asking his friend for her phone number before he dropped her off. They were less than three blocks away from her house and Tim still didn't have the courage to ask.

"Why are you always so quiet Tim?" Andrea asked.

"I don't know. I guess because I don't have much to say." This was his cue to ask her. He looked out the front windshield as he spoke. He could not look directly at her, but finally the words eased out. There was a slight tremor in his voice.
"Why don't you let me have your phone number so I can call and talk to you sometimes," he said.

"I guess," as if his question shocked her. She knew Tim had a crush on her and she liked him a little, but she wasn't going to say anything unless he said something first. She ripped a piece of paper from a small organizer inside her purse and scribbled her name and number on it and handed the paper to Tim. He accepted it and smiled as he pulled in front of her house. Andrea grabbed her things and jumped out of the vehicle smiling. Tim pulled away from the curb as Andrea ran up the path. She should have told Tim it would be a while before she could have phone calls considering how late she was returning home. She already knew she was in trouble. At least she would still be able to see Tim at school every day.

Caroline was in the kitchen fixing herself something to drink when her defiant daughter walked into the house with a small department store bag in her hand. Caroline slammed her glass on the counter and demanded that Andrea tell her where she'd been and why she was so late. Her daughter waved her empty hand into the air.

"I was at the mall, and before you even start, I lost track of time and I'm sorry." Andrea avoided her mother's eyes.

"Girl," Caroline said, "you had your father and I worried to death about where you were, and here you come prancing up in here all late and waving your hand." Caroline approached her daughter as she fussed. Angrily, she said. "Girl, you better get out of my face before I hurt you."

Thomas walked into the kitchen. He'd heard the commotion and figured Caroline was fussing at Andrea. He also needed to pour some milk into his son's trainer cup. Andrea stomped off to her room when her dad walked into the kitchen.

Thomas rushed upstairs to his daughter's bedroom and opened the door. He was losing his patience with the girl and went off on her.

"All right, Andrea I want some answers from you and I want them without any lies. I don't understand why it's so hard for you to do as you're told!"

Andrea didn't say anything, but he continued yelling.

"You know we wanted you here at a certain time to meet your brother and you made it your business not to be here! Just for being late you're not allowed to have any phone calls, no visitors, and no allowance! You will be confined to this bedroom until you can learn to act like a civilized young lady. Do you understand?" And turn around and look at me while I'm talking to you!"

Andrea hesitated, then turned to face her father. He was so angry he didn't wait for her to respond, he just walked out of the room. He was so predictable. Andrea knew she was home free because her daddy was soft when it came to discipline.

Love Hurts

Deshawn was lying on his dad's twin bed asleep and Monet was lying next to him. Derrick was downstairs somewhere. Monet and the baby were spending the day at Derrick's. Although she was bored, Monet didn't want to stay home alone. Her family left early that morning so she decided to catch a cab to Derrick's house.

Her boyfriend walked into the bedroom bopping to a beat heard only by him. He said, "All right, my mother finally left and Deshawn is sleeping, so what's up?"

"Ain't nothing up. I'm on my period."

"Man, stop lying."

"I ain't lying."

"Man that's messed up," Derrick moaned.

"Don't let it disappoint you because we are about to leave anyway."

"Dang, y'all getting ready to leave already?"

"Well, it's getting late and I don't want Deshawn out in the night air. Could you call us a cab?"

Derrick looked disappointed, but he picked up the telephone and started dialing. Monet rose from the bed and gathered her son's things and put them in his diaper bag. Then, she sat on Derrick's lap so she could get her smooch on. Within a couple of minutes she heard the cab outside blowing. She jumped up and lifted Deshawn from the bed and handed him to his daddy, then grabbed the bag and her jacket. Monet followed Derrick out of the room. Deshawn wiggled as his dad kissed all over his face. "Daddy's lil' man 'bout to leave. I'm gone miss you."

Monet put the car seat in the back of the cab and Derrick strapped Deshawn into it. As she climbed in Derrick kissed her and handed her two twenty dollar bills. He asked Monet to call him when she got home. He grasped his sagging jeans and ran toward the house. Derrick was a good provider, but Monet was tired of calling herself Derrick's girlfriend when she knew their relationship had been more a friendship.

Every time she saw Derrick, he wanted to have sex. They'd only been together once since Monet had the baby and she was tired of their so-called relationship. Besides, he wasn't in school or working, and Monet felt he would be a bad role model for her son. She believed Derrick was content with his lifestyle. He had no goals or plans for the future, so they had nothing in common.

This was her last year of school and she had worked hard to catch up on her work after having her son. She planned on going to community college to become a physical therapist. Dorothy had agreed to help with Deshawn and Monet was determined to become successful. She did not want to be just another statistic. Her son's unexpected birth gave Monet inspiration to succeed, if not for herself, then for him. She even had a part-time job lined up at a nursing home after she graduated. Her friend, Channel's mother, was a manager at Central Manor and guaranteed Monet a job. Monet hadn't figured out how to get rid of Derrick. Even though she would always love him, she didn't want to be with him anymore.

"That will be seven dollars and thirty cents," the cab driver announced as he parked the car, turned off the meter, and turned to Monet. She handed him a twenty-dollar bill, grabbed her baby, and waited for her change. She got out of the car and walked toward the front door.

Deshawn whimpered and squirmed in the car seat. He was so heavy Monet couldn't wait to put him down. Now that he was almost five months old, it was more difficult for her to carry him in the seat. Deshawn weighed almost seventeen pounds. She took the birth control pills every day, and even considered getting the Depo-Provera shot. That way she wouldn't worry about popping pills every day and she would be protected for three months at a time.

Once inside, Monet put Deshawn's car seat on the floor and sighed. Tonya walked up to Monet and told her big sister no one else was home. "Did you go to the mall with Andrea," Monet asked.

"Yeah," Tonya answered. "Do you want to see what I bought?"

"Sure," Monet took a seat on the sofa and waited for her sister to return. Tonya bought a real cute hot pink and black Limited sweater, and a pair of flare jeans to go with it. "That looks real cute together," Monet said. "I hope those jeans ain't too tight because you know Mama will make you take them right back."

"They ain't tight," Tonya said. "I got a whole lot of room in these jeans." She folded her outfit neatly and placed it back in the bag.

"How much did you pay for the whole outfit?" Nervously, Tonya answered.

"All together it came up to fifty-two dollars."

"Dang, girl, you had a whole lot of money saved up, didn't you?"

"A lil' bit," Tonya mumbled. Before she could finish, Monet asked, "Has mama called?"

"Not since I've been here," Tonya answered. She asked Monet if she wanted her to carry anything upstairs for her.

"Yes, I am about to go upstairs and give this boy a bath, then I can take a bath and get ready for bed. Mama 'nem should be back pretty soon." Tonya grabbed the diaper bag and Monet unfastened the car seat, picked up her baby, and started up the stairs. Deshawn was waking up. He began to cry and Monet patted him on his back. "Shh, Mama knows."

Monet was on the phone when Dorothy and the kids came home about an hour later. When hearing the racket downstairs, she told her friend she would talk to her later. Monet hung up and ran downstairs. "Where have you guys been all this time?" Monet asked.

"Everywhere, chile. How long have you been back?"

"A little over an hour!"

"Where is my baby at?"

"He's upstairs sleeping. I not too long ago gave him a bath."

"Where's Tonya?"

"She's upstairs in her room."

"I hope she has her stuff ready for church tomorrow. We are all going over to Caroline's for dinner after church. When you go back upstairs make sure you tell your sister what I said."

"All right," Monet said. "Let me go back upstairs and find something for my son and me to wear. If we are going to Aunt Caroline's I better dress Deshawn in his best clothes." Monet burst out laughing at her own comment as she started back upstairs.

The next day after church, everyone climbed out of the car at Caroline's house. The lingering smell of soul food had every-body's stomach growling. Dorothy walked into the house and asked if she could help with anything, as her husband went to the den to watch television.

Delvin walked down the hallway admiring the fine hand carved masks and paintings on the wall. He peeked into Caroline's formal living room beautifully furnished with antique furniture made of cherry wood with cream colored imported silk. The old family pictures and heirlooms gave the room a homey feel. When Delvin stepped down the steps into the den, he noticed the swim-ming pool shaped like Africa in the backyard. Caroline's back yard was huge and professionally manicured.

Thomas Jr. was posted to his dad's leg, staring at all the unfamiliar faces. Caroline's friends had arrived and were getting acquainted with everyone while Dorothy helped set the table.

Thomas and Delvin talked about old times. When the dining room table was set for twelve, everyone piled around it as Caroline led a blessing. The guests all helped themselves to the wholesome meal Caroline had prepared. The table was nicely decorated with a large variety of food, collard greens, baked chicken, roast beef, cornbread dressing, sweet potatoes, baked beans, and baked macaroni and cheese. For dessert Caroline made a huge banana pudding and a mouthwatering butter pound cake.

Everyone stuffed themselves and complained about how full and tired they were. Dorothy whispered to her sister that she wanted to hear the whole story about the baby before she left. Caroline shh'd her and said she would tell her later.

When the baby started crying, Thomas decided it was time to get him back to his mother. He'd been away from Sheila for two days and missed her. As soon as he was out the door, Dorothy pulled her sister into a private room, requesting to hear the whole story. Caroline told Dorothy about the baby. After their talk, Dorothy and her family left. Caroline walked upstairs to use her private bathroom.

Caroline could swear she smelled marijuana. The smell became stronger as she tip-toed to her daughter's bedroom door. She burst open the door, but didn't see anyone. As she stepped inside, the smell got stronger. Andrea was standing by the opened window looking very guilty.

"Andrea, why do I smell weed in here?" Caroline asked.

"I don't smell anything!" Andrea said.

"Do not play with me Andrea Tishon. Why in the hell are you standing over there with that window wide open?"

Caroline sniffed.

"And I do smell weed?"

Andrea didn't budge. She stared at her mother with a vicious look.

Caroline walked up and grabbed Andrea's jaw. She got a

whiff of the girl's breath and snatched her hands to smell them.

"Have you been in here smoking weed?"

"You don't see any weed, do you?" Caroline slapped the girl across the face. "You smart mouth heffa!" she yelled. "Who in the hell do you think you're talking too? Do you think I'm one of your friends in the streets?"

Caroline moved the girl out of the way and looked out the window to see if Andrea had dropped the marijuana on the ground. It was getting dark and she couldn't see too well. Caroline grabbed the girl's clothes. "So you think you're grown now. You think you're so grown that you can disrespect me and smoke weed in my house, while I'm home."

Caroline left the room and came back swinging her husband's leather belt at Andrea. Andrea tried to get away but Caroline stopped her by grabbing her shirt. With all her strength, Caroline pulled the girl toward her and swung the belt. She continued striking Andrea with the belt. Andrea kept yelling and trying to get away, but her mother wouldn't let her. Every word from Caroline's mouth was accompanied by a hit with the belt.

"I," smack, "told you," smack, smack, "not," smack, "to," smack, "play," smack, smack, "with," smack "me," smack. Yelling and squirming, Caroline accidentally hit herself with the belt, upsetting her even more. Caroline was so pissed, she threw down the belt and grabbed the girl's shirt. She drug the girl to the bed and threw her down, shaking her and shouting.

"You are going to learn to stop misbehaving. You have been walking around here getting into trouble for the last couple of months and I'm tired of the shit. Do you understand?"

"Yes, Mama," the girl screamed. "I promise I'm not going to get into anymore trouble. I promise!"

"From now on you're going to be confined to this house like a prisoner, since you want to keep acting like a criminal. I didn't raise you this way Andrea." Caroline walked out of the bedroom. Her blood pressure seemed to be soaring. Andrea laid across the bed and bawled until her eyes were bloodshot red. Caroline sat at the edge of her bed crying, and thinking to herself. "Lord, what am I going to do with that girl?"

Delvin got off work and rushed home. He changed into the outfit he'd bought the week before. Dorothy made sure he spent most of his check on her and the kids when they went shopping. This week he was hanging out with his boys and they were going to celebrate Tyrone's birthday. Delvin couldn't wait. This would be his first night at a club since getting out of jail.

When he got out the shower, Delvin called Dorothy and told her that he'd talk to her tomorrow. She was babysitting Deshawn while Monet went out with her friend, Channel. Dorothy let Monet and Channel use her car to go to some school party. Brandy was supposed to meet them there. Dorothy told Monet to be home by 2 a.m. Monet wore jeans and a shirt that didn't even reach her belly. Her stomach was so flat, it looked like she'd never had a baby.

At the party, the girls parked as far away from the building as possible. They appreciated Dorothy letting them borrow the ride, but it was a hooptie and they had a reputation to uphold. They climbed out of the car and started toward the party hall. Channel wore blue jeans and a white cut-off shirt like Monet's. Her stomach was flat too. Both girls looked nice and couldn't wait to get inside. Monet's hair hung down and Channel had twists in the front, and the back of her hair was flat-ironed.

All evening Monet and her friend were admired by all the guys. The girls didn't know anyone at the party. Monet danced a few times, but Channel was busy collecting phone numbers. She was dating the guy who invited her and Monet to the party. Channel figured she could date anyone she wanted since she didn't have a ring on her finger. Monet hadn't been out in awhile and planned on making the best of her free time.

As Monet walked away from the concession booth, Malcolm asked her to dance. He was about five-foot eight with light brown, smooth skin and big dark, brown eyes. Malcolm had the body of a professional football player. Monet needed a cold drink; she'd danced two songs non-stop, and her throat was dry. If Malcolm wasn't so fine, she would have refused to dance with him. After their dance, Monet and her new friend sat at an empty table and talked. Malcolm seemed smart and disciplined. He was a star quarterback on Central's senior football team and played point guard on the basketball team. He planned on studying dentistry at The Medical College of Georgia, in Augusta. After graduating, he wanted to join practices with his mother who was already an established dentist. Unlike Derrick, Malcolm had plans for his future. He also worked three days a week as a bagger at Clark's Supermarket when he didn't have homework or practice.

Out With the Old, In With the New

James sat outside Delvin's house blowing the horn as if his hand was glued to the steering wheel. Delvin ran to the car and told James he didn't have to be blowing like that. Delvin knew James and Tyrone were already buzzing because the car reeked of alcohol. Tyrone handed the newcomer a Budweiser from the back seat and told him to get his drink on. "It's party time, man."

Delvin popped open the can and took a long gulp. He burped loudly and sighed as he finished his beer. The club was about twenty minutes away, but with all three of them drinking, the twelve-pack would be gone before they got there.

"Man, y'all want to go in on a sixteenth?" James asked. Delvin didn't answer; he was ignoring James comment. Delvin hadn't gotten high since the day after Punkin's party and he'd promised himself he wouldn't do it anymore. He now realized that it wasn't a good idea to go out with the guys, but it was Tyrone's birthday and Delvin didn't want to disappoint him. He decided to go in on the sixteenth, but he would just let his friends toot it.

James said, "Good! We can pick up a package from one of the boys on Lafayette."

Delvin pulled a ten dollar bill from his back pocket and handed it to James. He had a hundred and forty dollars left to play with. Thank God, he'd handled all of his business earlier.

They traveled down the dark street about two blocks before they turned onto Lafayette Street. It was cold, but the boys on the block were well prepared with their big, puffy, Starter and goose down coats on. They paced to keep warm as they talked.

James pulled up behind a car that looked familiar. There were four or five guys in the car. They were obviously smoking because the inside of the car was filled with a gigantic cloud of smoke. James flashed his headlights to get the driver's attention. He hoped they didn't start shooting at him. Suddenly, a boy jumped from the passenger side sporting a wicked frown on his face. His blue jeans sagged and his coat was about three sizes too big. The boy appeared to be about nineteen or twenty years old.

A big puff of smoke spewed from the vehicle before the boy closed the car door. The boy walked up to Tyrone's side of the car and asked him what was up. Tyrone cracked his window and said, "What's up, man, can we get a nice sixteenth?"

"Let me get in," the boy said.

Tyrone opened the door and D-Slim climbed into the back-seat beside the birthday boy.

James turned to the boy, "I'm sorry, young blood. I know your face, but I can't remember your name."

"D-Slim," the boy responded, searching through his sack. He pulled a plump individual bag of powder from the big sack and clipped it on to a pocket sized scale. Tyrone checked the scale to see if it weighed up correctly before he handed D-Slim the money. James and Delvin didn't say anything. Tyrone handed D-Slim the money. D-Slim told the guys to holler at him later if they needed to get straightened out again.

James let the boy out of the car in a hurry. He was anxious to get him a bump before pulling off. When he closed the car door, James reached for the bag in Tyrone's hand. He scooped up some of the powder with his driver's license and sniffed it up his nostril. "Damn," he replied. "That right there is the shit."

James passed the bag back to Tyrone, who snorted a one-on-one. He handed the sack to Delvin. Delvin hesitated, then took a hit as the car slowly started rolling down the street.

When they arrived at the club, each one did a one-on-one before getting out of the car. James grabbed some cologne from his glove compartment and sprayed it all over himself. Tyrone took a small bottle of cologne from his pocket. It was one of those slender little tubes that came attached to a department store pro-motional item, the ones with the price list and picture. It was a new fragrance called Miracle and it smelled good. Tyrone said the smell was gone attract all the women to him. "Don't y'all think nothing strange is going on when all the honies start flocking my way," Tyrone teased. "That'll just be my new cologne working its Miracle on them."

Inside, they mingled and enjoyed themselves. The club was krunk and Delvin saw a lot of people he hadn't seen in a long time. At three in the morning, the guys staggered out of the club. Delvin told James to drop him off at Dorothy's house and not at his sister's. He didn't feel like riding across town. Delvin wanted to lie down as soon as he could.

Delvin's friends dropped him off at Dorothy's. Irritated that someone was knocking on her door at this hour, Dorothy looked through the peep hole and saw it was Delvin. She instantly caught an attitude. Not only was her husband disrespecting her by coming to her house at this hour, but he was staggering drunk. After she let his pitiful looking ass into the house, she scolded him. She said what was on her mind and jumped back into bed, throwing the covers over her face. She asked Delvin not to touch her.

Delvin got undressed and into the bed, but he couldn't sleep. After a minute or two he got up and went to the bathroom. Delvin sat on the toilet with his head buried between his legs. Denial was kicking in. He felt bad about disrespecting Dorothy and upsetting her. Dorothy stuck by him no matter what, and now he was taking her for granted. She wouldn't have let him in the house if she had known what he had done earlier. He regreted blowing all the money he left home with. Instead of allowing his friends to influence him, he should have stuck with his first thought. He made a promise to God, right there on the toilet that last night was his last time getting high. He knew he could do it. Delvin had gone almost eight years without dope and knew he had the power to continue. He couldn't go back. He just couldn't.

There was no way he would allow himself to transform back into the monster he was when he was getting high. He couldn't let his family down again, and he needed to be part of his son's life. Dwayne was growing up and needed a father he could look up to and depend on. Dorothy couldn't have those father-son conversations with him, and he'd be damned if another man raised his son. Dwayne didn't deserve to have a father who was a liar or cheater, or a cocaine fiend. He tried to wipe away the guilt, as he wiped away the tears. He walked back into the bedroom and fell into bed with his eyes wide open. He worried that Dorothy knew he'd been getting high. She knew him better than he knew himself.

Dorothy wasn't sleeping but Delvin didn't know. As he walked back from the bathroom, she wiped away her tears. His behavior was familiar. She knew he'd been out drinking and getting high. She knew the signs. He was probably in the bathroom getting high because he was restless. If he'd just been out drinking he would have come there either horny or sleepy and he was neither. She remembered when he was getting high before, and how he would rarely get any sleep. Dorothy wanted to believe her husband would change but, for the umpteenth time, she felt like a sucker for love. Delvin had not been out of prison even six months and he was already defiant. She had no proof, but her intuition told her that her husband was using again. She'd been through it too many times to count. She would stay on Delvin like white on rice, to see if her instincts were correct. She needed to prepare herself instead of getting caught off guard like in the past. If Delvin was getting high again, she would file for divorce even if it cost her every penny she had. If the fool chose dope over her and the children this time, she was cutting him off. She didn't have time for the lies and excuses. She absolutely refused to let him take her down again.

When Dorothy woke up, she decided to see what information she could get from the junky in her bed. She asked Delvin for fifty dollars for groceries. He hesitated before telling her he did-n't have any money. "I ain't gone have it until Monday because I put all my money in the bank yesterday and I don't have an ATM card." He said he only had fifty dollars last night, and lost twen-ty of that. Dorothy's anger turned into a verbal explosion, as she accused him of spending his money to get high. Delvin said he didn't feel like arguing and asked Dorothy if she could take him home. She was happy to take him home because she didn't feel like hearing anymore of his lies.

Four days passed. Dorothy still hadn't talked to her hus-band and that was fine with her. If she could go seven years with-out seeing him, four days without him wasn't shit.

She picked up the telephone to call her sister as she heard a knock at the door. It was Tony, Monet's father, doing his once a year surprise visit. Monet came downstairs immediately with her baby and talked with her father about her plans for college. She was really excited because she would soon be graduating from high school.

Tony told Monet about the new love in his life and that he couldn't wait until the two of them met. Before he left, Tony gave Monet two-hundred dollars and told her that he would see her later. For the first time ever, he gave Monet his phone number and told her to call if she needed anything. Now that she was almost grown, he was trying to act like a father.

Monet was so excited. With the money her father gave her, she could get the dress she wanted to wear to the prom. She hoped the dress was still at the store, since she saw it over two weeks ago. Malcolm had asked her to the prom but she'd been afraid to say yes because she couldn't afford the dress. Besides, it was still over six months away.

Monet enjoyed spending time with Malcolm. He was as different from Derrick as night and day. Malcolm had his own automobile and he had goals. Like Monet, he was enthused about going to college. On the other hand, Derrick had a problem getting up for school every day. Monet wondered why she was attracted to him in the first place. Her feelings for Derrick were decreasing. They had nothing in common. They never went anywhere anymore, and every time Derrick saw her he wanted to sleep with her, and she wasn't with that. Monet wished she never had a baby by him. She was falling in love with Malcolm because he was so different. Monet was embarrassed to admit that she was ever with anyone like Derrick.

After she'd found out where Malcolm lived, Monet was afraid to invite him to her house. She doubted whether she was good enough to be his girl. He lived in an upper class neighborhood with his parents and little sister. He planned to go to college and become a successful dentist. So why would he want a seventeen year old girl from the projects with a baby? Monet had avoided mentioning the baby to Malcolm. He was so smart and such a good conversationalist, Monet enjoyed listening to him talk. She only spoke when he asked her something, and he'd never asked if she had children. She and Malcolm had only been seeing each other a couple of weeks and she didn't feel like telling him her life story.

Over the next five weeks, Monet and Malcolm became better acquainted. She wondered how long the relationship would last since he would soon be going away to college. She knew Malcolm would be around a lot of females at college and probably wouldn't even think about her there. Monet didn't think it would be hard for him to leave her and a baby, to be with a college girl with no children and big plans for the future. Monet wished she had the opportunity to go away to college, instead of staying home and going to community college. If she'd never had a baby, she probably could have. Monet didn't want to be pessimistic but she didn't want to get her hopes up for something that wasn't promised to her. She knew it was a possibility that she and

Malcolm would go their separate ways because he was too good for her and they had such different backgrounds. Besides caring for one another, they had nothing in common.

Malcolm called Monet and invited her to McDonalds. Deshawn was with Derrick so Monet accepted. When Malcolm pulled up outside Monet's house, she told her siblings that if Derrick called to tell him she would be back in about an hour. "If he asks where I went, tell him that you don't know."

Malcolm watched as her slim hips swayed back and forth to his ride. Malcolm was turned on by what her body was doing to the jeans she had on. They snugly fit to her body's perfect curves. The brown in her shirt brought out the sexiness in her eyes. Her face was glowing, and her persona was friendly. Malcolm was so pleased with her appearance, his eyes smiled and invited her inside his vehicle.

Monet felt butterflies in her stomach as she climbed into the car. She knew Malcolm had been watching her every since she stepped out of the door and wondered what he was thinking. "Hey," she smiled.

"Has anyone told you how good you look today?" Malcolm asked. She was too nervous to answer, but he continued to flirt. "That outfit looks really nice on you."

"Thank you," Monet's eyes glistened, her teeth sparkled, and she couldn't stop smiling. She was starting to like Malcolm a lot. He'd given her a compliment, something she hadn't heard in a long time. Malcolm made her feel like the most beautiful girl in the world. As they rode down the street, Malcolm peeked at his beautiful passenger every time his eyes had a chance to shy away from the road.

Monet bobbed her head to the music from Malcolm's six by nine's. Neither of them said a word, the music was so loud. Monet smiled as she pondered how she'd tell Derrick that she didn't want to be his girlfriend anymore. She had fallen out of love with him and was infatuated with Malcolm.

Finally, they pulled into the parking lot of McDonalds on the corner of Division and Hall. He eased the car into an available parking space and Malcolm and Monet climbed out of the car walking side by side toward the entrance. They jumped into the shortest line and waited their turn. Monet ordered a double cheeseburger combo and Malcolm said he would have the Big Mac combo. The cashier said it would take a few minutes for the fries so if they should take a seat she would bring their entire order to the table when it was ready. They sat down and waited for the girl to bring the order. The server had a royal blue and black ponytail sticking out of the top of her visor. The heffa was so rude she started flirting with Malcolm right in Monet's face. Monet looked up and said, "We're all set." The server rolled her eyes and smacked her heavily, platinum painted, lips together and stormed away. Her lipstick clashed with her complexion and Monet laughed, "That color is just not for everybody."

They talked in between gulps, discovering they had a lot in common. Time passed like a swift wind in Chicago. Monet reminded Malcolm that she was only supposed to be gone an hour. She realized they had been in McDonalds for over two hours. She dismissed herself to go the ladies room and Malcolm cleared the table. When Monet returned he was waiting for her at the door.

They pulled up in front of Monet's house and her date asked when could he see her again? "I don't know. Call me," she said as she hopped out of the car and ran to the front door.

The car pulled off as Monet walked into the house smiling. Once inside, she was surprised to find Derrick sitting in the front room frowning. Deshawn was sitting on his lap. When he saw his mother, he started crying for her. Monet grabbed for her bundle of joy.

"Hey, mama's scooka wooka. Mommy missed her baby,

yes she did."

Derrick was angry. "You got a lot of nerve trying to walk up in here and act like you didn't have me waiting here all day for you. While you are stepping up in here acting all hunky-dory did you forget that I was bringing Deshawn home at seven o'clock? And I seen that nigga' you got out of the car with. Who the fuck is that, Monet?"

"You gone watch yo' mouth up in here Derrick and I bet ya. Don't even trip because I ain't even trying to hear what you're talking about."

"Don't trip! Don't trip!" Derrick snapped. "How are you going to tell me don't trip when it was you who neglected to come home and tend to your son because you were out with that buster?" Deshawn's cries grew louder.

"Watch your mouth in front of my son, Derrick. I don't know where you think you are but you're not going to be coming up in here disrespecting me or mine by trying to regulate. You ain't up on the block."

"Man, whatever Monet. I caught a ride over here to drop him off and when I got here you wasn't here. My ride left me because you weren't here to get this boy. Now I have to find another ride home."

"I'm here now so you can call your ride and tell them to come back and get you." Monet yelled and her son cried harder.

"So, Monet, is that the punk supposed to be yo' man now?"

"That's my friend."

"So when did you get this friend?"

"When I stopped having a man," she argued. Derrick's eyes grew wide with amazement and turned red as her words finally registered. Derrick got up and started fussing. Monet was standing guard because she wasn't sure what he was about to do.

"So when did you stop having a man?" Monet didn't

answer. Derrick asked again, but this time he put his finger in her face. Monet slapped it down with her free hand. Derrick suddenly burst out laughing.

"If that's the way that you want it to be Monet, that's fine. It don't matter to me what you do. Just don't have my son around that punk."

"Whatever, Derrick. It ain't no telling how many stanking tramps you've been with, and now you're trying to come up in here checking me."

Derrick was so upset he could have slapped Monet in her smart ass mouth. Instead, he sprinted to the front door. "You're lucky man. You're real lucky," were Derrick's lasts words before he slammed the door and left. Monet laughed as she kissed her son on the forehead and tried to shh him. "That's what yo' daddy get boo." She let a few minutes pass before she looked out the window and saw him walking up the street toward the bus stop.

Tonya paraded into the room deliriously.

"I didn't know if y'all was gone get to fighting or what," she said, "I was right there on them stairs waiting to see if he was gone hit you so I could run in here and beat his head in with this skillet."

"Girl, please, Derrick ain't gone do nothing to nobody," Monet mumbled.

Later that evening, Monet was lying on her bed when Tonya came in and said Derrick was on the phone. Monet did not feel like being bothered with him, but she drug downstairs to the kitchen phone. "What." Derrick began yelling.

"I wasn't playing with you Monet when I said I didn't want that punk around my son. I can't believe you gone try to kick it with somebody else and me and you ain't even broke up. Did you call yourself trying to play on me, Monet?

"How many times do I have to tell you that he is just my

friend? If you can't accept it, that's on you. I mean, it ain't like you've been breaking your neck to try and spend any time with me. You ought to be ashamed to call me your woman because who can say that they've seen us together. I feel like all I am is your baby's mother, not your girlfriend. Every time I want to do something with you, your claim is you're doing something with your boys, and I'm tired of that excuse."

"Monet, are you trying to say you don't want to be with me anymore?"

"Derrick, when are we together? Malcolm asked me out and I didn't see anything wrong with it. I don't see anything wrong with going out on a casual date with a friend. I bet you have done that plenty of times, haven't you?"

"Monet, you think I'm gone have another punk all up in my woman's face and taking her out and shit," he avoided answering her question.

"Hell naw! I bet not ever see you with that punk again or I'm gone mess you and him up." Derrick slammed the phone in her ear.

"Oh well," Monet thought as she hung up the telephone and went upstairs while laughing at the fool. She was too busy thinking about Malcolm to let Derrick stress her out. She was dreaming that some day Malcolm would be Deshawn's stepfather.

———————

Thomas and his wife sat in bed talking. It was getting late but they were discussing whether they would let their daughter go to the dance. She'd asked if she could go when she got home from school, but her parents hadn't given her an answer yet. Caroline didn't see the problem with Andrea going to the dance, but she wasn't sure if Andrea had learned her lesson. She wanted to have faith in her daughter, but based on her past, it was hard to do that. Before turning off the lights, the Smith's decided they would let her go. "This will be her trial," Caroline commented, lying back in bed. They would tell Andrea in the morning. "If she tries me this time, I'll kill her," Caroline concluded. Thomas leaned over and kissed his wife.

The next day, Andrea couldn't wait to get to school to tell Tim the good news. She could hardly sit still on the bus ride. When she arrived, Andrea hurried inside the building to find him. She headed toward his locker. As she passed the ladies' room, Andrea heard Tim call her name from behind. When Andrea turned around, Tim signaled for her to stay there.

"What's up?" he said as he approached.

"As a matter of fact," she said, "you're just the person I was looking for. I was coming to tell you that my parents said it was okay for me to go to the dance with you."

"All right then," he was so happy, he asked Andrea for a hug. She hugged him and when the bell rang, they went their separate ways and agreed to meet at lunch.

Dorothy's mind wandered as she pushed her shopping cart down the aisle. She still hadn't talked to her husband and he hadn't come over or called her to come get them fifty dollars. She hadn't heard from him since she accused him of getting high. That was her sign that her husband was back up to no good. She was tired of giving in. Although she wanted to deny it, Dorothy had a gut feeling her husband had started back using. She couldn't think of anything else that would cause him to behave that way.

A voice called out from behind! "Excuse me, ma'am, but I was wondering if I could get over there and grab a bag of that rice." Bewildered, she froze in the middle of the grocery aisle, blocking the rice section.

"I'm sorry," she apologized, snapping back to reality from her daydream. She turned in his direction. His deep, masculine voice sounded like jazz in her ear. The gentleman was tall and conservative, brown-skinned, and highly attractive. The brother had it going on. He was wearing a pair of navy blue slacks and a white Polo shirt. Dorothy pushed her buggy forward. The gentle-man threw his bag of rice into his shopping cart and smiled.

"I'm sorry to have interrupted what seemed like a pretty deep thought," he said. Dorothy revealed an embarrassed smile. The man extended his hand and introduced himself, "I apologize for being rude. My name is Sullivan, Sullivan Edwards."
She extended her hand to shake his nicely manicured hand.

"I'm Dorothy Johnson. What a way to meet someone," she giggled. "I'm sorry, but my mind drifted off for a minute." Trying not to be obvious, Sullivan studied her body, up and down. Even though he was clean cut and polite it didn't stop him from being a man. His staring was borderline rude. Dorothy didn't feel she looked her best. She had on an old blue jean, button down dress that was faded in front. She wished she was prepared to meet this sweet brown hunk of delicious standing in front of her.

"Well, again, Sullivan, I apologize for blocking your view. Please forgive me," she said, slowly pushing her cart down the aisle. The impromptu meeting with Sullivan caused her to forget why she'd come down the aisle in the first place. She grabbed a box of macaroni and hoped he wasn't looking, even though it felt like he was. Before she could leave the aisle, she heard his voice.

"Dorothy, if you have another minute, I was wondering if I could ask you something." Dorothy immediately stopped to let him catch up. She was curious about what he wanted. "I wanted to invite you somewhere."

"Where?" She asked defensively.

"Well, I attend the First A.M.E Church, right over there off Wealthy and I would like to invite you to my church." Church, she thought. Even though Dorothy attended her own church reg-ularly, this brother was so fine and well groomed she couldn't refuse.

"I just might do that," she finally answered. He reached into his pocket and handed her a business card. Dorothy read it and looked back up at him with a wiry expression.

"You know the area?"

"I'm trying to place it."

"Well, my home phone number is on there just in case you need a ride or directions." As Dorothy dropped the card inside her purse she told Sullivan how nice it was to meet him, and that she would love to see him again soon. She smiled and pushed her buggy around the corner and down the next aisle. Sullivan watched her until she was out of sight.

Malcolm sat in the boutique as Monet came out of the dressing room modeling different dresses and asking which one he liked. They weren't in the store long before Monet found a dress similar to the one that she'd wanted, which the store had sold out of. She walked out wearing a red satin dress. It was back-less with a long split up the side. The bodice of the dress was accentuated with white beads and glimmering pearls. Malcolm told Monet it looked beautiful on her. The dress was on sale for a hundred and forty-nine dollars, so Monet found the matching hand bag and put them both on layaway. Next, they had to probe the mall for a suit for Malcolm.

The first store didn't have much of a selection, so Monet and Malcolm headed for another formal menswear store across from the Gap. As soon as they walked into Gingiss, Monet spot-ted a suit she wanted Malcolm to try on. The salesman helped the young man find his size, then he escorted Malcolm to the dress-ing room. When Malcolm came out wearing it, Monet decided the suit didn't look as nice on her boyfriend as it did on the man-nequin. When the teens told the sales associate exactly what they wanted, he walked over to a black double-breasted suit with red pin stripes. He asked Malcolm to try it on. When Malcolm came out of the dressing room with the second suit on, Monet couldn't believe her eyes. Malcolm looked like a savvy businessman.

Although the suit had to be fitted, he wanted it. He could have it fitted at the cleaners by his house. He paid for the suit with his parent's credit card and they left the store. They looked for shoes and found a pair for Malcolm first, and then Monet. Malcolm put both pairs on the credit card and they left.

The night of the prom Dorothy helped her daughter get dressed. Monet was moving about like she had molasses stuck to her feet. She'd been at the beauty shop all day. Though she was pressed for time, Monet was still moving slowly.

"Monet, you need to hurry up because Malcolm will be here in a minute," her mom said.

Keisha and Tonya sat on the edge of their sister's bed watching her in the full length mirror.

Finally, Monet felt prepared. She wore her imitation pearl necklace with the matching bracelet and earrings. Her seventy-five dollar hairdo was hooked up, not a strand out of place. Her flawless skin was glowing. Dorothy had even convinced Monet to wear ruby red lipstick to match her dress. Her mother told her to stand so she could take one final look. Dorothy grabbed her camera so she could take a picture of her daughter looking like a younger version of herself. Joyful tears dripped down her face. She could not believe that her first born was old enough to go to the prom. Dorothy figured she must be getting old.

The doorbell rang, and Tonya and Keisha broke their necks running down the stairs to be first to let Malcolm in and see what he was wearing.

Dorothy yelled, "When one of y'all bust your asses don't think I'm taking either one of you to the hospital. He ain't even coming to see your hot tail behinds."

Dorothy hugged Monet before they went downstairs.
When Malcolm walked into the house, Monet's little sisters stared at him. Dwayne was sitting on the couch with Deshawn. He didn't understand why everybody was making such a big deal about

Monet going to a stupid dance. She reached the last step and turned toward the door. Malcolm looked so tall and handsome with her corsage in his hand. Monet walked over to him smiling. She was extremely nervous. He placed the corsage around her wrist as Dorothy's 35MM froze time. She really liked this young man a lot. She was happy that her daughter was not with that good for nothing Derrick anymore. Malcolm had high expectations and goals, and Dorothy admired that. The teary eyed mother hugged them closing the door behind them, she warned, "Don't forget to have her home by two o'clock, Malcolm."

"Yes, ma'am," Malcolm replied as he and Monet climbed into the limo his parents ordered. The car pulled out of the driveway and Dorothy stood in her front room smiling as big as Texas.

"I can't wait until my prom, Mama," Tonya said.

"Me either," Keisha replied.

"Well, I'm glad that neither of you will be going for awhile because this is too overwhelming. It's giving me a headache."

Ten minutes later, Derrick called. "Is Monet there?" he asked.

"No, she isn't," Dorothy happily answered. "She just left for the prom." Derrick didn't say anything. He hung the phone up in Dorothy's ear. He couldn't stand her any more than she could stand him.

He laid on his bed thinking about Monet being with that punk. Derrick mumbled, "Man forget her! There are plenty girls out here that want to be with me. I ain't got time to be sweating no Monet." He knew the punk his ex-girl was with had to go to school with her. Maybe that was why Monet had chosen him. Derrick wondered if her new boyfriend had a job. He was probably a hustler, just like him. He almost certainly had other females too. Derrick turned over on his bed and decided that he wasn't going to worry. He knew Monet would find out sooner or later that her new friend wasn't about shit, then she would be running back to get some more of his dick.

———————————

Delvin sat in the basement of his sister's house drinking a forty ounce Colt 45 out of the bottle. The room was dark and gloomy; the only light came from the 19" television on the small table near his bed. He sipped from the bottle and wondered what was happening. He was slowly sinking back into the same lifestyle he lived before he went to prison. He hadn't seen or talked to his family in months and it was killing him. Delvin felt so guilty he couldn't face Dorothy or the kids. Soon he would work up enough nerve to call his wife and tell her the truth.

The following Saturday afternoon, Delvin was sitting on his bed trying to figure out what happened to his whole paycheck. He'd gotten paid the day before and had only twenty-two dollars left. He hadn't even paid his sister yet. He and his buddies hung out all night getting high, and now he was feeling sorry for himself again. Even though he could still pay his sister next week, Delvin hated the fact that he'd blown almost four hundred dollars in one night. He gulped from his beer until the bottle was empty. He thought of a million things he could have done with the money he'd blown. He thought about his family. He wanted to hear Dorothy's voice, and he missed seeing his children. He thought about calling several times, but lost the nerve every time he picked up the receiver. He knew Dorothy wouldn't have sympathy for him, considering how he'd messed up. He loved her too much to take her through his mess again. After about ten or fifteen minutes, Delvin picked up the phone again and dialed his wife's number. He didn't know how many times the phone rang but he heard someone pick up. It was a man! He said hello.

"Who in the hell is this?" Delvin angrily asked.

"Man, this is James. What the hell are you yelling for?"

"Man, what in the hell are you doing over there?"

"Nigga', I live here. Why are you dialing in my ear and

I'm steady saying hello, hello?" Delvin hadn't realized that James was on the phone when he'd picked it up and started dialing Dorothy's number. Delvin had picked the phone up just as it was about to ring. When he figured out what was going on he laughed.

"Man, I thought that you were over at Dorothy's house. You was about to make me come over there and kick yo' ass."

"Man, quit trippin'. I was calling to see how much money you got on this package me and Tyrone was about to get. So far we got seventeen dollars."

"I ain't got nothing but ten dollars to my name."

"We on our way over there." James hung up the telephone before Delvin could say another word. Delvin reached under the bed and grabbed his shoes. He put them on, then reached into his pants pocket and pulled out twelve dollars and placed them in his top drawer. Next, he ran up the stairs and out the front door to wait for his friends.

Andrea and Tim had a great time at the dance. They strolled in together and all eyes were on them for the rest of night. They ignored all the bad vibes and comments from fellow class-mates. No one at the party could ruin Andrea's or Tim's night.

One of her so-called friends walked up to her when Tim was away and asked, "Girl, don't you feel uncomfortable walk-ing up in here with that white boy?"

"Why should I be ashamed of being escorted to the ball with my man?" Andrea commented boldly. The girl looked dumbfounded as Andrea sashayed away with her nose in the air. Tim was approaching. They eyed an empty table and walked over to take a seat.

When they sat down, Tim whispered to Andrea that his buzz was starting to wear off. She looked at him and smiled, but didn't say anything. They had smoked a fat blunt before coming in, but Tim was ready to smoke again. They were only at the party for a couple of hours before deciding to bail out. The two of them jumped up from the table at the same time and exited the auditorium without saying goodbye to anyone. It was a little past nine and Andrea had a twelve o'clock curfew. The school party was extremely bunk and she and Tim knew how to have more fun by themselves. "Tim wasn't so bad after all," Andrea thought as they walked through the parking lot toward his car. She wondered if he enjoyed her company as much as she did his. Tim unlocked the passenger side door and opened it for Andrea. As he walked to the other side, Andrea pulled out the goods and started breaking down the buds to roll a phat one. Tim climbed in and drove out of the parking lot. They drove around the city for the next hour, smoking and listening to music and bobbing their heads to the beat. At a quarter after ten, Andrea was so high and tired of riding around she asked Tim if he could drop her off at home. He pulled up in front of Andrea's house and thanked her for the good time. He sounded kind of corny, but she smiled and said she enjoyed herself as well. Andrea gave Tim a quick peck on the lips and told him she would call him tomorrow.

The next day was Sunday. Dorothy sent her children to church with Caroline and rode by herself to Sullivan's church. When she walked to the door, he was waiting for her, as he said he would.

The pastor preached a good sermon and Dorothy told him so when Sullivan introduced the two of them after service. He seemed like a respectful older man who ran a decent congregation. Sullivan invited Dorothy out to eat afterwards. Dorothy drove her own car so she could go straight home after eating. She knew Sullivan was going to the evening service and she wasn't.

While they waited for their food, they got better acquainted. She was embarrassed to tell him she was in a dysfunctional marriage and that she was a grandmother, but decided to tell him anyway. It couldn't hurt too much since it was the honest to God truth. He said he could relate to what she was going through. He told Dorothy that he'd been through some stormy weather himself. He was forty-one, working as a juvenile probation officer. He'd been divorced six years from a one year marriage to a lawyer. She left him for another lawyer he'd caught her cheating with. He lived by himself, in a home he purchased after his divorce. He told Dorothy that he'd gone through a stressful divorce and was glad that everything was finally settled.

"Sometimes people don't think about the consequences of their actions until it's too late." Sullivan said he respected her dedication to her husband. "No matter what the situation was, you've stuck by his side and that's the pure essence of a marriage, loyalty." Dorothy told him she was finally throwing in the towel. "But there does come a time when one becomes fed up," Sullivan said. She laughed and their conversation continued well after their meals were served.

Three hours later, Dorothy was still in the restaurant, deeply involved in conversation with Sullivan. Discovering what time it was, Dorothy told her new friend she had to leave before her family put out a missing persons report on her. Sullivan laughed so hard he had to take a sip of lemonade to catch his breath. "I need to be getting back to the church as well, and, by the way, our night service is just as good as the morning one."

"I'm sorry, Sullivan, but I must get home to my children."

"Okay, but we will have to continue this conversation another time."

Dorothy jotted her phone number on a napkin and handed it to him. "You can call me when you get home from church," she said. Sullivan took the napkin, folded it, and stuck it inside his jacket pocket. Dorothy gave him a thank you for dinner hug and they exited the restaurant smiling.

As she sat waiting for her car to warm up, Dorothy thought, "Sullivan is a really nice guy."

It was ironic that she'd met a saved brother in the grocery store who had no kids or a wife. Was God trying to tell her something? Was this her ideal man?

During her ride home lots of thoughts ran through her mind. She wondered what her husband was doing and where he was. She thought about Sullivan. She hadn't had a man ask her out in over ten years. Dorothy realized she must still be semi-attractive to have a man as fine as Sullivan ask her out, but maybe she was overreacting. Since meeting him, Dorothy had a feeling that things in her life were about to change. She prayed and had faith that change was coming soon.

Coming Out of the Shell

Andrea was on punishment for well over a month, still confined to her bedroom for smoking in her room. Her parents were sticking to their word this time and giving her no slack. Once she was off punishment she was going to chill out on the foolishness. It wasn't worth her wasting her life in her boring bedroom day in and day out.

She walked down the hallway of the school and saw Tim standing outside the classroom talking to a friend. Andrea and Tim had a second hour English class together but Tim rarely showed up for it. He said Mr. Braggs, the English teacher, had it out for him since day one and there was no point in going to the class if the man was going to fail him anyways. Andrea felt special when he told her that he only showed up to talk to her.

"I haven't seen you in ages," he teased.

"Yeah," Andrea mumbled. "My parents were really fed up. The only thing I've been allowed to do in the last couple of weeks is come to school and go back home to prison. Trust me, I feel this punishment. The day after I was with you guys my mom caught me smoking in my room and I've been on punishment every since."

Tim said he was sorry to hear the bad news and his facial expression was in compliance. "So were you coming to class today or did you really just come here because you were worried about me?"

Tim blushed in silence. She'd caught him off guard. His nervous hands were buried into the pockets of his jeans.
Tim smiled. "You know the school dance is coming up real soon."

"Yeah, I know. I don't know if I'll be off my punishment by that time, so I haven't made any plans. I am going stir crazy because I'm not even allowed to talk on the telephone."

"That's too bad! I hope you're off punishment before

next Saturday. If you are, I would like to know if I could escort you to the dance."

Andrea didn't say anything. She was in shock. She'd always thought Tim was cool and good looking, but dating him never crossed her mind. He was white! Andrea stared Tim up and down without opening her mouth. Now that he'd asked her out, he looked totally different. She stared into his ocean blue eyes, vigilantly observing his curly blonde hair, his long, narrow Caucasian nose. Tim waved his hand in front of Andrea's face trying to distract her from her daydream. She was taking so long to answer, his smile turned into a disappointing frown.

"I have to ask my parents first," she blurted as the bell rang. Andrea left Tim standing in the hall as she ran to take her seat in the classroom. Tim walked away before the teacher came. Andrea looked baffled. Her friend Mary asked if she was okay. As the teacher began calling names off the attendance sheet, Andrea turned to Mary and said, "Just fine."

Tim sat outside the school in his car listening to music. He was humiliated because he'd made a complete fool out of himself by asking Andrea out. He should have known that she would refuse. She said she had to ask her parents, but what she meant was no. He didn't know how he'd had the nerve to ask her out in the first place, especially since she was black. Why would a fine, smart sister like Andrea want his white ass? Tim knew he'd stepped out of his boundaries, but every since meeting Andrea, he had a secret crush on her, but was afraid to tell her. Tim thought she felt the same way, but apparently he was wrong.

After the final bell rang, Andrea stopped by her locker to pick up a book. She saw Tim in the hallway talking to a friend. She politely walked up to them, "Excuse me, Tim, but I was wondering if I could talk to you for a minute." The boy shook Tim's hand and told him he would see him later. "Tim, I was just shocked to learn that you were interested in me. It never crossed my mind that you wanted to be anything besides friends. Now that I'm over my shock I would like to say I'm sorry, and I would love to go to the dance with you if my parents say it's okay."

Tim smiled. She had made his day. At first, he was a little upset, but now he was content. "Of course the offer is still good, and it'll be good whether you can go to the dance or not. If you can't, we'll just have to wait until you're off punishment to go out."

Andrea smiled, "When I go home tonight I'll ask my parents."

"That's cool."

"I'll see you later Tim. I better go before I miss the bus." Andrea ran down the hall.

Tim called out to her, "I got something for us." He held his hand in the air balled up into a fist. It looked like he was holding something.

Andrea shrugged her shoulders, "I've got to pass. You know I'm trying to stay out of trouble." She turned around and ran down the hallway toward the bus line up.

Tim was so excited he jumped when Andrea was out of sight. After all this time he finally told her how he felt. Tim headed toward his locker, grabbed his English and math book, and started to his car.

———————————

Caroline sat in the counselor's office waiting for her husband. He had called earlier to say he was running late. The receptionist offered Caroline a cup of coffee but she refused. All she wanted was for the meeting to be over. Today, she just wasn't in the mood. She just wanted to relax. Moments later, Thomas walked in. "Baby, I was starting to worry," Caroline said.

"You shouldn't have. You know how traffic is this late in the day."

The receptionist buzzed Dr. Marshall to let her know the couple was ready. Thomas grabbed Caroline's hand and escorted her in.

"Good afternoon," Dr. Marshall said. They sat down and she asked how the home visits with Thomas Jr. were going?

"Thomas Jr. is really starting to enjoy coming over," Thomas began, "As soon as he sees his sister Taylor, he goes crazy with excitement. He follows her all around the house and even tries to say her name."

"That's good," the doctor commented. "I promise you that before it's all over he'll be crying when you take him back home."

Dr. Marshall was pleased that the couple's relationship was starting to mend. She believed everything would be back on track soon. When the meeting was over, the doctor told the couple to schedule an appointment for two weeks.

Taylor ran into the garage when she heard the door open. She hugged and kissed her parents and they went in the house. Thomas went upstairs to change for dinner. Caroline told him to check on Andrea.

"She's on the telephone," Taylor reported.

"Make sure she shows you her finished homework since she's sitting up there yapping away on that telephone. On second thought," Caroline continued. "I'll go and check myself" She followed her husband upstairs. Andrea was in her bedroom on the bed with her leg propped up on her stuffed animals. Her ear was glued to the telephone and her eyes focused on her mother. Since she and Tim started dating, she was on the telephone all day.

"Is your homework finished?" Caroline inquired. Andrea nodded and her mother demanded to see it. Andrea held it up in the air. "Is that all of it?" Andrea huffed and asked the caller to hold on.

"This is it, Mom." Her mother walked over and scanned the homework. Looking into her daughter's eyes, she sensed that she was telling the truth, so Caroline decided not to pry. She quietly walked out of the bedroom.

When the girls went to bed, Thomas stepped into the room where his wife was sitting on the edge of the bed. Finally, they had some alone time. Thomas popped a slow groove into the Bose player and walked into the bathroom. He undressed and turned on the shower. Caroline imitated him and stripped. Her husband became aroused by her naked body. He grabbed her and they danced in the middle of the floor. Once R. Kelly's voice faded and he let out his last "step right in," the blissful couple entered the shower. Thomas was so excited he washed quickly and jumped out. He grabbed his wife's arm and escorted her to the bedroom. Before she could get comfortable, her husband was inside her. His strong hard penis rocked in and out of her wet coochie causing it to make a squishy sound. The comforter was drenched from their dripping bodies. She made soft satisfying noises as Thomas gently stroked her body and the headboard beat up the wall. It was a good thing the children were asleep. He was only in it for a short time before he dripped his juices into her and collapsed. Afterwards, Thomas ran downstairs to get something to drink and Caroline got up to go to the bathroom.

When she came out of the bathroom she put new sheets on the bed while Thomas changed the pillowcases. Soon, they were cuddled in bed, ready for a good night's sleep.

Delvin held the telephone waiting for someone to pick up. He knew Dorothy was home, but didn't know why she wasn't answering, Usually, she would be at home watching soaps and babysitting Deshawn. He hadn't talked to his wife in over two months and he missed her. Delvin yearned to hear her sweet, humble voice. For the last couple of weekends, Delvin had been jacking off his money by getting high and clubbing with his friends. This week, he wanted to get in touch with Dorothy because he didn't want to blow his money. He wanted to do something for her and the kids.

She answered on the sixth ring. She was saddened when she heard his voice. "Hey, baby," Delvin said. "You just don't know how good it feels to hear your voice."

Before she could answer, Delvin continued, talking. "I know I messed up with you and I'm sorry. I ain't trying to call you for no sympathy, even though, I miss you and the kids like crazy. I ain't calling to beg for your forgiveness or nothing like that."

"Are you in some type of trouble that you need your wife to get you out of?"

"Don't start Dorothy," he warned. "I did not call to argue with you. Like I said before, I apologize for my behavior."

"Apologize," she yelled. "I think you're about a month too late to be calling here talking about an apology. What do you expect me to tell our children? Am I supposed to say to them, kids I apologize for your father's behavior, but excuse him because he's been getting high again. Hell no, Delvin! I ain't doing that shit no more. I am tired of apologizing to my kids because of their father's mistakes." He was silent, but Dorothy continued.

"You know, Delvin, I was trying real hard to believe that you were going to change once you got out this time, but you know what? I must have been a motha' fucking fool to believe yo' ass would change. I mean, why would I believe that you would choose to play a part in your three children's lives verses snorting that white shit up your nose all day, every damn day, or have you went back to smoking the pipe too Delvin?"

She took a deep breath. "You want to know why I would think some dumb ass shit like that Delvin, because I was a stupid ass fool, that's why, and I'm fed up with playing the fool. I'm fed the fuck up!"

Breathing heavily, Dorothy said. "Delvin, let me tell you one more thing. I don't think it will be good for you to call here anymore, because after today you no longer have a reason."

"Dorothy, please give me a chance to talk," Delvin pleaded. "Dorothy began to cry." "I can't go through this anymore. I just can't. I think the best thing for us to do now is to go our separate ways. You have your life, and me and my kids, we have ours. I'm going to file for a divorce as soon as I get the money." Dorothy took another deep breath to calm herself down. She'd finally gotten that off her chest and felt better. She wiped her tears away with the back of her hand and spoke in a soft friendly tone. "Now what was it that you wanted to say?"

He tried to speak, but it was hard talking after hearing her paralyzing words. Delvin tried to hold back the tears. Dorothy's words had pierced his heart. Delvin had no hope for their relationship.

"Dorothy, I just called to let you know that I get paid Friday and I want you to come to my job before you go to work, to pick up some money for you and the kids."

"You think that's going to make up for your behavior Delvin?"

"Dorothy, meet me in front of the building at four o'clock." Those were his last words. He had already heard all he needed to hear.

Dorothy was furious that Delvin had the nerve to hang up on her. She felt like an atomic bomb ready to explode. Tears ran down her face. No matter how indispensable she tried to pretend she was, Dorothy was hurting. She was feeling hurt and relieved at the same time. No matter what, she was through. She was tired of going through the bullshit and tired of taking her children through it. Friday, she was definitely going to pick the money up as he requested. If he was going to blow his money, it may as well be on something necessary.

The telephone rang, distracting her. Dorothy was sure it was her husband calling to apologize for hanging up on her. She picked up the telephone on the second ring. It wasn't Delvin; it was the secretary from Dwayne's school telling her that Dwayne had gotten into a fight and been expelled. He was sitting in the office waiting for a parent or guardian to pick him up. Dorothy told the woman she was on her way. She hung up the telephone, got Deshawn out of her bed, and rushed out of the front door.

When she arrived at school, Dorothy walked into the office with an evil frown on her face. If Dwayne had been kicked out for misbehaving, she was going to get in his behind as soon as they got into the parking lot. Dwayne knew Dorothy didn't tolerate acting ignorant at school, period. Her kids knew better than to make her look bad. If he was at fault, he was about to be sorry.

Dwayne was sitting in a blue chair with his head down when Dorothy walked in. She didn't understand what was going on; Dwayne was usually a good boy and kept to himself. She couldn't wait to get the story from the woman.

Mrs. Sutten invited Mrs. Johnson and her son into her office and introduced herself to Dorothy. Dorothy slung Deshawn to her left hip and walked into the office. Mrs. Sutten explained what happened, repeating the story she had heard from the teacher. A boy, Melvin, and Dwayne had a disagreement and Melvin got mad and pushed Dwayne. "Dwayne hit the boy in self-defense."

"Is that what happened?" Dorothy asked her son.

"Yes ma'am," he answered, his head down.

"Excuse me," Dorothy snapped. Dwayne heard the elevation in his mother's voice and lifted his head.

"The only reason your son is being expelled," the principal continued, "is because the school policy is no fighting allowed. Besides, the brawl interrupted the whole classroom and we can't allow that." Dorothy remained calm, but looked upset.

The principal said, "If it'll make you feel any better, Mrs. Johnson, I am glad to inform you that Melvin has been suspended longer because he started the commotion." Dorothy was relieved to hear that and rose extending her hand to the woman.

"I'm sorry. My son and I will further discuss this matter once we get home."

Mrs. Sutten thanked Dorothy for coming and for being so cooperative. Dorothy and her son left the building. Outside the school, Dorothy told her son she wasn't mad at him. "I don't think you did anything wrong, baby. If this happens again while you're at school, walking away is the wisest choice."

"Yes ma'am," Dwayne said and grabbed his nephew from his mother's hip as they headed toward the car.

When she got home she called Sullivan. She'd been waiting all day to talk to him and couldn't wait to hear his sexy voice. He always lifted her spirits. Impatiently, she dialed the telephone and waited for him to pick up. When he picked up and recognized it was Dorothy, he perked up. His voice was friendly and masculine. "How was your day?"

"Oh, it was good, although the most exciting part of it is being able to come home and hear your voice." He moaned seductively.

"Oh, yeah, it's good to know you were thinking about me because I've been thinking about you all day." Her smile widened with amazement. She felt like an adolescent in love. They talked for about fifteen minutes before Sullivan asked her about her plans for the weekend. When Dorothy told him she didn't have any, Sullivan invited her to a play Saturday night, performed by the children from church.

"Well, I don't have anything else to do," she answered.

"Then it's settled. I'll pick you up at six o'clock on Saturday."

"That sounds wonderful." Dorothy smiled and her brown

skin turned red. She wasn't used to being asked out on a date. Sullivan was becoming a part of her life when she needed him most. He was filling the void of her absent husband. Dorothy had been telling herself she needed to stop moping about Delvin. This was Sullivan's third offer to take her someplace, and she'd only known him a month. She liked talking to him, and enjoyed his company. She was happy that Sullivan wasn't the type of man who wanted to come over and sit in her face for a couple hours. The next thing you knew about that type they'd want to spend the night, and before long would be a part of your family.

Before hanging up the telephone he asked, "Could we meet tomorrow for lunch? I've got free time right before Bible study."

"Well, tomorrow I have to work, and my only free time will be during my break. That is the only free time I'll have tomorrow."

"That's cool," he agreed.

Dorothy told him to meet her at the job around five thirty. His Bible study wasn't until six thirty, so he would have a whole hour to spend with her. He wished her a good night and said he would see her tomorrow. Dorothy hung up the telephone and went into the bathroom to run some bath water. She had to get the chicken smell off her before she went to bed. The thing with Sullivan could be serious, so she had to make some decisions about Delvin. She damn sure didn't want to get hurt. She and Sullivan were just friends and there wasn't any harm in going out with a friend. Their dates had been totally innocent and that's the way she intended it to be until she figured out what to do with her crackhead husband, who she was slowly falling out of love with.

Delvin must have seen Dorothy pull up because he ran to her car before she even parked. She pulled the car into an empty space and her husband jumped into the passenger side. Before he even said hi, Delvin handed Dorothy three crispy one hundred dollar bills. "Even though they ain't seen me, I want you to tell the kids that this was from me."

"When do you plan on coming to see your children, Delvin?"

"Just tell them I'll see them soon. I don't want to make any promises I can't keep."

The visit was brief. He said he had to get to work.
She stopped him as he was about to leave.

"Delvin, can you just answer one question for me?" He just stared toward the factory and waited for her to continue.

"Have you started back getting high?"

He clutched the handle of the door and opened it. He refused to answer her question.

"Tell the kids it was from me Dorothy," then Delvin got out and walked away. She burst into tears, started her car and pulled out of the plant's parking lot.

As she drove down the street crying, Dorothy asked herself. How could she have been so stupid to think he was going to change? How could she have thought things were going to be different when Delvin had been the same way their entire marriage? She was so hurt she felt like driving back to the plant to argue with him for not answering her question. But she didn't have the time or strength for more heartache, especially when she already knew the answer. She had to pull herself together before she made it to Kentucky Fried Chicken to start her shift. She had to get herself together before it was time for her to meet with Sullivan.

Saturday evening finally came and Dorothy was excited about going to the play. She searched through her wardrobe to find an outfit that still fit. She wanted to look sexy, but in a nice way. She wanted her ensemble to be as beautiful as she felt. She asked Monet to choose one of two outfits she had lying on her bed."You should have bought something new," Monet said.

Dorothy rolled her eyes and held up a navy blue mini-skirt. She should have never asked her daughter because her advice only made Dorothy feel more insecure.

"What's wrong with this one?"

"It depends on what shirt you wear."

Dorothy looked dumbfounded. Monet walked to the closet, searching through her mom's antiquated wardrobe. She slid each item down the pole until she found a shirt that would possibly go with the skirt. It was a cute, black, rayon blouse with small flowers embedded across the front. Monet looked through her mother's shoes and came across a nice pair of black Nine West pumps. They were sharp and expensive looking.

Dorothy tried on the shirt and skirt before ironing it. Her daughter said, "That's tight." Dorothy guessed that meant the outfit was all right because Monet was smiling.

"Good," Dorothy said, and instructed her daughter to iron it while she jumped in the shower. Sullivan would be knocking at the door in a minute and Dorothy wanted to be ready."

After her shower, Dorothy wrapped herself in a towel and opened the medicine cabinet. She pulled out her occasionally used make-up compact and applied foundation. She bumped a few touch-up curls in her hair with the electric curling iron. Dorothy headed back to her bedroom to dress.

Tonya's nosy behind walked in the room, startling her mother as she tried squeezing into her skirt. When she got it zipped, Dorothy looked in the mirror on her bedroom door. Not bad, she thought after having four children and being on a stress diet called going through changes with your husband and kids. Dorothy maintained a comfortable hundred and fifty-six pounds. When satisfied with her looks, she sprayed on some of her Gucci Rush cologne which had been sitting on her dresser collecting dust. She only used it on special occasions. It was a gift from her sister Caroline.

Dorothy strutted out of her bedroom like a diva. She

walked into the front room so her children could see her. In unison, they shouted. "Mama, you look good."

"Thank you." She smiled as she looked through her purse to see if it contained everything she needed. Dorothy sat on the couch and waited for her date.

Sullivan pulled up shortly. When he came in and saw Dorothy, he was amazed. She looked beautiful, and Sullivan wasted no time telling her. As they left, the children stood in the door watching and waving. They yelled, "Have a good time!" Dorothy and her friend got into his midnight black Yukon. He said. "I love the perfume you have on. It smells real good on you. What is that fragrance?"

"It's called Gucci Rush," she blushed.

"Hum, Gucci Rush," he repeated suspiciously as they drove off.

Sullivan chose a restaurant not far from the theatre so they wouldn't have far to drive after eating. He said the small soul food restaurant had good food and wonderful service. Sullivan ordered a fried catfish dinner and Dorothy ordered BBQ chicken with baked macaroni and cheese and candied yams, her favorite. They sat in silence until Sullivan finally sparked a conversation.

"So, tell me more about your family. I know your days are never lonely with your children and grandchild around."

"You're right, but trust me, it has gotten better. When they were all small, it was really hard, but now that they're older, things are a lot easier on me; and Lord only knows where I would be without Monet. She helps me out a whole lot. She is a good girl. She does a great job taking care of her son, and she works hard in school. Having Deshawn put her behind a little, but she worked hard to catch up. She will still be able to graduate on time."

"That's really good that you support her the way you do. A lot of youngsters these days are the way they are because they have parents who don't care. Most parents don't know where their children are half the time." He nodded and added that he was impressed with how well behaved and respectful her children were. Sullivan knew it had to be hard raising four children on her own and he wanted to congratulate her on doing such a fine job. Dorothy thanked him and relaxed in her seat. Those were the last words they shared. The server came to the table and placed their dinners in front of them. Sullivan's eyes were on Dorothy, as her eyes nervously wandered about the room. Dorothy and her date chomped into their dinners. The food was delicious. They didn't stay long after eating because they were pressed for time. Sullivan paid the check, tipped the waitress and they were out the door. They wanted to get to the play before the crowd. When they got out of the SUV, Sullivan grabbed Dorothy's arm and wrapped it around his, then escorted her down the street through the crowd.

Shortly after leaving the play, the duo pulled up in front of Dorothy's house. She thanked Sullivan for a wonderful evening. Dorothy felt totally mesmerized around him. Sullivan told her he hoped they could do something together again soon. "I know you're not officially a single woman and I don't want to cause any problems, but I will warn you. When you're free I want to spoil you rotten."

Dorothy tried hard not to show her nervousness. She smiled and nodded because she had no idea what to say. He was coming on to her in a sly way and her game was so weak she was speechless. This man was totally out of her league. Timidly, she reached for the doorknob to open the passenger door. She had butterflies, but she played it off. Sullivan grabbed her arm and pulled her body toward him. She had no choice but to look him directly in the eye. Her look was shy, but permissible. Without warning, his juicy lips collided with hers. His tongue swirled inside her mouth in a way that intoxicated her entire body. Her head fell back and their lips moved to the rhythm of love. After her first kiss with Sullivan, Dorothy was flustered. She eventually climbed out of his SUV and walked to her front door. He said goodnight and waited until she was inside before he pulled off. Sullivan blew the horn and thought, "She was a wonderful kisser."

Dorothy couldn't believe what she'd done, but it felt right. She hoped she hadn't scared him away.

Her children were in bed when she came in. It was after ten and Dorothy was exhausted. She plopped down on her bed and recaptured the moment when his lips collided with hers. She felt like a teenager in love. She shook her head miserably and wondered if Sullivan was as infatuated as she was. Only time would tell. She would have to observe him for awhile to tell what he was really about. She wondered if he was a sly, dirty church boy, like the rest of the dogs in the street. She prayed he wasn't there to waste her time or cause her any drama.

Church let out on time and Dorothy, Sullivan, and her children packed into Sullivan's vehicle and headed to the Woodland Mall. Dorothy divided the money Delvin had donated among all the children. Before she released them, she told them to get whatever they wanted. She instructed them to meet her back at the eatery in an hour and a half. She and Sullivan sat with Deshawn, who was chomping on some french fries. When Deshawn finished eating, his grandmother cleaned him off and placed him in the stroller so the three of them could walk through the mall and window shop. By the time they made it back to the food court, all the children were there and ready to go.

She heard her telephone ringing as she walked into the house. It was Caroline and she wanted to know every little detail about Sullivan and their trip to the mall. "What did he buy you?" was the first thing out of Caroline's mouth. Ignoring her sister, Dorothy asked, "What was it you called me for again?"

Caroline smacked her lips. "Anyway, girl, I called to let

you know that we are leaving to go on our family trip soon and I was double-checking to see if you're still keeping the car and checking on the house for me. You know I must have you over here to water my plants. We are going to be leaving right after Monet's graduation."

"All right then," Dorothy answered. That was all Caroline had to say. Dorothy hung up the telephone. She knew her big sister was ticked off because she didn't feel like sitting there discussing her business. Shit, it wasn't like Caroline broke her neck to tell Dorothy about Thomas Jr.

The weekend before the graduation, Dorothy had a barbeque to celebrate her daughter's victory. Sullivan cooked the meat and the guests had been instructed to bring a dish. Deshawn tried to catch his uncle, who was running around the table trying to get away from him. Dorothy was tickled to death. Her grandson had grown up so fast, was spoiled rotten, and as bad as he wanted to be. Dorothy saw Monet and Malcolm sitting alone at a secluded table in the shade. Earlier they had been talking about school. Malcolm had been accepted to the Medical College of Georgia and Monet was staying home where she would be attending community college.

Now that they were alone, Monet asked Malcolm what she'd wanted to ask him for a long time. "How are we going to hold on to this relationship when we'll be a thousand miles away from each other?"

"We will be able to talk on the telephone and see each other on vacations and holidays when I come home. You don't have to worry, Monet. You, Deshawn, and I are going to be a family as soon as I graduate college and come back to marry you."

Monet smiled, but she knew better. She knew that as soon as he got to Georgia and was around all those eligible females he would forget all about her and Deshawn.

He kissed her. "You don't have to worry because I love

you and that's the way that it's going to stay. Those other women are not going to phase me because I want you."

Monet stared dead into his eyes as he recited those lovely and heartfelt words.

"The only thing you need to worry about is keeping Deshawn in line." Before he could finish, Deshawn ran up and grabbed Malcolm's leg. Dwayne was chasing him, so the baby ran to Malcolm for protection. His mama picked him up before her little brother could grab him. She giggled and kissed him on the cheeks. She couldn't believe how fast her baby was growing up.

Dwayne ran to Monet and grabbed his playful nephew. "Put him down, Monet," Dwayne complained. Monet waited until she thought her brother wasn't looking, then she released her son so he could get a head start running away.

Back at Dorothy's, everyone helped carry all the stuff from the park back into the house. After Dorothy put everything away, she took a deep breathe. She still couldn't believe that in four days her daughter would graduate from high school. The thought of it made her feel proud, and like an old woman at the same time.

That Wednesday, everyone gathered at Dorothy's before heading out to see Ms. Monet walk across the stage. All of her and Dorothy's friends congratulated her on her big accomplishment. Monet was proud of herself and got teary-eyed along with her mother. Dorothy eventually broke up the ruckus of the crowd by announcing it was time to go to the graduation. "We want you to walk across the stage with your head held up high," the guests cheered as they left the house. They piled into their vehicles, one behind the other, pulled away. Soon they were in a procession on their way to the graduation.

The departing students lined up in the hallway of the auditorium, eager to walk across the stage. They had waited for their whole lives. Some were still getting into their caps and gowns.

Others were doing anything they could to kill time until the ceremony started.

Monet remained calm. Instead of lollygagging with her classmates, she stood in a frustrated trance alone. She had so many things on her mind that her hands were sweating. She smeared them onto her gown and waited patiently. She wondered how much this day would change her life. From this day on she would be responsible for her life. Her days of wasting time and making mistakes were over. It was time to be serious about life. From this day forth her life would be about learning and planning. She was the second of three generations who'd made it to high school, let alone to graduate. To her, this moment was surreal.

School staff walked through the hall trying to quiet the students and let them know the ceremony was about to start. The theme music started and the soon to be graduates slowly marched into the auditorium. Even though friends and family were warned ahead of time not to applaud until all the students walked across the stage, no one followed instructions. Monet walked, with dignity and pride, as her mom had instructed. Her guests cheered so loud that people in the audience stared at them. Monet smiled, received her plaque and walked the platform with joyous tears. The ceremony only lasted about an hour and a half. Afterwards, all the students left the hall and gathered in the hallway. Some left and others stood around talking. When Monet came out of the buildings, her family and friends were gathered waiting for her. Caroline made sure that Monet opened her gift first. She was so proud of her oldest niece she even shed a few tears. Her auntie handed her a gold envelope and gave her a big hug. Monet looked inside and pulled out the card. Once she opened the card, three crispy, one hundred dollar bills caught her attention. Excited, the girl gave her auntie another kiss and hug. Sullivan was next to hand Monet an envelope. Inside was a one hundred dollar bill.

"I hope you get yourself something real nice with that. I

didn't know what to buy you."

Monet gave Sullivan a big hug and thanked him.

"Okay, guys" Dorothy yelled. "Let's get back to the house before people start getting all sentimental and stuff."

Caroline handed her sister the keys and she and her family headed for the highway. Monet drove Dorothy's car home and Dorothy rode with Sullivan to her sister's house. When they arrived, Dorothy reached over and allowed her lips to meet his for a brief, innocent kiss. She pushed the garage door opener and walked inside to the Lexus. Dorothy climbed in and started it up. She adjusted the mirrors and the seat, put the car in reverse, and backed out of the garage. Sullivan saw her pull out of the driveway, so he blew his horn and headed down the street. Dorothy blew back as she put the car in drive easing down the street after him. She smiled. She would have ten whole days to ride around in luxury.

Dorothy walked into the house after she heard the car alarm arm itself. Tonya was sitting on the couch, yapping her lips off on the telephone. Dorothy heard Dwayne splashing in the tub. Dorothy asked where were the others?

"Keisha is downstairs putting a load of clothes in the washing machine, and Monet is upstairs giving Deshawn a bath," Tonya said.

Dorothy walked to the front door and glanced out the window to see how pretty the car looked sitting in her driveway. After a minute, she closed the curtain and walked toward her bedroom. She collapsed on her bed, relieved that Monet's graduation had come and gone. Words could not express how proud she was. She wished she could have done more for her daughter than just throwing the picnic at the park, but her money was low. As soon as she got paid, she would give Monet some cash to buy herself something. She closed her eyes. Sullivan appeared in her thoughts. They had been friends for

198 It Just Gets Better With Time

over two months and Dorothy was starting to have strong feelings for him.

The doorbell startled her. She sat up in bed and waited to
see if Tonya was going to answer the door. It rang again, but
Dorothy didn't feel like getting up. "Girl, see who is at the door,"
she yelled to Tonya and thought. Now that's was one advantage
of having older children.

Tonya dropped the telephone and ran into her father's
arms. Delvin picked up his over grown daughter and stepped into
the house.

Dorothy heard a man's voice and walked out of her room.
To her surprise, her soon to be ex-husband was sitting on her
couch. Tonya ran into the kitchen yelling, "Daddy's here,
daddy's here."

Dorothy was in shock. She could not believe Delvin had
showed up unannounced. The children ran into the front room
where Delvin was. Dorothy couldn't believe what she saw. He
had abandoned them for months and here they were greeting him
like he was the king of the world or something. Disgusted,
Dorothy sat in a nearby chair and shook her head. She finally
said, "So, what wind blew you this way?"

"I came to see my kids," he answered defensively. "I also
came to let you know that when I get paid this week, I am gong
to give you some more money so you can get the kids some summer clothes." Dorothy grit her teeth and turned her head. Delvin
didn't say anything. He was too busy acting like he was concerned about his children. Monet walked into the living room.
Tonya beat her telling Delvin that she graduated. Delvin hugged
her and told her he was proud. "I'll put something extra in for you
when I give your mother the money at the end of the week."
Dwayne frowned and stared at Monet, who was getting presents
from everybody because of her funky little graduation.

"She doesn't need anymore money. She already got

enough from everybody," Dwayne said.

"Oh, yeah," Delvin gasped.

"Yeah, Daddy, Aunt Caroline gave her some money, Mr. Sullivan gave her some, and her daddy."

"Okay, Dwayne, you can stop running off at the mouth," Monet threatened. Dorothy was evil-eyeing Delvin out of the corner of her eye. She hoped he didn't ask Dwayne who Mr. Sullivan was. Instead, her husband sat on the couch inhaling all the exciting rapture from the children. Dwayne and Tonya started arguing and Dorothy warned them to stop. The telephone rang and Dorothy ran to the kitchen to answer it. It was Sullivan. She nervously whispered, "I was wondering when you were going to call."

"I was getting around to it. I got caught up on the other line but you know I was going to call you no matter what," he said with compassion.

"Aren't you thoughtful?" she spoke in a hushed voice.

"Did you enjoy your ride home?"

"I did. I was thinking of joyriding for awhile, but I was a little tired so I just came on home. My husband just showed up on an impromptu visit and I'm sitting in here listening to the children worship him." Sullivan started laughing because he sensed in her tone that she was pissed.

"Well, since you have company, why don't you call me back later?"

"Okay," Dorothy hung up the telephone and pranced back into the living room. She walked in just as Dwayne explained to his dad why he got kicked out of school. Dorothy rolled her eyes. She couldn't wait until Delvin left so she could call Sullivan back.

Buck Wild and Outta Control

Elaine tapped her nails on the bar to the beat of the music. Her friend Sheila was sitting beside her trying to shoo off a scrub who was mumbling lies in her ear. The Squeeze In was krunk as usual, and as soon as one of her songs came on Elaine headed toward the dance floor to get her groove on. She glimpsed around, searching for someone to accommodate her once she got ready. She scanned the dimly lit room one more time. It was occupied by mostly regulars. In the lounge, the walls were painted an ugly mango orange color, bright enough to reflect light on all the scally-wags there. Irritated, she sucked her teeth. The Squeeze In was truly a hole in the wall hang-out.

The fifteen or so tables were taken up by loud talking hoochies, made up from head to toe with their expensive weaves and discount outfits. The men were smooth talking, perpetrators acting like they had plenty of money to spend on any female willing to fall for the lies. These men were out prowling to recruit a trick for the night, or get a phone number for the night after next.

The dance floor could use a make-over but that didn't stop anyone from getting their groove on. The Squeeze In was still the shit and Elaine and Sheila always came early so they wouldn't have to pay the ten dollar cover charge. Since they frequented it often, Elaine knew just about every face in the place. They were the same old faces she was tired of seeing. Elaine turned toward the bar and signaled the bartender to bring her a drink.

A few minutes later Elaine felt a gentle tap on her shoulder. She turned around to look into the eyes of a tall, handsome unfamiliar face. She smiled at the gentleman when he asked if she wanted to dance. Elaine didn't hesitate. Sheila looked from the corner of her eye and saw Elaine approach the dance floor. She looked away rolling her eyes, because another aggravating ass man with no game was sitting beside her, talking her ear off.

Elaine and her dancing partner bopped until the song went

off and Elaine exited the dance floor fanning herself with her hands. When they sat down, the guy asked Elaine if she wanted something to drink.

"Pina-Colada," she answered, then raised her hand and signaled for the bartender. It took fifteen minutes to take their orders, and by the time the drinks arrived, Elaine and her friend were engaged in conversation. He asked if she frequents the club often and Elaine knew he wasn't a regular. He seemed cool, but he wasn't her type. He was too conservative and proper. He didn't have enough thug in him. When she saw that Sheila was finally alone, Elaine tried to figure out a way to shake Antoine. She grabbed her drink and told him she needed to see how her friend was. Before she walked off Elaine thanked Antoine for the drink and said she would look for him later for a dance.

Elaine sashayed to the other end toward her friend. Antoine couldn't believe that he'd just gotten played. He couldn't believe how rude the girl was, and he was just trying to be nice to her. He glanced around the club to see if anyone had observed the diss. "It just goes to show how some women don't recognize a good brother when they see one," he mumbled.

The two women watched as the man walked away from the bar inconspicuously. They cracked up as he disappeared into the crowd. The music was so loud Sheila had to yell to Elaine.

"Well at least he bought you a drink. That scrub sitting here talking me to deaf didn't even offer." They burst out laughing.

"Girl, let's go to the bathroom. I need to check my make-up," Elaine said. They headed toward the bathroom.

———————

It was Andrea's sixteenth birthday and she and Tim had been out all day celebrating. They saw a movie and went to TGI Friday's for dinner. They left the restaurant a few minutes after 9:00 p.m. and Andrea's curfew wasn't until 12:00 a.m. Tim's friend was having a party and he wanted to check it out before he took her home.

The music was pumping so loud they could hear it when they pulled up. Cars were parked up and down the street. Tim got lucky and got a nearby spot that someone was pulling out of. He parked his car and they got out. He grabbed Andrea's hand and escorted her to his friend's house. The couple walked into the foyer where they were greeted by a tremendous cloud of smoke. The party area was packed with just about everyone who went to their school, and then some. It was humid and dark. A myriad of odors lingered from perspiring, drunken, and drugged teenagers. Andrea appeared to be the only black person, but she didn't feel uncomfortable because she was used to that since she went to a predominantly white school.

Tim slipped away from Andrea as soon as they got in the door. She looked around the room for a spot to sit until Tim was ready to go. There were all kinds of drugs being passed around. Some were on Ecstacy, others were smoking pot, and a bunch of kids were gathered around the table sniffing lines of cocaine. There was so much smoke in the air, Andrea began to cough. She changed her mind about sitting and went to the patio door where there was fresh air circulating. It was a chilly night, but the patio doors were wide open. She could feel a breeze of clean, fresh air.

Andrea stopped a girl with a pack of Newports in her hand and asked if she could have a cigarette. The girl passed Andrea one and flicked a lighter in her face to light it. Andrea took a pull and inhaled the smoke until the cigarette was fiery orange at the tip. She exhaled the poisonous smoke and thanked the girl for the cancer stick.

"No problem," the girl said. Then, she walked away nodding to the loud music. Andrea took another pull from the cigarette and exhaled. The next song that came on was Jay-Z's "Hard Knock Life." Andrea bobbed her head because that was her jam. The party wasn't so bad after all. She didn't really know anyone but since there was good music playing and no one was bothering her, Andrea was cool.

Tim walked over to her with a lit blunt in his hand. He took a long pull, then passed it to her. She took a hit and dropped the cigarette in an empty cup. Tim asked her if she wanted something to drink. "Why not? It's my birthday."

"All right then, follow me," he said. They walked to the mini bar and he dipped some drink from the punch bowl into some plastic flutes. He passed one to Andrea and took a sip from the other. Andrea took another pull from the blunt and passed it back to Tim. They took their flutes and toasted. Tim said, "I hope you've had the happiest and the sweetest sixteenth birthday, and I hope it's the one you'd always wished for." Andrea smiled bashfully and sipped her drink. When she removed her cup from her mouth, Tim snuck a peck on Andrea's lips. She retaliated by accepting. After the kiss she mumbled, "Thanks for tonight."

A boy standing by the front door, waving his arm, caught Tim's attention. Tim excused himself and told his date he would be right back. Andrea nodded, although she was slightly disappointed. She gulped down another long sip of her drink. She tried not to think about her parents or anything else besides enjoying herself. It was her day.

A girl walked behind Andrea and introduced herself.

"Hi, my name is Lisa, and yours?"

"I'm Andrea," she extended her hand to the girl.

"I saw you over there standing by the patio earlier. By the time I made it over to say hi, Tim walked over and you guys disappeared through the crowd."

"Yeah, and he hasn't stood still a good ten minutes since we've been here," Andrea commented.

"That's Tim for you. He has what everybody wants so he'll be running back and forth all night." Andrea smiled. The girl stopped talking and threw her hand in the air as the next song faded in. She danced in place, jukking her shoulders up and down. For a white girl, she wasn't stiff at all. When the song faded all the way in, Lisa started breaking it down. Lisa stood about five foot seven and weighed a good ninety-five pounds soaking wet. She had pale white skin with long, skinny arms. Her hair was ash blonde, very thin and long, with brittle ends. As she danced in place to the music, Andrea noticed the cup in her hand.

"What are you drinking?" she asked Lisa.

"It's the mystery drink Bobby serves at all his parties. Nobody really knows what's in it but it tastes really good and it gets you fucked up. Would you like some? They have a big bowl of it on the bar over there."

"Oh, well, I guess that's what I was drinking."

"Would you like a refill then?"

"Sure," Andrea answered as she passed her glass to Lisa. When the girl came back she handed over the drink and said,

"There is no need in us just standing here. Let me take you around to meet a few people."

"Okay." Andrea followed the girl through the crowd. They said hi to Tracy first, then Rebecca and Lindsey. After them, Lisa introduced Andrea to Billy and Tom. She told them Andrea was there with Tim and the guys were like, that's cool. "Tim is the man."

Lisa shook her head and told her new friend to follow her upstairs. She said. "I have to go to the bathroom, what about you?"

"I guess I could freshen up a little," Andrea said as she followed the girl to the top of the stairs. Lisa got excited when she saw two girls near the bathroom door. She introduced Andrea to a strawberry blonde named Angie. Andrea didn't know Angie, but the girl with her was in Andrea's second hour English class. Her name was Suzy Thompson. They greeted each other and faked some smiles. Lisa told the other two girls that it was Andrea's birthday. The three girls looked at each other and started giggling.

"Since it's your birthday," Angie said, "we have a special surprise for you." Andrea was curious. She looked at the girls, wondering what they could possibly have for her since they'd just met.

The girls stood by the bathroom door and patiently waited. Within a couple of minutes, a girl came out and walked past the four girls. They huddled in the bathroom, and Suzy locked the door behind them. Angie took a folded dollar bill from her purse and laid it on the counter, then fumbled through her Dooney & Burke for something else. After a few seconds her hands became visible again. She pulled out a quarter and a pile of lint. She dropped everything else back inside her purse. The other girls stood by waiting with excitement. Angie took the quarter and pressed it across the dollar bill, then opened the package, revealing the powdery substance inside.

Andrea's eyes grew wide, as if they were about to pop out of her head. Angie took half of a drinking straw and a razor blade from her purse and put them on the bathroom counter. Suzy poured the white dust on the countertop and parted it into four lines with the blade. She placed the straw under her nostrils and sniffed a small portion up the left side of her nostril, the rest went up the right one. She laughed. "Now it's your turn, birthday girl."

Andrea was so nervous, she didn't know what to do. She'd never actually encountered cocaine and never thought about getting high, but when Suzy handed her the straw she grabbed it. Andrea held the nose hose in her hand and stared at the powder on the counter for a minute. She looked at the others. "Go ahead," Suzy said. She was sniffing and looking in the mirror.

One of the girls tried enticing Andrea. "Go ahead, you'll like it. It's a much better high than weed. Go ahead, try it," she urged.

206 It Just Gets Better With Time

Andrea stepped up to the counter. She figured, what could a tiny sniff hurt? It was her birthday.

Angie mumbled, "Go ahead, birthday girl. Your mind and body will be unbelievably relaxed for the rest of the night."

"For real, you'll feel like you're on cloud nine, Andrea," Angie encouraged. Andrea didn't want to be the only lame in the room so she placed the straw at the end of the next line and rushed the powder straight up her nose. As the drug went down, it burned her nose membranes and made her cough, although it was stimulating and caused a head rush. She passed the straw to Angie as she grasped her flaming nostrils. All the girls clapped to congratulate Andrea on taking her first hit successfully.

Lisa said, "It burns because that's good shit. Tim keeps the good shit." Andrea slowly let go of her nose and held her head high. She felt an enormous rush. She closed her eyes. Her body was calm, but her heart pounded like it was about to jump out of her chest. She opened her eyes and saw other girls passing the straw. Her eyes suddenly closed again and stayed that way. She closed her eyes. Andrea waited for the drug to take control. It was her birthday, the day that started a new chapter of her life.

PART TWO

Time Changes People

Nine months after Monet's graduation, Dorothy and Sullivan had a private wedding ceremony at his church. A new year had come and gone and new days were dawning. Soon after her graduation, Monet moved into her own apartment. She visited her mother and new stepfather often because they kept her son while she worked and attended college. Monet really liked her new stepfather. He was good to her mother. Even though the marriage was a bit premature, and totally unexpected, they had the ceremony only a week after Dorothy's divorce. Considering they only knew each other for less than a year, on March 3rd they went to the church and were joined together, as one, by Sullivan's pastor, in his office. There was no one present but the preacher's wife and Punkin. After the ceremony, Dorothy and her new husband went back to her house and told the children to get the empty boxes from the basement and pack their things because they were moving. Dorothy showed off her half carat diamond solitaire saying she would explain the new living situation after she got back home. Later that evening, Dorothy called her oldest daughter and told her what she had done. Monet was shocked. When Dorothy asked if she would baby sit while the newlyweds honeymooned for the weekend, Monet agreed, although she was still mad at her mom for not letting her know. She packed an overnight bag and waited for Monet.

She and her husband spent the whole weekend together at his, and her soon-to-be, new place. Dorothy wanted them to break in every room of the house before the children came and they'd never have the opportunity again. In the kitchen, he stripped her of her shirt and eased her skirt off her hips and down to the floor. His tongue slid into her mouth, salty and warm. He licked her ear, blew on it, then spoke. His voice was ear delicious. His words were tantalizing. He foretold what he was about to do as he took her hand and led her to the wall. He spread apart her hands flat against the off white enamel. Taking off his shirt, he got down on the floor, sitting on his butt. Next, he took her scissors and spread them apart as he stuck his tongue out and it wiggled its way inside her. She screamed a sweet melody and gripped the wall, securing her weakening knees. His fingers dove into her mounds as his tongue tickled her clitoris and sampled her juice.

When they made it to the living room, Sullivan sat on the couch, and she stood over him. Straddled on top of her husband, his lips and tongue teased her nipples. He grabbed one and pulled it into his mouth. She threw her head back and closed her eyes, placing her hands around his neck. One of his hands gripped her behind, and the other delved between her thigh, sweeping her G-spot with just the right strokes. She purred like a kitten, and he moaned while licking his lips; his fingers indulged in her wet cream. Passion seared through her body as she lifted herself and slid down onto his chocolate base. As she rode him, her thrusts of desire set her legs in motion. She wanted all of him, all eight inches. His stick dove into her cave of intoxicating pleasure. She slowed down and leaned against him to catch her breath. He continued his thrusts as she cried out from a pain all too good. Before either of them reached their highest peaks, Dorothy rose to her feet. Her knees gripped the floor as the delicious taste of her husband lingered on her tongue. His sucker filled her jaws, and she indulged on it like it was her favorite flavor. When she got up again they kissed and verbally expressed their love for one another. His freshly groomed mustache tickled her face as their tongues locked. He grabbed her hand and escorted her upstairs to the master bedroom. Sullivan picked her up and placed her firmly onto the bed. He climbed in and, like lighting, his palate struck her gently. It slivered in and out of her mounds. Her fists cringed together and her toes curled. Her body wiggled back and forth across the satin sheets as Sullivan reveled in her warm ocean. He plunged in as if it were a mouth-watering treasure.

He climbed in and fulfilled his wife in military position. Passion transferred through them as they rocked and intoned together. Her body melted as he pampered it perfectly. She yelled out with an intense "ooh" when her sweetness flowed onto the sheets like a torrential river. His body contracted. He climaxed, and collapsed on top of her with his head down. Dorothy made him feel like a new man.

When Dorothy came home from the weekend rendezvous, she explained the new arrangements to her children. They were all excited. They all loved Sullivan as much as Dorothy did and since he spent more time with them then their own father, Dorothy's children were thrilled that he was their stepfather. The girls were enthused about moving from the projects, although they didn't want to leave all their friends. They were excited to be going to a new school.

Everyone except Caroline seemed to adjust to the change. She went off on her sister saying that she hadn't known Sullivan long enough to marry him. "Girl, how are you going to have a man around your kids who you barely know? He can be an ex-convict or an ex-murderer or something and you got him all up in the house with your children. More or less, he could have dozens of children running around. Girl, you do not know him like that." It would have been too much for her to be happy.

"Well, if some children do pop up out of the blue, I'll just have to learn to accept them just as you have learned to accept the outside one your husband's got," Dorothy said. Caroline didn't say anything. Dorothy hated for it to come out the way it did, but Caroline pushed her. She needed to learn to tend to her own business. If she did, her child wouldn't be in the predicament she was in. Caroline was mad that Punkin knew about the wedding and she didn't. In a couple years her children would be out of the house and Dorothy and her new husband would be able to enjoy their future together.

Dorothy's son Dwayne was in the seventh grade, Tonya was in the ninth, and Keisha was a sophomore. From day one Sullivan treated Dorothy's children like his own and she knew in her heart that her new man was a good one. He was heaven sent and she deserved him, with as much as she'd been through. Now that Dorothy had a halfway decent man, she could see why her sister wasn't trying to let go of hers even though he did what he did. Things sure were a lot easier when you had a dependable, extra income.

Living

Caroline and her husband seemed happy again for a change. Since their counseling, things were back on track in their lives, not to say their marriage was perfect, just better.

Andrea was another story. She was becoming more and more out of control. She was a disgrace to her parents. She skipped school so much, her parents dropped her off on their way to work in the morning, but lately that didn't even work. The school was always calling to say their daughter was still not showing up for classes. Andrea became out of control after her parents forbid her to see Tim. Thomas threatened that he wouldn't do anything for her if she continued to see the boy. He told his daughter not to ask him for anything, but Andrea didn't care. Caroline and her husband had a hunch that Andrea was stealing again, and maybe even smoking weed on a regular basis. Caroline knew from the time she'd caught Andrea with the marijuana that she probably hadn't stopped, but she wasn't certain.

Andrea was never able to keep money. If she wasn't begging her parents for money, she was scamming money from her little sister. Andrea no longer acted like the smart and ambitious daughter Caroline and Thomas once knew. They couldn't wait until she turned eighteen so she could run the streets however she desired.

One Saturday afternoon, Caroline was getting dressed to have lunch with one of her girlfriends. It was a warm spring day so she decided to wear her white DKNY tennis skirt. She had a white and navy blue print cotton blouse that matched it, so she pulled that from the closet and slipped it on. Caroline probed in her closet for her white leather Coach bag to accentuate her outfit. She felt around on the shelf, picking up different purses, but not the one she was looking for. Puzzled, Caroline sat on the bed trying to remember the last time she remembered carrying the bag. She remembered lending it to her daughter a month prior.

She jumped up from her bed and dashed into her daughter's bedroom. As she stormed down the hallway, Caroline remembered that Andrea wasn't home, but that didn't stop her from searching her bedroom. She flung open the closet door hoping to find Andrea's purse, since Andrea wasn't carrying it. After discovering it wasn't in the closet, Caroline searched the room but could not find her purse. She left the room, closing the door behind her. After finding a substitute bag to accentuate her outfit, Caroline carried on with her plans for the day.

When she returned home that afternoon all her family was home. Caroline had been anxious to get home so she could confront her daughter about her purse. She didn't see Andrea when she first got in, but Thomas said the girl was upstairs mad about somebody meddling in her things. Andrea came downstairs dressed as if she was prepared to go somewhere.

"Where do you think you're going young lady?" her mother asked.

"Oh, I was just about to run somewhere with Tim right quick."

"I don't think so," Caroline retaliated. "I need to talk to you."

"Well, can't it wait until I come back, Mother?"

"No, it can't, and you're not going anywhere anyway."

"Mom, yes I am," Andrea argued as she walked past her mother. "I am not a baby and you keep on trying to treat me like one." Caroline grabbed the girl by her collar and jerked her body toward hers. Andrea pulled away, losing her balance. She grabbed her mother's shirt as they stumbled down the stairs. At the bottom of the steps, they tussled. Caroline tried to pin her down but Andrea kept swinging at her. Thomas ran in and attempted to break them up. Thomas got his wife to take her hands from around Andrea's neck, and Andrea ran out, vowing never to come back.

"Don't bring your ass back until you have my damn purse with you," Caroline shouted. Thomas ran after Andrea but she had already jumped into Tim's car, and they quickly sped off. Two days later, Andrea called home crying and begging her dad to convince Caroline to let her come back home. Thomas convinced his wife to let the girl come back, but their relationship was never the same.

A week later, Thomas and his wife sat down to talk with their insubordinate child.

"Andrea," Thomas began, "your mom and I love you with all of our hearts and it's normal for us to worry about you, but we can't help you if you don't let us know what's going on." Andrea didn't look at her father while he spoke, but when he finished she burst into tears.

"I don't know what you guys want me to tell you. If you want to know if I'm on any drugs, I'll tell you. Yes, I do smoke a little weed from time to time."

"Well, if smoking weed causes you to act out of control and disrespect your parents, then you don't need to smoke it."

"Dad, I made one little mistake by smoking weed and you guys are acting like I have killed someone. I'm sorry to disappoint you but I'm just not that perfect little girl you want me to be. This is the twentieth century. Everybody gets high on something."

"That's absurd," Caroline shouted. "Neither of us use drugs, Andrea, so don't even try it."

"Oh yeah, I forgot Mom. You guys are without error."

"Don't even try it, young lady," Thomas interrupted.

"We are not saying that we don't make mistakes. It's just that you can't solve a problem until you deal with it head on."

"Is that what you did Dad? Did you learn your lesson after you stepped outside of your marriage and got another woman pregnant?"

Smack went Thomas's bare hand across his daughter's face. Caroline could not believe what had come out of Andrea's mouth. After Thomas slapped her, he went upstairs. He was finished with the conversation. He wasn't getting through to Andrea, and she'd hurt his feelings. After that he decided to let Andrea live her life exactly how she thought it should go. In the end, she would realize her mistakes and would need her parents' support. He hoped she would realize how deep a ditch she was digging before it was too late.

"A hard head makes a soft behind," he said.

Caroline and her daughter continued arguing. Andrea was going on and on talking about how her parents were always bothering her. Near the end of the conversation Caroline stood up, and walked into Andrea's face.

"As long as you are still living under my roof," Caroline said, "I don't think you should claim to be so grown. All grown people have their own shit, and they pay bills. If you feel like you've reached that level of maturity then why did you beg us to let you back in our house? How come you didn't stay with that white boy you keep running around here with?" Andrea didn't answer.

"Yeah, that's what I thought. I don't know what gives you the audacity to say that someone is bothering you. We're constantly going out of our way trying to make sure that Taylor and your ungrateful ass have the best of everything. What do you do to repay us? You walk around here disrespecting your father and me. You've been stealing my shit and borrowing all of your sisters extra money, that you never pay back, so how and the hell can you fix your mouth to say that someone is bothering you?"

The girl had nothing to say; she sat in the kitchen chair balling her eyes out.

"Like I told you before," Caroline continued, "Andrea, what you do in the dark will eventually come to light and it's not going to hurt anyone but you. My only advice to you is this. When you get caught up in some more shit, you can forget that you even know this number because neither my husband nor myself will be coming to bail you out."

Caroline walked away shaking her head in disgust. The next day, Andrea left for school and never came back home.

———————————

Delvin stepped out of the shower and grabbed the peach and white striped drying towel from the rack. He patted himself down with the towel as he glanced in the fogged up bathroom mirror. With his spare hand, he wiped a small section of the mirror with the end of the towel until his dark, wet body appeared. Delvin got another good look at his freshly cut fatback and his clean new shave. His sideburns set off the masculinity of his attractive facial features. He and some of the guys from his job had agreed to meet at this new club everyone was talking about. Delvin had been completely sober over seven months and tonight he was going to enjoy himself.

He'd been working hard to clean up his act since his ex-wife divorced him. Dorothy had truly broken his heart when she finalized things and Delvin was doing all he could to stay afloat, after all he'd lost. Time was healing him slowly and as long as he stayed focused on the important things, he would be all right. Delvin knew he took Dorothy for granted all those years and he was sorry now. He knew deep down in his heart that she deserved someone better and he hated to admit it, but Sullivan seemed like the perfect man for the job. He loved Dorothy and he was good to the kids. He treated them like they were his own and Delvin respected him for that.

This year he had different goals. Delvin was faithfully paying his three-hundred and sixty one dollars a month child support and spending a lot of time with his children. Before, he spent every dime he could get his hands on getting high. Since he'd strayed from his old crowd, he had things to show for his hard earned money. He still saw James every now and then, but basically Delvin stayed to himself. If he could live without the women and children he was deeply in love with, it was easy not to see a friend. Losing his family had opened his eyes and made him snap back to reality. He heard that his friend Tyrone was strung out on rocks. He hadn't seen him in a while, but Delvin heard that Tyrone was looking pretty bad. That was somewhere Delvin wasn't trying to go anymore.

When he finished dressing, he dabbed some Gucci on his neck and down the front of his shirt. After taking a good look at himself, he headed upstairs to wait for his ride. In about two weeks, Delvin would no longer have to wait for transportation because he was soon getting his own vehicle.

Sheila stood in front of Elaine's bathroom mirror applying her makeup. It usually took her a good forty-five minutes to get her face on. She had to make sure that every little stench of make-up was applied perfectly.

Cherhonda, Elaine's oldest daughter, was baby-sitting Thomas Jr., so Sheila was getting dressed there. Elaine was in the bedroom putting her clothes on. Before they got ready to leave, Elaine went over the rules with her daughter, like she always did. Cherhonda nodded in agreement to everything her mother told her. Before they left, Sheila went into Cherhonda's bedroom and kissed her son on the forehead. As she and her friend headed out the door, they transferred from caring mothers into two divas of the night. It was time to get their party on. Elaine acted like she was single, just like her husband did all of the time.

They walked through the first set of double doors of the night club. After paying, the two women got into the second line to get their hands stamped. Sheila got to moving and shaking as soon as she heard the music. She pulled open the last door and entered the club. The place was beautiful. Even though the room was dark you could see the dance floor was packed.

Immediately to the right was a gigantic aquarium filled with dozens of tropical fish in an array of radiant colors. About five feet away from the aquarium were four stairs going up to the bar and four going down onto the dance floor and lounge area. It was nothing like the bars they were used to. This was the first real club they had in town, unless you wanted to go to the other side of town and party at one of those clubs where same sex dancing was uninhibited and techno music played all night.

The friends chose to step up the four carpeted stairs toward the luminously lit carousel bar. Sheila anxiously led them straight to the bar where she ordered a shot of brandy and coke. Elaine ordered her usual Pina Colada. Both women grabbed their glasses and turned around to look at the dance floor. There weren't many people standing around; everyone seemed to be mingling, dancing and having a good time. They didn't see any familiar faces right off, but by the end of the night they were bound to see someone they knew.

Sheila danced in place to the music, but not for long. Some attractive, light skinned brother approached her and asked if he could escort her to the floor. Sheila smiled as she bopped away with him.

Elaine glanced around for an available table. She didn't see one right off, however, she did see an angry lady who appeared to be putting some man in straight check. The woman trotted onto the dance floor where he was dancing mighty close with another woman, he must have had no business talking to. He and the woman that broke up the slow dance were standing close by the dance floor arguing. The other woman walked right off like she hadn't even been dancing with the man. Elaine learned from that mistake a long time ago. She and her husband used to clown so much in public that Elaine was embarrassed to go anywhere with him. It was actually funny to see someone else in her shoes. Elaine knew from experience that it was because that female had a no good, lowdown parasite who wasn't about nothing, just like her husband, and nine times out of ten he was a creeping dog that would screw anything that had a coochie.

Sheila walked toward Elaine who was fanning herself. "Girl, it's hot in here," she yelled over the music.

"The only thing that's hot in here is your ass," Elaine joked.

"Girl, you need to be getting your dance on instead of standing here wearing out them pumps."

"Girl, for real, my feet are starting to hurt."

A couple got up from two bar seats nearby. Elaine and Sheila rushed over before someone else got them. Before they could even sit down good someone else was asking Sheila to dance; within seconds she was out of sight again. A guy walked up behind Elaine and tapped her on the shoulder.

"Would you like to dance?"

Her drink was almost gone, so Elaine didn't mind. She got up hoping she and Sheila would still have seats when they finished dancing.

It bothered Elaine that the guy kept trying to get close to her while dancing. He was all up on her like he was her man or something. Several times she had to back away to leave some space between them, but the guy kept getting close and grinding on her. When the song was over, he invited Elaine to sit at his table on the other side of the club. He said there were extra chairs for her and her friend. Her chair at the bar was probably taken, so she said, "Well, I guess I can come to your table, but I have to keep a look out for my friend so she'll know where we're sitting."

"That's fine," the man said, "and by the way my name is

Edward."

"Nice to meet you, Edward. I'm Elaine."

"Elaine and Edward, sounds good together, ha."
Since Elaine didn't laugh, his smile dropped and he escorted her across the room to the table. She was starting to get the carpet burn feeling at the bottom of her feet, otherwise she would have shook him. Sheila saw Elaine and waved as if she was trying to stop a cab on a New York street. When she saw where Elaine was headed she continued getting her groove on. When Sheila got to the table, she looked at Elaine like, who are all these men you're sitting with. Elaine introduced all the guys to her girl. Sheila said hi to everyone.

"What do you drink?" Edward asked Sheila. Sheila ordered the same thing she'd had earlier and took a seat in the empty chair. When the waitress brought the drinks, Edward sent her to get Sheila's drink. As the waitress took off, Delvin walked up to the table. Edward introduced the women to Delvin. He shook their hands and sat directly across from Sheila. Sheila thought, "damn, Delvin is a fine chocolate brotha; he has it going on." Sheila excused herself to go to the bathroom, to freshen up. She didn't want to sit next to that scrumptious looking brotha looking all sweaty and hot. Sheila strutted off like she was walking down a runway. She wanted to make sure that Delvin had something to think about until she came back.

Delvin did take a good long look. Sheila was thick in all the right places, and she knew it. When she was out of sight, Delvin asked Elaine, "So, is your friend single or what?"

"You can ask her all the questions you want when she comes back." Elaine smiled.

Sheila looked in the bathroom mirror. Her makeup had started to run so she took her MAC compact from her purse and touched it up. She dusted, and put on Lipglass, then dabbed on a touch of blush and of course, put on eye liner. Her face looked brand new and she was ready to get better acquainted with Mr.

Sexual Chocolate.

When she got to the table, Elaine and Edward were on their way to the dance floor and Delvin handed her the drink she had ordered. Sheila took her seat soon after Delvin inconspicuously tried to get up in her business. He wanted to know how often she came to the spot. "Do you have a man in your life, Sheila?"

"What do you mean?" she asked like she didn't know what he was talking about.

"I mean, are you currently seeing anybody?"

"No, not lately." The only man I'm seeing is my son's father who comes to visit his son a couple times out of the week."

"So you have children."

"I have a son. He's almost four years old."

"Well, does your son mind you giving out your phone number?"

"Now see what mama does ain't got nothing to do with son. Son ain't grown." Delvin laughed as Sheila took a sip from her glass. Her lips were so big and lusciously painted strawberry red that they called attention of his manhood. Delvin hadn't been this turned on by a woman in a long time.

Delvin lifted a napkin from the table and asked Sheila if she had a pen. She answered no. Without taking his eyes off her, Delvin fumbled through his pocket for a pen. He didn't find one. Sheila told him to wait until Elaine came back and she would have a pen. He made her promise that she wouldn't forget to give him the number before they left the club.

Can't Give Up

It was Friday night and Dorothy and her husband were getting ready to have dinner with Caroline and Thomas. They were supposed to meet at Friday's twenty minutes ago and Dorothy had just gotten out of the shower.

Sullivan looked at his watch. "Hon, you know your sister is going to be upset if she has to wait on us to eat."

Within minutes, Dorothy was out of the bedroom, dressed, and ready to go. As they were about to leave, the telephone rang. Aggravated, Sullivan picked up the receiver. It was Monet. She said hi to her stepfather and asked for Dorothy. Sullivan covered the mouthpiece and whispered, "We were just on our way out the door."

"Baby, I'll be in the car, okay?" Dorothy nodded.

"I'm sorry, Mama, I didn't know you were about to leave, I just have one quick question."

"What is it?" Dorothy asked in a motherly tone.

"I just wanted you to tell me how to make the gravy for my roast before I put it in the oven. Dorothy laughed and explained it step by step. She told her to season and flour the roast on both sides. "You know that cast iron skillet I bought you when you moved?"

"Yeah," Monet answered.

"You need to heat up a little cooking oil and onion in that skillet then put the roast in there. Cook it on both sides until it turns brown. Take the roast out the skillet, make your gravy from the trimmings in the skillet, then put the meat and the gravy in a roasting pan and put it in the oven with some aluminum foil over it. Keep flipping it, and stirring the gravy so it can thicken and start sticking to the meat."

Before she finished reciting her recipe, Dorothy asked, "What are you cooking with it?"

"Some mashed potatoes and green beans."

"Um," Dorothy replied, "Well, let me go. I'm already running late and you know Caroline is going to be talking crazy. I'll call you later, all right?"

"Okay, Mom," Monet said, and they hung up. Dorothy ran to the car where her humble husband was patiently waiting.

At Friday's, Caroline sat tapping her two-hour-old, manicured nails down on the table impatiently while she waited for her slow ass sister. She was ready to eat. Becky, the skinny white waitress, kept coming to her table asking if she could get them something, as if Caroline hadn't told the broad before that they were waiting for the rest of their party.

"Would you all like to try an appetizer while you wait?"

"No, we will not," Caroline muffled rudely.

"No problem," Becky answered and tip-toed away.

"I'm sure that we'll get good service now," Thomas implied.

"Whatever," Caroline huffed.

"With you treating her like that, we'll be lucky if she doesn't spit in our food."

"Whatever," Caroline hissed. "I told her once. Apparently, she didn't understand. I guess she was waiting for me to get indignant."

"Baby, why don't you calm down? I know you're hungry but chill out, okay? If you want to do something to kill time, let's talk about Andrea. I'm really worried about her."

"Well, I'm not. If she wants to act like she's grown, then she will get treated like an adult. The way she disrespected me, I don't want to see her for a minute. I need some time to heal. I still can't believe she hit me."

Thomas looked at his wife surprised. He didn't know if she was talking crazy because she was hungry or if Caroline was really serious. He didn't say anything, instead, Thomas looked away from the table with a stern look on his face.

Caroline was happy that he turned away because she didn't want him to sense her concern. Of course she worried about Andrea, every minute of the day, but she wouldn't admit it. She pretended to be unbreakable, only to cover up the worry and frustration. She was disappointed in what her daughter had become. Caroline wished she could rewind the hands of time and have the old Andrea back. The old Andrea was sweet, kind, and determined to grow up and become a successful lawyer. Caroline wondered what happened to that dream. In her heart she knew her daughter was like many lost souls on the streets. She prayed that Andrea had somewhere safe to lay her head every night. She missed her daughter so much that thinking about this made her eyes water. She hoped her daughter wasn't strung out on drugs, or worse, selling her body to survive. She knew that living on the streets and prostituting was the only way most young girls survived. Caroline took her napkin and wiped a tear away before Thomas noticed.

"It took y'all long enough," Caroline shouted when her sister crept up to the table behind the hostess. You guys have had us sitting up here with our stomachs growling for over forty minutes, and Dorothy I know that your slow ass was the reason you guys are so late." Dorothy didn't answer. She and her husband sat down while Thomas busied himself trying to get the waitress' attention. When she recognized he needed her assistance, she sighed, "It's about time." She put on her fake smile and pranced over to the table. The group ordered their drinks and meals at the same time. The waitress repeated the photographically recorded order to her guests. They agreed she had everything correct, then the girl walked away from the table. Caroline demanded an explanation from her sister and brother-in-law for being late.

"Girl, first I was undecided about what to wear and since Sullivan was rushing me, I put on the first thing I pulled out the closet and didn't have to iron. When we finally were on the way out of the door, Monet called and asked how to cook a roast."

"Since when did Monet know how to cook a roast?"

"Honey, my baby is almost twenty years old and she has known how to cook every since she was about eleven. You know she learned from the best." The sisters burst out laughing as their husbands stared at them.

Their waitress came back to the table with a girl behind her carrying half their orders. Thomas and Caroline were handed their New York strips with baked potatoes and rice pilaf. Sullivan ordered salmon, and Dorothy had a combination plate with bar-beque chicken and fried shrimp. Everyone dug into their entrees. Within ten minutes worrisome was back at their table seeing if everything was okay. Everyone nodded and Becky pranced away.

After dessert, the check was delivered. Thomas told his party he would handle it. Thomas handed Becky his credit card and walked away from the table. Even though she was collecting fifteen dollars and some odd change for a tip, she was ready for the group to leave her table. They had been there over two hours and she could have flipped the table two or three times. They did-n't realize how they were messing up her money for the night.

They sat in the restaurant chilling for about thirty minutes after dessert. Dorothy was so full, all she could do was lean her head on the back of her chair and listen to her husband and Thomas talk. She busied herself by drilling a toothpick through her teeth. When they walked out of the restaurant, Dorothy told Caroline she would call her tomorrow, and the couples went their separate ways.

Rolling down the street in silence, Thomas broke the monotony. "I wonder where Andrea is right now." He knew Caroline didn't want to discuss the subject earlier, but he figured she was trippin' because she was hungry. He knew his wife would have a comment.

"Thomas, the subject is taboo. When Andrea gets herself

together and wants to come back home, she knows where we live. She must not be ready."

"But, I can't just let it go, Caroline. Andrea has been gone for a long time and I'm worried about her. I don't know what your beef is but something deep inside of me is telling me that I need to find her and bring her home. I love my daughter and I have a gut instinct that she may need me, and I can't ignore it. I want to go out and look for her."

"I'm tired," Caroline mumbled.

"So, are you saying that you don't feel like driving around for a little while to look for her?"

"No, I don't feel like all of that Thomas. I want to go home and go to bed; you can go if you want t..." He cut her off before she could finish.

"I can do that," he said abruptly. He didn't say anything to his wife until she climbed out of the car in front of the house. He said, "I'll be back in a little while," then he backed out of the driveway and pulled off.

His first stop would be Ottawa Street, where a lot of teenagers hung out. If he saw Andrea, he would talk her into coming home so they could get her some help. If the whole family needed to go to counseling, Thomas was willing to do that. He wondered if his daughter had been eating, and where she was sleeping. He wanted to know how she was surviving, because the last he knew, Andrea didn't have a job. She was probably with Tim, so maybe the boy was taking care of his little angel. Thomas hoped he would see Andrea so he could bring her home with him.

He turned right on Ottawa and drove down about two blocks before he slowed down and pulled over to the curb. Thomas pulled up in front of a brick apartment building and stopped his car. Children stood in front of the apartment. He was uncertain what to do so Thomas sat back and contemplated a plan. A couple minutes passed so he turned off the engine and climbed out of the car. He hoped his daughter wasn't living in a place like this. This was a side of town that Andrea should be unfamiliar about. It was run down and dirty. Everybody was walking around outside looking at the ground as if they'd lost something.

Thomas asked one of the kids if they knew Andrea. One boy ignored him and turned his head. Another guy pointed toward the house. "Thanks," Thomas replied and started toward the door. Someone else was walking inside so Thomas followed the guy and asked if he knew Andrea.

The dismal hallway reeked of urine and vomit. Graffiti covered the walls and there were gigantic holes filled with empty bottles and trash. The boy walked toward a door, saying nothing to Thomas. He knocked and went inside. Thomas stood motionless for a minute before deciding to walk to the same door and knock. Before long a girl came to the door and yelled,

"Who's there?"

"I'm looking for my daughter." Thomas yelled. "Her name is Andrea. Do you know her?"

The girl opened the door enough to see Thomas' face and tried to close it back. Thomas forcefully pushed it open. The girl had given him a reason to be suspicious so he had to intrude. He pushed the girl out of the way and stepped inside the dilapidated apartment. The teenager looked as if she hadn't changed clothes in months. Thomas looked at the girl with disgust. He couldn't believe these kids would rather live somewhere like this than to follow rules and live at home with their parents.

"I don't know any Andrea," the girl fussed. She appeared to be about thirteen or fourteen and terrified, but she tried to act brave. "Are you a cop?"

"Look, young lady, I am not here to cause you any problems. I just want to know if my daughter hung out around here. I came here simply to take her home. By the way, what is your name?"

As if saying the first thing that came to mind she answered,

"Shelly."

"Well, where is she, Shelly?"

"I don't know who you are talking about, but if you want you can look around. People run in and out of here all day."

The walls had holes the size of tires. The floors were nasty, and the carpet was so filthy it was almost black. Two or three people were piled up sleeping on a soiled brown couch where the girl named Shelly joined them. The apartment smelled more like a pet store, than a place for human dwelling. Thomas walked toward the back and stepped over kids lying on the floor sleeping. They had no sheets or blankets, nothing but bare, nasty, smelly carpet under them. Another girl walked from the bathroom into another room and closed the door behind her. Thomas peeked in that room and called out his daughter's name. A voice yelled back at him,

"There is no Andrea in here. Now get the hell on."

The rooms were so dark Thomas could barely see. The farther he went, the worse the smell got. It was so bad he had to plug his nose. He walked out of that room down the dim hallway and into another bedroom. He didn't see his daughter. Everyone in this room was apparently sleeping because no one said anything. The only light came from a guy sitting in the corner striking a lighter, while smoking what looked like a crack pipe. He didn't say anything to Thomas. He didn't even look at him when he asked if he knew Andrea. After Thomas left that room, he stood in the hallway in disbelief. The next door was the second from the last down the hallway. Thomas turned the knob, covered his nose and slowly crept inside. The screeching of the door caused the teenagers to cry out.

"Who the hell is it?" The girl looked up to see her father. Andrea couldn't believe her eyes. There was a small candle burning in the room and Thomas could clearly see his daughter straddled on top of some boy. When she noticed her father in the door-way, the fornicating teens jumped up from the floor and tried to dress.

"Dad, what are you doing here?" Andrea yelled. Thomas walked over to his daughter and snatched her up by the arm. Tim was standing with his mouth wide open, but he was without words. He quickly put his clothes back on. Andrea began yelling as soon as her furious father approached her. When Tim saw Thomas grab her, he ran out of the room.

"What has gotten into you girl?" her father scolded. He jerked her body, "How can you have any respect for yourself if you are lying up here in this dilapidated house, having sex with this boy?"

"Daddy, I'm sorry," Andrea screamed. "I'm sorry."

"Get your damn clothes on," he said," You are about to take your butt home rather you want to or not, and I am taking you to see a counselor first thing in the morning. I am fed up with you and this nonsense."

"You can't make me, Daddy," she fussed. As he dragged her out of the apartment, Thomas turned to the others and said,

"If you guys think this is some type of life, then you're all wrong. You children need to go home to your parents. It makes no sense what you are doing here." Thomas opened the door and drug his daughter out with him. Andrea tried to jerk away from her father's grasp as he drug her down the dark hallway and out of the building.

"I am not going anywhere," she argued. Thomas stopped in his tracks and smacked his daughter across her face.

"You may have lost respect for yourself, but as long as you are my daughter you will respect me." Before they got into the car, he told Andrea, "Until we get home, I'd advise you to remain silent from here on out."

He put her in the car and got in the driver's side. Thomas drove off, daring her to move.

Fed Up

Elaine and Sheila sat outside of a white two level apartment watching Dennis' parked car. He had not come home last night. That morning, Elaine called Sheila to ride with her to look for him. Her first hunch was where they found his car. Elaine had been to the same place before. She knew the car belonged to her husband because of the license plate. Dennis was supposed to be at work, but obviously he wasn't.

"So, what are we going to do now?" Sheila asked. "I am tired of sitting out here in this car. Are you going to go up to the door or not?"

"I don't know! If a woman comes to the door, girl, I think I'll go crazy."

"Do you suspect that a man's keeping your husband out all night?" Elaine looked at her friend with a devious frown, but didn't say anything. "Look, all you have to do is ask is he in there, and if he is, you tell her to tell him to bring his cheating ass out. Don't front like this is your first time having to do this shit. Hell, you ought to be good at it by now."

"Don't even start," Elaine warned. "I'm not in the mood for your sarcasm." She and her friend had been sitting in front of the house for over an hour and Elaine still hadn't concocted a plan.

"Don't you have a spare set of keys?"

"Yeah!"

"Well check this out. Why don't you get in the car and start blowing the horn until he comes out?"

"Girl, please, it's too early in the morning to be doing some shit like that. These people will have us locked up for disturbing the peace."

"Well, why don't you just take the car and drive it home? I'll drive yours. That'll teach his no good ass a lesson. You would think with all you've been through, you'd have left him by now."

Elaine threw her hand up! "Please Sheila, I don't feel like

hearing it right now." Sheila mumbled something as Elaine pulled opened the car door and climbed out. She walked toward her husband's car while her friend tried to figure out what Elaine was about to do.

Before unlocking the car door, she glanced at the white building to see if anyone was looking. She stuck the key in the lock and opened the door. Her hands were trembling with fear. Elaine slid into the driver's seat, closed the door, and went crazy on the horn. Sheila laughed her stomach into knots until it dawned on her how childish they were acting. After all, they'd been together thirteen years and Dennis hadn't changed yet. Elaine used to believe everything he told her, but as the years passed and the lying and cheating got worse, she wizened up. She'd endured too much disrespect. That was the main reason Sheila enjoyed being by herself. A piece of mind was way more comforting than the load of stress endured with trying to turn a boy into a man.

Her friend was right. She should have left him a long time ago. She stuck by him even after finding out about the countless women he'd been with. She'd forgiven him for all the lies, but was that enough? No, he still wasn't satisfied. She was finally realizing that he wasn't worth all the pain.

If Dennis was in the house, he sure wasn't planning on coming out. Elaine wore his horn out for a good five minutes, so whoever was sleeping was awake now. In her friend's car, Sheila observed a couple of people looking out their windows, but none of the shadows fit Dennis' profile. Elaine became so disgusted she started the car and prepared to pull away, signaling for Sheila to follow her. They took off down the street. She was too old to be running him down and acting silly, like she was. This time she had to retaliate. With tears in her eyes, she drove the Cadillac down the street, not paying attention to the road. She had to get it out of her system while she was alone because with Sheila, she played the tough role. She tried to act like the shit didn't hurt.

When they arrived, Elaine ran into her house to get Sheila's baby, who her daughter Sheronda was babysitting. She soon came out with Thomas Jr. in her arms. Elaine passed Sheila her son and asked her to drive her car home. Elaine said she would get it later. It was almost time for her children to leave for school, which would allow her time to come up with a possible plan. She told Sheila she'd call her in an hour.

Shanice lifted herself from the bed. She glanced over to see if Dennis was awake, but he was still sleeping. When she leaned over to kiss him, his right eye popped open and stared at her. "You're awake?" she asked.

Dennis flipped his body over and replied, "Damn, you let me go to sleep. What time is it?"

She looked at the clock. "It's five after eight."

"Damn, I'm late for work. I know Elaine is gone be trippin' about me not coming home." Shanice frowned.

"Why is it that every time you spend the night over here, you always wake up talking about her? Do you think I want to hear that shit?"

"You just don't know Shanice. This back and forth shit between you and her is starting to put too much pressure on me. If she ain't the one trippin', it's you."

Shanice smacked her lips and yelled, "Well, boo, you can take yo' ass right on home to her. I don' know why you keep running over here, since I'm always trippin. If you stayed at home with your wife, then I wouldn't have to worry about y'all's problems."

Dennis got up from the bed and shook his head. It was a shame, he couldn't even get the stank off his breath before Shanice started talking shit. He said, "Why are you trying to start something, when you know it ain't even like that? I just need some time to think this all out, that's all."

Her neck and head rolled, her lips smacked. "Think," she huffed! Shanice got up from the bed and walked toward the dresser. She snatched a Newport from its pack and held it to her mouth. She took the lighter and struck it. The flame ignited the tobacco, turning the end of the cigarette from a dark brown to a fire red. She took a long drag from the cancer stick and a whirl of smoke filled the air, then evaporated. She began to speak again, this time in a calmer manner.

"You know what? I think I need some time to think too. I need time to think about why I keep allowing you to take me through this bullshit, and while I'm at it, why don't I think about why I feel like I have to come second to her? I also need to ask myself why I'm putting up with someone else's man in the first place, and to top it all off, you expect me to sit up here and listen to you talk about her. I ask myself, why do I sit up here and keep playing the fool for you, Dennis when I know you ain't trying to leave her." He stepped into his jeans and zipped them.

"What are you talking about? All I said was that she's going to be ready to fuss because I've stayed out all night. I don't know where all that other shit is coming from." He put his shirt on, and turned to his lover. "Where are my keys?"

Her eyes bucked and her head jerked in his direction. She grabbed his keys from the dresser and threw them at him. Dennis knew she was about to act crazy because they went through the same thing whenever it was time for him to go. They'd been kicking it for three years so you'd think she'd be used to him going home. He started toward the door.

"Oh, that's fucked up, Dennis. You're steady walking out of the door when you hear me trying to talk to you." Bobbing her head, she continued. "Oh, my time is up now, ha. Now that it's time for you to go back home to your family, you ain't got no words for me, ha."

As Dennis reached for the door knob, Shanice stood

behind him with her cigarette burning between her fingers.

"That's all right," she said, "gone ahead and be with your family. And don't call me no more."

Dennis ignored Shanice and walked down the street. He didn't feel like arguing with her. He'd already missed work and that was unfortunate because he hated when his check came up short, and hated when his wife questioned him about it. Shanice flicked her cigarette into the yard and slammed the door after going back inside.

Dennis walked down the street two blocks, then turned left at the corner. He headed to his usual parking spot when he stayed at Shanice's house. Just in case Elaine was out looking for him, which she usually was, he parked far away from where he was actually staying so she wouldn't come knocking on no doors and acting crazy.

When Dennis approached the white house, he was stunned. He stood in place, then looked in all directions, but there was no car. "Wait a minute," he thought scratching his head. "Where in the hell is my car?" Frustrated, Dennis threw his hands in the air and looked heavenward. He repeated,

"What in the hell happened to my car?" He knew he was in the right spot because he parked there every time he came to Shanice's. He looked up to see if there was a No Parking sign posted, but there wasn't. He knew there wasn't, but Dennis was checking to be sure he wasn't going crazy.

He stood there in shock. He looked up and down the street, but there was no sign of his car. "Damn," he shouted. "Somebody done stole my damn car." Instantly, he thought negative. God musta' been punishing him from not taking his black ass home to his wife. Dennis looked up into the air and confessed, "I'm sorry, Lord, please forgive me."

Dennis didn't know what to do but start walking. There was no way he was going back to Shanice's to hear her bitch. He was already too upset. He figured he'd just start walking until he could get to a phone booth to call one of his boys to come get him. He couldn't believe someone had stolen his baby. Marching down the street, Dennis concocted a plausible story for his wife, and for his job. He would tell the job that his car was stolen, and he'd have to take the day off. He could tell Elaine that his car being stolen was the reason he had not come home. At least he had that advantage. His wife was going to cut up a hell of a lot worse than Shanice did, so he really had to come correct.

Brandy and Monet drove down the highway headed to a party. Monet never met the birthday girl, but was looking forward to doing so. Brandy said she was real cool.

"I really miss Malcolm," Monet said out of the blue.

"I will be glad when he comes home because I am tired of you talking about him," Brandy told her friend.

"Girl, I know, but I really do miss him. I love him, Brandy."

"Girl, please, after he gets home and hits that thang a few times, he's gone start getting on your nerves. You are going to be happy when it's time for him to leave again. You know that's one thing about a man I had to find out for myself. Once he's gone you miss him like crazy, but as soon as he comes back and starts talking about baby get me this, or baby fix me that, and after you get tired of cleaning up after him, you gone be praying that his departure day will hurry up and come," Brandy said.

"Girl, you are crazy," Monet burst out laughing.

Brandy turned the stereo up and eased down the road, bumping "In Da Club" by 50 Cent. They pulled up outside the rented reception hall. There were not many cars in the parking lot, but it was still early. Monet was relieved to see that the party was at a hall because she thought they were going to a house party and she didn't like being cooped up in a crowd of sweaty people in a dark and congested living room.

The party hall was spacious and well lit. It was decorated with happy birthday decorations, confetti paper on the table and chairs, and balloons hanging from the ceilings with colorful streamers. There was a sizeable dance floor and a small kitchen with an open window used as a bar.

Brandy looked for the birthday girl. Once she spotted her, she grabbed Monet's arm and pulled her toward the guest of honor. Brandy introduced her two friends. They smiled at each other and exchanged greetings. Nicky told the two girls to fix themselves a plate. Her Auntie and Mother had cooked all kinds of delicious dishes. Monet wished Nicky happy birthday, as Brandy reached into her purse and pulled out a ten dollar bill. She pinned it on the birthday girl and gave her a big hug, then walked off trailing Monet's greedy behind toward the food table. Monet and Brandy helped themselves to the food. They spotted an empty table and went to sit down. Before long, Nicky came along smiling. She appeared to be having a good time. The girl took a seat. As Brandy dug her plastic fork into her plate, she noticed that the birthday girl wasn't getting her buzz on. She yelled over the music.

"You stopped drinking."

"Girl, I have a legitimate excuse not to."

"And what's that?"

"Girl, I'm pregnant."

"What?" Brandy blurted.

"Yeah, girl," Nicky sighed.

"Well at least you are out of school," Brandy said.

"I know," Nicky replied as Brandy scooted in closer to receive an earful of gossip.

While the two friends caught up, Monet sat quietly at the table bopping her head to the music. She looked around the room to see if she noticed anybody she knew. Brandy soon dismissed herself to get a refill on her drink, leaving Monet and Nicky at the table. Nicky turned to Monet. "Aren't you going to go out there and dance?"

"No, goodness, "Monet replied. "I have to go out there when the dance floor gets packed so nobody can see me." As Nicky continued talking, Monet didn't say anything. She wasn't really listening, because her mind was on a journey that involved only her and Malcolm. Nicky soon became distracted by more guests. Once she got a good view she excused herself from the table and told Monet she would be right back. Monet smiled and watched the pregnant girl walk away. Monet was happy she was leaving because she talked too much.

Brandy came back to the table with two cups in her hand. She kept one for herself and passed the other to Monet. "Girl, this stuff is good," Monet said.

"What is it?"

"Something from the punch bowl. I'm not sure what but I like it because it has a fruity flavor."

Out of the blue Monet asks,

"So, when and where did you meet motor mouth Nicky?"

Brandy burst out laughing and said. "Oh, Nicky used to work with me at the movie theatre. I guess I met her..." she paused. "It was almost a year ago. She didn't work there long though. She said she got tired of always having to work weekends so she found herself another job. I gave her a ride home a couple of times and she was cool. As a matter of fact, I hadn't heard from her since she quit. She just called me the other day telling me to come to her party."

"Oh, yeah," Monet mumbled.

"Yeah, sometimes she used to get on my nerves at work because all she ever talked about was her man. You know how females always be bragging on a man that no one ever sees them with." She paused. "I guess all my friends be having the Love Jones." Brandy emphasized all, staring at her friend to see if she caught on to what she was implying. When it sunk in, Monet cracked up laughing.

"Forget you. Love is going to catch up with you one of these days. As soon as you find somebody you can tolerate after two dates." Both girls giggled as Monet took her first sip from the drink Brandy brought her. She suggested they get up and mingle. Brandy saw a guy drinking the same thing she was, and asked, "Do you know what's all in this drink?"

The man answered. "It's a secret." The girls rolled their eyes and walked away.

Brandy spotted Nicky on the dance floor so she stopped walking and stood there to watch. Monet stood beside her friend when some guy walked up and asked if she wanted to dance. The dance floor was packed and Monet had a good buzz going on so she figured why not. She asked Brandy to hold her drink as she bopped to the dance floor behind the young man.

The song stopped, but Monet and her dance partner remained on the floor throughout the next song. More people piled onto the floor when Saturday by Ludacris started playing. Nicky left the dance floor, fanning her face with a napkin. While on the dance floor, Monet noticed a guy walk up to her and pin money to her shirt. Monet turned around and did the dip on him. She came back up from the floor shaking her body and swinging her arms in a funky rhythm. The guy she was dancing with was good. He was competing with every one of Monet's jazzy moves. When the song was over, Monet was hot and thirsty and looked for her friend with her drink. Her dancing partner's name was Toby. He thanked her for the dance, then walked away. Monet searched for Brandy. She walked by the bathroom and spotted her. As she walked up, Monet recognized the guy Brandy was talking to. It was Jamil. She crept up behind her and Brandy turned around. Monet said what's up to Jamil as she reached for her drink in Brandy's hand. Jamil said hi and asked Monet how her lil' shorty was doing.

"He's all right," she smiled. "He is as bad as I don't know what."

"Yeah, Derrick said he was gone come and get him one day soon to spend some time with him. He said he ain't seen 'em in a minute." Monet's smile faded.

"So, when's the last time you seen my baby's daddy?" Monet asked.

"Oh, Derrick came here wit me. He's around here some-where hollin' at people."

"I haven't seen him up in here," Monet muffled.

"He up in here somewhere. You'll see him before the night is over." He hesitated, "You know this is his girl's birthday party."

"What?" Monet chided.

"What," Brandy hummed. Monet stared at Brandy. "Why are you looking at me like that? I'm just as surprised as you are. You know if I would have known, you would have known."

"Now don't y'all be up in here tryin' to start nothing," Jamil warned. "Monet, you wit' somebody new and so is my boy. Y'all bof doing y'all thang so don't trip." Monet spotted her ex hugged up with his pregnant girlfriend Nicky. His ass wasn't shit. She hadn't seen Derrick since he found out somebody else would actually spend time with her. She felt sorry for Nicky for not knowing that all she had was a lying ass sperm donor.

She told Brandy. "Let's go!" Brandy looked over toward Derrick and Nicky and then at Jamil. She was like, "We'll holla at you, Jamil." She and Nicky sat their drinks on the table and headed toward the door. She could not believe what they'd just discovered. They left without even telling Nicky, goodbye.

———————

After Elaine's children left the house for school, she was

ready to pursue her plan. She'd figured out what she had to do and her time was limited, so she had to move fast. She called her job and told them she wouldn't be coming in. Her boss was cool with it since Elaine had been with the phone company almost fourteen years, and rarely called off. She breezed through the phone book searching for a locksmith. There were dozens listed, so she went down the first page calling one after another. She came across one that could come out right away to change all the locks at a reasonable price. Elaine ran up to the bedroom to pack her husband's things. She was going to pile his car with his personal belongings and drive it back to where she found it. She would leave a note in it so that when he woke up to leave the female's house, he would realize that home was closer than he expected.

At 10:30 a.m. her friend returned. Sheila helped Elaine load the car while the locksmith changed the locks. Once the job was done and the man left, Elaine rushed to her husband's car and took off. Sheila jumped into her car and trailed. She couldn't believe her friend was finally getting rid of that no good husband of hers.

When they pulled up in front of the apartment building, Elaine parked Dennis's car in the same place she found it. She didn't immediately get out, instead Elaine sat there contemplating if she should go through with her plan or not.

Sheila was wondering why Elaine hadn't gotten out yet. What was going on? Had she copped out? Impatiently, she blew the horn to see what was up. Elaine held her hand up signaling for Sheila to chill. She sucked her teeth as she impatiently waited in the car, mumbling. She had no choice but to wait for Elaine to make a move.

Inside her husband's Cadillac, she scribbled a note. Her tears, poured onto the paper. The sheets became soggy and harder to write on. Elaine tore the paper up and wrote a note on a clean sheet. After composing her Dear John letter, Elaine placed the paper on the steering wheel and read it out loud.

I married you years ago because I thought you wanted to spend the rest of your life with me. Over the years you have proven the total opposite. I wish you and your new woman the best of luck and I hope that you guys have that wonderful life you once promised me. She obviously can give you everything I never could. Perhaps standing by your side through good and bad times, and baring your children wasn't sufficient. You've proven that my love wasn't enough to bring you home last night and many others. Then, she signed it, your long time and faithful partner.

The tears fell as Elaine stuck the note on the dashboard and climbed out of the car. She left it running, but locked all the doors. Hopefully, all the gas would run out by the time he came out of the house. Elaine couldn't believe that after all this time she was really letting go. For her piece of mind, she had to do what she had to do.

She climbed into Sheila's car and told her to drive. Since she was crying, Sheila didn't say anything. She just did as she was told. The car pulled away from the curb with Elaine staring at Dennis's running car packed with his belongings. It was all his fault. He shouldn't have tried to be a mack when he had a good woman at home. It was a shame men didn't see things for what they were until it was too late.

Getting By

As soon as Thomas got home from enrolling his daughter into rehab, they called to say she'd escaped. Andrea hadn't shown up at home and Thomas wasn't expecting her. He was tired of dealing with her ungratefulness. If Andrea didn't want to help herself, Thomas wasn't going to bother. He should have listened to his wife when she told him to let Andrea go about her business.

Tim grabbed two pair of men's Guess jeans and stuffed them down the pant leg of his oversized jeans. Andrea grabbed a couple of large shirts and stuffed them, then the couple dashed toward the front of the department store. At the car, Andrea was able to relax and calm her nerves. She was extremely paranoid because she didn't know if an APB was put out on her or not.

After the couple unloaded their stolen merchandise, Tim started the car and pulled away. Andrea calculated the items to see how much money they could make from selling them. The total came to two hundred and twenty dollars. They could at least sell the items and get a hundred dollars.

The couple sold the merchandise for less than a gram of cocaine and sixty dollars in cash. This gave them enough collateral to get a room and something to eat so they could enjoy the sack they'd copped. Tim and Andrea would do anything to avoid sleeping in the car or going home to their parents. It was the middle of fall and in Michigan sleeping in the car wasn't ideal.

Before settling into the hotel room, the couple opened the bag of cocaine. They were no longer able to restrain from sniffing it. Tim had so much respect for Andrea, he let her get the first hit. When it was his turn, he did a one-on-one. Andrea's first toot of the powder rushed to her brain, transforming her untamed reality into a tranquil hallucination. Tim, on the other hand, always went through a highly dramatic stage of revelry after taking his hit. He would clinch up and his head would shake. His body would spasm, as if he were going through electro-shock therapy. He would moan so loud it sent chills up Andrea's spine. She would be so irritated, she'd just look at him with a distasteful expression. She never understood why one lil' ole bump would cause him to act out so.

The two of them got high for a couple hours and talked about their plans for the next day. It seemed the minute they got to sleep, room service called to let them know it was check out time. Tim hung up the telephone and dialed the number on a small piece of paper. It was Mont's pager number. Mont bought the clothes from them the day before. He told them to page him when they wanted to pawn their car for a night or two. He suggested Tim let him borrow the car in exchange for the dope, a hotel room, and food. After checking out of the hotel, the couple picked him up. When he dropped them off at the Motel Six, Tim told Mont that he would page him the next day, an hour prior to check-out time.

The next morning, Tim dialed the pager number. When the recording came on he punched in the digits, pressed the pound key, and hung up. The young man picked up the brochure on the bedside nightstand, which held his rolled dollar bill and last few rows of cocaine. Tim snorted a line up his nose and went through his routine ritual, then relaxed on the comfy mattress. Andrea walked cheerfully out of the bathroom and hopped onto the bed. She was already dressed and ready to go.

"Wasn't Mont supposed to be here by now?" she said.
Tim handed her the brochure. She took a hit and passed the brochure back to him. He never answered her question. They sat quietly, lost in separate worlds. The moment was pleasureful and calm. When his head rush settled, Tim paged the boy again. As he reached for the telephone, it rang. It wasn't Mont. It was room service. Tim told the snotty woman on the other end that he and Andrea were on their way out. The boy hung up and paged Mont a second time. Tim took a quick shower, brushed his teeth and put on his same outfit, no underwear. He opened the bathroom door

and came out with his wet hair dripping onto his clothing. He stroked his hair with the drying towel so it would dry faster.

"Has Mont called back yet?" he asked Andrea.

"No."

"Damn," Tim sighed.

It was a quarter after one when room service knocked on their door. The housekeeping lady was ready to clean, so Tim and Andrea had to leave. They went across the street to McDonalds to eat. Andrea ordered a double cheeseburger and super size fry. A Big Mac and a cup of water was all Tim could afford. After paying, he had only nine dollars left. They gobbled down the food and headed toward the bus stop. They were going to catch a bus to see if Mont was with their car. Andrea cursed the whole trip. All Tim thought about was the possibility of never seeing the car again. He should have known not to trust a street hustler. He should have gone with his first thought and said no to the offer. His instinct told him that the recovery of his vehicle was wishful thinking.

The bus stopped at the intersection of Lafayette and Eastern. Tim was relieved to see his car parked up the street. He and Andrea marched toward it quickly.

One of the boys saw them coming. "Ay, ole girl is kinda' fine. It's too bad she be getting high." He was referring to Andrea. He and his buddies directed their attention to the couple walking toward them. When Tim and his girlfriend approached, Mont and his friends were all leaned up against the car talking.

"Thanks man for letting me use yo' ride." Mont handed Tim his key ring.

"That mug running too. You want to sale it?" Tim retaliated.

"Man, why didn't you call me back when I paged you? We sat at the hotel waiting on you and you never called or showed up." Mont stopped smiling and stood up straight.

"You call yo' self trying to check me white boy?" Tim was nervous, but he didn't back down.

"Man, I just wanted to know why you didn't keep up your end of the bargain."

Mont's voice returned to normal. "Man, I'm sorry. That shit slipped my mind. Just for my fuck up though, I'm gone look out for you." He pulled Tim to the side and said, "Let me holla' at you for a minute."

He placed his arm around the white boy as they walked up the street to talk in private. Andrea opened the car door and sat inside waiting for her man.

"Why you struggling with that punk when you can have a brother on your team treating you like a queen?" the boy said. "That white boy got you out here hustling to get a bump," said a young man approaching. Andrea swung her head in the direction of the insult.

"Do you know me?"

"Naw, I don't know you," Rae-Jay spit back, then laughed and said, "I think you have potential though. Wait until he ain't around. I got a job for you."

All the guys burst out laughing. Andrea rolled her eyes and closed the car door. She rolled down her window and looked down the street to see if Tim was coming. She overlooked the ignorant ass lowlifes by playing like they weren't even standing before her. She was too busy wondering what was taking Tim and Mont so long. Andrea didn't really trust the guys around here. Mont could have been trying to do something to Tim.

Mont reached into his pocket, pulled out a small plastic bag and handed it to Tim. "I'm giving you this on the strength of, and I apologize for your inconvenience."

The boy grabbed the miniature zip lock bag and said to his homie, "Nice looking out, dude."

"That's almost a quarter; I'm in a generous mood today. Besides, my boys did leave your ride a little messy."

"That's all right," Tim said, walking toward his vehicle.

"We'll take care of the mess." He hurried to his car where his girlfriend was impatiently waiting. He jumped in, and pulled off down the street. Excitedly, he showed his girlfriend the sack, and her eyes widened with pleasure. Tim pulled out what they had left from the previous night and told Andrea to mix the two of them together.

"Don't you even want to see which one is the best?" she said. She dipped into the sack and pulled out a sample, snorting the powder up her nostril and leaning back in the car seat. When they came to a red light, Tim took a hit and did his thing before the light turned green. As they cruised down the street, Andrea complained that her stomach hurt. She told Tim that her period was about to start and they needed to stop at a store. Tim was distracted by the mess in the back seat.

"Baby, why don't you jump back there and see if those guys left us any goodies?" Andrea frowned but didn't say anything. She climbed into the back seat. Tim pulled the car over into a grocery store parking lot. The car rolled into an available space and the engine aborted. He turned toward Andrea in the back seat. "Did you find anything?"

"No, they haven't left shit back here but a damn mess. Those nasty ass dogs," she fussed.

"Well, I guess we better go in here and get the stuff you need." Andrea climbed out of the car. Tim took the leftover powder and stuck it into the glove compartment. "My mouth is dry as hell."

"Mine too." He turned away and began hawking, hoping to produce some moisture in his mouth. Andrea removed a few things from her purse and threw them on the seat. She patted the purse flat and closed the car door. They walked toward the store to gather her things.

"We are going to have to get something to wear before we go back to the hotel. I've worn this outfit for a couple of days and

I'm ready to change. Besides, this was my last pair of underwear so I definitely need to get to the mall, Kmart, or somewhere." Her boyfriend didn't say anything; instead he grabbed a shopping cart and waited for Andrea. She got behind it and pushed it into the store.

She headed for the aisle with feminine products and grabbed a jumbo box of super Tampax and threw them into the buggy. She grabbed a box of Lightdays panty liners and a bag of Always Thin maxi pads with wings. She needed the pads for the first couple of days of her menstrual, and the tampons for the last two. Andrea threw all the items into the cart and drove to the next aisle. Tim had already started stuffing small packaged food, granola bars, honey roasted peanuts, and cheese and crackers in his clothes. When the coast was clear Andrea dropped the things she needed into her purse and pushed the buggy to the side. She and her boyfriend proceeded to the front door. Her heart pounded when Andrea heard someone over the loudspeaker call for security. She tried to reach the door as quickly as possible. Tim saw a white man in a suit approaching. He glanced around the room to see if anyone was in back of him. He and Andrea were about ten feet away from the automatic sliding door. Tim wasn't prepared to be caught so if anyone approached, he was prepared to run. A women's voice rang out, the loudest amongst the other patron in the crowded store. Andrea looked toward the woman and thought, Three more steps and she'd be out the store. Tim was right behind his girlfriend.

"It said a dollar ninety-nine on the sign that was hanging up on the shelf, so you better call somebody because I'm not paying no three-fifty nine for no damn Ritz crackers."

The lady standing in line three was causing quite a commotion about being overcharged for some crackers. The couple saw their escape and took it. While the upset lady was fussing and creating a scene, Andrea and Tim dashed through the automatic doors and began to jog to the car. They were both wound up and flustered. Once the lady started yelling, Andrea thought for sure that her and Tim were about to go to jail.

In the car, their hearts were racing. As she unloaded all of her stolen items, Tim started the car and screeched out of the parking lot. By the time they got on the freeway, his fidgety accomplice had the sack out of the glove compartment and was about to do her a one on one. When she finished, his passenger passed the bag of leftovers to her man. He pulled the car into a gas station and stopped at pump eight. The boy took a quick hit and placed the bag on the front seat. He pumped five dollars worth of gas and hung the handle into its holder. When he came out of the store, Tim placed two ice cold Mountain Dews on the seat and climbed in. One bottle was already open, so Andrea took a big gulp from it. The drink was very cold and quenched her dry mouth and throat. The car headed to the closest mall.

They hit a couple stores in a hurry and went back to the car to unload. When the couple re-entered the mall, they went to the Guess Store. Tim distracted the nosy sales lady, getting her to assist him. Andrea got away with two pair of jeans and a shirt. The two walked into Banana Republic. Andrea boosted a pair of jeans and a shirt for Tim and he grabbed some things. Tim and his girl hit a lingerie store. He gripped his baby about ten pairs of underwear. She grabbed some bras. Bonnie and Clyde were out of there and back in the car in minutes. They had enough merchandise to exchange for eighty-five dollars worth of nose candy and a little cash for a room. They each had enough clothes to last a few days.

It was a quarter after seven when Andrea and Tim got back to the hood in search of Mont or his boys. When Mont noticed the car, he walked toward it to see what the two of them wanted. He approached the driver's side. Tim told the boy that he and Andrea had some things he might be interested in. Andrea held up the jeans and asked Mont to get in the back seat.

The boy yelled to his buddy, "Ay, man, they got some gear for sale." His friend ran toward them. The boys climbed into the back seat of the car and looked over the clothing.
Mont's friend asked, "How much y'all letting these go for?"

"You can get those jeans, and that Levi outfit in exchange for a whole, and a quarter gram of dust."

"Bet," Andrea said to Mont.

"You can get the other two pair of jeans for... I'm gone give you the hook up." She paused, then negotiated. "Just give me sixty-five for both of them." Mont dug into his pocket and pulled out a wad of money. His friend handed Andrea two sacks. She checked them out while waiting for Mont to give her the money. Finally, he tossed her the cash and got out of the car. Andrea separated and counted the wadded up bills carefully before Tim pulled off. He had remained silent throughout the transaction because Andrea was better at working deals than he was. She confirmed the money was all there and the car rolled down the street. Now it was time to go and chill and get high all night.

The couple relaxed in a bath together and enjoyed their drugs. Afterwards they made love and did a few more lines. They were so busy getting high, they hadn't touched their fast food. Tim grabbed the remote control and turned the television on. He flipped through the channels to see if he could catch a good movie. Andrea told him what she'd been thinking about.
"You know what, baby? I'm getting tired of sleeping from hotel room to hotel room. I really do think it's time that we tried to get our own place."

"I know," Tim sighed. "I wish Erin and I had never fallen out. At least I could have gotten a sack on credit, that way I could hustle up on us a place." Tim used to sell for Erin until he messed up his money by using too much of the product, and going overboard on splurging on Andrea. He held his head downward in disgust. "That's all right, though, because I'm going to start looking for a job so I can get us a place to call our own. As a matter of fact, I'm going to start looking tomorrow. Since I have new clothes, I can get up early in the morning and look for a job."

"I can get a job too," Andrea got up and reached for the magazine with the drugs on it. She did half a line and fell on the bed. Tim didn't take a hit this time, he continued lying in the bed in silence. Andrea took the remote from him because she wasn't interested in watching the channel he'd stopped on. He closed his eyes and fell into deep thought. Andrea was talking, but he was deep in thought and didn't hear her.

Tim was thinking about his life and how it had changed so quickly. He'd traded riches for rags, to be with Andrea. If he had stayed in school, he could be graduating and going to college this summer. He used to have big hopes and dreams, but now his days consisted of hustling and stealing to get by and to support his and his girlfriend's constant cocaine appetite, a habit he'd once had control of. He remembered when every female wanted to be his girl and every guy wanted to be him. Tim hated what he'd become!

He forced back the tears by burying his face into the pillow. Tim could remember himself not long ago, living happily with his parents. He was going to school every day, and getting good grades. He was making good money and had finally gotten connected with the girl he'd always wanted. But then something happened. His dad could not accept the fact that he continued to see Andrea, so Tim had to go. No one in his family had ever dated outside their own race, and Tim was the rebel. He and his father stayed into it so much, he finally left to have some peace. He'd grown tired of sneaking around to be with the girl he loved. He didn't care what color Andrea was; he loved her with all his heart. At the time, he thought he had to leave home to be with her, so that's what he did. Now, Tim was having second thoughts. If he had known he would end up in the situation he was in, he would have never left. He'd gone down skid row in a few months shy of a year and had taken Andrea with him.

"Now look at you," the voice inside him cried. "Look at what you are."

Tim thought about his parents, recalled their disappointment when he admitted his drug use. That was one more reason for his father to remind him what a failure he was. Instead of trying to get him help or talking to him, Tim's parents disowned him. He missed his family and his younger brother Bobby. He had not seen or talked to him since he left home. He was tired of the life he was living. He wanted out.

His ambition to be anything was gone, and he'd long ago stopped caring about his appearance. He had no place to call home and no one who cared about him besides Andrea, and she was in the same predicament as he was. They needed a change of pace. The time they spent stealing and getting high was getting them nowhere and Tim acknowledged that. He had to make changes in his life.

All night he sat up searching for answers. When morning came, Tim was too tired to get up. Andrea jumped up chipper and jolly. They showered together and got dressed to get something to eat. The hotel offered free breakfast and Andrea wanted to get down there before it was all gone. When they finished eating, they decided to fill out some job applications. By the end of the day they had no money, no hotel, and the car had only a little over a quarter tank of gas. Andrea became irritated because she wanted to get high. Not having a place to stay rattled her more. The couple sat in a vacant parking lot trying to decide their next move.

An hour later, Andrea became so aggravated that her skin itched. Her aggravation was from wanting to get high. She told her man, "Maybe we can ride over to see if Mont wants to get the car tonight. That way we can at least get enough cash for a room."

"Well I guess it's worth a try," Tim said. When they arrived in the hood, Andrea jumped out of the car. She didn't see any of the boys standing out. It was about thirty- six degrees, so the guys were probably up in the house on the corner where all the junkies got high. The tenement was rented by some fiend named Betty who let in anyone who had dope.

Andrea walked up the stairs to the house. When she got to the front door, she looked back at Tim before knocking. He sat anxiously awaiting some good news. A guy asked who it was before opening the door and saw Andrea standing there. He didn't know her name, but remembered her face. She asked if Mont was around. The boy said that he'd ran somewhere real quick.

"What you need?" he asked just as Rae-Jae walked up. "I can straighten you out." Rae-Jae stared her up and down and Andrea turned away from him. He was making her nervous, and she didn't like him. She didn't want him saying anything to her, but he did anyway.

"What up, shorty?" Rae-Jae chanted.

She spoke in a low voice. "I was just coming to holla' at Mont."

The other boy walked off and Rae-Jae walked toward Andrea. He dug into his pocket.

"How much you want?" he said after he pulled out the sack. Just looking at the dope was enough to make Andrea's skin crawl. Her face was so wet with perspiration she looked as if she had been running a marathon.

"Well, I was coming over to see if he wanted to get the car tonight," she said.

"Mont just rode out in a ride, so he ain't gone need y'all tonight." As Andrea turned to walk out, Rae-Jae asked, "Where is your boy?"

"He's outside," she answered and continued for the door. "Tell Mont I stopped by."

"What if I say I have a proposition for you?" Andrea turned the door knob and stopped to hear what he had to say. She did not turn around.

"You can get some work up in here."

"What about some credit? I can get you some clothes tomorrow if you front me something until then."

"I don't do credit."

"Well, what kind of work you talking about?" Rae-Jae had a big grin on his face. "Come on over here and I'll tell you," he said. "I'll give you something that's way better than that powder."

She hesitated, then said, "What do you mean?"

Rae Jae held his hand out to reveal a handful of manila colored pebbles. Andrea's reaction was ghostly. Her small frame fidgeted nervously. She knew what he had in his hand was rock cocaine and to accept it would be crossing the line, but she desperately wanted to get high. She fished a little bit to see if she could get what she really wanted.

"I don't want that, I want some soft," she said.

"Well, this is all I got, and like I said, this gone get you way more fucked up than that soft." Andrea looked at him with a weary expression. Rae- Jae had grown impatient and had closed his hand. "Look, you can just come back when..." She cut him off!

"You wanna use the car?"

"Naw," he responded. "I wanted you to do something else."

"My man is waiting for me."

"I know," he smirked as he walked closer to her. Andrea walked backwards, he was invading her private space.

"You don't have any powder for real?" Rae -Jae started, unbuckling his pants.

"I might find some if you give me a lil' head." He'd totally disrespected her! She looked toward the front door and back at the thug. Her feelings were hurt. He persisted pulling down his pants and gripping his piece in his hand, massaging it as he walked closer to her.

"How you just gone come out and talk to me like that. You know I got a man," she said.

The boy walked up to Andrea and grabbed her arm. She stared at him, and then toward the door. Her eyes watered as Rae-Jae pulled her closer to him.

"My man is in the car waiting on me," she yelled.

"It ain't gone take that long, he whispered." He spoke as if she was his girl and he was trying to get her to go all the way for the first time. "Come on now." He gripped her wrist tighter and escorted Andrea toward the wall. She was so scared she didn't know what to do. Her eyes stayed focused on the door. She wished Tim would blow the horn. Rae-Jae reached into his pocket, but kept what he had in his hand concealed. "Come on," he said.

Her body shook like a wet puppy. She wished she could get high just to escape this situation. Andrea's awareness evaporated. Her mind focused only on getting high. Her mouth became moist just thinking about what Rae-Jae might have in his hand. She thought about how a hit would make her feel. Her most passionate moment was when the dope traveled up her nostrils and dispensed a relaxing sensation throughout her body. Andrea thought about how the cocaine would last through the night and put her out of her misery until morning. She took one more look toward the front door, and back at the boy. Andrea allowed him to have his way. She got down on her knees and her mouth grabbed hold of his chocolate stick. She didn't mean to betray Tim but her actions would benefit the both of them.

Minutes later, Rae-Jae was hooping and hollering like he'd lost his mind. He sure didn't sound like the same punk who was always talking like he was so big and bad. Andrea got up and held her hand out. After relieving himself, he reached into his bag of tricks and passed Andrea one of the miniature zip lock bags. He also gave her one of the smallest rocks he had and told her to try it. Andrea briefly inspected the rock and threw it in her pocket. She kept the small bag of powder in the palm of her hand and rushed to the door. She had been inside for about twenty minutes and knew Tim would be wondering what was taking her so long. She had to make up a story by the time she got to the car, but her mind was too crowded. She briefly thought about what she'd done and the tears poured down her face. She felt so humiliated that she needed a hit. She opened the bag and dipped her pinky finger inside. Andrea dug out a small bump and snorted it. She waited for the hit to take effect. Wiping away the tears, she ran to the car where her boyfriend was waiting.

When she climbed in, Tim asked what had taken so long. Andrea threw him the sack and said that one of the boys had given it to her on credit. She stated that her taking orders for the next day was what took her so long. They rode off, with no place to go and not a whole lot of gas to get there.

Tim looked at the gas gauge and told his girlfriend, "We can't get too much farther because we don't have any gas." Tim's voice distracted her hypnotic daze.

"Wha, wha...," she answered.

"We don't have any gas," he repeated. Andrea leaned over to see what the gauge was reading.

"My cousin Monet lives about ten minutes from here. Do you think that we can make it over there?" she asked.

"Does she still live over there off of La Grave?"

"Yes."

"Do you think she'll let us stay at her house for the night?"

"Yeah! That's my family. We're cool like that." Even though Andrea hadn't talked to her cousin in six or seven months, she knew Monet would house her and her man for the night. "You know the way don't you?"

"Yeah," Tim answered as he turned left onto the main street. In about seven minutes, the couple pulled up in front of Andrea's cousin's apartment. Monet lived in a small place right on the border of the ghetto. It was 9:47 p.m. Andrea and her boyfriend hoped Monet was home and up. Monet was in college, so she was likely to be in bed. The girl got out of the car and walked up to the door. She tapped her knuckles on the plexi-glass window and stepped back. After standing there for about thirty seconds, Andrea banged a little harder. Soon, a small section of the curtain opened about a third of the way. Monet's eyes peered through the tiny lookout hole. She could see it was her cousin and a white guy. She shook her head and took a few steps back after she unlocked her front door.

"Girl, I have to be at work at eight in the morning," she said. Andrea retaliated. "I'm sorry, cousin, but Tim and I needed a place to sleep tonight because we're too tired to drive all the way on the other side of town to our domains." Monet looked at Andrea suspiciously.

"It's cool, but y'all have to leave in the morning when I leave for work." Andrea sounded just like her mother.

"Fine." Andrea and Tim followed Monet into the living room.

"I'll get you guys some blankets and you can sleep in here." Tim sat on the sofa and Andrea asked where was the bathroom. Monet turned toward the hall and pointed her finger. Andrea excused herself, leaving Monet and Tim staring at each other. They were strangers, and Andrea had not introduced them.

Andrea sat on the toilet and pulled out her bag. Nervously, she reached into the bag and dug out a small portion with her finger. She did a quick one on one and let her head fall back on her shoulders. Out of her pocket came the rock she'd worked for. She wasn't planning on smoking it, or telling Tim she had it. Rae-Jae was trying to get her hooked and she wasn't falling for it. The thought of him nauseated her and brought her to tears. Yeah, he was trying to make her sink but she was going to turn the tables. What she had done to satisfy her horrible habit, made Andrea sick. She slid the rock back into her pocket. She got up from the toilet hoping to use what she had as collateral to get what she really wanted.

As she reached for the doorknob, out of the corner of her eye Andrea observed a pair of her cousins' blue jeans hanging on the dirty clothes hamper. She paused and listened for voices on the other side of the door. Andrea reached for the pants and probed through the pockets to see if there was anything interesting inside. To her surprise, she stumbled upon a folded crisp twenty-dollar bill in the back left pocket. She looked toward the door again. As bad as she hated to steal from her cousin, she knew her and her man needed money. She pocketed the twenty, took the jeans, and stuffed them into the hamper. She figured if they weren't visible Monet wouldn't think about them. Deep down she knew what she was doing was wrong, but Monet wasn't going to miss it. Shit, she had a job so how could she miss twenty measly dollars? Andrea finally flushed the toilet and turned off the bathroom light.

Monet woke them up right before she was ready to walk out the door. Andrea jumped up from the floor and nervously folded the blankets. She started a conversation with Monet to see if she had discovered her missing twenty dollars. "Do you have to take Deshawn over to Auntie Dorothy's?"

"Yeah, and I am kind of running late. I hate to put you all out like this, but I only have one key and my door has to be locked with the key, otherwise you know I wouldn't mind doing a favor for my cousin."

"It ain't no big deal, Monet. We just needed to rest our eyes. We appreciate you for letting us stay."

Tim got up from the floor and headed to the bathroom. He wanted to rinse out his mouth and splash some water on his face. He was hoping Andrea could get a few dollars from her cousin, otherwise they weren't going far. He was praying the car would start. As they waited for Tim to come out of the bathroom, Monet asked Andrea, "So where exactly do you guys live? Auntie Caroline says that you and her don't really speak anymore. She says that she hasn't heard from you in months."

"Well..," Andrea stuttered, hoping an answer would pop into her head. It was too damn early for Monet to be nosy.

"We live over in Wyoming."

"Dang, you do live far." What were you guys doing over this way?"

Andrea had to think of another lie.

"Ah..., we were visiting one of Tim's friends."

"Oh, okay." Tim came out of the bathroom. Andrea quickly jumped up.

"Let me use the bathroom real quick, and I'll be ready to go," she said. She ran into the restroom and closed the door. Five minutes later she stepped out of the bathroom and said she was ready to hit the road. Monet grabbed her son and the four of them walked out the front door toward the car. Tim and Andrea sped off to the gas station. Andrea told Tim that Monet loaned her twenty dollars so they had enough money to get some gas and something to eat. Then they could go to the mall and get some stuff to sell. They had to make some money or they'd be sleeping in the car come night fall.

The Encounter

Sheila and Delvin had been dating several months and were becoming close. On her birthday, Delvin decided to take her out. Sheila made an appointment to get her hair done. She would have loved to hang out with her girl, but she hadn't talked to Elaine in a long time. Since her husband talked his way back into the house, Elaine had been trying to reconcile her marriage. She did a good job of avoiding her friend. Sheila was tired of being in the middle of Elaine and her husband's disputes, just so they could get back together anyway. She was disappointed that her girl hadn't called her and wished her happy birthday.

Delvin drove Sheila to the beauty shop, and went to pick up a dress Sheila had on layaway to wear for the night. He also wanted to get her something special for her birthday so he needed to be alone to do that. When Delvin dropped her off in front of the beauty shop, he told her he would be back as soon as he left the mall.

She pranced into the beauty shop with a smile that spread all the way across her face. The owner, Niecy, had a contemporary style expressed throughout her exquisitely decorated salon. The reception counter glimmered like gold glistening on the bottom of a wishing well. Behind the desk were glass shelves that had an attractive display of all the products available for purchase. Off to the left was a voluminous waiting area with a couch large enough to seat four women comfortably. Folding chairs were lined up in rows. In the back of the shop was a little room with a soft drink machine and microwave. In the corner was a small square table with four chairs for customers who brought in food, which was not allowed in the salon area. African paintings lined the spacious walls and healthy green plants hung from the ceiling, giving the salon a comfortable, homey feeling, and every seat held a different class female ranging from ghetto queen to a business buppie waiting to get her hair either silky weaved, chemically straightened, or cut and curled into a short wispy millennium style.

She refused to accept who she saw in the waiting area. It was her vicious enemy whom she had not seen, in over a year. Why did she have to run into this huzzy on the day she was supposed to be happy?

Caroline, along with the rest of the patrons, had their eyes glued on Sheila as she stepped up to the receptionist's desk in her super tight jeans and sweater. Sheila saw Caroline eyeing her and thought. "I don't want yo' man, I got my own." The only thing Sheila wanted from Thomas was that one seventy-five a week child support check.

Caroline stared at the tramp and thought, "She must have tricked up on enough money to get her hair done." She couldn't wait to tell her sister about this.

Sheila's stylist met her just as she was about to take a seat. Trisha was escorting someone out and was ready to shampoo Sheila before her next client showed up. Sheila followed Trisha back to her station where she caped her. After that, the two of them headed to the shampoo bowl.

Two hours later, Sheila was all done up and ready to go. She had her hair cut into a layered bob pressed silky smooth with whispy flat iron strips. As she walked toward the reception area to pay, Sheila noticed that the beauty shop was more crowded than it was when she came in. It was to be expected, being that it was a Friday evening. She looked around the room for her enemy, and within seconds, Caroline was spotted. She was in Lonnie's chair. Sheila walked toward the bathroom passing Caroline and rolling her eyes. When she stepped out, she closed the door and sighed angrily as she walked toward the door. She wished Delvin would hurry up.

Delvin stepped in the door of the beauty shop and stopped. He glanced around the room filled with women. He was looking for his. As he scanned the beautiful surroundings, Delvin was astonished to observe his ex-sister-in-law occupying one of the chairs. Caroline waved to him once. She said to Delvin. "What in the world are you doing here?" she asked. He looked for Sheila.

"Oh I'm here to pick up my friend," he said. Sheila walked toward Delvin wondering why he was talking to her enemy. Delvin said, "What a coincidence. You two get your hair done at the same place."

Caroline was thinking. Now when the motherfucker was married to her sister, for damn near fifteen years, he ain't never took her to no beauty shop. Caroline was ticked off just thinking about it and hoped her anger didn't show.

The nosy hairdresser listened as she added the final touches to Caroline's do. She knew about her client's relationship with the infamous Sheila and that they couldn't stand each other.

"Ex-sister-in-law," Sheila reiterated shockingly.

"Yeah, that's my ex-wife's sister." Caroline rolled her eyes and smiled.

"I guess you get around, ha Sheila?"

Sheila frowned, threw her hand on her hip and was about to straight read her opponent just as Delvin said,

"You two know each other?"

Sheila looked at her man with an "I can't stand this bitch" pronouncement on her face that was strong enough to kill. She answered, "You can say that," as her arm reached out and wrapped around Delvin's waist. His voice calmed her and brought her back to her senses before she embarrassed herself and him in a shop full of people. Delvin wondered if it was safe for him to say anything else.

"Well, I guess we better be going," he said. He reached toward his back pocket. "How much is it?"

"Oh, baby, I already paid." She looked toward her friend in the chair and continued. "Let's go, baby," then said another goodbye to her stylist, rolled her eyes at Caroline one more time, and walked out. Caroline figured it was the best thing for her to do because she was burning to tell Delvin exactly what kind of slut he was dealing with. She couldn't wait to call her sister and let her know who her ex was screwing. She was so anxious, she handed Lonnie three twenty-dollars bills and left.

Later that night as they prepared to go out, Delvin asked if Elaine was going to meet them at the club.

"I doubt it," Sheila confessed sadly. Since her man came home, I haven't heard from her. I thought, since it was my birthday, she would at least have given me a call, but she hasn't. I guess she doesn't have time for me anymore."

"It's doesn't matter. I am more than delighted to spend your special day with you." Delvin said as he walked up and planted a big kiss on her soft lips.

Bad Luck

The frantic girl grabbed three pairs of denim jeans and stuffed them into her oversized purse. Her hands trembled as she zipped the bag halfway and walked down the narrow aisle of the store. Tim had walked off. She preferred they stay together so she could watch his back and he could watch hers. Andrea's head rotated from right to left as she came upon a table loaded with name brand men's jeans on sale for fifty dollars a pair. That was a come up because she could still sell them for half of the regular price. She fumbled through the garments for her size. She couldn't get anything under size thirty six because the smaller sizes were too hard to get rid of. Guys liked jeans a couple sizes bigger. She bundled up three pair and stuffed them under the sleeve of her jacket. Her heart pounded as if it were about to jump out of her chest. She was so paranoid. It seemed everyone knew she had store merchandise in her purse. She had to get out of the store without the nosy store attendants seeing her. The door was only about fifteen feet away and she was ready to make a break for it. Glancing around the room, Andrea spotted Tim. She signaled to let him know she was headed for the car. When she made a move for it, Andrea looked back to see if anyone was following. Tim looked through the jeans on the table she'd just left. Another guy was standing beside him so Andrea couldn't get his attention.

Tim waited for Andrea to get to the door, then he started toward it. Andrea was outside already. She unlocked the car door and ducked inside. Tim hadn't come out yet. She wondered if he had gone back to get something. Frantically, the girl unloaded her stolen goods into a shopping bag and sat back trying to calm her nerves. She wished Tim would hurry up because he was making her nervous.

She waited for him in the car for what seemed like twenty minutes before she decided to go in and see what was taking him so long. She hoped she wouldn't have to look for him. As she reached for the door handle, Andrea felt an excruciating pain in her stomach. She leaned forward placing her hand over it. "Please God," she moaned. "Please let this awful pain go away."

She remained in that position until the pain was bearable, then opened the door. She climbed out, shut the door behind her and walked toward the store.

A police car drove up and parked in front of the door. Andrea looked down and did a three sixty in the parking lot. She patted her pockets as if she had lost something. When the officer got out of the car, she turned around and walked back toward the car. Her heart pumped out of control as she climbed into the vehicle. She leaned back in the seat crying. What was she going to do if her man had gotten caught shoplifting?

The officer came back outside exactly thirty-one minutes later, and her boyfriend was walking beside him in handcuffs. Tim mouthed something to her as he waited for the officer to open the door, but Andrea couldn't quite make out the words. As she waited, her man got into the cruiser. She felt alone and lost. She didn't know what to do. The police car pulled away. Andrea leaned her head back into the headrest and cried. The harder she cried, the more her stomach ached.

She cried even harder when she thought about what Tim might be going through. He had never been to jail and now was not the time to be going. He and his parent weren't on good terms. How would he get out? She didn't have the money or anyone to call. She remembered getting caught shoplifting and how awful the experience was. At least she was still a minor then, but Tim was not.

"Oh no," she, punched the dashboard. "Tell me this is not happening!"

It was getting dark so Andrea drove away from the mall parking lot. She decided to drive to the hood and get rid of the merchandise she had. She had at least three hundred dollars worth of stuff that she wasn't letting go for nothing less than one fifty;

she needed all the money she could get.

Monet sat on her sofa eating a bag of microwave popcorn and talking to Malcolm on the phone. He was telling her how nervous he was about a history final he had the next morning. He'd only been studying an hour before Monet called. Her voice took his thoughts away from his studies, and he wanted to give Monet his undivided attention. He had told her he couldn't talk long, but they'd already been on the telephone over thirty minutes. She told him she couldn't wait for him to come home and she missed him very much. Monet said she was counting down the days until he came home. He said he was too, and that he had a surprise for her.

When Malcolm hung up the telephone he began to smile. What Monet didn't know was when he got home his dad was going with him to pick out her an engagement ring. Malcolm told his father that he was going to marry Monet once he graduated from college and buying the engagement ring would make it official. He wanted the whole world to know that he planned on spending the rest of his life with her.

Dorothy and her family arrived home from Bible study. Sullivan carried in their dinner as everyone headed for the kitchen. Dorothy washed her hands and took five paper plates and plastic forks from the pantry. She brought them back to the table and fixed everyone a portion of the KFC meal they picked up on the way home. After dinner, she told the children to take their baths and get ready for bed. Dorothy checked their homework, put them to bed then joined her husband in the shower.

After selling the merchandise she lifted from the store, Andrea drove to the Rainbow Motel. It was probably the cheapest hotel in town and a haven for twenty dollar prostitutes, twenty-four seven. The woman at the front desk munched on some spicy pork rinds and watched a small thirteen inch television. The front counter was an old wooden desk covered with piles of dusty papers, empty Coke cans, ink pens, paper clips, Vienna Sausage cans with only juice left in it, and a half eaten box of imitation Ritz crackers. Off to the side was a grey desktop index card holder. Guests still filled out index cards. In the middle of the desk sat a Soap Opera Digest magazine.

The dark skinned woman eyeballed the girl up and down. Her mouth was filled with rotten, crooked, partially missing teeth. "Can I help you?" she asked, wiping her greasy hand on her right pant leg.

"How much is it for a single room?" Andrea asked.

"Twenty-two dollars a night," the woman replied.

Andrea looked around. The place was a total dump. To ask for twenty dollars a night was insulting. The woman's eyes remained glued to the television.

"Are the rooms clean?" Andrea asked.

"What do you mean are the rooms clean?" the clerk asked angrily rolling her eyes. It was obvious Andrea was in the wrong neck of the woods. She was too finicky, looking around as if the place was contagious.

"Can I look at one?"

The woman snarled. Too pretty bitches got on her last nerve.

"Do you have an ID?"

"No," Andrea answered.

"Well, no you can't look at one."

"You have to have an ID to get a room here?"

"It's a motel, ain't it?" Andrea wanted to curse her out, but it would be worthless. The ugly ass woman probably never asked anybody for identification. The girl sucked her teeth, turned away and mumbled. "Hater."

She realized she wasn't old enough to rent the room, and she could think of no alternative. Andrea decided to drive to where she sold the clothes to see if somebody there could get a room for her. She asked a wandering junky if she would get the room in her name. The lady agreed, only after Andrea showed her the rock she had. The girl hopped into the car and sped down the road.

The lady, Mary, begged for the dope. Andrea told her to calm down, she was making her nervous.

"Just let me have a piece of it right now, and you can give me the rest later," Mary begged.

"All right," Andrea shouted as she passed the dope to the lady. "Break off a piece."

"Okay, okay," Mary whispered and pulled out her pipe. She broke off a small piece and handed the rest back. Before she knew it, the woman had loaded up the glass tube. She lit the end of it and sucked down the thick smoke. She took a long pull and threw her head back. Andrea looked at her and then back at the road.

Mary looked over and said, "You want a hit?"
Andrea didn't say anything. The fiend turned her head and struck the lighter again, igniting the fiery orange flame. She inhaled until the pipe made a hollowing noise as it emptied. She exhaled. "Damn, that's some good ass dope." Andrea pulled up to a red light and stopped. "So, that dope is good, ha?" she asked.

"Yeah, let me break off another small piece," said Mary as the light turned green.

"So how does it make you feel?" Andrea asked.

"It makes you feel good. It makes you feel good all over." Mary moaned and wiggled her body. She continuously rubbed her legs and arms. "You got to try it for yourself." Mary soon broke out into a song. "It makes you feel good, it makes you feel good all over," she sang, mocking the lyrics of one of Stephanie

Mills' songs. Her voice sounded really nice too. Andrea looked at the woman as if she were crazy.

"You have to calm down!" Mary became serene as she sat back in the seat. Thirty seconds later, she asked, "Are we almost there?"

"Yeah, I'm going to stop at this one right over here." The girl put on her signal light and pulled into the right lane. The hotel was about a block up the street.

It wasn't much better than the motel with the hating desk clerk, but it would have to do. Andrea needed someplace to sleep. She pulled into the parking lot and told Mary to tell the receptionist she needed one single room for two nights. When the check-in was complete, Andrea handed the clerk the money and they got the key. Mary asked Andrea if she could come in her room and smoke the rest of her dope before she hitched a ride back to her neighborhood. She didn't really want to be alone, so Andrea invited her in.

The young lady kicked off her shoes and fell onto one of the twin beds. She'd had a long depressing day and couldn't wait until it was over. She closed her eyes, thinking about her man. She wondered if he'd made his first phone call and, if so, who he had called. She didn't know how long it would be before she'd see him, but she hoped it was soon because Andrea was going crazy.

Mary asked if she could have the other piece of the rock since she had completed her job. Andrea got out of bed, dug into her pocket, and took out what was left of the rock. Mary grabbed it and walked to the table. She pulled some utensils from her purse and removed the screen from the pipe, replacing it with a new one. Her new friend asked.

"Let me try it."

"Say what?" Mary was shocked.

"I might as well try that shit since everything is fucked

up anyways."

Mary looked at the pipe and then at the young girl sitting on the bed. She got up and walked toward her. She handed the pipe to the girl. Andrea froze for a minute. She wiped the mouthpiece off with her shirt, before placing it in her mouth.

"Gone head, hit, Mary said." The young lady placed the lighter at the end of the glass tube and ignited it. Andrea inhaled and passed it back to her friend. The lady took the pipe and it finished off. Andrea felt so hype after hitting the rock that she wanted to hit it again, but it was all gone. It was a good high but, she had no intentions of getting hooked.

She told Mary. "That is the shit."

"Yeah, it's the shit all right." Her eyes watered, and her voice was hoarse. "It's the shit that will break you down to the lowest you can go." Tears filled her eyes.

"Once upon a time, I was a legal secretary living happy with my husband and two kids. Well, he up and left us one day, saying he was tired of being married and he needed some time to sort things out. My life was in shambles! I felt like living was no longer important, and I needed a way out. A friend from work suggested I try this new drug that would mellow me out and relax my body. It was supposed to take my mind away from all the problems I was going through. That day I became the same person that my husband was. I left my kids with my mother and haven't turned back since. I've been on this shit for almost ten years and now it's all I got to live for, but I ain't mad, though."

She perked up and wiped away her tears. "My mama is taking good care of my kids and I'm gone be all right. I got my life and they got theirs. I feel like staying out of their lives, while I'm like this, would be best. I don't want them to see me like this."

Andrea grabbed her purse and searched through it frantically looking for the package she'd bought.

"My man just went to jail today," she confessed, "and I don't have shit either. The only thing I got is forty funky dollars that ain't gone last me too long."

She opened the package and scooped up a small amount of the dope with her pinky finger. She snorted up her nostrils and offered it to her friend. Mary jumped up and grabbed it. She did a one on one and handed the package back to the girl. Andrea closed the bag and stuck it in her purse. Mary whipped out a pack of cigarettes, passed one to her new friend, and lit another one.

They exchanged sob stories, snorted cocaine, and smoked cigarettes for hours. Finally, Andrea passed out on the bed. Mary left at 3:41a.m.without telling Andrea she was leaving. She didn't have time to spend in no hotel room all night, especially not with a kid who needed to go home to her parents.

When Andrea woke up the next morning, she turned on the television to the local news station. It was eight-forty. She felt like shit and had a pounding headache. She wiped the sleep from her eyes and looked toward the bathroom. Since the door was open, she knew Mary had left. She tried to stand, but sat back down because her head was spinning. She sat on the edge of the bed, drained and exhausted. Her stomach growled as she tried again to stand up. Andrea was probably having these weird symptoms because of smoking that rock with Mary.

The girl drug her tired body in the bathroom and flicked the light switch. She stared in the mirror before sitting on the toilet. She thought about Tim. Today was the second day he was gone. If only they had some way of communicating.

Andrea flushed and washed her hands. She ran out the bathroom and to the main room. She ran toward the nightstand and reached for the phone book, searching for the number to the county jail. She wanted to call and find out about her man. She found the number, picked up the telephone, and dialed. An operator answered after about the seventh or eighth ring. She asked the name of the inmate the girl was inquiring about. "Timothy Doberson, please."

"Do you know what he's being charged with?"

"Shoplifting!"

Andrea could hear the woman typing. A few seconds later the woman came back stating that Tim's bond was twenty-five hundred dollars.

"Thank you," Andrea hung up. She fell back on the bed and burst into tears. He would never get out. How was he going to get out when his family didn't have anything to do with him and there was no way she could come up with the money? Andrea wept until her throat was dry. She hadn't spoken to her family in over four months, and she didn't have any friends. She spent all her time with Tim, and living without him seemed like the end of the world. She couldn't even go see him because she didn't have identification.

Her stomach growled. Andrea needed to get herself together and ride to one of those fast food restaurants to eat. She wiped away the tears and went to the bathroom. The mirror reflected her swollen face and red eyes. She drug her body back to the main room where she grabbed her duffle bag from the chair and fumbled through it for something to wear. She pulled out a new pair of blue jeans and a sweatshirt she had racked the day before and took the tags off. Andrea took out underwear and laid her outfit on the bed. She walked into the bathroom and turned on the shower. What is life like on the street when you have no one? All she had was forty dollars, and if she didn't make something happen by the next day, she would be homeless.

She climbed out of the shower and got dressed. Her thought was to shoot down the street to the Checkers to grab a Big Buford combo meal. She brushed her hair into a ponytail and cleaned out her bag. She pulled out of the hotel parking lot and down the street. She had no license, or insurance on the car, and the tags were expired, so she had to drive carefully. Five-O would pull you over for anything at the beginning of the month.

She pulled into the drive-up at Checkers and ordered a Big Buford combo with cheese and a vanilla shake. The worker recited her total and Andrea pulled the car around to the window. The cashier opened the window. "Three ninety-one, please."

The aroma from the grilled burgers smelled good. The worker stood in the window waiting as Andrea was pulling out everything but money. The employee sighed and Andrea said to herself, I know I didn't leave it on the bed with the rest of the stuff.

"Damn," she moaned and "I'm sorry, but I think I left my money at home on the bed. I'm going to have to come right back."

"All right," the girl said aggravated. As Andrea pulled off she heard the fast food lady yell. "I need a manager over here for a cancellation."

Back in the room, she dug through the purse that she emptied onto the bed earlier. There was paper, empty candy wrappers, and some change, but no money. Andrea dumped her purse onto the bed and still did not see her money. She got down on her knees and looked under the bed; there was no money. She went into the bathroom and grabbed the jeans she wore the day before, searching through the pockets, and found no money. Andrea went back and sat down on the bed. She realized that Mary must have robbed her. There was no other explanation. She beat her legs with her fist. All she could think about was riding into the hood to find Mary and beat the shit out of her crackhead ass. It was hard to believe that Mary had robbed her when she'd given the whore a whole twenty piece just for renting her a room; and let the bitch toot some of her powder. "Just wait until the next time I see that trick," Andrea moaned.

She needed to eat. Her stomach was growling so she

decided to go to the grocery store to boost something to eat. Then, she would hit the stores so she could make enough money to keep a roof over her head.

In the grocery store, Andrea boosted a few packs of lunch meat and some cheese, and whatever else could stuff into her purse. She headed for the car. Once she got to the car to eat her Sardines and crackers, she chomped down a couple of cracker sandwiches before rolling out of the parking lot. Now, all she had to do was find a store where she could boost some small items that would add up to some money. She was too paranoid to go back to the mall, so she went to a nearby Wal-Mart.

Andrea walked into Wal-Mart with her Coach bag on her shoulder. After finishing the drink she had bought outside in the machine, she placed the empty can on a shelf and went to the music department. If she couldn't sell anything else, music was sure to go fast. She searched for the most popular CD's and grabbed seven good ones and stuffed them into her purse. Her mission was successful. She headed for another aisle where she could conveniently pick up more small items. She looked for things she could easily lift and sell.

She came upon the men's underwear. Her sticky fingers searched the racks for the most expensive and most popular sizes. Andrea grabbed some boxer briefs in packs of three because those were what Tim wore. There were different assortments, so she grabbed several packs of each. After she stuffed those items, her bag was getting full. She decided to finish in the clothing aisle. She could return the clothing for cash because she knew no gear from Wal-Mart could be sold on the street. She looked at the price tags on two shirts. They were each seventeen ninety-nine. She balled them up and headed toward the door, trying to disguise the clothes. A woman was walking behind her, but Andrea just kept on going. She looked to the left, then to the right. Her hands were sweating. She didn't have time to get caught and if that woman tried to grab her she would swing on her and run. As she got closer to the exit, Andrea took another look behind her and stuffed the shirts as she rushed through the garden center. She took this exit because those damn buzzers weren't blocking the doors. When she reached the parking lot, she ran to her car. She got in, and raced off.

Driving down the street, the girl unloaded her purse, throwing the items onto the seat beside her. Her heart was racing so fast she had to pull over to calm down. When she gathered her composure, she pulled the gear back into drive and was on her way again. The gas hand was kissing E. She knew she had to get some cash quick. After she sold all the CD's and underwear, she went back to Walmart to get cash for the two shirts she lifted. That was a guaranteed thirty-five dollars she could desperately use.

She got rid of all her items successfully. Back at the room, Andrea tallied her money. She had been generous by letting all the CD's and underwear go for seventy dollars, and she got back thirty-eight dollars and some change from Walmart. In the morning, she would pay for the hotel for two more nights so she had an extra day to decide what to do. She had taken twenty-five dollars to buy a sack, three-ninety one for that combo from Checkers, and some money to fill the car with gas. That hundred and eight dollars sure went fast. Her mom always used to say, "Fast money doesn't last long," and now Andrea knew what she meant.

Hustlin

It was Friday night and Caroline didn't cook on Fridays. Her daughter, husband, and she sat at Red Lobster eating some delicious, mouthwatering seafood. They shared a platter of fried shrimp. Taylor ordered a lobster dinner, and her parents ordered combination plates with steaks cooked medium well, huge, stuffed baked potatoes, and a basket of crab legs on the side. The family always splurged at whatever restaurant they agreed on. It was Taylor's choice so she picked Red Lobster because it was her favorite.

"Mom," Taylor said. "I really miss Andrea. Is there anyway you can get in touch with her so we can talk? I just want to know how she's doing and stuff."

"No, I don't have a way of getting in touch with her, Taylor. When Andrea gets a chance, I know she'll call you."

"She doesn't ever call," Taylor whined sadly.

"When she gets ready, she'll call Taylor," Thomas said to his lonesome daughter. "In the meantime you better hurry up and eat that lobster before I get to it."

"No, Daddy," she smiled as she put seafood on a cracker. The two of them laughed and dug into their food. Caroline was glad that Thomas consoled Taylor because she hated talking about Andrea. She had not seen her daughter in months and it saddened her when anybody brought up her name. She wished she could drag Andrea home, clean her up and turn her into the sweet innocent child she once was. On their way home after dinner, Thomas and Taylor talked and laughed. Caroline rode silently, tears running down her face.

Andrea was only able to live in the hotel for six days before her luck ran out. On the sixth day, she could not come up with the forty dollars to rent the room another night, so she had to go. It didn't seem like a big deal until night when she discovered she had nowhere to sleep. She only had ten dollars to her name. She planned on using half for gas and food the next day.

She'd gone to the mall earlier, but was only able to get a pair of pants that nobody wanted to buy. It was eleven seventeen p.m. and she was sitting in the parked car on the hottest block in the neighborhood because she had no place else to go. She felt safe here because the area was always busy. Junkies probed the streets day in and day out. When she saw Mont or one of his boys, she would see if one of them needed a ride anywhere, which would give her something to do besides sit in the cold lonely car.

She must have drifted off to sleep because when Rae-Jae tapped on her window, Andrea jumped. Her eyes focused on Rae-Jae and she wiped her mouth with the back of her hand and unlocked the car door to see what he wanted. Rae-Jae jumped into the passenger side and slammed the door. He smiled like the devil in disguise. "Why are you smiling?"

"What's up?" he asked.

"What do you mean, what's up?" she frowned, while sitting up straight in her seat.

"Why are you sitting out here in the cold car sleeping when you can be in a warm room relaxing?" Andrea didn't say anything. She lurked an unfriendly expression at him.

"Why you gotta' be looking like that? You act like I did something..."

"What's up Rae-Jae?" she interrupted, "What do you want?" Andrea could not stand the sight of him. He was the only person who had something to hold over her head, and he was manipulative. He might even assume she'd do anything, to get high, and she didn't like him having that incentive. She knew he would only show her the respect he showed the rest of the junkies he sold to.

"Look, you ain't even got to be acting like that. I'm trying to be nice to you."

"You must want something."

"Well, I figured what I wanted was gone benefit the both of us."

"How?"

"Well, since I don't have no wheels and you do, it would be really nice of you to give me a ride out by 28th Street. I got a room out there with double beds, and since you are out here sleeping in the car as cold as it is, I figure both of us could benefit from my proposition."

"How you know I ain't already got a room?"

"If you did, I don't think you would be out here sleeping in the car at something to three in the morning."

"Damn," she thought. She must have dozed off because the last time she looked at the clock it was eleven something.

"You think you're slick, don't you? I am not trying to screw you, Rae-Jae."

"Man, ain't nobody trying to get in your draws." He dug into his pocket and pulled out a small sack. "Look, I'll even give you this, plus a couple dollars for gas. I just want to get to my room so I can go to sleep. Ain't nothing going on out here and these motherfuckas is getting on my nerves coming with less than ten. They must think I'm a nickel and dime hustler or something. He sucked his teeth. Man, they ass got me twisted."

"Where is your room at?"

"The Lands Inn, on twenty-eighth and Wilson. You can take Grandville all the way out there and we'll be there in twenty minutes."

Rae-Jae was comfortable in his seat. His head was relaxing on the head rest. He was waiting for her to start the car and pull off, he was certain she wouldn't turn down his offer.

"Give me the sack, plus twenty dollars," she said.

"Girl, please, I wish I would give you twenty dollars and a whole quarter." He handed her the bag and dug into his pocket. "I'll give you these six ones right here." He handed them to her.

"Six dollars."

"Yeah, six dollars! I'm giving you a whole quarter, and

I'm gone let yo' ass stay in my room for free. If I give yo' ass an additional twenty dollars, we fucking." Andrea snatched the money from Rae-Jae's hand. She rolled her eyes and started the car.

The music played softly as they rolled down the street. Rae-Jae was snoring so loud, Andrea turned the radio up louder to drown it out. She was ten minutes away from the hotel when Rae-Jae's eyes popped open. "Where can we get something to eat?" he said.

"It ain't nothing open this late."

"Ain't it a Denny's out here somewhere?"

"I haven't seen a Denny's," Andrea said, "but I am a little hungry myself." The nap had given her energy, besides she'd hit the powder and was feeling good. Usually, the powder would take away her appetite, but she hadn't eaten anything besides the egg McMuffin she had for breakfast the day before. There wasn't a restaurant open in the direction they were going, so Andrea drove straight to the hotel.

She pulled into the parking lot, parked the car, and followed Rae-Jae to the room. They walked through the lobby. The desk clerk was watching television until she noticed the patrons. She greeted them. Rae-Jae noticed the complementary snacks and coffee on the table. He grabbed a few donuts, a bowl of cereal, milk, and an orange juice. He had to put the carton of milk in his pocket so he could carry everything at one time. Andrea grabbed a few snacks and they headed toward the elevator.

When they walked into the room, Andrea kicked off her shoes, put her donut and juice down, and raced toward the bathroom. When she finished, she whipped out her little sack and took a couple of hits. She looked in the mirror. Her bulging eyes made her look like her father. She wondered how her father and the rest of her family were doing. She wondered if her father had forgiven her for leaving and for finding out she wasn't a virgin anymore. She missed them, missed having a guaranteed place to lay her head everyday, and she longed for a home cooked meal. Andrea reminisced about family trips. On the streets, she had no love.

Rae-Jae poured milk into his bowl of Raisin Bran and began undressing. He unbuckled his belt and his pants dropped to his ankles. He kicked the jeans to the side and took off his shirt. He sat on the bed in his underwear. He opened the package of plastic silverware on the nightstand, digging into the personal sized cereal bowl. Within minutes, it was gone.

The boy pulled back the bedspread and hopped under the covers. Andrea sat in a chair with the remote control to the television in her hand. She was doing anything she could to avoid looking over at Rae-Jae. His frame was small, but muscularly enticing, although Andrea wasn't attracted to him. She was aware of what he was doing at all times, in case he tried something. She stopped flipping channels when she saw the BET logo pop up on the screen as a commercial faded away. She put down the remote and watched the countdown of hip-hop videos.

Rae-Jae's eyes were closed. The empty cereal bowl was still on the table and the trash can next to him.

"Guys were such pigs," she thought as she dipped her finger into her little sack and sniffed a small portion up her nose. Rae-Jae turned over on the bed and said, "If you need somebody to keep you warm you can come lay over here with me." She rolled her eyes.

"Don't even play. I'm straight."

"You need to stop acting all stuck up like that, girl. I just thought you might need a lil' lovin since yo' man is gone and all. Oh, by the way did y'all break up or what?"

"No, we didn't. He's just has to do a little time."

"What he do, get caught stealing?"

"So many questions," she thought. Andrea shook her head.

"Do you work for Channel Eight or something?"

"All right, I ain't gone say shit else to yo' high yellow ass. I'm tryin' to be nice to you and your sitting up here treating me like I'm the enemy. You act like me and you ain't never been close, and that's cold blooded because I really appreciated the time we spent together."

"Quit trippin'. You acting like we done had a relationship or something. What we did was strictly conduct business, other than that, ain't nothing."

"Whatever, man, I'll holla at you in the morning." The boy then turned toward the wall and pulled the covers over his head.

Andrea grabbed her bag and carried it into the bathroom. She locked the door behind her. She looked through her dufflebag for something to sleep in and found a pair of boxers and a t-shirt. She had a new pair of stretch pants and a t-shirt she could put on in the morning. After that, she only had one more clean outfit. She needed some money ASAP.

Rae-Jae woke her the next morning. He was standing over her with his dick sticking straight out, hard as a brick.
"Why don't you give me a little bit to take care of this." He was holding himself.

"Man, would you get out of my face?" Andrea warned as she turned away.

"Come on, man, you shouldn't even be like that. I'll give you fifty dollars right now if you just let me have a little bit."

"I should have known it was a trick to you letting me stay here."

"Man, it ain't no trick, girl. I'm trying to give you a chance to make some money."

She let him beg while she thought about his proposition. It wasn't like it was the first time she'd been involved with him.

"Where is the fifty?" she asked.

Rae-Jae reached inside the pillowcase and pulled out a big

knot. He counted out fifty dollars and handed it to the girl. She hated having sex with him, but she desperately needed the fifty dollars, so she turned over on her back and he pulled down her boxers. He wasted no time entering her from behind. Andrea remained on her knees the whole horrible seven minutes it took for Rae-Jae to handle his business. He howled and Andrea jumped up from the bed and ran into the bathroom. He used his hand to finish off his pleasureful moment.

Naked, he waited for Andrea to come out. She was in the bathroom so long, he threatened to come in. She finally, came out and the relieved young man went inside to take a shower and get dressed. His big smile made her nauseous. When Rae-Jae finished dressing the two of them grabbed their belongings and left. Rae-Jae was still smiling from ear to ear.

After Andrea dropped the boy off at "work," she cruised away down the narrow street. It was a fairly nice day, so all the regulars were on the block early. She decided to go to the mall and see what she could rack. Rae-Jae giving her fifty dollars was cool, but she gave half of it back for another sack, so all she had left was twenty-five dollars. The dope he'd given her last night was so good she'd snorted it all up before she went to sleep. She was so high she didn't even go to sleep until a quarter to seven and was up at eleven.

She needed some money to get her own room. That way she could be by herself to think about how much she missed Tim. Living on the streets wasn't the same without him. They'd both left home for the same reason, their parents refused to face reality. Her parents seemed to think not having money meant that you were nothing, and Tim's parents didn't want to face his interracial relationship.

Tim was Andrea's backbone. With him she felt she could get along fine without depending on her parents. Without him, Andrea had to do degrading things. Turning tricks was not part of her plan. A life like that would quickly make her break down and go home. With Tim around, Andrea felt loved like she felt at home. Without her man, she felt alone and afraid. All Andrea had the desire to do was get high to escape the escalated loneliness.

Just thinking about being without Tim made Andrea feel heartbroken and angry. Her stomach ached. She was having terrible cramps. Andrea bent over in the driver's seat gripping her stomach as tears ran down her light brown face. Having no friends or family to tell her everything would be okay was unfair. She felt like she'd hit rock bottom. She desperately needed Tim back in her life. She was on an emotional roller coaster, her thoughts spinning out of control. She felt tension in her forehead. She had to stop worrying to prevent a migraine from coming on.

She wiped the salty liquid from her face. Either the breakfast she'd had with Rae Jae or the coffee wasn't agreeing with her stomach. It felt like a rumbling war going on throughout her abdomen. She had to hurry and get to the mall so she could use the bathroom. She took a dip out of her package and snorted it up her right nostril. She then took two Tylenols from her purse and sipped them down with the watered down orange juice she'd taken from the restaurant. She had to prevent the headache before her muscles stiffened and ruined the rest of her day, which wasn't starting out too good in the first place. Andrea had to make some money to avoid sleeping in the car or having to deal with Rae-Jae again.

She wasn't focused on stealing. She was too depressed. She went into the ladies room, took a quick hit, and felt a burst of energy. After that she was too paranoid to boost anything. She came out of the mall empty handed.

Back at the car, Andrea took out her sack and took two hits, then sat back and tried to de- stress. Andrea cleared her mind of the pitiful reality of her life. She thought about going home. Maybe God was trying to tell her something. She knew she always had a place at home, but she didn't want to hear her mother bitch about she told her so. If she didn't go back to her parents', Andrea would need a hell of a plan, one that was going to get her paid quickly. She thought about hitting up a little shopping center, but she didn't want to risk being caught. Since Tim's arrest she'd been extremely careful and twice as paranoid. Her last resort was to drive back through the hood to see if one of the boys would want to rent the car for a small fee.

She pulled out of the drive through at Burger King and headed toward the neighborhood. It was a little after four in the afternoon and she wanted to be in a hotel relaxing, by six. She pulled up in front of the dingy white house where all the street boys probed. Andrea rolled her passenger side window down and yelled to one of the boys, "Come here for a minute." Three boys looked at each other wondering which one of them she was talking to.

"Who you talking to?" yelled one.

"I got to ask you something."

"Man, get out the car," the tallest boy with the black jeans said. Andrea huffed and cut the car off. She jumped out with the keys in her hand and walked to the porch. They were staring at her. She was acting very strange.

"What's wrong wit you? You 5-O or something?" one boy asked.

"Man, whatever," Andrea sighed. "I was trying to see if one of you guys wanted to rent my car for a night or two." One boy started smiling.

"How much?" he asked.

"Fifty dollars, plus a fat quarter."

"Man, whatever."

"Man, whatever nothing, I got to get me a room."

"Well, if I give you fifty, plus a quarter, I'm definitely keeping the car until tomorrow about this time."

"I have to check out the room at twelve so what am I suppose to do until then?"

"I ain't got nothing to do wit that. I'm just letting you know what the deal gone be."

Andrea thought for a minute and decided to take what she could get. Having a place to stay was the most important. "All right then," she agreed and held her hand out. "Deal."

The boy smiled, dug into his pocket and pulled out a big wad of money. He sorted through it, then gave her two twenty dollars bills.

"I said fifty."

"Hold on and let me find a ten. Shit, you act like somebody tryin' to get over on you or something. Yo' ass better hope that ride don't break down either."

Andrea rolled her eyes as the boy handed her a five and five ones. He bent down, digging in his shoes. He pulled out a small plastic sack tied in a knot. He opened the bag, took out a rock and held his hand out.

"I don't want no rock," Andrea yelled.

"Look, this is all I sell so yo' ungrateful ass can take this shit or leave it. You out here begging and still trying to act like you got choices. You better take what yo' ass can get."

"How you gone try to serve me some hard and I don't fuck with that shit. Does anybody out here have some powder?" she yelled.

The boy put his dope back in his bag. "Go ask one of them den, and give me my damn fifty dollars back."

Andrea didn't want to let go of the loot so she looked around at the other boys. They were not about to be bothered with her. She felt nervous and her blood was pumping fast. She was so desperate to get high she could taste the powder on her tongue. Her hands trembled and her mind raced. She thought about the last time she'd tried rock and how good it made her feel. If she took what Mark had to offer it wouldn't be like she was going to get strung out; she hadn't had even wanted it since. She'd had a very depressing day, so anything would do. She was dying to take a shower, and get a cool buzz going, and urgently needed to get some rest.

"Well, you are going to have to find somebody to get me a room too." The boy whistled, and several heads turned.

"Peppa," he yelled. "Come 'ere for a minute." The skinny, dark skinned woman ran up to the porch. The boy said something to her and she shook her head yes. "Let's go!" the boy said.

Andrea took the rock and headed to the car. The boy and the woman followed. He jumped into the passenger side and the lady got in back. The car pulled off down the street. Andrea finally asked, "What's your name?"

"Mark."

"Mark who?"

"Damn, man, I swear yo' ass is 5-0. Mark Doe. Is that good enough?"

Andrea shook her head in disgust and looked out the window. Her stomach was hurting and she didn't feel like arguing with his ignorant ass. After the Burger King food she had to use the bathroom.

Peppa came from the office of Motel 6 with the key to the room. She handed it to Andrea. The worn-out misses got out of the car and said to Mark, "I'll see you tomorrow at twelve."

The boy adjusted the car seat. Andrea dragged her body to room 210. Having to pawn Tim's car made her feel terrible, but she had to do what she had to do. Tim would have wanted her to do what was best.

Andrea headed to the bathroom and turned on the shower. She shuffled back into the sleeping area and threw her purse on the bed. She kicked her shoes off, sighed and sat on the bed. As she began to undress, she thought of going home. Life, on the street was not what she'd hoped. She was tired of hustling to barely get by. Soon she would be eighteen. She had nothing going for herself and no plans for the future. She had not finished school, never thought about going to college, and was alone in a big ole world. Tim had been locked up for almost two weeks and she longed for him. She moved out of her parents home to be with him. They agreed to quit school and eventually get married, but none of that happened.

She sat naked on the bed, in silence, as tears began to fall from her eyes. She opened her purse and pulled out the dope she'd gotten from Mark. She didn't even have the utensils to smoke it with. She fell back on the bed and let her tired body unwind. She didn't even have the energy to get high. All she wanted was to mend her broken heart.

She took a shower and dried off, then wrapped the snow white towel around her naked body and sat on the side of the bed. She grabbed the telephone and dialed. When the operator answered, Andrea asked if Tim was still at the facility. The women told her to hold on. A minute later, the woman came back on the line saying he was still there and had been sentenced to serve two hundred- forty days. Andrea hung up, leaned back on the bed, and cried.

New Found Friend

The next morning, after crying herself to sleep, Andrea felt rested and somewhat relieved. She got up and dressed, and watched television while waiting for Mark. She watched The "Young and The Restless" while gathering her belongings. She confiscated a face towel, took the unopened bar of soap, and the unused roll of tissue, she could use these later. Since the boy wasn't there with her car like she'd asked him to be, Andrea went outside to wait. By two o'clock, she assumed Mark wasn't coming. She should have known he wasn't to be trusted. She broke into a nervous frenzy as she started toward the bus stop. She stopped a pedestrian and asked if she could bum a cigarette. Andrea wished for a little powder to calm her nerves. One little hit would make her feel so much better.

Cocaine was Andrea's escape from reality, her journey away from reality when she wasn't high, and, ooh she wanted some badly. The rock she had in her purse was not her drug of choice, but right now anything would calm the craving. After taking a long drag from the borrowed cigarette, she exhaled and flicked the butt. She dug through her purse for fare as the bus approached. She knew the car thief was in the hood and as soon as she spotted him she would curse him out for not following instructions. When the bus stopped on the corner, Andrea got in line to board. She had to find somebody who would give her some powder instead of the rock cocaine she had. The pebble in her pocket wasn't enough to kill her desire for her powdery, beloved white friend.

Downtown, she transferred to the number seven bus since the five was running behind schedule. Andrea departed the bus at the corner of Wealthy and Lafayette. She sprinted down the uneven sidewalk like a gold medalist. She was nervous and upset and couldn't wait to get her car back. She glanced down the street hoping to see the Chevy parked out front, but she didn't. As she approached, she saw the usual crowd standing around, but not the punk she was looking for. She stepped onto the porch. Two guys saw her and started laughing. When she asked them where Mark was with her car, they look amused.

"Man, I'm sorry to tell you," one said, "but 5-0 rolled through last night and scooped up a few homies who wadent quick on they feet. Yo' boy got out of the ride and ran but the police caught him. They searched and impounded the car for having an expired tag and no proof of insurance. I don't know if he was holding or not, but the po po's caught him hiding and took his black ass down. You could have at least told my man that yo' shit wadent legit."

"I'm glad it wadent me' cause I would get out of jail looking for yo' ass." The guy gave his boy some play.

"Whatever!" Andrea said as she looked down the street. Her eyes filled with tears. Now she really didn't know what to do.

A blue four-door Corsica pulled up and two girls jumped out holding bags filled with items they were trying to get rid of. Andrea's mind escaped to a place far, far away.

What in the hell was she going to do now? She had no car, no man, and no place to stay. She felt a sharp pain and she bent over, clutching her stomach. She really did need to get high. Her body was experiencing withdrawal. Andrea couldn't believe that her transportation, the only form of hustling she had left, was gone. Where was she going to go? She couldn't call her family and tell them she wanted to come home. That would make her feel like a failure. She wished for serenity. Now a victim of the streets, she wanted to turn back time to before she ever thought about stealing, getting high, or being rebellious. She longed for her mother's strong shoulder to cry on, and her father's encouraging, comforting words. Andrea wished she had never messed up, had never lost her parents' trust and respect. She missed having her privacy, her own room, and her aggravating sister getting on her nerves. Living at home with her parents, she was free. It was comfortable and guaranteed. The fear and distress of being homeless, and alone brought out the young child crying for help. Andrea wasn't the grown woman she claimed to be. Being grown came with too many obstacles and decisions. She wanted to be under the wings of her loving parents.

Flo and Stephanie traded off their merchandise for a couple of twenties. They danced down the stairs and off the porch. After wiping away her tears, Andrea stopped one of the ladies.

"Excuse me."

Flo turned her skinny neck so fast it was almost spinning like the girl's did in "The Exorcist."

"My name is Andrea and I know you don't know me, but I was wondering if you all were on your way to the store?"

Flo looked to be about thirty something years old. She was very dark skinned, about a hundred and twenty pounds with slightly bulging hazel brown eyes. Although she had on name brand clothing and wasn't what you would call ugly, she could trick someone into thinking she wasn't a user. It was obvious that she cared about her appearance.

Stephanie wasn't as attractive as Flo but didn't look like she got high either. She had a very attractive figure and fair skin complexion that would make her popular with the guys. She too was dressed real nice. Her hair was cut in a becoming sophisticated style.

"Why, what you need?" Flo asked, assuming she was about to take an order for a potential sale. Stephanie trotted to the car.

"Well...," she hesitated. "I was wondering because I boost too, but I don't have a ride. I need to make me a few dollars so if you were on your way to the store, I was wondering if I could ride with you" Flo looked suspiciously. She'd never been approached in this manner by anyone and she was skeptical.

"Do you get high?" Andrea asked, as she reached into her purse and pulled out the rock. Flo's eyes opened wide when she saw the rock.

"I was waiting to smoke this, but I don't have anything to smoke it with." Andrea said.

Flo looked up at a guy listening to their conversation, then looked out toward the car. "Come on," she said. "I got the shit you need in the car." Andrea jumped up from the step and followed her. She didn't know either of the women, but it didn't matter. She would do anything to avoid sitting at the hot spot all day.

The women approached the Corsica and Andrea climbed in the back seat. Flo introduced Andrea to Stephanie. The car pulled off. Flo passed the residue filled glass pipe to her back seat friend. The girl grabbed the pipe and stuck the semi-white devil inside. Andrea was so desperate to get high, it didn't matter what drug she used. Putting the dope inside the screen, the girl grabbed the lighter and started puffing. She had no idea she was taking the puff that would make her life even more miserable.

She took about four hits and passed the pipe back to the front seat. Flo grabbed it without hesitation and inhaled the awful smelling drug.

"So where you live at Andrea, and do you have a nick name or something because Andrea sounds too damn proper?" Stephanie asked waiting for her turn.

"No," the girl muffled.

"Well, I'm just gone call you, —let me see, what would be a good name for her, Flo? I'm gone just call you Ann. Is that cool?"

"Yeah, I guess."

"So where you live, Ann?"

"Well, nowhere really. I've been living from hotel to hotel for the last couple of months."

"Damn, you got it like that?"

"No, that's why I asked if I could go ride to the mall with you." They pulled up to a red light and Flo passed what was left of the dope to Stephanie.

"I need to make some money or I'll be sleeping on the street tonight."

"Who are your folks?"

"Nobody you all would know. The only somebody I had was my man and he got locked up a couple of weeks ago."

"For what?"

"Boosting."

"How much time he get?"

"Seven months."

"Damn," Stephanie sighed as the car turned the corner.

"Well, we ain't going back to the store tonight, but you can stay at my house if you want to. I live over in Stonegate Apartments and ain't nobody gone be there but me and Stephanie 'cause my mama got custody of my kids. I'm on Section 8 chile and don't pay a dime of rent so we just kick it there doing our thang." Stephanie and Flo began laughing. Stephanie said she'd invited over a couple of friends and they were about to kick back and get fucked up. "I got three bedrooms, so you can sleep in the extra one."

"Cool," Andrea smiled as she kicked back in the seat and got comfortable. Her high was kicking in. Andrea was feeling like a great burden had been lifted from her. Somebody must have been praying for her. They stopped at the store to get some drinks, and headed for Flo's place.

Before they were even settled in the apartment, the doorbell rang. Flo answered. Two guys entered, carrying brown paper bags. Stephanie was in the kitchen filling five glasses with ice, and Andrea helped Stephanie bring the glasses from the kitchen. They brought them into the living room and sat them on the coffee table. Flo's apartment was nice, clean and elegantly decorated. She had cream leather furniture and accessories in the living room. After placing the glasses on the table, Andrea went into the bedroom that Flo assigned her. She wanted to get comfortable and change her clothes. Flo had given her a new Gap sweatsuit to wear since they were around the same size. After Andrea changed, she walked back into the living room where the music was bumping loudly and everyone was drinking and getting high. They had plenty of drinks, rock cocaine, weed, and her favorite, powder. When Andrea saw the dust on the table, her eyes brightened as if it was Christmas morning and she was about to open the gifts. Flo introduced Andrea to the guys as she took a seat on the floor and joined the free festivities.

For the next two months, Andrea hung out with her new buddies like white on rice. Andrea experienced some things she'd never thought she would. They got high more than a little bit. When they weren't at the malls stealing, they were busy with whatever man came over with dope. At first it was hard for Andrea, but after Flo and Stephanie hooked her to the rules of the street, she caught on. Flo explained that nothing in life was free and if she didn't do what she had to do, she would end up where she was, before, on the street begging and stealing.

"And for what," Flo finally said to Andrea who was sitting on the sofa feeling sorry for herself. "A nightly hotel rental?"

"What else you gone do, go back up to the spot and sit on the stairs praying for a place to lay your head every night? You got it good here. You eating everyday, you got a comfortable bed to sleep in every night, and you're meeting nice men who come over here to show you a good time. Girl, please, you looking one hundred percent better than you were two months ago and I know that you can see that improvement. You done gained about ten or fifteen pounds, your new hairdo is the bomb, and you dress like one of the best bitches from head to toe. What else can a girl ask for?" Stephanie smiled, turning up her twenty-two ounce bottle of Colt forty-five.

"Girl, you better pick yourself up 'cause this is the good life," Flo slapped hands with Stephanie and walked into the living room. She reached for the remote control to the stereo and pushed a couple of buttons. The music pumped loudly out of the speakers. Stephanie stood in the middle of the floor dancing to the beat of the song as Ann and Flo looked on and laughed.

The next night no one had company but Flo. Andrea wasn't in the mood for company. She watched the thirteen-inch television on the dresser of what probably was Flo's daughter's bedroom. Stephanie was in the living room with Flo and her friend Deontae. Andrea had been in her room for over an hour. The beer she was drinking caused her to keep running to the bathroom. She decided to go one last time before turning in.

Her urine burned coming out. Her stomach and lower abdominal area ached. Since she slept with Flo's friend's cousin, her body had been feeling funny. Even though he promised her he'd worn a condom, Andrea's body hadn't been feeling the same. She hoped he hadn't given her a disease, but nine days had past and her pain was becoming unbearable so she asked Stephanie to take her to Saint Mary's.

She placed her hands on her stomach, allowing the warm secretions to exit her aching womb. When she looked into the toilet, she saw that the bowl was filled with blood. She shouted "AWWWW," as if she was crying her last breath. Flo rushed to the bathroom door.

"Girl, what the hell are you doing in there?" she yelled.

"Flo, I got to go to the hospital. I can't take it no more." Flo burst open the door and saw Andrea lying on the floor in front of the toilet in a fetal position, her underwear wrapped around her ankles. The rug was full of blood. Flo ran to her friend and helped her up. She said, "Girl, you are burning up!" Andrea wept.

"Please, Flo, take me to the hospital. I don't know what's going on. I'm scared."

"What happened?" The distressed young lady didn't answer and Flo screamed, "Stephanie."

Stephanie rushed into the bathroom and saw Flo pull up Andrea's clothes. There was so much blood on the floor, Stephanie assumed that Andrea had tried to commit suicide.

"Girl, we got to take her to the hospital. She is burning up and I don't know why she's bleeding like this."

"Damn," Stephanie moaned.

"Let me get Deontae so he can help us get her to the car." She had no idea what was going on, but it didn't look good. Deontae hurried to the bathroom after Stephanie. Andrea was on her feet, but her legs were weak, her shirt was wringing wet, and she was fading in and out of consciousness. She was delusional, seeing double, her speech was slurred, and no one could understand her. Andrea was minutes away from passing out.

They carried the girl to Stephanie's car and laid her across the back seat. Flo had placed some drying towels on the seat to stop the blood from soaking in. Stephanie jumped into the driver's seat and sped off.

When they arrived at the hospital and went inside, Flo yelled for help.

"What's wrong with her?" a woman wearing a white overcoat asked as she approached.

"She needs help."

The woman signaled for someone to bring the girl a stretcher as she grabbed Andrea and asked what happened. The girl's body reeked of alcohol and vomit. The smell was so stench, the doctor held her breath while helping the young girl onto the stretcher. "How long have you been bleeding?" The resident whipped out her stethoscope and pressed it into the girl's abdomen. She discovered a feeble heartbeat. Another staff member accompanied the first physician and asked the status of the patient.

"She's hemorrhaging. We have to get her to the OR stat."

Flo and Stephanie stood in the entrance area as the hospital staff raced down the hall through the double doors. As they rolled away on the wheeled bed, her periodic outbursts faded as the bed vanished.

She momentarily dozed off, but when her eyes opened doctors and nurses were scattered around her bed like ants on a leftover piece of a picnic sandwich. Andrea had a nasal cannula in her nose and an oxygen mask over her mouth. She looked at the tubes of liquid being pumped into her veins and closed her eyes. She heard someone say that she was extremely dehydrated and her blood pressure was high. She was hooked up to a telemetry machine to monitor her heart. There was a level two ultrasound machine and a large cord running from it was positioned in the doctor's hand. It was used to detect birth abnormalities or fetal deformalities. The physician moved it around on Andrea's stomach and watched the screen, looking disturbed. The girl began to wail again and one of the members of the medical staff said, "As you can see, the baby is appearing to be breach. The feet are right at the tip of the uterus. We are going to have to take this baby by Caesarean section. There is no time to waste. There still is a good possibility of this baby surviving."

"Ma'am, how long have you been using drugs?" The doctor asked Andrea.

Andrea tried to raise her head, but it was so heavy it plopped down onto the bleached white pillowcase. All she managed to get out was another pitiful moan.

"We have performed a chromatography test and cocaine has been detected in your system," the woman said. Our diagnosis is that you're about twenty-seven weeks pregnant. Have you had any prenatal care?"

Andrea cried when she heard she was pregnant. She was hurt, ashamed, and full of guilt. She had no idea she was pregnant, let alone how far along she was, and God only knew who the father was.

"You're in labor and we're trying to do all that we can to save this baby. You have caused a great deal of trauma to your unborn child. There is a condition called abruption placentas. It is when the placenta starts tearing away from the uterine walls causing premature delivery and that's what's going on now. Your baby is trying to come before it's time. It's crying out for help." Tears rolled down Andrea's face as she closed her eyes.

An anesthesiologist walked to her bed. Andrea felt her arm being lifted and the prick of a sharp needle. Her head became heavy and lifeless, her vision blurred, and she felt restful and sleepy. She tried opening her eyes, but they were too heavy; she had no strength to lift them. The anesthesia was pumped into her vein as she tried to speak, her words were inaudible. For the first time in her life, Andrea felt totally helpless. Her last wish before shutting her eyes was for her baby to survive the trauma she'd taken it through. If she had known she was pregnant, Andrea wouldn't have continued getting high. She couldn't recall the last time she'd even had a period. When she could fight no longer, Andrea mumbled, "Please call my mother." The rush she experienced made her close her eyes. She felt herself fading from reality. She felt as if the world was slipping away from her. "4...5..6...9.....1...8......7," she murmured. The whole room seemed to fade into total darkness.

Flo and Stephanie sat in the waiting area wondering what was going on. Flo was so stressed, she began chewing on her fingernails. She needed to know the status of her friend so her nerves could rest. She walked up to the information desk and asked the receptionist what was wrong with the girl her cousin had brought in.

"What's the young lady's name?" The woman asked in a

tone that Flo didn't appreciate.

"Remember my friend you just seen me rush in here, you know the same one they just flew back there without telling me anything?" The woman looked at Andrea's register, then back up at Flo.

"They just took her up to the fifth floor," she said as if Flo was irritating her.

The ghetto girl placed her hands on her hips. "What is telling me that she's on the fifth floor supposed to mean to me. What the fuck is on the fifth floor?" she cursed.

"Ma'am, you're going to have to watch your language or I'll have to ask you to exit the premises."

"All I asked you to do was tell me what's going on with my friend and you're the one acting all snotty and stuck up and shit." The curse words slid from Flo's tongue as another woman rushed up to the counter with a man behind her. Ignoring the sister standing beside her, Caroline pressed her way forward and asked the receptionist to help her find her daughter.

"They just called me and told me that my daughter was at this hospital. They said she was in surgery and is going through an emergency C section. Her name is Andrea Smith."

Flo silenced her trap to listen to the woman. She knew this couple had to be Andrea's parents because the man standing beside the hysterical woman looked like he'd spit Ann out. He looked worried and sad, trying to avoid breaking down and crying.

While his wife asked the questions, he stood to the side listening without saying a word. When the couple walked away from the counter, so did Flo. She went to fill Stephanie in on this new information. Stephanie became paranoid and suggested they leave. She said as long as Andrea's parents were there she would be all right. Stephanie said she wanted to get out of the hospital before the girl's parents came back asking questions.

"Ann is cool and all that, but I ain't got time to be answering no questions. Let's go."

Stephanie got up and Flo followed her out of the hospital. In the parking lot the thin cousin turned toward the hospital and said. "I hope Ann is gone be all right."

Since they weren't allowed to go in, Caroline and her husband sat outside the operating room waiting for the doctor. They were deeply concerned about Andrea and their unborn grandchild. Caroline couldn't believe the girl was pregnant, and to carry a baby, while on cocaine was a sin and a shame. Just two days before, an officer had come to the house looking for Andrea with a warrant for her arrest. Since she'd run away from home she hadn't been reporting to her probation officer so he had a warrant put out. When the officer knocked on her door, Caroline thought he was coming to tell her that something terrible had happened, but when she found out the visit was a result of a probation violation she was relieved. She prayed her daughter would contact them soon. Caroline had no idea it would be under these circumstances. Poor Thomas was so worried. He sat next to his wife in complete silence. He hoped his daughter would make it through the ordeal so she and the baby could come home where they belonged.

At 1:47 a.m., the doctor came out and introduced herself to Andrea's parents. She said they had a tiny baby girl who was fighting for her life.

"Although she came into the world successfully, her chances of survival are volatile. She was born addicted to cocaine, and your daughter delivered a little over two and a half months early. The baby is extremely malnourished and also has an underdeveloped lung and kidney. Her heart rate is irregular so we're rushing her to the NICU ward where she'll have a CAT scan to check for respiratory distress. In the NICU, she'll be continually monitored twenty-four hours a day. She's a tiny two pound, seven ounce warrior struggling for dear life."

Caroline collapsed after the doctor walked off. Her husband caught her and the doctor ran back to see if everything was okay. She helped her husband coach her back to her feet.

Staff members came out of Andrea's room looking drained and discomforted. Before the resident doctor walked away she said, "I'm sorry to be the one to tell you this, but a social worker and a police officer are on their way. It's hospital policy for us to contact them in situations like these. The baby will probably be in the hospital for the next couple of months. We have her hooked up to several machines assisting in the function of her organs until they're developed enough for her to use them on her own. Right now, were hoping for a miracle."

Since Andrea was still out, her parents rushed to the neonatal unit to see the baby. Through a big glass room they observed the tiny new member of their family. Caroline fell into Thomas's arms crying when she saw the undeveloped little infant. "Why, Thomas, why did Andrea do this to this baby?"

Thomas was crying. The baby was just big enough to fill the palm of an adult hand. Her head was very tiny, about as big as a balled up fist. Her miniature body was frail, and white all over.

Her tiny limbs trembled as the physician stuck a needle here and there. People ran in and out with buckets of waste or bags filled with clear fluids. Her arms and legs were no bigger than a grown man's fingers. The sight was so depressing that all Caroline could do was turn away and weep. Seeing this baby hooked up to so many tubes was unbearable. Caroline could take no more and left the room. If the baby survived, it would be a miracle.

That night, Caroline got down on her knees and asked God for that miracle. She told him that everything was her fault. If she hadn't put her daughter out, this would never have happened. She prayed he would forgive her and give her precious grandbaby a chance to survive. She was sorry for Andrea's behavior and promised God that from that point forward, life would be different. She would make some serious changes to prepare herself for what was about to come her way.

Testimony

Andrea got out of the hospital seven days later. She named her daughter Timya Angel Doberson. The following morning, she had to see her probation officer. She arrived early and sat in his office for ten minutes before she was called to the back. The secretary escorted Andrea to an empty room, asked her to have a seat, and told her that Mr. Beasdon would be in shortly.

About fifteen minutes later, the door opened and two police officers walked in. One read her rights and handcuffed her, and the other one told her she was under arrest. Thomas was in the waiting room when the officer escorted his daughter out. She was in handcuffs, but she wasn't crying. She was cooperative. One officer told Thomas to meet them downtown to see if Andrea would be released on bond. At the station, Andrea found out she was being charged with a felony charge of child cruelty and abuse along with the felony probation violation. Thomas was there to bail her out, but at her probation officer's request, she was to be held without bond. He wanted to make sure she would show up for court. There was nothing her parents could do to get her off; money couldn't help her out of this one. This time Andrea had to pay her debt by doing time.

Two long days past before Andrea opened up to Velma, the woman who shared her cell. She'd cried the whole time she was there. She wanted to go home more than anything in the world, but it was unlikely. The prosecutors were doing all they could to hold her until she turned eighteen so they could charge her as an adult. She wept as she told Velma how she became strung out on drugs, and had a drug addicted baby. She told the woman she deserved to be punished for what she'd done to her daughter.

"After seeing my child inside the incubator, with all the tubes hooked up to her, I felt like dying. It disturbed me emotionally like nothing else ever has. My carelessness and stupidity resulted in my daughter possibly being damaged for the rest of her life. She will never be able to have a normal life like all children deserve. They said that having a baby while on cocaine deconstructs the baby's neurological, developmental, and behavioral functions. If I hadn't been so disobedient to my parents, this never would have happened. If I had just listened to them, I wouldn't be in this terrible situation. I feel like I have nothing left to live for. I have disappointed my parents and everyone else around me. It saddens me when I think of the trauma my daughter has been through. It is not fair what I did to her."

Andrea closed her eyes as she thought about her daughter lying in bed with her weakened heart. Andrea fell onto her bottom bunk crying. "Oh God, I am so sorry. Please watch over my little Angel. Please give her a chance. I promise to never touch another drug in my life, if you just let her live. I'm sorry that I didn't do right, but it's not her fault, please don't punish her." She rolled on her side and yelled, "Please help me."

"Shut up, people are trying to sleep," someone from another cell yelled.

Velma dropped her magazine on the mattress and jumped down from her bunk. She held the young girl in her arms as if she was her own child. The girl's body was hot and trembling with fear. Her cellmate was worried about her and wished there was more she could do. Since Andrea had been incarcerated, she'd been in her bunk crying. Velma knew from experience that she'd adjust soon, but for some, it took more time than others. Only God could see her through it. Velma knew the girl was severely scorned, but the crying wouldn't do her any good. As the old saying goes, when you make your bed hard, you're the one who has to lie in it. Velma rocked the girl, hoping to console her.

For the first two weeks, Caroline and Thomas were at the hospital every chance they got. They even designated specific times to sit with the baby. After the third week, they took Taylor to see Timya. Taylor couldn't take seeing the baby hooked up to all the tubes, so her parents immediately took her home and did not bring her back. Taylor asked all kinds of questions and even had nightmares. She told her mother she saw Timya crying in her sleep.

After leaving the hospital one night, Caroline was so distraught, she could barely drive. She hated seeing Timya in so much misery and discomfort. The whole time Caroline visited, the baby did nothing but cry because her tiny little body was going through substance withdrawals. She hadn't gained any weight since birth because her body wasn't craving food like normal. It was craving the drug, so she wouldn't eat. Even though she despised leaving her side, Caroline needed a break or she would have to be admitted for emotional stress. Not seeing the tiny infant suffering would partially ease her mind.

After the third week, the baby still wasn't improving. Not only was she still fighting to survive, but she was also yearning for the awful drug her body was addicted to and could no longer have.

"We're hoping for a miracle," the doctors said. Once her body learns to cope without the drug, her possibilities of surviving will increase. No matter what we do she'll continue to show her urge for the drug by crying continuously like she does. It's her expression of grief."

Caroline was brokenhearted, confused, and needed a shoulder to lean on. Her life had changed so much in the last few weeks, she was contemplating ways to rid herself of everything. Her granddaughter was fighting with all her might just to take a breath and Caroline heard her whimpers of pain. Andrea was in jail, which left all the decisions and concerns about the baby, to her and her husband. Caroline was worried about how much time her daughter would get. She'd never experienced such a depressing two and a half weeks, not even when her mother passed, not even when her husband cheated. She shed a few pounds. She was lost. She didn't know how to resolve the situation. She felt sorry for her granddaughter and what her mother had put her through. It made her so angry she wanted to choke Andrea until she answered why she'd done such a terrible thing to an innocent, harmless baby. Andrea wasn't raised to be inconsiderate and ungrateful. Even though she was spoiled, Caroline knew she had taught the girl morality. If Andrea had been home, Caroline would have noticed the pregnancy and gotten her help. Andrea knew she could always come back home. Lord knows that girl got those selfish ways from her mother.

By the time Caroline pulled up in her sister's driveway, her face was completely wet. She looked as if she had been standing in a rainstorm. Her hands were trembling and her mind was restless.

"Oh, God," she cried. "I thought you said you wouldn't give us more than we could bare." She needed comforting, sisterly advice, and she owed Dorothy an apology for the way she'd treated her over the years. She'd been holding a grudge against Dorothy for something she couldn't even control. Caroline always treated Dorothy like she was beneath her and nothing her sister did was ever good enough. She wanted to apologize for the awful things she said to her when she found out Monet was pregnant. Caroline now realized that a parent could only do so much. It dawned on her that even children raised in fine homes, with two caring parents, didn't mean they would automatically turn out perfect. She seriously thought that's all it took. All the love in the world didn't mean children wouldn't grow up and disappoint their parents. Caroline had been so far up on her high horse that it took this unforeseen tragedy to bring her back to reality, where people weren't perfect. A drink would ease her mind and help her see the truth. She needed to come back to the world where material things were not the essence. Caroline learned the hard way that an upscale lifestyle certainly didn't solve all your problems.

Caroline apologized to Dorothy for being a total bitch over

the years, and they cried together.

"Sister, I have to admit I'm not perfect, and neither are my children," Caroline said. "If I had never thought that, then my daughter would have never rebelled and turned to the streets. I realize now that I don't have to play like everything is all right when they're not. I accused you of not being a good mother when Monet got pregnant and look at my situation. I can't tell you how proud I am of my niece who graduated from high school, is attending college, and is taking care of her son. She's trying to have something. You raised her right, Dorothy. I have to give you that. All the time I spent judging you, I should have been looking at my own situation. Now you're happily married with a good husband and your kids are doing well, and look at me. My husband is the one who went out and had a baby on me, my daughter is the one strung out on drugs and having crack babies, and now I have no other choice but to stick by her side. Now I know why you stuck with Delvin all those years. You did it because of dedication to your relationship, not because he'd done something wrong that you couldn't sweep under the rug. You didn't care who knew, and you didn't let it get you down and I'm proud of you. You are stronger than I'll ever be and I love you, and I am sorry."

"It's all right, Caroline," Dorothy mouthed. "I always knew you meant well. You just have some ugly, selfish, ways that you can't control. I know we have our good and our bad times, but I still love you. You're my big sister and you'll always be no matter what."

Their testimony session wrapped up and Caroline tried getting herself together before driving. She didn't want Taylor to see her like this. Things were hard enough as it was. Caroline told Dorothy that she loved her and asked for her forgiveness again.

Andrea's court date followed thirty days later. As the judge got ready to sentence her, Andrea stood with her head held high.

She held back the tears and prepared to take her punishment like a grown woman. She was ready to get it over with, so her life could move forward. She had been clean for almost two months, which gave her time to think about what she'd been through and where she was going. Her mind was made up. She was going to do the right thing. Even though her daughter was still in the hospital, she was showing signs of improvement. She didn't have to live in the incubator anymore but was still in the NICU. If Timya kept improving, she'd probably be home in another couple of weeks. The good news helped Andrea to be strong.

The judge announced her name before he recited her penalty. She was sentenced to one hundred and thirty days in the county jail, and had to participate in a twenty-four week drug rehab and parenting class. The judge also ordered her to complete her GED before she could be released. Caroline cried and hugged and kissed Andrea before the bailiff escorted her away. Thomas did the same and told Andrea to call them when she made it back to the county. Andrea would make the best of her situation. Soon her time would be served and she would be home with her baby.

Timya's grandparents were able to bring her home nine weeks after Andrea was sentenced. When Caroline and Thomas came home with the baby, Taylor, Dorothy, and her entire family were there to welcome her. She had gained four pounds and had been taken off the machines she had depended on. She still looked more pale than black. She was still on a heart monitor, but at least she was home. Caroline took a leave of absence from work to take care of the baby. Her husband worked his normal schedule. Everything worked out fine.

The baby stayed up many nights going through withdrawal. Timya cried so much, even holding her didn't calm her. Some nights they rode in the car during the wee hours of the night to calm her, but that didn't work. They gave her warm baths and played music, even read her stories, but nothing helped. Many nights the baby cried for several hours straight. Caroline would become so frustrated that her only relief was to go into the bathroom and scream. The crying was more than she could handle. She had no way out, and longed for peace. Sometimes she would become upset with Andrea because she wasn't there to see her own child go through the withdrawal. She often wondered why she had to be the one to carry the burden of her child's mistake.

Only time would tell how things would turn out. She didn't know if Andrea would do the right thing when she got out or not. But one thing Caroline knew was that she was not going to turn her back on her granddaughter like she did with her own daughter. She'd learned a powerful lesson and almost lost a lot in the process. No matter what the circumstances were, Caroline would deal with it like a woman. Caroline had the faith to go on, knowing things would only get better with time.

THE END

Discussion/Writers Group Questions for IJGBWT

1. When Andrea was admitted to the hospital what were your first thoughts of what possibly could have been wrong with her?

2. Who is Andrea's baby father?

3. Do you believe that the only time Thomas was unfaithful to his wife was the one night he spent with Sheila and conceived his son?

4. Do you feel that Dorothy overreacted when she divorced Delvin or did she have just cause?

5. Do you think Dorothy made a wrong decision by allowing her daughter to have a baby? How do you feel she should have handled the situation?

6. Do you believe Thomas and Adell were really having an affair?

7. Do you believe Delvin would have cleaned himself up if Dorothy hadn't left him, or do you feel their breakup was his incentive to change?

8. Dorothy felt that moving into the projects was a better living opportunity for her and her children, but the projects are usually stereotyped as one of the worst places to live. In her same situation which route do you feel would have best benefit her and her children.

9. Through the book we got to know Caroline pretty well, was her apology to her sister in the end really sincere?

BOOK ORDER FORM

Make check or money order out to Maseyree and mail to
Tongue Untied Publishing, PO Box 822 Jackson, Georgia 30233

For Purchase of book It Just Gets Better With Time $12.95

Georgia sales tax 7%

Postage and handling . . . .$ 1.95

Total . . . . $ 15.80

Name_____

Address_____

_____

Enclosed Amount for:

Book purchase only___$15.80_____
BookQuantity_____

Total Enclosed_____
Visit our website at www.tongueuntiedpublishing.com for other
products

Thanks for supporting my vision,
Maseyree- President
www.maseyree.com